"It is time someone taught you to do as you are told,"

Darcy said.

He lifted Merry as if she weighed no more than the paper she clasped. The house spun by as he carried her up the creaking attic stairs to his hidden loft above.

Suddenly, she was afraid. Not of him, really, as much as of herself. Had she come for this? The message written on the paper she clasped might have been invisible, but she knew her feelings for this man had never been.

"I only came with a note," she said, but her voice was raspy and not her own.

"I know. I prayed you would come."

His hot breath, his sure hands on her, were madness. Months of pent-up longing poured through her. "Oh," she sighed. "Oh, that feels—so strange—so wonderful!"

"Mmm! Tell me more how you feel, *ma belle*. What you want!"

But she only wanted him.

Dear Reader,

Once again we stand prepared to transport you to other places, other times. Let the summer heat, the hustle and bustle of everyday life, disappear from your mind as you journey into the past.

Kathleen Eagle has been one of your favorite authors since her first appearance, and in *Heaven and Earth* she will once again touch your heart. Young missionary Katherine Fairfield must deal not only with being widowed but with her forbidden attraction to rugged Jed West. Jed is rough-hewn and strong, a perfect match for the Oregon wilderness where he makes his living as a trapper. But he is also tender when he needs to be, and more loving than any man Katherine has ever known. Somehow these two must move heaven and earth to spend their lives together.

Caryn Cameron returns with *Freedom Flame*, a sequel to her earlier *Liberty's Lady*. This book is just as exciting as its predecessor, so don't let yourself miss it. In months to come look for new favorites like DeLoras Scott and perennial crowd pleasers like Kristin James. There's always something special going on at Harlequin Historicals.

Leslie J. Wainger
Senior Editor and Editorial Coordinator

Freedom Flame

Caryn Cameron

Harlequin Books

TORONTO • NEW YORK • LONDON
AMSTERDAM • PARIS • SYDNEY • HAMBURG
STOCKHOLM • ATHENS • TOKYO • MILAN

Harlequin Historical first edition July 1990

ISBN 0-373-28649-X

Books by Caryn Cameron

Harlequin Historicals

Dawn's Early Light #11
Silver Swords #27
Liberty's Lady #39
Freedom Flame #49

CARYN CAMERON

is a former high school and college English teacher who now writes full-time and is the author of best-selling historical romances under her own name, Karen Harper. She is a lifelong Ohioan who, with her husband, enjoys traveling and family genealogy. She also plays the piano and keeps in shape with Scottish Highland dancing.

My special appreciation
to my supportive Harlequin Historical editor,
Eliza Shallcross.
And as always,
to my proofreader, business manager,
traveling companion and dear husband,
Don Harper.
Caryn Cameron and Karen Harper thank you both.

Prologue

New York City
July 2, 1776

He was, quite simply, the handsomest man Merry Morgan had ever seen. Broad, hard-muscled shoulders stretched his elegant coat taut; long, strong legs swelled his satin breeches and molded his silken hose. His powerful thighs were made for hard riding, graceful dancing, and lap-sitting to pleasure a woman. His hands were large and square, entirely capable and masterful. His high cheekbones, aristocratic nose and finely chiseled lips reminded her of a bust of Caesar. A prominent brow made him appear brooding, but she knew how to tease forth the smile that softened that stern visage and heated her heart.

His deep-set but widely spaced eyes were dark, so different from her own sky-blue ones. His hair, drawn straight back in a black-ribboned queue, shone like polished onyx. He was a complete contrast to her pale blondness. He was the missing part that made her feel the gaps in her existence just waiting to be filled.

He was always polite with her in public, but when they were alone his passion for her shattered his poise—and hers. His mere presence, with that masculine tang of leather and the outdoors—and that vibrant essence of danger he evoked—inflamed her senses. It was as if they were linked by an invisible cord that was always ready to snap taut and tumble her into his arms.

The thought made her smile. Whatever would her family, and all of nervous New York City, waiting so solemnly for the American war for independence to come here, say if she staged her own little war for independence and rode off with her lover on his horse?

Tonight he was riding through the pounding rain to be with her, here in her private bedchamber at the Broad Way Street town house. Though the night was not cold, she sat staring into the hearth fire with her embroidery in her lap, waiting, knowing he would come.

He never asked for permission to enter. He strode in past her family and the servants. He swept off his black tricorne and knelt on one knee before her. He was so close that his dripping, rain-swept raven locks wet her green dimity dressing gown to her thighs. She trembled with anticipation of the time when she would hold that big, wet body completely to hers. His hand cupped her knee, sending sparks skimming her skin. His eyes, hooded with thick lashes spiked by the rain, burned flaming oranges and reds into the very core of her being. He spoke.

"My beloved Meredith, forgive me! I should never have gone away."

"I had unshakable faith in you from the first," she assured him. "I knew you left because you must be someone special, doing what you had to do. But I've missed you so!"

"My duty to our new nation called me away, or I never would have gone!"

"I understand, my darling," she said soothingly, her hand in his slick hair. "I vow to do anything to help our country, too. What matters is that you have come back to me again!"

"I'm so grateful you waited for my return. I never want to do anything again without your knowledge and approval. I will strive to make you happy. Live with me forever! Let me make amends for our sad separations, now, on that bed, while we listen to our heartbeats and the rain drowning the night!"

She pressed her thighs tightly together and shifted on the needlepoint chair seat. She bit her full lower lip to stop her lips from trembling. "Yes, my darling," she whispered as the flames burned higher inside her. "Let me prove my faith and love to you! Hold me, take me now!"

She stood to wrap her arms around his powerful neck as he reached to lift her. One of the logs on the fire settled noisily, scattering sparks at her feet. Her sampler cascaded from her lap to the floor. And her latest beautifully embroidered fantasy went *poof*!

"Drat!" she cried to the empty room.

Merry Morgan scrambled to save her sewing from the shower of sparks. As she scuffed at them on the tiles, their crimson pinpoints ebbed to nothing, just as the vision of her fantasy man had again.

She could hardly picture what it would be like to really meet him. He just had to be out there somewhere, praying she would find him, too!

Meanwhile, molten silver still scalded her insides, just from another daydream of him. Always, when she envisioned him, he demanded her eternal love and her body to seal that promise. Yet, when he reached for her or carried her up some dark, winding staircase to the curtained bed of her heated reveries, she had no notion of what came next. Ah, but when she found him, she would discover all that—as soon as she learned where and who he was!

Chapter One

New York City
July 9, 1776

N ow, Merry," Georgina Morgan scolded her younger daughter, "I cannot believe you are prancing about yet in your corset and petticoat. You're going to make us all late for the reading of that Declaration of Independence, and I'll not allow it. Today's a day that would have made your father proud."

"I know, and I won't be much longer," Merry promised her mother, who was standing in the door of Merry's bedroom at the Gant town house. "You just go on ahead with the others, and I'll catch up with Libby's maid. She just went to press my dress, and then she was going to look in Libby's wardrobe for a bigger modesty piece for me. You don't want your only unwed daughter showing too much bosom with all those soldiers on the Commons, do you now?"

Georgina was tempted to give Merry a tongue-lashing for her pertness. The country's newly declared freedom seemed to have gone to her daughter's pretty blond head. Perhaps it was the excitement of just over a week ago, when Merry and her sister, Libby, had rescued Libby's new husband, Cameron Gant, from the British. Or perhaps it was a result of living here in wicked Manhattan with the newly wedded Gants, to whose house Georgina and Merry had moved after the British had taken over Staten Island.

But Merry's smile bathed Georgina's heart with hope and happiness. Her love almost made her forget her shortness of breath and her recent chest pains. At nineteen, Meredith Morgan was a grown woman. And what had it ever profited her, Georgina thought, to try to control her second daughter's exuberance? It had worked no better than when she had tried to control Libby's stubbornness. But Libby had turned out so well and made such a fine match with the wellborn, wealthy Cameron Gant, perhaps there was hope for Merry yet!

"My, my, I pity the man who tries to tame you, Merry Morgan," she chided gently.

Merry returned her smile. "War or not, I'm going to find one *I* can tame, you wait and see! I'll be right along with Penelope!" she called as her mother shook her head and slowly walked away.

Merry knew everyone but she and Penelope had left the house for the public celebration now. For one moment she could pretend she was mistress of this lovely New York town house—and that she had a handsome, dashing husband stowed away, just down the hall.

But Merry Morgan had things to think about besides a husband. She badly wanted to help win this war, just like Libby, who was a patriot printer. Why, Merry would be willing to face more British than she had on Staten Island rescuing Cam. She'd even spy for General Washington, if only he'd ask her! Now what was keeping Penelope? Still in the disarray of undress, for it was a warm July day, she stepped boldly out into the upstairs carpeted hall and headed for Cam and Libby's room.

"Penelope!" Merry called. Drat, she was going to be late!

Puzzled that there was no response, Merry shoved open the door to Cam and Libby's room. Except for a handwide split in the front draperies bringing in light and breeze, the room lay in shadowed silence.

"Penelope?" Merry's voice quavered as she stepped in. The door to her brother-in-law's study, just beyond, stood ajar. "Where are you?"

Everything happened so fast. Big, hard hands flashed out, one to clamp her arms to her side, one to pull her head back against a sturdy shoulder. Fingers pressed her lips against her teeth as she tried to turn her face so that she could see.

"Don't make a sound and don't struggle," a deep, rasping voice ordered. Her captor was so close that his hot breath stirred the tendrils of her hair against her temple. "The other housemaid is unharmed. It will be far better for us all," the voice whispered, "if you do not see my face. But I must say I have seen yours. And, considering the rest of you on display, I regret I have not the time to savor both!"

There was something alarming and distinctive about the voice that she could not place—something about the way he pronounced his words. If it was an accent, it was not British. At any rate, his voice, his touch—so commanding and strong—rattled her in a way that pure fear would not have. Her blood thrummed through her veins; her pulse pounded; her skin broke out in a fine sheen of sweat the sultry day could never have caused.

"Who—?" She tried to speak against his warm palm. He wore a thumb ring on his big, square right hand. It had a sort of gold lily embedded in black onyx. So close to her eye, the onyx was almost a dark mirror to catch his reflection, but she could not see him in it.

"Silence, I said!"

A scent emanated from the man, an outdoor scent of mingled leather and something alarming and forbidden that she could not quite place. Danger . . . that was it, the smell of danger, somehow, just like her mystery man. Was that why she was strangely more intrigued than afraid?

But when he walked her over to Cam and Libby's big bed and pushed her facedown on it, she panicked. She twisted, kicked—and felt herself land a good one in the softness of his groin.

"*Sacrebleu!*" he swore, and she wondered what that meant. He shoved her down harder on the bed and straddled her, his hard knees on either side of her squirming hips. He groaned and gasped in ragged breaths. She wished she could free her mouth from his hard hand to bite him. She was glad she had hurt him, yet suddenly even more afraid of what he would do in return. She even wished she had a gun or knife hidden somewhere on her person, but of course it wouldn't have been hidden with the little she had on.

"I just . . . need to tie and blindfold you, woman!" he whispered through gritted teeth. "Not to be . . . unmanned!"

All too adeptly he pulled her wrists behind her hips and wrapped them with what she realized must be the velvet ties of the draperies. He used another to blindfold her, then wrapped a third around her ankles.

"One sound and I shall have to gag you, too!"

He rose from the bed, and she heard him brushing himself off. He must be quite a macaroni to do that at a time like this, she thought.

She lay still, listening acutely as he opened drawers and rifled about. Then he walked away to shuffle through papers in the next room. He must be spying on Cam, who was one of General Washington's aides, so he had to be British. How she detested the British! She'd find some way to expose this man, to capture him!

She heard his muted footfalls approach the bed again. She tensed every muscle and stopped breathing. She could almost feel his eyes. What color would they be? The curled hairs on his fingers had been darkest sable.

She jumped when he put his hands on her corseted waist to turn her faceup again. She cursed her blindfold.

"Please . . . don't," she pleaded quietly.

"Just looking. So high-and-mighty for a housemaid, but I should have expected that here."

"What do you mean?"

"Enough!"

She went hot and pink all over at the thought of how she must look, half-attired and disheveled, under this stranger's gaze. A chill made her shudder. Hair prickled on the back of her neck. To her embarrassment, she could feel her nipples pointing against her thin linen bodice.

She longed to see what he looked like, but even tilting her head back she could not. She wanted to demand what his business was. But at least she knew he did mean business. If he thought she was a housemaid left behind today, so much the better. There was a strange, musical cadence to his rasped commands. He was not the usual sort of thief. She jumped when he touched her, but it was just a quick hand in the hair that his rough treatment had tumbled loose.

"I regret holding anyone prisoner," he whispered, as if in apology. "Especially on this, your day of independence here. And so, goodbye, rebel vixen."

He turned her over on her stomach again and loosened the bonds around her wrists just a bit. "Do not cry out, or I shall have to come back." His words were threatening, but his tone was etched with bitter amusement now. He gave her bottom an outrageous little pat, and then she heard him hurry from the room.

She lay panting, struggling with the bonds around her wrists in feverish silence even as she heard the front door calmly open and close below. The man had dared to casually stroll out the front door!

"Penelope? Where are you?" she cried, freeing her wrists and yanking her blindfold down. As she untied her ankles, she heard Penelope's muffled cries.

She ran into Cam's study and found the maid tied, blindfolded and gagged. She pulled the gag down and hugged the shaking girl.

"Did you see his face? Did you?"

"No! No, mistress . . ." Her voice was quavering. "When I came in the bedroom, he was just there, and he grabbed me. Did he hurt you?"

"No, but he'll be sorry he ever so much as touched me without my permission!"

"But if we don't know him, mistress, how—?"

"Never mind. Just help me get dressed, or we'll miss General Washington's appearance and the reading of the Declaration." Merry helped Penelope to her feet. Now she had two men she was looking for, one a fantasy she had to bring to life and one who was all too real. And she'd seen neither of them. "We'll have to lock the doors when we go out, for sure. I think that rogue walked right in and out, brazen as you please! I don't care if I don't know who he is. I'm going to find out!"

* * *

Though her legs still shook and her heart pounded louder than her flying shoes on the cobbles, Merry searched the cavorting crowds for her family. Almost everyone had traipsed down Broad Way Street toward old Fort George after the reading of the Declaration, so she hurried that way, too, searching faces, wondering if *he* was here, too. She gaped in surprise, then joined in the cheering, when the decapitated gilded head of King George II's statue went by on rebel shoulders, having been removed from its once lofty marble perch on the bowling green. And then Merry saw her sister, standing outside General Washington's headquarters at Number 1 Broad Way.

She weaved her way toward her through the crowd, waving and calling her name. "Lib! Lib!"

When Libby saw her sister, she hurried to her, the blue bells of her skirts swishing. "Merry! Mother's all right, isn't she? We sent her back with two maids. I can't believe you missed the reading of the Declara—"

"I didn't even see Mother. A man was in the town house looking at Cam's papers! He seized me and the maid and bound us both, Lib, and we've got to tell Cam!"

Libby grabbed Merry's shoulders. "Praise Providence you're safe! He didn't hurt you, did he? A thief? Or a British spy?"

"I don't know. I didn't see him, but he has dark hair, I think, and a raspy voice with a different lilt. Where's Cam? Maybe he has a hint who he could be or what he's after."

"As usual, we'll just have to wait on war business," Libby replied stoically, and hugged her sister to her. "General Washington sent a man out to fetch Cam in the street. Oh, Merry, this whole thing just saps my strength sometimes, and it hasn't even really started yet, even if we have won the siege of Boston. All that so-called victory has gotten us was the Royal Navy and Army coming here now!" Libby moaned as, setting propriety aside, they sat down to wait between two Continental Army guards on the broad stone steps of Washington's headquarters.

* * *

"Needless to say," Washington was saying inside to his aide, Lieutenant Cameron Gant, "we're desperate for everything in this army, including more soldiers. Desperate enough that we will be using the best system of spies we can put together. I'm relying on you to keep my correspondence of all that completely to yourself."

"I understand, sir."

"We are desperate enough," the commander-in-chief of the infant Continental Army went on, "to traffic with the French, even if we did fight them in the Indian Wars only twenty years ago. But 'the froggies,' as we used to call them, hold our interests very much at heart of late."

"Anything to torment the British," Cam interjected.

"Precisely."

Washington gazed past Cam out the window, noting that the crowds had not yet dispersed on the street below, then turned to face his young aide again. Cameron Gant was a tall blond man, almost the equal of the six-feet-two-inch white-wigged Washington. When talking war business, both men remained crisply formal and stiff in their blue-and-buff uniforms, despite the warm mutual respect they enjoyed. Cam Gant had done New York and the cause of independence a great service these past long months by playing Tory royalist when in fact he was a staunch colonial Whig through and through. He had fed Washington vital information about the British movements and about temperament here in this key city. But now, heaven help them all, Washington mused grimly, the redcoats were coming back in force.

"I must tell you, Lieutenant," he continued, "there are already a few French agents in the colonies. And certain funds, ships, engineers and officers have been promised through secret channels, although the public policy of King Louis XVI and Versailles is still to take no apparent part in this 'colonial squabble.' We must convince him and his ministers to a more public support."

"I see."

"Of the influential Frenchmen already in Philadelphia, one's supposed to be sent here to assess the New York theater of war and to work with me and my top men. I don't know whether

he'll be returning with me after my quick trip to Philadelphia
to report to Congress or if he's already here. The French un-
derground operatives—especially this man, it seems—work in
their own ways and times. At any rate, the word on him indi-
cates he's quite a dangerous fellow.''

"Dangerous? To us, sir?''

"He's what we used to call a loose cannon. Apparently he's
a bitter man with quite a scandalous and tragic past. So you'll
forgive me for saying I've sent your name on to him. Officially, he is to report to you for an overall view of things when
he arrives. But I also want you to watch him until we're certain
he's one to really trust.''

"He sounds a paradox.''

"Even to his French superiors, I take it. Yet if they put up
with all that he must be exactly the sort we need. Let's just hope
the man's cold-blooded menace will be a boon to our cause and
a boot to British bums. I repeat, his country's help is absolutely essential to our future victory.''

"I understand," Cam said as he watched Washington pick
up a paper and reach for a quill. "And do we know this dan-
gerous-if-helpful loose cannon's name, sir?'' he inquired as he
stood.

"Ah, yes, here it is," the general said, reaching for another
paper. "Would you believe this note was written in a mixture
of milk and something secret and had to be heated against a hot
surface to be read? Makes our fledgling covert information
service look like merest babes lost in the woods. I shudder to
think what we shall learn from these French, like it or not. Read
this, then tear it up, and tell no one—especially not your lovely
printer wife, if you please. By the way, I saw her outside with
that pretty blond sister of hers a moment ago.''

"Meredith. We call her Merry.''

"Ah, yes. Anyway, the bold and beautiful Morgan sisters are
evidently awaiting your unfair detainment here with me. Dismissed, and keep a sharp look for that Frenchman, Lieutenant.''

Cam took the paper, saluted and went out. As other aides
passed him on their way into Washington's office, he glanced
down at the spidery writing on the folded vellum page. Moody

and dangerous, but the very best we have, the cryptic words declared. Louis Philippe D'Arcy Montour, comte de Belfort, passing in these colonies by the name of Darcy Mont.

Cam's hair prickled along the back of his neck as he read those words, but he had no idea why. Hell, he thought, trying to buck himself up, he was the man who had finally tamed Libby Morgan! He'd survived dangerous months spying for Washington himself! So what problem could some French "loose cannon" possibly cause him or his family of three Morgan women?

He stuffed the note down his polished boot and clapped his bicorne back on as he strode out into the warm July sun. As he walked down the steps, Libby and Merry sprang up to meet him. But surely they weren't so glum-faced just because Washington had kept him a few moments!

Merry's words stopped him in his tracks. "Oh, Cam, some man who was looking for something in your study—at least I think he was—broke in and tied me up!"

"He didn't hurt her, but he blindfolded her," Libby put in. "He didn't sound British, she said. Why, if he'd come across Mother there, she might have had another heart spell! Who could it have been, Cam?"

Cam shook his head. His gray eyes narrowed. His jaw set hard. He could almost feel the note in his boot burning a hole in his leg, but he was sworn to secrecy.

"Come on home, you two, and we'll see if he took anything," he said, his voice catching. "And I'll make certain it does not happen again. The thing that matters is that Merry's quite unharmed."

But Merry was not so sure she had not been harmed in some way. And she could tell she was not the only one seething. She noted well her brother-in-law's dark mood as he marched them home. When she fell silent, Libby told Cam every last thing she had related about their visitor. He only nodded grimly. Merry was burning with curiosity to find out if Cam knew more than he was telling, but she wasn't going to ask him until she had him alone. She knew that more than once in her sister's tumultuous courtship days he had hesitated to tell Libby something volatile, fearing her duty as a printer to share the truth.

Merry studied men's faces they passed for telltale suspicious, dangerous looks. She craned her neck to squint behind them. Maybe they were being followed! Deep down it infuriated her that this real mystery man had dared to come and go as fast as the mystery man of her dreams did. Illicitly entering the house was one thing, but that rude, crass, strange-speaking man had no right to intrude on her perfectly tended and controlled fantasies! Drat that dark, dangerous stranger!

But Merry's agonizing over her mystery man soon paled beside family concerns. Her mother's heart spells worsened, and she and Libby took turns tending her day and night. Georgina Morgan drifted between heavy sleep and the desperate desire to talk. Suddenly the threat of British invasion took second place to the threat of death's invasion in the Morgan sisters' lives.

"Meredith, you know how much I loved...your father," Georgina muttered. Trying to hear the whispered words, Merry leaned closer to the pale face framed by plump bolsters on the big bed. Only a moment ago Merry had been certain her mother slept.

Merry bathed her feverish brow and said comfortingly, "Just breathe easy, my dearest. You don't have to talk. It's after midnight, and you need your sleep. Shall I fetch Libby for a sleeping potion?"

"No... I'll sleep soon.... My, my, I loved that man...."

"Yes, I know, Mother. Both Lib and I know that." Merry's voice caught in her throat. Her fingers curled around her mother's hands, which twitched on the bedclothes now and then, as if they longed to ply a needle or tend beehives, as they had for so many years.

"I want the same for you, my girl. Libby has Cam, but I want you to have one—just like your father. He was exciting to be with, he—" She gasped for breath.

"Mother, please just rest. You're getting yourself all worked up—"

"He had such dreams for us!"

Those fervent words wavered in the warm air like the flickering candle flame on the bedside table. At first Merry felt relieved that her mother had quieted, and was breathing easier now. Then she realized that she was not breathing at all and that her hands lay still.

"Mother? Mother! Oh, no! No! Libby! Libby! Come quick!" she cried as she hurried out into the dim hall.

In her night rail, Libby came flying, her hair loose and wild. The sisters stood together in a taut embrace at the silent bedside. Then Penelope came in and closed their mother's eyelids.

"I'm sorry I wasn't here, too," Libby choked out as tears ran down her cheeks. "But you were always her comfort and joy."

"Oh, Lib! You were, too!"

"No, it's all right. She's at rest now, and we have a lot of grieving to do. But a lot of joyful remembering, too!"

Trembling, Merry nodded through her tears. Her mother's last wish for her had been the object of all her dreams—the legacy of love.

Merry tossed her blond curls, her skirts swishing about her legs as she walked. A month since her mother had died, and still her heart raged like the weather outside. She paced back and forth during yet another summer night's storm as she glared at the wag-on-the-wall clock on her bedroom wall.

"Drat!" she said. The worst thing was that there was so little for her to do that she considered important. If she had a purpose in life, like Libby, that at least would make her feel that mourning her mother was not time spent just in remembrance of loss. Time was passing her by! Nineteen years old and still a naive—and motherless—spinster! And one not even living up to her mother's final wish for her!

Granted, she had led a few lads a fine chase back on rural Staten Island, where she'd been reared. She could have wed any of them. But she had cared for no man that way, not the way her mother had cared for her father, even at the very last moment of her life. Not one had stirred her passion until that dark stranger had entered this house and briefly held her prisoner. And, though she had fought against it, somehow in her mind he had dared to merge with the beloved man of her dreams! It had been forty-eight days and—she glanced at the clock again—six and one-half hours since the mystery man had held her captive, and she still had no idea who he could have been!

Worse—since, in her dreams, she had always forgiven her fantasy man for fleeing, only to return again and again to beg for her love—she had somehow partly forgiven the intruder. After all, perhaps, in these terrible times, he had good cause. He had stolen nothing, had left nothing amiss, Cam had reported. The stranger had quickly released her and Penelope unharmed—and had left her, she thought, somehow reluctantly. When she'd tried to pin Cam down, it had been useless. He had wanted to dismiss the whole incident as if it had never happened. How she wanted to hate the intruder, but it just wasn't in her, especially when her mother had spoken so fervently of love! Even at the very end of one's life, that was obviously what lasted.

Merry sighed from deep within as the sounds of the storm beat their way into her consciousness again. The night rain gusted outside as if some hovering giant's fist were tossing handfuls of drops against the windows and then, on a whim, batting the next away.

She glared at the ticking clock again. Fourteen minutes after nine of the evening, fifteen minutes after... She felt trapped here, suspended in time, longing to find that man, waiting to find herself. Even the rich, sedate elegance of this house and the kindness of Libby and Cam only stoked her impatience to get on with her life.

Those around her were living out their passions, but she had not yet found hers! Cam had his dedication to his service with the army; Libby had hers to freedom and her powerful, popular Whig newspaper. And they both had their burning love for each other.

But she, Meredith Prudence Morgan, had only the *desire* for service, the *need* for freedom, the *lack* of a burning love. She had a personal score to settle with the vile British, who had taken her home of Staten Island for their own. And, for the way he had captured her mind, she had a score to settle with the intruder.

Her nostrils flared as she paced. Even up here she could smell the aroma of the hearty supper Libby had ordered prepared in the hope that Cam and his officer friends would make it back tonight. With Washington and the army, Cam was making a

bold stand against the encroaching British across the East River
on the Brookland Heights. And this infernal waiting—for information about the army, for her sister to return from her
print shop, for her own life to begin so that she could make
some worthwhile contribution—was driving Merry to utter
distraction!

She even missed her mother's scoldings, almost as much as
she missed her mother. She could just hear her eternally si-
lenced voice lecturing her: "Meredith, now you listen to me, my
girl, and just settle your fractious spirits! You cannot possibly
be thinking day and night about a man you have not been introduced to properly, especially when you don't even know his
family!"

But that bittersweet fantasy, too, faded into the ticktock of
the clock and the perpetual patter of the rain. Because the
British still held Staten Island, they had had to bury Mother
here on Manhattan instead of over there with Father, as she
would have liked. Now, if the British broke through and the
patriots had to evacuate Manhattan, too, Merry would be going
south, alone, to the home of Cam Gant's merchant friends in
Philadelphia, while her sister and her newspaper staff fled north
with the precious printing press to other trading partners of
Cam's in New Haven.

Libby and Cam had both agreed that Merry would be safer
farther away from the fighting, in the new nation's bustling
capital of Philadelphia. Merry, who had fallen in love with the
big-city excitement of New York, agreed it would be a marvelous adventure. Surely the British would never manage to storm
that city, as they might others here along the coast. Cam had
known Judge Shippen for many years, and knew him for a sober, responsible man who kept himself clear of the vagaries of
politics. He would take good care of Merry. And he had three
motherless daughters much of an age with her to keep her
company.

So, initially, the idea of going off alone to fashionable Philadelphia had thrilled Merry. But now, as the possibility of
leaving neared, it tied her stomach up in knots. After all, if she
were sent off to safety in the City of Brotherly Love, how would
she ever find her own husbandly love *here* so that they could

come back here to live after the colonies won the war? Before she left, she would at least make certain Cam told General Washington she would do anything she could to help the cause of freedom in Philadelphia. Or, if Cam would not tell Washington, she would do it herself!

Her impassioned musings scattered at a flutter of knocks on her bedroom door. The young, dark-haired maid, Penelope, darted in, words tumbling from her mouth faster than raindrops.

"Oh, mistress, news just come our army's trapped something terrible over there 'cross the river. Your sister's 'prentice from the print shop's here with a message for you, dripping all over the front hall from the rain he is, and I told him—"

But Merry was already partway down the staircase, her slippered feet pattering softly on the deep carpets, her hand skimming the green-and-gold-striped paper hangings on the wall. Though Penelope had clearly identified her visitor, and she knew the tow-headed boy called Coll quite well, there was one flaming moment when Merry Morgan willed her dripping night visitor to be quite another.

The boy recited his message. "Mistress Merry, Mrs. Gant says tell you to send someone for her the minute word comes of Lieutenant Gant's return. She'll be home in a flash when he gets here, she says. We're puttin' out another issue, then packing if the bad news is true."

Merry squeezed the boy's soaking shoulder. "Bad news? Tell me! What have you heard?"

"That them Brit gen'rals Howe and Clinton somehow trapped a lot of Washington's boys over on Long Island. Some's shot up bad, too. But our gen'ral, he's gonna retreat here to Manhattan. He asked for any kind o' craft that floats to get them 'cross the river. Gonna 'vacuate and then fight from here, I bet. Gonna land the whole army down by the wharves 'fore them lobsterbacks get the rest of them. Say, what's that real good smell?"

"It's a late supper held for Mr. Gant, and I'm going to see you get a big plate of it before you go out in this mess again," Merry said with a pat on his shoulder. "I'll wager," she went on, more to herself than the boy, "our soldiers are every bit as drenched and hungry as you are. And if they're wounded, too..." Her words trailed off as she hurried Coll ahead of her to the kitchen.

"Mrs. Gates," she told the portly cook, who had been nodding on her bench by the broad hearth, "please feed the mistress's apprentice. Then gather up whatever of this food can be carried—all the bread and pastries in the pantry, too—and wrap it in two sacks to keep it dry. I know the master would approve. If I find him down on the wharves, I'll feed him, too!"

Merry was on her way out the door in a flurry of blond curls and ruffled dimity before the old cook's sputtered protests reached her ears. "Penelope!" Merry called on her way up the stairs. "Fetch that linen we've been tearing for bandages and get your weather buskins and cape on. We're going out!"

Despite the old butler's protests and Mrs. Gate's dire mutterings, Merry and Penelope were out on the streets in a quarter hour carrying two heavy sacks filled with food, bandages and clean rags. They'd even packed candles and a flint kit in case hot tallow was needed to stanch bleeding. Merry had changed to her only remaining homespun gown and had left her bulky hoops, panniers and whalebone stays behind. Despite her leather buskins, her sturdy, square-toed shoes were soon full of rainwater. And her wheat-hued hair, carefully curled with iron and papers, hung dank and straight around her face every time her hooded wool cape slid back.

When they reached the formerly bustling New York docks, the truth of the boy's words struck them both. The two women stood awed, shoulder to shoulder, staring out over the slips, ferry moorings and wharves that the British blockade had nearly shut down months before. But now the waterfront stirred with all sorts of sailing and rowing vessels desperately shuttling Washington's trapped troops before the British could close their net across the water.

In the dark and the rain, the homespun shirts and random-hued uniforms of the fledgling Continental Army all looked a shiny black. In this dark, sodden disgrace, no more the proud colors of the brown-smocked marching Marylanders or the sharp blue-and-red caps of the Delaware regiments or Virginia and New York's own blues and buffs. Now hundreds of men, standing, limping or lying on makeshift litters, created churning chaos on the docks.

"Not a very good start to our war for independence," Merry allowed, "but we'll fight and win another day!"

"*We,* mistress?" Penelope asked. "Them army boys, you mean."

"It's our war, too," Merry insisted. "Tote that bag. Come on now."

They walked among the clumps of men, offering hunks of cheese and bread and sweet cinnamon rolls meant for the Gant breakfast table. Merry was moved by how young, stunned and frightened the troops looked. Her stomach twisted in trepidation when she thought of how they would have to face down the massive, veteran British army, with its hated Hessian mercenary troops. Amid the babble of men's voices, she found herself straining her ears for one distinctive, whispering, lilting voice. But, when she came across the first badly wounded man, tears stung her eyes, rivaling the sporadic raindrops.

She knelt beside him on the cobbles to wipe his face with a damp linen rag. She couldn't see where he was wounded, but it must be a gash on his head hidden in his sopping hair somewhere. Rain and blood had turned his forehead pink. He looked so pale, so young, so afraid.

"Say, what's a lady doin' here, and a real pretty one, too?" he asked.

"Just trying to help, my friend. What really happened over there?"

"Damned lobsters snuck 'round and trapped least eight hunnert of the boys, when we can't spare none. Shot up the ranks of the Pennsylvania rifles some. That's me."

"I'm sure you were very brave. I envy you the chance to fight."

"Only a few of us run, but not me, ma'am. Some wounded's still over on the Brookland side. They're having a real bad time loading them to come over. Have to patch 'em up on the run 'cause the whole army got to be over by daybreak or we're doomed. Doomed,'' he concluded, and he closed his eyes with a racking shudder.

Someone shouldered her away, and two men carried the boy off. She moved on to comfort others. At first she was afraid she would be ordered away, but everyone ignored the two women in their frenzied haste. When she looked around for Penelope, she couldn't find her in the press of people.

She edged her way along Murray's Wharf, where the pitiful collection of quickly gathered boats were putting in or setting out. Sailing craft of all sizes struggled with wet, flapping canvas in the gusts of wind, and a smattering of rowboats rounded out the motley fleet. At least the fitful wind was moving them quickly and—for the moment, at least—keeping the big vessels of the British fleet from entering the river.

The Pennsylvania soldier's words about the wounded men over there echoed in Merry's mind. She walked farther out on the rain-slick wooden wharf, bucking the torrent of newly landed troops. The murmur of many men's voices swirled around her, dominated by the strange, flat-accented voices of the Massachusetts Marbleheaders Washington had asked to captain the largest of the requisitioned craft.

''All right, out, boys,'' they intoned nasally. ''Move on...now. We've got to go get ourselves another load 'fore the tides and this nor'east wind shifts. Careful with that wounded man...now, boys. Move on now. We've got to go get—''

She knew then how she could help the cause right now. She hoped Penelope would not worry if she didn't see her in the crowd for a little while. It surely must not be taking more than an hour for one trip over and back. She could aid the wounded over there and help them board. Her sack still held rolls of linen strips, and bandages must be gravely needed. If the rain stopped, she could light a candle and seal wounds with hot tallow. She could not hear any guns firing. Everything was moving smoothly and safely under cover of darkness. Just the other day, Cam had said that every patriot must do his part! Surely that meant women, too! But could she talk one of these dour New Englanders into letting her ride over with him to help?

She moved closer to the numerous vessels bumping the wharf and each other. Then she saw someone she recognized standing with a newly emptied craft. "Mr. Rappaport! Clinton Rappaport!" she called.

The old man, whom she'd known during her girlhood on Staten Island, squinted up at her through the glaze of rain. She grasped a mooring post and jumped down into his single-sailed barge.

"You?" he cried. "Missy Morgan! What in creation—?"

"Go ahead. Push off! I've got bandages here that have to go over, and I can patch up our boys while you bring them back. Hurry now!"

The old man glared at her and shook his head, spraying water like a dog. "Lieutenant Gant send you?" he asked. "Just saw him on a ferry that came over."

She breathed a sigh of relief. Cam was safe! And she wouldn't have to worry about running into him over there. Suddenly she was overwhelmingly convinced that she had to get across this rainy river to help. So she crossed her fingers behind her back the way she and Libby had when they were girls. Even with her rich imagination, she never told untruths anymore—except right now.

"Yes," she blurted. "Lieutenant Gant wants me to help. Don't delay. Shove off."

Shrugging, the old man obeyed. He looked more stooped, more exhausted, than he ever had in all the years he'd hauled Staten Island firewood over to Manhattan. And yet that strange light burned in his eyes that she'd seen in so many others' lately. She thought of it as the freedom flame. It made old men young, shy folk bold, the uncommitted fervently patriotic. And it made Merry Morgan brave enough to risk herself for something bigger than just staying home to tear linens and pray for all these boys.

She nodded and smiled her encouragement and gratitude to him. Mr. Rappaport turned to his task with vigor as they sailed out through the gray curtain of rain and night toward Brookland.

Chapter Two

Merry huddled on the single plank seat in the back corner of the small barge as it plunged across the East River, shoved along by the northeast wind. The very core of her being had come to life. This was real! She was actually doing something to help! She would comfort and bandage the wounded. She had no doubt that Cam and his officer friends, even the grim-faced General Washington, whom she had met once at the house, would be appalled at the thought of a young woman heading over toward the enemy, but she did not waver in her belief that she was doing the right thing.

She closed her eyes against the push of the dark, damp wind. The rain was merely sputtering now. The night felt black and close, like a blindfold pressing in on her, shutting out the world. It was like that time last month when the man had surprised her in the town house. Strange how that memory warmed rather than chilled her, even now. When the man had stood, looking down on her, while she lay blindfolded in her petticoat, he had admitted he was "just looking." And she meant to keep looking for him, though she would know him only by his whispered voice and by the onyx ring she had glimpsed on his hand.

She jumped at the sound of Clinton Rappaport's voice. "Brace yourself, missy. We're here!"

The draft of the barge was so slight that they did not have to put in at the crowded ferry landing like other vessels. "Hang on!" Clinton added as the prow crunched against the beach. Immediately clusters of waiting soldiers, a few of them holding horses, all of them with muskets and powder wrapped to keep them dry, emerged from the darkness. Like nervous cattle, they surged forward to be rescued by the ramshackle "navy" of the new American nation.

The wounded were lying on the shore, so Merry climbed out, helped by someone's hand. There were a few surprised gasps when the soldiers realized that she was a woman, but they generally ignored her in their haste to clamber aboard. Breathing a prayer of gratitude that her sister's husband was on the safe shore, Merry bent over the wounded, wrapping wounds, dispensing words of courage.

Finally the rain stopped completely. She saw that a bullet had plowed through one rifleman's shoulder. She put down her sack and fumbled with her flint kit to light a candle. Her hands were shaking, but she knew the tallow in the wound would stop the blood until he could be bled properly later.

Her heart thudded in her breast, making her entire body shake. With the hand not holding the candle, she ripped the man's shirt away from the wet gash. She bit her lower lip to calm herself. She had never seen so much as a man's naked chest—save her father's years before—let alone a bullet hole. She lifted her candle higher to see where she should dribble the tallow. And then it happened.

"Curse you!" a harsh voice hissed. "Get that damned light out, you fool!!" A man knocked her over, and his big, booted foot stamped her candle in the mud, just missing her fingers. On her hands and knees in the slick mess, glaring up at him, she tried to stand. He looked like some black, faceless giant that had emerged from the river's depths.

"I was only trying to help!" she insisted. "This man could bleed to death and—"

"Sacrebleu!" the man clipped out. "A woman! And over here at a time like this! How in blazes—?"

It could not be, but that voice, that word . . .

She tried futilely to claw his hand away as he reached roughly for her elbow and dragged her to her feet. He peered into her upturned face, then muttered something she did not catch. Oh, no! Not this rough, rude monster! He could not be the man she sought! Her mind was playing tricks on her!

He was still only a big, dark form, a face she could not see in the looming dark. But she had no time to question or protest as he hauled her like a sack of booty down to the crowded shore. She slipped more than once in the slick mud, but he pulled her on. Her cloak, soaked with mud and rain, pulled away and fell behind.

"Who are you? I demand you loose me!"

"You demand nothing! You could have signaled the British with that light! Gotten us and yourself killed! Some men have orders to bayonet anyone with a signal light! The enemy may discover us at any moment and pound us with their artillery! Damn you, woman, this is no evening soirée!"

Her insides cartwheeled and her head spun. She would have seethed at being cursed and handled so roughly by anyone—and when she only meant to help!—but the fact that it was this man made it worse. Even in his rage, his voice had that distinctive foreign lilt to it. But she had imagined he would truly be more gentle and gentlemanly when they met again, even more solicitous of her than he had been at the town house. But now—   Before she could again demand his identity, he dared to toss her over his shoulder and stride out into the dark water with her. He plunked her in a sloop like a sack of potatoes, then hiked himself up and in after her. She was already drenched, but he sprayed river water on her when he swung his booted legs over and plopped down beside her in the corner of the crowded sloop. The troops had one nervous, snorting horse, covered piles of muskets and several barrels of gunpowder aboard, and they were all wedged in tight.

The sloop's two small sails flapped, catching the breeze, and the vessel put out at once. The stranger dared to prop his arm behind her on the gunwales as if she sat willingly in his embrace. And through it all she squinted in the dim moonlight that filtered through the river mist to see what he looked like, praying she was mistaken about who he was.

He seemed all raven dark. She could see that much. Black garments that he was brushing mud off of, as if he were going to the palace to see King George himself. Black leather riding boots, ebony hair pulled tightly back in a queue that looked as if it would not dare let one strand loose. A swarthy, forbidding face, with a rough shadow of beard and a flash of white teeth that she'd have called a snarl.

If only she could get him to whisper instead of raving at her like a lunatic, perhaps she could assure herself that he was not the man she sought. If only she could touch his right thumb to see if he sported an onyx ring there. Surely he could not be the intruder who had merged with the courtly knight of her fondest daydreams, the man who would seek her forgiveness and vowed to be her humble, adoring love forever! After all, his raw anger and his obvious dislike for her were what she saw best in the dark.

"You realize you are taking a soldier's place here," he clipped out coldly. "One place, perhaps one life, eh?"

"I only meant to save lives. I didn't think of that."

"Certainly not. Just jump ahead. Do not think."

"You have no right to speak to me this way and—"

"Besides, women are bad luck on a sailing vessel," he said smugly. "Bad luck anywhere."

"You surely don't believe—" she began, but the horse's wild neighing drowned out her words before someone soothed it and held its muzzle closed.

And then the wind died completely.

They bobbed, everyone unspeaking save for a few whispered curses, somewhere in the middle of the East River. Despite the patches of floating fog, the sky was brightening, so they could see other sailing vessels, likewise perilously becalmed. Merry looked everywhere but at the stranger. Did he really think she had caused this bad fortune?

Occasionally rowboats, loaded to the gunwales, went creaking by, but everyone knew sails were needed to get the rest of the army across by dawn. The water all around them looked as flat as pounded pewter.

"Hell," someone whispered, "the bloody Brits'll see us and drag a few good pieces to the shore to pick us off like damned sittin' ducks out here."

Merry's heart was thundering so hard in her breast that she was certain the men would hear. The stranger had said her presence was bad luck. She hoped no one else believed she might have caused the calm. She knew none of them felt one bit calm inside. She prayed harder than she ever had that this rude, crude ruffian beside her was not her mysterious stranger. The war had shattered her once placid life; she could not bear to have the private world of her dreams shattered, too.

Packed like a herring in brine, Merry thought as she sat wedged between the stranger and the hull of the craft. She shifted in her seat, trying to move her hips away from the persistent press of the man's rock-hard thigh. It radiated heat to her leg and bottom, a heat that spread upward, inward. She dared not move or even breathe too deeply. This was not the way she'd imagined she'd react when she met the man of her dreams. This was a nightmare! But when he whispered to her she knew he was, curse him to the devil, the man she had sought.

"You can berate me later," he whispered, as if he had read her thoughts. "Voices carry on still water, even with no breeze."

Yes, that very voice! Despite his warning, she almost stood up in the boat and screamed.

"You!" she croaked. "It is you!"

"I have not the vaguest notion what you mean. Silence!"

He turned away. He was a mocking man, perhaps even a bitter man. Fiercely bitter—at her, at the war, at the lack of breeze, at life, she did not know. Even in the misty air, she stared at him, memorizing the ghostly profile of the man who had haunted her. The wretch was indeed, she admitted grimly, the handsomest man she had ever seen, just as she'd imagined he would be. But he was certainly not what she had expected, what she had longed for. Nor had she conjured up his true appearance.

His nose was not patrician, as it had been in her fantasies. It was a bit crooked, with one small bump. Surely someone had broken it for him, and she understood all too well that someone might want to. His brows were thicker than she had pictured. With no aristocratic arch, they went straight across above his eyes, making him seem vexed. His face was lean and austere, with prominent brow and cheekbones. That much she had envisioned. His mouth was more than taut-lipped; it was set harshly now. His slick hair was blacker than the night, as were the eyes that had burned her when he'd glared her way.

Somehow, when they got ashore, she had to find Cam and tell him she knew who the intruder was. He could be a British spy or a rabid Tory sympathizer now passing as a friend to the army, in which case Cam could take him into custody tonight, before he ruined this entire endeavor. Luckily, she was safe—at least from him—on a craft loaded with Washington's soldiers! Yet, sitting so close, she trembled deep inside at something more awesome than fear.

"There will be a reward," she whispered to him when she found the courage, "if you deliver me ashore to my brother-in-law, Lieutenant Cameron Gant."

He deigned to slant a narrowed glance her way again. "You are fortunate," he rasped, with a tug at one sopped and muddy shirt cuff, "not to be delivered over the side of this sloop into this river. You have risked not only your own life but all of ours." After that, chastised and crushed, she kept turned away from him.

They all sat unspeaking, awkward, tense, while the eastern sky grayed and the rain began again. From somewhere down the small sloop came the distinctive sound of more than one soldier unbuttoning his breeches and making water over the side. Her elbows propped on her knees, Merry slunk lower and covered her eyes with her hands.

"No manners in war, eh?" her rude rescuer said.

"You ought to know," she shot back without uncovering her face.

Events around her were spinning out of her control, so unlike the daydreams she had embroidered as cleverly as she did her needlework. She felt only panic and anger at having discovered him this way. No sunlight, no flowers, no proper introductions, no civil, polite, flirtatious smiles in the beginning. Only brutality, war, danger all around, and the prospect of worse. Despite what she had thought was her iron stomach, the gently rocking craft began to make her queasy in a way that the plunging barge on the way over had not.

"Ohh!" she muttered as she twisted over the side to be sick. To her amazement and dismay, the stranger held her shoulders and offered her a sodden cambric handkerchief. Shaking, suddenly weak, she clung to his proffered arm. His words, however, were anything but comforting.

"Always trouble."

"You don't even know me—"

"Women are all the same when it comes to a crisis. Complications and foul luck from the very first."

Just then the breeze lifted, as if from the gray river itself. It cooled her hot face. A fist of wind pushed the sail and moved the becalmed vessel forward. The entire stranded, makeshift flotilla started toward Manhattan again. Merry sat up and shrugged the man's arm off, and he seemed glad enough to pull it back. Everyone squinted to pierce the rain and fog toward freedom's shore. She felt better now, and she cursed the fact this man had seen her weakness and felt her need for him. And if he ever guessed how passionately she had been searching for him, she would be mortified to her very grave!

An interminable trip later, the sloop butted Murray's Wharf. The craft emptied as if a cork had been pulled from a bottle. When Merry stood unsteadily in the rocking craft, the man's hard hand returned to her upper arm, and he half lifted, half escorted her forward.

"I can make it myself, sir!"

"Admit you almost did not. Not only could the enemy have gotten you, but if you had been a soldier waving that candle, you could have been court-martialed, even bayoneted, for putting us all in danger. No noise or lights—those were strict orders over there."

She tried without success to loose her arm from him. "I demand that you return me to my brother-in-law, Lieutenant Cameron Gant!"

"Indeed I shall. Poor man. A willful wife, and you in his house, as well."

He'd tipped his hand, admitting he knew of them. She had him now! Cam could seize him, if she could just get them together! At least then she'd find out who he really was!

"You admit you know of him, then. That you've been in his house," she declared triumphantly, though she fully expected the wretch to try to lie his way out of her discovery.

"Certainly," he replied as he hustled her down the swarming wharf. "Such a lovely town house, with a beautiful—if nosy—female running about *en déshabille*."

His honesty—and that bitter, teasing tone again—set her back. Perhaps he was not all bad after all. Perhaps he had been assigned to make sure no lights were lit and had only been doing his duty over on the Brookland shore. But, no, the man had been entirely insufferable to her, a lone woman, even after that. How could she have been so stupid as to think she could care for someone like this? He obviously hated her, and perhaps all women for all she knew. What had she ever done except light one candle to help a bleeding soldier?

If she ever saw this man wounded—drat him, whatever his name was, whatever foreign country he had crawled out of— she would not stop to help him if he lay bleeding hard enough to fill the entire blasted East River! She was embarrassed and ashamed that she had ever indulged in fantasies about this rude oaf. Her face flamed and perspiration rolled between her breasts at the mere thought.

To her amazement, he seemed to know exactly where to find Cam in this hubbub. Well, at least Cam would help her now! This man would finally get what he deserved, she thought smugly when he freed her nearly numb arm at last.

"Merry!" Cam said, shocked. His blond hair, which made many people think she was his sister rather than his sister-in-law, shone white in the foggy dawn. "What in the world are you doing here? And with— Do you know this man?" he demanded, looking even more surprised.

"He's the one who broke into the town house last month, the one who tied me up!"

"I know. I'll try to explain later," Cam muttered, looking shamefaced, and put a hand on her shoulder. Merry's mouth dropped, but neither man so much as looked her way. "I take it you've just been across, Mont. What's it look like over there?"

"Perhaps with the fog they shall all make it—if Clinton and Howe keep late to their beds, eh? I found her over there, Gant," he continued, with a toss of head and a sniff that she considered the ultimate in brazen arrogance. It was as if he could just dismiss her as having no right to help. "She could have been killed, the little fool!"

Strangely, his words and his frown softened her heart. He did at least care that she might have been killed. "Cam," she said, "you're friends with this man? But he's the one, who— Drat it, Cam, who is he? He's not a Brit—I can tell that—though he has the manners of one!"

Cam dared a quick laugh. Mont's eyes glittered harshly as he looked at her. Unlike some men, who dimpled when they smiled, this one had a tiny cleft in his chin that appeared when he set his jaw in a frown—which was all the time, as far as she could tell! But when he looked at her like that she began to shiver, and not from fear. It's because I've been soaked to the skin for hours, that's all, she told herself. She was furious at both Cam and Mont. Mont—what sort of name was that, she wondered, her thoughts jumping about. Libby read a lot. Maybe she would know.

And then she realized with a start that Mont's eyes were not dark at all. Even in the pearly gray of fog and dawn they were stunning, the clearest green! When his sharp gaze took in the way her sodden garments clung to her shapely form she began to shiver even harder. When he lifted his right hand to his square chin, as if to peruse her at his leisure, she saw the tell-tale onyx thumb ring.

"He's just a friend from Europe named Darcy Mont, Merry," Cam was saying. "That day in the town house—a misunderstanding. I know he regrets it." He turned to the man. "I'll get someone to take her all the way home, Mont. I can't thank you enough for—"

"Thank him!" Merry cried. "For tying me up at the town house? For dragging me around tonight? I was coming right back on the barge. I was only helping our men! And he terrified me speechless!"

"You? Speechless?" Mont said mockingly. "You were only really speechless once, when I threatened to gag you. And, as your brother-in-law says, I regret that."

The fantasies in which he always apologized to her washed over her in a warm rush. He was not on bended knee, but he had, more or less, said he was sorry. Yet she fretted at having been played for a fool, not only by this man, but by Cam, too. Worse, she was enraged at herself for pining after such a smug, insufferable man.

"I'll get home on my own, thank you both!" she managed. "You'd best see to your men, Cam, and not let a 'foolish woman' take any more of your time, either of you," she insisted, drawing herself up proudly, despite her bedraggled appearance.

"Not with the entire army wandering loose!" Cam declared.

"I am going that way to send a rider for Franklin, Gant," Darcy Mont said, as if he hadn't heard her protest. "General Washington said he could help parley if the retreat worked. And I believe it has."

Merry's thoughts whirled again. This man was an intimate of Washington's? And he knew Ben Franklin, the greatly revered Pennsylvania patriot and statesman?

"Mistress Morgan, after you," Darcy Mont declared grandly, as if they had just met at some well-chaperoned ball and he'd asked to partner her in a quadrille. "At your service to escort you to the house where fate first brought us together," he added under his breath, his face straight and stern.

She glanced at Cam. He looked suddenly uncertain that she should walk off with Mont again. She had almost decided to refuse and stalk away from both of them, but then Darcy Mont removed his coat and swung it around her shoulders like a big cape. Despite its dampness, its warmth and protection enveloped her. And it smelled deliciously of river air—and the tart tang of intrigue and danger.

She would have liked to shove him to his knees so that he could apologize properly for all he'd put her through. But, she supposed, if she played her cards right, there were other ways to bring a proud, even arrogant, man to his knees. And he had as many questions to answer as Cam did.

She bade Cam good-night. Then, her chin angled, she thanked Darcy Mont stiffly for the use of his coat. She drew herself up to her full five-foot-six-inch height, which he beat by a good six inches. Then she gathered up her muddy, sodden hems from the running gutters and walked like a countess beside him down the street toward home.

"I'm sorry, sister, but I couldn't find out much about Darcy Mont for you," Libby reported four days later. "After all, if you couldn't get much out of him during a midnight walk, what else would others around town know? He's just a rich, bored man touring the colonies, that's the word out on him. But I hear his English is quite good for a Frenchman."

"French? He's French?" Merry demanded. She felt a fool for not having recognized a French accent, but then why would she? And why had he refused to share even that with her on their awkward walk back to the house the other night? He had acted as if he couldn't bear even to look her in the face. He must think her the simplest colonial bumpkin. "But why would a rich man, a friend of Cam's, be sneaking into this house? And he's hardly bored, Lib! He seems to know everyone who's anyone in this war—Washington, Franklin, and *your* husband. Drat! If Cam hadn't been with the troops up by Harlem since the retreat I'd make him tell us why this Mont monster is mixing in our nation's business so!"

"Monster?" Libby said with a laugh. "But you said he was disgustingly handsome, I believe, and that hardly sounds like a monster to me! Now don't fret. When I get Cam alone some place besides in bed I'll ask him!"

Libby rolled her eyes and chuckled, so Merry laughed, too, as if she knew all about what went on in marriage beds. Merry yearned to know, but she had never worked up courage enough to ask Libby. Even her wildest fantasies—which she'd halted, of course, now that she knew what a lost cause her mystery man was—never got as far as a marriage bed.

"Besides—" Libby's words yanked her attention back again "—what with worrying about the war and evacuating us safely when the time comes, Cam has so much on his mind right now."

"Don't we all?" Merry muttered as the two sisters went into the sunny upstairs sitting room to take afternoon coffee together. Libby, ramrod straight, perched on one end of the green silk brocade settee to pour while Merry plopped down, one arm

along the back of the couch, one foot tucked up under her vo-
luminous blue satin skirts. When their mother had died, Libby
had adopted the maternal task of chiding Merry for her nonchalant demeanor and casual posture. Today she saw her sister's brooding look—a look she knew all too well—and held her
tongue.

Both were pretty women much of a height, but the Morgan
sisters were quite a contrast. Merry's shapeliness counterbal-
anced Libby's slenderness. Although more men tended to give
Merry slanted second glances, Merry had always envied her
elder sister for her naturally curly hair, for she spent hours
curling her own. Meredith's looks, pale, golden, almost angelic,
belied her exuberant, strong-willed nature. Elizabeth—
"Libby" was the result of the colonial penchant for nick-
names—had crimson hair and hazel eyes. Her heightened col-
oring suggested an impetuous, flamboyant temper. Yet she was
quite self-disciplined, circumspect and calm—at least compared to Merry.

Though the two sisters loved and admired each other greatly,
their early years had set them quite on diverse paths in terms of
personality: Merry was too clearly their mother's favorite, and
Libby their father's. The only things Merry had inherited from
their grandiose sire, Silas Morgan, were her generous streak and
her fertile imagination. Yet, unlike her dead father, Merry kept
her daydreams to herself and had long ago outgrown even little white lies—except those she generously told herself in her
search for a man to admire and love.

Merry was witty and bright, but she preferred to learn from
experience and people, rather than books. She navigated
through life with her womanly emotions and instincts, despite
the fact that both sometimes got her in trouble. Libby was a
deep thinker, a fervent reader who was content to spend hours
on her own—at least she had been, before she'd inherited the
Liberty Gazette and fallen wildly in love with Cameron Gant.
Still, she tended to be a rational, detached observer of people
and life, and she brought that talent to bear on her younger
sister now.

"A good American penny for your thoughts, as if I didn't know," Libby prompted when Merry just sipped her coffee from her saucer in uncharacteristic silence.

"Why would a Frenchman be all cozy with American rebels? After all, we fought *against* the French in the Indian Wars not so many years ago."

"But we were fighting for the British then. The French have always hated them much more than they ever hated us," Libby explained. "Indeed, it goes way back to Froissart's medieval chronicles and all of that."

"I'm afraid I haven't read it, Lib," Merry said testily, and put her saucer down a bit too hard.

"Well, let's look at it this way," Libby explained. "Our stand against the Brits has pleased the French. But, little sister, one handsome, brooding Frenchman mixing in 'all cozy,' as you say, hardly means a thing in international affairs. Maybe he just met and impressed General Washington. And, with the Brits knocking on the door again, our commander-in-chief needs every good, trustworthy man he can find!"

"Well," Merry declared huffily as she took another piece of buttered walnut bread, "I'm not so sure Darcy Mont's a good, trustworthy man yet. And, alas, I'm too busy with important things to bother to find out."

"Really, Merry! Methinks the lady doth protest too much. In the beginning, when I fell for Cam, I was always— Oh, I hear his voice below!" Libby cried, and leapt up to run for the door. "We can talk more later—"

Merry just shook her head as the door swung shut behind her sister. When Libby dropped all decorum to greet her husband like that, Merry knew better than to remind her to ask Cam about Darcy Mont again!

Later that day, when Cam had been closeted downstairs in his library with Libby for a very long time, Merry sensed that something special was afoot. Servants darted here and there; Libby sent her maid up for more quills and lots of paper and orders not to say why. Looking out the sitting room window into busy Broad Way Street, facing the parklike Commons, Merry noted that several of Washington's soldiers had ridden in to stand about in all-too-obvious nonchalance. Merry darted through the upstairs to peer out her back bedroom window. She could see no one near the mews from here, so she went to the single small oval window on the curve of the master staircase. Yes! A few more of Washington's smartly attired Virginia regiment, looking none the worse for their rainswept flight across the East River four days earlier, were clustered around a carriage that apparently had come down the back alley without a sound!

She plied her ribboned fan harder in the warmth of the afternoon as she put all the clues together. Her heart was beating very hard. She shook out her pale blue satin skirts and straightened the row of stiff pink satin bows on her quilted stomacher. General Washington had been here once for dinner and once for an unannounced meeting. Perhaps he had come again. If so, perhaps she could catch him as he left and tell him she would do anything she could to help freedom's cause, even after she went to Philadelphia.

And she intended to explain to him why she had gone across to Brookland during the retreat. News of her nursing the wounded had appeared in several New York gazettes. People had reacted strongly, one way or the other. Some declared her a heroine, an angel of mercy; others scolded that she had behaved scandalously, that young unwed women should be kept far from strange wounded men with their garments all in tatters. Libby had sided with her, though Merry surmised that Cam was upset. Perhaps after she discovered what General Washington thought about it all she'd just briefly ask him what he knew of Darcy Mont.

Merry started resolutely down the stairs. Muted voices rumbled from Cam's library below. His stiff-as-starch butler, Andrews, was placing a large silver tray of Madeira and some glasses—five glasses, to be exact—on the mahogany Chippendale table just outside the library door. Surprised, he looked up the half flight of stairs to where Merry stood, as if she had caught him in some devious act.

"Oh, Mistress Morgan. Just setting the things down here. The master's guests prefer to serve themselves inside, you see."

"Oh, yes, I do see. Things need to be a bit private with the general in attendance."

Andrews nodded, evidently relieved that she understood. He gave one of the glasses another quick polish with his linen cloth, then folded it neatly on the tray. "He looked rather grim, the general," Andrews whispered confidentially. "After that defeat."

"Not a defeat, Andrews, just a retreat until we face them the next time," Merry insisted with a nod and a tight smile.

Andrews nodded, too, almost proudly, a new gleam in his eye. After asking if he could fetch her anything and being assured that she was just fine, he left her. Merry stood stock-still, her heart racing, her brain building possibilities. And then she marched down the last of the steps, quietly opened the library door a crack and hefted the heavy tray to take it in.

"The British commander treated us like servants on Staten Island, General," an indignant but measured voice was reporting. "Made us stand like lackeys on the hot sand surrounded with his horde of Hessians and refused to listen to any terms of peace. I shall inform Congress that my report on the entire fiasco of attempted armistice with the British is 'We met, we talked, we parted. Now nothing remains but to fight!' "

"Well said, Mr. Franklin," Cam's voice declared.

"But not well fought so far," rumbled a stern voice that Merry recognized as General Washington's. "As one of our critics said, and rightly so, 'In general our generals were outgeneraled back there on Long Island.' But I intend to make another stand for this city and to hold the field this time! Tell that to Congress, and to Versailles, too, Mr. Franklin!"

Wherever was Vair-sigh, Merry wondered. Holding the big, unwieldy tray, she shoved the door open with her panniered hip and stood as it swung inward and bumped the oak-paneled wall. Libby, who was taking notes, looked up and saw her. Her eyes widened. Cam frowned. And Merry almost dropped the glass and silver all over the floor when she saw who else sat there.

It was not Washington's sharp eyes that startled her; nor was it the amused gaze and quick smile of the elderly Benjamin Franklin. Darcy Mont, who had been sitting with his back to her, twisted around in his chair. She felt as if his eyes undressed her on the spot.

"Good afternoon," she managed. "I saw the drink tray quite unattended in the foyer and felt Cam's guests would want it now. Really, no one told me—I had no idea," she floundered as she set the tray on the big polished sideboard, "just exactly who all was here."

Her hard gaze dared Darcy to protest before she looked away. Libby dropped her quill pen and jumped up to help with the drinks.

Ben Franklin's voice broke the awkward silence. "And who, may I ask, is this charming young lady?"

Merry answered for herself. "A patriot, sir, who has come to help any way she can!" She shot a dimpled smile the old man's way. She was grateful to have found an ally in the midst of these stares.

Cam rose and made hasty introductions all around. He saved Darcy Mont for last, saying merely, "I believe you've met Mr. Mont."

"Ever my pleasure," Mont muttered properly, though she knew that was a bald-faced lie. Merry retreated to the sideboard and busied herself with glasses so that he could not possibly take her hand and bow over it as Ben Franklin had. She dared not let Darcy touch her; each time he so much as looked her way her knees turned to water. He, too, looked uncomfortable, however, and she took heart from that. Perhaps he was ashamed of the way he had acted on the two strained occasions they had met.

"Just let me serve you before I leave you to your work," Merry told them as Libby helped.

"I didn't know *he* would be here, honestly," Libby whispered to Merry when their backs were turned to the men. "Not any of it, until Cam told me just a bit ago. And I'm not to put a word of what's said in the gazette. The notes are for Congress in Philadelphia!"

The two smiling sisters served the drinks. Unfortunately, Merry smacked Darcy Mont's Madeira down just a bit too hard and splashed half the glass's contents in his lap. She stared down at his wet crotch, which was outlined and flaunted by his tight breeches, for one instant before she jumped back.

"Oh, sorry," she said. "I'm sure they don't make such mistakes in France." She felt a rush of triumph that she had told him—all of them—that she knew where the man was from. But the revelation was apparently not appreciated at the table, and an awkward silence followed. Why was it supposed to be such a secret? Merry fumed.

Her eyes jerked up to meet Darcy's, and she read stark challenge in them. Libby noted their locked, defiant gazes well, as did bespectacled, gray-haired Ben Franklin.

Quickly, in an attempt to smooth things over, Libby offered Darcy a linen cloth from the tray. "I understand you've met my sister twice before, sir," she blurted.

"Indeed," Darcy replied, his voice a study in taut control. He did not use the towel. Merry had the strangest feeling that he wanted to dare her to do so, despite all the stares. "If she is still angry I dragged her back from Long Island before she could become cannon fodder, I apologize publicly," he continued with surprising politeness. "The truth is, she looked quite the golden angel of mercy in the hell over there. You see, General," he said to Washington, "I feared your wounded colonial boys would look up into her lovely face and think they had glimpsed heaven already. And then they would too readily give up the ghost when they are needed to fight another day."

The clever compliment seemed to break the tension for all but Merry. Washington and Cam went back to whispering, Ben Franklin chortled, and Libby's silver laughter laced the air. But Merry felt herself blush hot. The prickling telltale warmth she had thought she had outgrown years before started. The blush began just above her breasts, so carefully powdered to look fashionably pale, and spread up her ivory throat. It heated her cheeks crimson and inflamed her all over. It was either that or the way Darcy Mont was still glaring at her.

"My sister-in-law's going to stay with merchant friends of mine in Philadelphia soon, the Shippen family," Cam put in, and Merry blessed him for the shift in the conversation. When Darcy Mont heard her destination, Merry saw his thick, straight brows bob once, though she was trying not to gawk at him.

"And what a delightful addition she will be to my home city!" Ben Franklin declared with a shake of his straggly gray locks. No one in the room wore a proper wig but Washington. Indeed, in the age of wigs, Mr. Franklin seemed to flaunt his baldness. His plain, dark Quaker garments stood out, as well, especially next to Darcy's elegant attire. "And she will fit right in at Judge Shippen's big house," Mr. Franklin went on with another nod and smile for Merry, "as his three lovely daughters will surely welcome a companion. Mr. Mont and I will be delighted to show you about town if we're still there, will we not, sir?"

"If I am not kept busy day and night having to improve your schoolboy French, Mr. Franklin," Darcy Mont said.

Merry bit her lower lip to keep back a gasp of surprise. Franklin laughed loudly and pounded his gnarled hickory walking stick on the floor. So that was it, Merry thought. For some reason, Ben Franklin was to be instructed in French, and Darcy Mont was his tutor. But Mont in Philadelphia, too? Perhaps they were meant to keep on meeting! Still, he was not what she wanted, was he? However would she tame a man like Darcy Mont!

"Well, Mr. Franklin," she said, "I can only wish you good fortune and much-needed patience and perseverance in learning French with Mr. Mont. And so I shall leave you to your refreshments, sirs—and your planning. I just want General Washington to know I would like to help the cause in any way I can in the future."

Chairs scraped back as the four men stood. "Mistress Morgan," General Washington said from his place at the head of the table, "we thank you for your aid and your spirit—even risking involvement in a battle, as you did the other night. And I shall remember your brave offer to help, though it shall not be on a battlefield again. At least," he added when he noted how Darcy stared yet at Merry in the first moment when she was not staring at him, "not on a battlefield of war."

Merry's lips curved into a satisfied smile that General Washington had taken her seriously—and that he had done so in front of the French tutor Mont. But, despite her desire to exit ignoring the Frenchman, she could not resist a curious glance back at him to see if he felt reprimanded that Washington valued her service to the troops.

The glance was a grave mistake. She felt sucked under, pulled back, as if Darcy Mont had physically reached for her and given her a rough shake. Her feet seemed to disappear from beneath her, as if she could not leave his presence, as if the wind had died, becalming her ship again while she waited for something more between them to begin.

Then she fled, closing the door just a bit too loudly.

Chapter Three

Two days later, Merry stood with Cam and Libby in the early-morning light under the tall tower of the Provincial Arms Hotel and Tavern in central Manhattan. The New York City landmark had long been known as the King's Arms, but had been quickly renamed when King George III became their reviled enemy instead of revered sovereign. The Arms was famous as the tallest spot in town from which to "take the view" or, these days, to watch for the approaching foe by land or sea. It was from the front steps that the fast "flying" coach set out each morning for the two-day trip south to the new nation's largest city, Philadelphia.

Because Cam was now often away from home with the army, he thought it best that he send both his wife and her sister out of town before the British drew their net even tighter. He regretted that there was not extra room for Merry where Libby would be staying with his friends in New Haven. But he assured himself that his lively sister-in-law would be better off in the more pleasant company of three young ladies and their watchful father than mixed in with whatever burly men Libby hired to work her press in New Haven. Merry's coach was being loaded now, and Libby was sailing for New Haven this afternoon, with the remnants of the gazette's staff, on one of Cam's merchant ships, now converted for smuggling goods past the British naval blockade. Both Morgan sisters, for their own reasons, were unable to hold back tears.

"But you should have told me sooner about an escort!" Merry protested shakily to Cam. "I don't need one at all, and certainly not Darcy Mont! Strange he's such a 'friend' of yours, when he as good as broke into the house.''

"I told you I can't share more on that now, Merry," Cam replied. "Let's just say that war makes strange bedfellows. That aside, the British and their Hessian cohorts may attack any day now. What was I supposed to do when I heard Mont was heading for Philadelphia by coach this very week?"

"Put me alone on the last coach if you had to!"

"Meredith Morgan!" Libby scolded, just as their mother would have. "I thought you were interested in knowing more of Darcy Mont. And this may *be* the last coach for all Cam knows!"

"I can't believe that man said he would escort me," Merry said, trying another tack. "He detests me."

"I'm sure your sour face and stubborn attitude will win him over," Cam replied pointedly. "Besides, the way he looked at you the other day was not exactly hateful."

"Oh, drat," Merry murmured, dabbing at her eyes. "I am sorry, Cam. You've been so wonderful to me, done everything to help. I know that was your intent here, too. I'm just so nervous about leaving."

Cam put one arm around her shoulders and the other around his sniffling wife. "I know. And I only wanted what was safest for you. Mont's a real loner, but he was reared to be a gentleman through and through. Don't give me that look. I mean it! I feel better to know you'll be traveling together. It's only two days. And I believe he won't be in Philadelphia long. He's sailing back to France, so if you really dislike him so much you won't be in agony long."

That good news made Merry's tears flow even harder. She hugged Cam goodbye and thanked him again for his care and generosity. She held tightly to Libby, as if she could cling to the stable, peaceful past of her girlhood, before the war and her mother's death had changed everything. If only her mother had lived, she'd be making this journey with her. That would have kept Darcy Mont's tart tongue in its place!

Cam helped her up the iron steps into the high wooden coach. Phil.-N.Y. City Flying Coach was painted in bold red-and-gold script on its side. Two men—one quite elderly—and two women were already settled inside. Merry rolled up the canvas flap beside her to smile down at her family's dear upturned faces. Fortunately, Darcy Mont was yet nowhere in sight and so could not witness this scene. Merry was quite convinced he had no warm sentiments of his own. Suddenly her stomach flopped over in a flash of cowardice at the thought of facing him again.

"The war's going to make this separation hard, but it's for the best," Libby called up to her as she dabbed at another wayward tear. "Just think of it as a great adventure."

Cam reached up to pat Merry's gloved hand on the sill. "You're strong, like your sister, Merry. I was never prouder of you than the other day, when you volunteered to help General Washington. And," he went on at his wife's prompting, as if he'd told her something privately but hesitated to admit it, "I greatly admire your bravery in thinking to help our wounded boys across the river, even at great risk to yourself. But take care of yourself, my dear. Don't do anything foolhardy, even in pursuit of freedom. The army will win the day! And if I get south to defend the capital, I'll come calling at Judge Shippen's!"

"Oh, yes, do, Cam! I wish you could bring Libby, too!" Merry called down to them. "And don't worry about me a bit. I'll write, and I won't cause the Shippens a bit of trouble!"

Behind her family, she saw Darcy Mont approaching. Was that smirk on his face because he had heard her last passionate vow and believed there was no way she could keep out of trouble? Or was it because he intended to be that trouble himself? He strode forward to bid polite farewells to the Gants and heft his leather satchel up to the luggage boy on top. Then he climbed in.

The coach rocked once under his weight, bumping Merry's shoulder into the wall. She had chosen her seat so that Mont could not sit beside her or facing her. But the passengers on the opposite side moved down so that he was directly across from her by the still-open door.

It did not seem to bother him one bit that his long, booted legs took up most of the meager space between their hard benches. Well, she thought, staring boldly back so that he would not think he had bothered or bested her, at least now he'll have to tell me all about himself.

He tipped his black velvet tricorne to her and straightened both lace-edged sleeves under a hunter green coat with huge, upturned brown cuffs. His boots looked like polished ebony; she could see her elongated reflection in them. At least she would not have to jog along tens of miles today with his hard hip rubbing hers again; that would not have been easy—especially in these narrow traveling skirts!

The door snapped shut. Merry waved her fan and called final farewells to Cam and Libby as the coach lurched away. She looked pointedly out the window as the city, which had become so dear to her, shrank behind them. Her stomach rolled a bit in trepidation at the thought of what she would have to face in this coach and beyond. She prayed fervently that the British and their looting Hessians never take New York—and that she would not be sick in front of Darcy Mont again.

Soon she found that the hot September sun and the bouncing of the carriage lulled her, despite the hard bench, her nervous stomach and Darcy's nearness. He had been too rude to make conversation, and she was stubborn enough to match his game. She had obviously made a serious mistake about his real character once, and she would not repeat that foolhardiness. Let him just keep looking out the window as if he expected danger around every bend. He seemed to her like one with a guilty conscience. Drat the Frenchman! She hadn't asked him to come along as her escort, anyway, and she'd tell him so privately at the first tavern stop they made.

She had managed to shift her feet and her dark brown skirts away from him so that they did not touch at all, except when an especially bad jolt in a hole in the road scrambled them all together. At least now Darcy Mont had tipped his hat down over those green, green prying eyes, as if he were asleep. Despite his presence, she, too, felt almost drowsy. Suddenly she had no desire to speak with the man, as what she had to say would no doubt upset these other, civil passengers.

Early on the journey, they crossed the Hudson River at King's Ferry and started down through New Jersey. Now why hadn't patriots renamed King's Ferry, too, she wondered, anxious to keep her thoughts on anything but Darcy Mont. They could have called it Freedom Ferry, or some such.

Then she wondered what this rolling farm country of New Jersey had been like even before they named it King's Ferry? Indians had, no doubt, possessed all this land at one time. She'd seen Iroquois braves on Staten Island once, as a young girl, Christianized ones visiting a church. But the Iroquois tribes had once been fierce, dangerous, warlike. Why, they would have attacked such a coach as this back then in a way the British never would, even if they were hovering around Manhattan these days.

Her eyelids drooped heavier, but she did not sleep. Through thick lashes she stared at her reflection in Darcy Mont's sleek boots. It was as if she were seeing another time and place, hearing the war whoops of painted Iroquois warriors as they stopped the coach with a barricade of tree limbs across the road.

She could not comprehend the language they spoke, but she knew that the tallest of the savages shouted to the passengers to disembark. She wished she knew what they were saying, wished she could converse in a foreign tongue. But the Indian leader's gestures and his men's muskets made it clear enough what they wanted. When they got out, Merry took some satisfaction in seeing that Darcy Mont was as frightened as she. He reached up to help her down the carriage steps, but she ignored his hand. She'd rather hold hands with that half-naked savage! Besides, in her skirts she was hiding the pistol she had begged from Cam at the last minute. If the Indians just meant to rob them, that was one thing, but if they intended other dire torments, she would have to shoot them.

Standing next to Darcy Mont in the hot sun with the fiends' eyes on them both, she felt the hot flare of danger race up her spine. The Indians grunted, rifling through the luggage, throwing Darcy's French tutoring books from his satchel all over the road, then setting fire to them and the coach. She realized then that she would have to flee into the thick forest before the red men turned on their victims. She fired her pistol once, then again, to wound the Iroquois warrior who gave the orders.

In the hubbub that followed, she tore into the thick forest along the path. Soon her sides ached from running; her breath came sharp and hot. Her legs shook. Tree limbs yanked her straw hat off and tugged curls free; her hair streamed back like a blond banner. She heard footsteps right behind her, keeping up. She was doomed, as good as dead!

But then she saw that Darcy had fled, too, and was sprinting after her. He seized and yanked her wrist to swing her back into his arms.

"*Sacrebleu*, you little fool! You will have the whole tribe after us now. We have to hide!" He tumbled them down into bushes on the slope of hill. They lay in thick, soft moss and leaves, and he held her tightly to him as the pursuing Indians thudded by their hiding place. Darcy's heart beat against hers where he pressed her breasts to his hard chest. His hands held to her desperately; he cupped her bottom to cradle her even closer to his powerful thighs. They breathed together in fear and passion. And then he shifted his mouth just inches from hers.

"You saved my life back there," he said. In French he told her that she was the most wonderful woman he had ever met, but she understood the tenor of his words. "I've been so wrong about you, about your bravery and wisdom, my darling Meredith. Forgive me. I am so sorry—"

"Sorry!" Darcy Mont muttered from the carriage seat across from her. She jolted upright. He had accidentally kicked her leg when the coach had jerked. His eyes went over her thoroughly, if briefly, before he repositioned his hat over his face.

"Think nothing of it," she managed icily as the heated daydream she had not wanted but had nonetheless welcomed fled.

A few miles farther into New Jersey, Darcy admitted to himself that it was hopeless. Somehow fate kept tossing this annoying, alluring woman in his path! Why was it that every time he looked at her it was so difficult not to be both lustful and angry? Damn her, of all the women in the world, why did she have to have *that* color of hair and look like *that*?

He regretted that Merry Morgan should be such a beautiful and beguiling woman. Her hair shimmered like the palest moonlight; her animated, heart-shaped face looked as if a sculptor had done his finest work. But her pert nose and her generous mouth—especially when she was pouting, as she was right now—saved her from a cold, classic look. Ah, yes, such a face and body could be—had been, he reminded himself painfully—the rage of the French court. As much of her skin as he could see, and no doubt all that he could not, was perfect, like porcelain. But he knew all too well that such physical enticements could be both deceiving and disastrous. Yet Merry Morgan seemed not to know that she was stunning. What a rarity that would be at the court of Louis and Marie Antoinette! Ah, what waves this young vixen, this *rebelle américaine*, would make among the courtiers at Versailles, just like the other who had deceived him and taught him to never trust again!

Besides her looks, so angelic yet so damning, what bothered him the most was that she seemed to embody all the things he admired most about America. Natural loveliness, untamed naiveté, a stubborn, touchy independence. But he wanted no part of her and the complications she could weave around his heart and soul. He could not risk letting her know anything about his mission, and she had a natural talent for making him want to tell her all kinds of things! Besides, he had been alone and bitter and vengeful too long to let her near the real Louis Philippe D'Arcy Montour, comte de Belfort. Despite the knowledge that Merry Morgan always came back to haunt his thoughts as if she had taken him captive instead of the other way around the first time they had met, he sought refuge again in thoughts of Amélie.

He missed Amélie very much when he let down the walls he had erected against memories of her. Her clinging sweetness, her adoring gaze, her beautiful face and her inherently flirtatious nature called to him. She would do anything to please, to tease, to distract him. And yet he had as good as imprisoned her at rural Belfort so that no one could harm her, no one could show her how cruel and crass life could be. Sometimes he could not bear the knifing slice of separation from her!

A voice shredded his thoughts. "Stand, there! Stand in the name of the king!"

His hat tumbled to the floor, and he twisted in his seat to gaze out the window as the coach jolted to a halt. Just what he had feared most! It could not be! Was this Morgan woman bad luck after all? At least twelve redcoats, backed up by a troop of green-coated Hessians! The British had evidently circled New York clear into New Jersey since the last flying coach had gotten through just yesterday!

He glanced at Merry. She looked more surprised than frightened, but the others in the coach were murmuring and clasping hands as if the British and their Hessian lackeys might shoot them on the spot. Well, he was one they would put before a firing squad if they knew the truth. And if Merry even blurted out that he was French, he was in for a brutal inquisition at the very best.

He caught Merry's wide, nervous stare and held one finger to his lips. "If worse comes to worst, follow my lead," he whispered. But he had no time to warn her further before the door next to them was pulled open.

"Out, out! Now!" a whey-faced British lieutenant bellowed as he yanked down the folding metal steps. Darcy dismounted first and put up his hand to help the others down. Merry came behind him, her head held high. To his relief, under the sharp eye of the British she took his hand until her feet touched the ground. He jolted at the energy that seemed to crackle to him through her gloves and right up his arm. They all stood along the roadside near a farmhouse and barn the British and Hessian had evidently overrun.

"Names, occupations, business in Philadelphia!" the lieutenant barked. "Line up here. Any weapons to be handed over at once."

Darcy and one other man relinquished their pistols. Merry had not noted that he had one stuck in his belt under his finely tailored waistcoat. She recalled her daydream about hiding a pistol from the Iroquois who stopped the coach and cursed herself for romanticizing such a thing. In the face of real danger, her knees were shaking.

She turned to glance behind them. From a prosperous-appearing brick house just off the road a hubbub floated to their ears. Merry squinted in the sun to watch Hessians carrying pewter and silver plate, piles of food, furniture, even feather beds, out onto the front lawn to cart them away, and calling to each other in guttural voices as they bagged squawking chickens in pillowcases to be taken off. The grim-faced, bulkily built soldiers divided what they wanted, terrorizing the farmer's wife and her two young daughters, who pleaded with them to spare at least some of their possessions. Merry's heart went out to them. British soldiers had briefly been quartered in the Morgan house on Staten Island. They, too, had acted as if they owned the place, but they hadn't looted so blatantly.

"Drat them," she muttered under her breath.

"What's that?" the scarlet-coated lieutenant demanded as he strutted her way. His white wig, cross belt, stockings and gaiters looked as pristine as freshly fallen snow, but Merry glared at him as if he were filthy from head to foot.

"I said, I'm ashamed our American nation was ever part of a nation that allows its hired hands to steal from women and children like that!" she dared.

"Silence," Darcy hissed, but it was too late.

"Real bold and brave, you rebel skirts, aren't you?" the lieutenant demanded, swaggering closer. His gaze was insulting; he leered at her so long she felt as if he'd plunged his hand down her bodice. For once Merry took Darcy's advice and held her tongue, though she could think of a great many things to say. She even kept her peace when a Hessian began to throw all their luggage down so that the brutes could smash the bags open with their rifle butts and toss their contents in the grass to plunder.

Merry's heart fell as her wardrobe, painstakingly remade from remnants of old curtains in these hard times and so carefully packed for Philadelphia, disappeared into Hessian haversacks. Her favorite ice-blue dressing gown went, draped over a green-coated back, down the road to where they were halting other traffic. Her insides twisted with anger and loss, yet she felt far worse for the pleading women in the farmhouse behind her.

"This one looks hale and hearty enough to make a sailor on one of our ships!" the lieutenant bellowed at Darcy when he saw that Merry would not rise to his bait again. Her head jerked around. Darcy was held immobile by two brawny, mustached Hessians, their bayonet points pressed to his broad back. "Send for someone to haul this big Yankee off to the harbor and we'll split the bounty!" the lieutenant shouted. "Let's make the rebel lout a British salt. Our navy will give him a real good taste of the lash till he comes to know his masters!"

Merry gasped, horrified. Whatever she thought of Darcy Mont, she was chilled by the idea these English and German brutes planned to haul him off. But, bayonets in his back or not, Darcy was not going without a fight.

"Now listen carefully, Lieutenant!" Darcy demanded. "Impressment of foreign nationals not at war with Britain is strictly forbidden."

"Laws, the rebels say it's forbidden to impress them, too—"

"But I am not an American."

"Well, what are you, then?" the lieutenant demanded, suddenly taken aback.

Merry saw her chance to help. Darcy had said to follow his lead. "Yes, it's true!" she blurted. "He's only a French tutor, just traveling through!"

Darcy's bitter glare was hardly the grateful glance she had expected. If looks could kill, she would be dead now. She recalled too late what Libby had told her about bad feelings between the French and the Brits, but hadn't Darcy himself been ready to declare he was French to save himself from impressment and a beating?

"French, is it?" the lieutenant sneered. "With all the rumors about French spies sniffing around to help the enemy, I believe we shall just apply the lash here until this froggie croaks out all his business," he said, and someone guffawed. "He'll tutor all of us in just what's going on back there in New York City."

"Oh, no!" Merry said, much too loud.

"Oh, yes! Haul them all into our new headquarters in that farmhouse there," the lieutenant ordered triumphantly. "And lock that mouthy rebel skirt there,'' he added with a pointed finger at Merry. "Separate from the others, too. She sounds like she knows all about our froggie, and I intend to question her, too. And see to it he's tied up tight until I get to him!''

The soldiers herded the six passengers and the coach's two drivers into the looted, vandalized house. As they passed the sobbing farmer's wife, Merry stopped to pat her arm and speak a word of consolation. She was shoved on for her pains, and she bounced off Darcy's back.

"Do not annoy them further,'' he mouthed to her as he reached out to steady her arm. Then, with a shake of his head: "I cannot believe you. I intended to tell them I was Italian.''

Before she could say anything, their captors shoved them up the stairs. She watched with a sinking heart as the Hessians tied Darcy's hands hard behind his back, bound his feet and shoved him to the floor in a small, slant-roofed room where they took his purse and rifled his coat pockets. One Hessian with a thick blond mustache came out with Darcy's fine velvet tricorne perched over his tall black plated cap, and the guards all laughed.

Merry felt sick all over. It was her fault. Darcy might well have talked his way out of this, and now she'd endangered his very life. If he had disliked her before, Darcy Mont no doubt detested her now.

She closed her eyes to pray but was rudely pushed into the small room next to Darcy's. The other prisoners were locked across the hall. The guards ripped her embroidered equipage, which held her only coins, from her arm. The door slammed in her face with finality, and she heard a guard put his rifle down with a smack just outside to guard her. Shocked at the quick twist of events, she stared dazedly around the ravaged room, which had evidently belonged to one of the daughters downstairs.

Drawers pulled askew from a tallboy dripped ruined ladies' undergarments. The bed was stripped down to its rope webbing. A fine sampler on the wall, much like one Merry might have done painstakingly herself, had been slit. If there had been heirloom quilts, homesewn curtains or lovingly woven rag rugs here, they were gone now.

Tears blurred her eyes as she leaned her shoulder on the single window frame to gaze out toward freedom. At the thought of that lewd-looking lieutenant questioning her in private, her skin crawled. She had no real fear that they would imprison her, too—unless they recognized her name from the New York papers. Libby said the British were always getting copies of New York gazettes on the sly for the news they gave.

But Darcy—to be lashed, questioned, forced to be a British sailor, maybe worse. If only she could help him escape and show him how wrong he had been about her!

She sniffed hard and dashed the tears from her cheeks as she stared out across the slanted slate roof a few feet below her window. The Hessians had evidently stripped the big stone barn out back of all its livestock. It looked deserted. If only they had left just one horse, they could have gotten away! And then her eyes jumped back to the slate roof.

It was not so very slanted! And Darcy was in the next room! There was a tree just beyond the edge of the roof that he could grab and slide down if she untied him! But she had to do it *now*, while they were alone! She had to risk it, no matter what it would mean if they caught her!

Merry's slippery soles were a great hindrance on the slate roof, and her skirts were worse. Cursing her need to hurry, she sat on the window ledge and pulled off her shoes. She hiked up her skirts and her single traveling petticoat and thrust them through and behind her legs. Holding a shoe under each arm, she half waddled, half shuffled along the sloping roof to Darcy's window. She squinted in, shading her eyes to ignore the silly picture she made reflected in the window glass.

He wasn't in the room! The window was slightly ajar, though, and she bent awkwardly to push it in farther to make certain. Even from here, she could hear the guards talking loudly to each other in the hall. Could they have taken him out for questioning already?

Then she saw him. He was kneeling on the floor, directly under the window. It was another looted room, stripped of everything but its heavy wooden furniture and a shattered porcelain washbowl in the corner. Darcy was using one of the shards to cut the bonds that held his wrists. He had positioned a large broken piece between his boot heels and was kneeling, straining backward to saw painfully at the ropes. His head thrown back, his eyes tight shut, he strained to control his movements. He breathed hard through gritted teeth; the sinews of his neck stood out like powerful cords. Then he opened his eyes and jerked his head around to see her as she half stepped, half tumbled in, almost on top of him.

"My angel of mercy from heaven," he muttered, still kneeling before her.

"But there will be hell to pay," she whispered back, "if you don't get away!"

"Cut my ropes," he ordered, but he looked dazed with relief to see her.

She knelt behind him and sliced at the triple cords with the shard. She was appalled to see that the ropes had turned his fingers as white as sausages. He gasped when his hands popped free, and he untied his own feet, despite the obvious numbness of his hands.

He stood slowly, pulling her up with him. "Merry, I cannot thank you enough!"

"I owed it to you for that mistake out on the road. I thought—"

"I know. Now listen," he whispered, so close to her ear that his hot breath bounced the corkscrew tendrils there. "If you go back to your room, they will believe I freed myself. I will have to run out there, and perhaps get caught. Otherwise, I would risk—"

"No," she said, surprised at her own determination. She hadn't really thought beyond freeing him. "They'll question me. And I do know a bit too much to stay—about your tutoring Mr. Franklin at General Washington's bequest."

His lips set in a firm, hard line. She had a point. But was she actually blackmailing him? He could not risk her life; if she stayed, they would soon enough release her. Still, the way that son of a bitch of a lieutenant had looked at her would haunt him. He had vowed to Cam Gant that he would watch over her, but his duty to France—and to freedom—came first.

He made the decision so fast he stunned even himself. "Get those shoes back on!" he whispered as he reached again for the sharp edge of broken porcelain. "Get out of that petticoat. I'm going to cut your skirt off above the ankle so you can run, and don't argue."

She didn't, but her heart took up a clanging so loud she thought she might as well have shouted at him. He sliced and tore her skirt hem off all around. The cool rush of air, the new ease of movement, felt so good. He helped her out the window and hand in hand they shuffled to the edge of the slate roof and looked down. They heard men's voices from the front, but there seemed to be no one back here.

Darcy stepped gingerly onto a creaking limb of the old apple tree that half leaned against the house. Its branches drooped with fruit. She stepped out boldly, too. She had to keep up. She had to show him that she was not afraid, even when her entire body trembled the way these leaves did in the breeze.

"Place your feet where I do. Try to hold your skirts in," he said, and started down.

Apples bumped to the ground with a sound like a muted drumming. Merry scraped her cheek and hit her head. But she climbed steadily down after him, even when a dried limb cracked as loud as cannonfire under her left foot. She heard him drop to the ground. He reached for her and supported her the rest of the way. His hands felt so steady on her hips, so sure. His eyes had never looked greener. At the heady taste of liberty—and with Darcy Mont—she almost laughed to see him stuff several fallen apples down the front of his waistcoat. And then they sensed that they were being watched.

Merry sucked in a breath as they both spun around. The woman Merry had comforted earlier stood there, alone and apparently very surprised that they had dropped from her tree. Her thin face, still streaked with tears, suddenly looked years younger.

"Go, run!" she urged them, gesturing wildly. Her eyes gleamed bright at this small shared victory. "I'll not let the thieving animals know! Godspeed!" Then they heard a shout from around the front and ran madly away from the woman and her ruined house.

Darcy pulled Merry so hard her feet almost left the ground. She expected him to break across the plowed field to the woods or duck into the orchard. But he pulled her straight into the deserted barn.

"No time to get farther now! Hessians!" he hissed as he shoved her ahead of him toward the ladder to the hayloft that covered half the barn floor ten feet above their heads.

They heard the alarm of shouted voices. A single gunshot. Running steps. Grunted German commands. Up in the loft, Darcy stopped Merry at the very front of the pile of straw. He clawed a place out for them. "Under, and do not move!"

Her heartbeat rattling her teeth, she helped him dig a burrow and huddled in it. "We could get way back in the corner," she began, her voice not her own, as he joined her and raked a thick blanket of straw over the top of them.

"No. The too-obvious strategy is always best—"

They heard the shrill voice of the farmer's wife as she told their pursuers that they had run into the orchard. More guttural shouted orders; more running, with the metallic sound of canteen and powder pouches bouncing. Merry breathed a prayer of thanks to the woman. The enemy could ruin her home and steal her goods, but they could not break her spirit.

Darcy moved closer behind Merry under their shared pile of straw. They were on their sides, and he held her tight, as if to fasten her to him. The backs of her legs bent against his knees, as if she were sitting in his lap. She almost forgot that she was clad in hacked-off skirts and being hunted like an animal. In those first moments in his arms she was a prosperous housewife in her own bed with the husband she would always love.

All too soon they heard the shuffling of feet below. "I wager the farm bitch was lying," they heard the British lieutenant say. "They could not get clean away that fast. A gold crown to the man that turns them up. And check the loft, too. You can poke those bayonets in any straw. That'll get them quickly enough. Then join me to search along the stream!"

They lay frozen in dread while the Hessians tramped the entire barn floor below, bumping stalls, swinging doors, jabbering to each other. Merry jerked in Darcy's arms, but he held her tighter. She kept her eyes shut tight. They breathed in unison, though she seemed to be the only one trembling. How she wished she could face this danger with Darcy's steely aplomb. They just had to get away from these villains! She could not bear not to know all about this man, perhaps to lie in his arms like this in safer times. But when would being near—and lying with—Darcy Mont ever be safe? How had everything spun out of her control and turned deadly dangerous so fast?

She did not know the struggle going on in Darcy's mind as he castigated himself for bringing her along. He must have been demented! He would never forgive himself if she was recaptured, bayoneted or shot. Yet he could not surrender, could not jeopardize his own mission. The fate of three nations, the future of thousands upon thousands of lives, the ultimate survival of American freedom, were at stake here. But if this woman, who felt so good in his arms even in these dire circumstances, did not shout out to them that he was French again, perhaps they had a chance.

But then the louts climbed the ladder, nearly at their feet. Darcy had gambled that they would search the back corners of the loft, where the straw was piled deeper. They did so first, grunting, sticking their long bayonets clear down into the wooden floor so that it shuddered from the strokes and from their shuffling tread. Four, maybe five of them up here, Darcy estimated. Too many to take on. Both Merry and Darcy held their breath now, as if they could already feel the sharp slice of bayonets in their quaking flesh. And then the Hessians moved even closer.

Chapter Four

Merry's nostrils flared as the Hessian jackboots stirred up dust on the floor. The urge to sneeze scraped far back into her head. She held her breath and bit on her lower lip until she tasted blood and the urge slowly faded.

"Dumkopf!" one soldier snarled at another as they evidently bumped or kicked each other. And then—blessed relief—their pursuers clambered back down the ladder and hauled it after them.

Merry and Darcy began to breathe again. They lay achingly still for the longest time, while the voices moved away and floated back, more muted now. When they had the nerve to uncover themselves and peek, the rust-hued rays of the setting sun stained the barn floor below. Darcy peered out through the single slatted window in the loft.

"Safe for now," he whispered. "I think we can talk."

Still trembling, she brushed herself off. "I kept thinking they might light the straw, and I was already so hot!"

He shot her a stiff smile, his eyebrows raised. He seemed to have had some impudent thought she could not read. "I felt hot, too. But as soon as the sun sets we shall have to put some miles between us and here, so lie back down and rest."

"Oh, I couldn't possibly. Not after that— You know what I mean."

His eyes went lazily over her in that challenging way of his, but he didn't answer. They moved into the back corner of the loft, and each of them ate an apple. Darcy peered out through the slats each time he heard voices outside. He took off his coat and waistcoat to give her a less dusty place to sit. As dusk deepened, his upper torso was a ghostly white in his wide-sleeved shirt and his cravat.

Merry saw a little garden snake slither across the floor in front of them, and she almost screamed, despite the danger of their situation. Darcy merely seized it and dropped it over the side into the straw below. "Ah, *quel bonheur*, our own little Eden," he whispered as he sat down beside her again, so close that their shoulders bumped. "We have seen the serpent and we have shared some apples. And here are Adam and Eve, half dressed," he said, daring to run his index finger up the bare calf her sliced skirts exposed.

"But they were naked!" she said, before she saw his flash of grin in the dark and knew she'd fallen right into his trap.

Drat it, she fumed silently, this was an impossible situation! She was forever blurting stupid and naive things to this witty, sophisticated man. And she was too ignorant to speak a word of his French. They were trapped together in a potentially fatal situation, and he was teasing her and making her feel dizzy and prickly hot! Fool that she was, she instinctively trusted him to outwit the entire British army, and even those ruthless Hessians. Worse, she cared even more for him now than she had at first, when she knew it would be both wiser and safer to detest him!

Darcy kept quiet after that. It moved him that this woman with ruined skirts, bruised cheek and straw stuck in her hair could look so artlessly beguiling. Her coiffure, awry and astray, was more charming than any of the ornately puffed, padded and powdered concoctions at Versailles. Her cameo complexion reminded him of a court painting by Boucher of a wonderful, free-spirited shepherdess—and not the painted, rouged kind Marie Antoinette and her *coterie* thought the rage at her private rural retreat, the Petit Trianon. Louis Philippe D'Arcy Montour, comte de Belfort, sighed and struggled again to erect a wall between his feelings and his actions, between this dangerous present and his destructive memories—and silently, soundly cursed Merry Morgan for ever having crossed his path!

* * *

When it was so dark that they could not see each other, they felt their way to the edge of the loft. "I am going to have to drop down to get the ladder they took," he told her. "It is probably down there somewhere! Sit still until I come back for you."

He patted her knee and hung over the edge. For such a big man, he dropped like a cat. She heard him shuffle around the barn and walk out. Then nothing more!

Her pulse thrummed like marching feet. Surely he would not leave her here like this for the British to find in the morning! Surely he had really meant to take her with him! But she knew so little—virtually nothing—of the man. Of course, he'd be much quicker fleeing without her. Tears stung her eyes at the thought. Drat him! Had he deserted her?

But then an eternity later, she heard steps, and the ladder bumped beside her. His face appeared. She was so happy she almost kissed him. "Our Hessian friends must have been looting the apple trees with it," he whispered as he reached for her trembling hand. "I will be under you, but be careful coming down!"

Outside, she followed him willingly while he propped the ladder back in a tree, then took her hand and led her at a quick pace through the orchard. They saw and heard no troops. Her joy, her surge of confidence, amazed her. Surely she was safe with this man! He had come back for her! She had not judged him wrong from the very beginning! But she hesitated at the edge of the creek.

"Are we going across?"

"In it for a way, in case we have left footprints or they use dogs in the morning. Come on."

Despite the ripple of the cool black water and the slipperiness of the rocks, she did not hesitate. Her deepest instincts told her that this was a man she could follow into the darkness at the ends of the earth and still be glad she had left all else behind.

They walked for several hours, wending their way through forests and fields, finally following a road southward, munching on the last of their apples. Huge, painful blisters made

Merry want to throw her shoes off, but she went on. Darcy stuffed leaves in them to cushion her heels the next time they rested. She ached all over, and she yearned to curl up in his arms and go to sleep, but her mind was alert. Several hours before dawn, as they approached a hamlet of scattered houses, they heard the rattle of racing hooves behind them.

He hurried them off the road to stand knee deep in another stream under a wooden bridge. He put his arms around her drooping shoulders and held her to him. She closed her eyes as if to shut it all out, while a band of riders came closer, then thundered past, right over their heads. When they had passed, he loosed her, and they both stood trembling in the cold water. He gently touched the cheek she had scraped an eternity ago climbing down the apple tree.

"You are a brave, beautiful woman, Merry Morgan," he whispered in the tar-black night. "And I am going to have to trust you with some very important things in case something happens to me before we get out of the enemy's reach."

He talked steadily to her as they climbed the creek bank and walked hand in hand across an open field. In just a few minutes her mystery man was a mystery no more—at least not as far as his mission here in the colonies went. The mystery of her sweeping feelings for him, the magnetic allure he held for her, still awed her. She wondered if, had he told her he was here to steal every last American musket and bullet, she would not have felt the same.

She vowed she would do her best to help him and their two countries. As dawn stained the sky orange and pink, he picked their breakfast from blackberry brambles and dropped them in her ruined skirt. Still he talked, explaining how the French were still smarting from their losses to the British in wars both in America and in Europe. Yet, he said, his country could not yet quite afford to face the risk and expense of open support of America and resulting war with Britain again.

Finally they rested beside a small, quiet pool in a grove of trees surrounded by open fields in all directions and quenched their thirst with drafts of the ice-cold water.

"And, unless he's already left secretly for France and you have to write him," Darcy told her as they sat wearily side by side with their backs against the same big oak, "never, *never* put any of this down on paper or trust it to any other soul but Ben Franklin. That wily old statesman is the link who has to make all this happen between our countries when he sails soon for Paris as American ambassador!"

"But you're the link, too," she added proudly. She had learned Darcy was much more than Mr. Franklin's French tutor! He was his advisor, and he would be the *liaison*—a new word for her—between General Washington and Congress and the French government. Darcy would be back and forth across the ocean, occasionally reporting to the French king and his ministers in person, and always keeping open the lines of communication between America and France.

"Then what were you hoping to discover rifling through Cameron Gant's things that day you were in his town house uninvited?" she asked.

"Besides a beautiful half-dressed woman?" he said teasingly. "I assured myself that the man I had been assigned to contact in Washington's staff was not any sort of spy, even though I had heard rumors earlier he was—how do you say—in tight with the British."

"A mere ruse to help our American cause," she added, pleased to no end to learn that she had been right from the first about the righteousness of Darcy Mont's cause. But she need not tell him all that quite yet.

"All right," he said when she gazed at him with a wistful smile that unsettled him to his very toes. "Now recite it all to me again. And then I must reconnoiter to choose our best way to Philadelphia."

Her intelligence and recall amazed him as she repeated it all: "Upon his arrival in France, Mr. Franklin must rely first and foremost on the Comte—that means Count—de Vergennes," she said, proud of the few French words she had just learned. "He's the minister of foreign affairs at Versailles. Mr. Franklin must ask Vergennes to help him obtain no less than one million livres from King Louis's treasury but ask Caron de Beau—Beau—"

"Beaumarchais."

"Beaumarchais for private donations. Namely for brass cannon and mortars, muskets with bayonets, thousands of pounds of powder, and tents for at least twenty thousand American soldiers."

"Exactly. And, most important, he must ask for a na—"

"The loan of a French naval fleet is the key to bottling up the British army here and cutting their supply lines," she continued smoothly. "Besides asking for public recognition of our cause, Franklin must appeal to King Louis and his ministers to send us a fully manned fleet!"

He smiled, more broadly than she had ever seen before. No mockery, no acerbic retort, no little telltale cleft in his chin, no hint of a frown. *"Sacrebleu!"* he muttered. "I should send you to the king to ask these things, not old Franklin. Still, the personal price you would pay at Louis's licentious court I could not allow."

She felt her cheeks heat again. She knew exactly what he meant this time, but she thrilled at the hint that he wished to protect her, even from his king! "We're both going to make it to Philadelphia safely, I know it, but perhaps I can help you afterward! And I will tell no one I knew but Franklin."

He sighed and flopped back wearily, his long arms thrown over his head in the shady grass. "Washington would be rather shocked, but he would understand dire necessity after the retreat he made the other night. And tell Franklin one more thing, if the Brits or Hessians retake me."

"Don't even think that! But what?"

"Tell him not to bother wooing the queen, however much he likes the ladies. Her political influence is little, and she leads the current fashion for things British over there. Her little *société* of wild, selfish friends is closer to her than the king is. Who can blame His Majesty for not having bedded his wife yet, even after five years of marriage. Women!!" he added grimly.

"You're certain it's all her fault, of course. Perhaps you had best tell me where you got this poor opinion of women!"

His gaze slammed into hers so hard that she almost felt as if he had slapped her. She felt the bloom of his candid trust in her wither again. She knew there was something very painful that he carried around with him, and she feared she might never know to help heal it.

"Feed me a berry or two, will you?" he murmured instead of answering. She complied slowly, picking the plumpest ones from her stained skirt and dropping them between lips he licked after each one. Then he gently seized her wrist and held her sticky palm to his lips to lick that, too.

A great surging jolt leapt up her arm and landed in the strangest places. Hair prickled on the back of her neck as if a chill wind blew. She felt her nipples turn to pearl-hard nubs. That rough velvet feel his whispered voice invoked rubbed across her belly and slid down between her thighs. It darted clear up inside her in a longing ache for all sorts of knowledge of him. Perhaps he felt the same way, for his free arm snaked up and pulled her down until their mouths met.

He tasted her dark stained lips lightly, then tugged her closer. He did not kiss the way she had expected, the way she had experienced several times before from suitors, mouth closed and dry. This was no peck, no brief caress. His mouth slanted to tease her lips open. His warm, berry-tart tongue darted into her mouth to skim her teeth and the slick inside of her lips. He tasted her and then devoured her as her tongue danced with his. How good he tasted, how delicious and dangerous!

"Mmm," she managed at last.

"Mmm," he echoed. "You learn all things so fast. Do you like French kisses?"

"Yours, you mean?"

"Yes, mine!" he said with a chuckle, and ravished her mouth again.

He tumbled her over him, and berries flew. She lay flat on her back in the grass by the pond, staring up at his mussed dark head and the swaying green leaves and the clear blue sky far above. He propped himself just barely off her on one elbow and kissed her again and again, until she couldn't breathe and felt quite giddy. Usually she kept her eyes closed, as his were, but she could not resist an occasional peek at him so close. She could see each raven lash lying against his rough-bearded cheeks; when he moved his mouth over her she reveled in the brush of stubble on his chin. His free hand gently roamed the supple length of her, lingering at her breasts and waist and belly. She was floating, mesmerized. Something deep inside told her she should stop him, that she should protest. But something even deeper told her this was the man she had been born to help and please and love.

His breath singed her skin. He ran his tongue down her arched throat to the barrier of the square-cut bodice of her gown. "Mmm, more sweet berries here for the taking," he murmured, lightly flicking her peaked nipples through her gown. She held her breath, thinking he would plunge fingers or lips even below her bodice, where she ached almost painfully for his touch, his lips. His hand dropped to her bare leg, where her knee-length skirts slid higher up her thigh. He obviously knew a great deal about how to make a woman happy. He obviously appreciated women. She could attest personally to the fact that women must adore him. So why did he say such disparaging things of her sex?

"We have shared so much in a short time," he muttered. "I am desperate to share more!"

Her heavy-lidded eyes popped wide open. "About why you speak that way of women?" she asked trustingly, her voice slow and lazy.

To her dismay, he loosed her and sat bolt upright. She felt utterly bereft without his touch. He looked away, then back down at her, as if he were seeing her for the first time. His eyes, soft and green as grass a moment ago, now glittered like cold, cut gems.

"I did not mean to become—what is it?—taken away." He stood. "Insane in our predicament, insane anyway." He turned away quickly, cursing himself for the blatant thrust of desire for her that he could not hide in the taut stretch of his breeches. But she seemed not to have noticed. The French women he knew would have been clawing at him and demanding their due after what he had started here.

"That's all right," she floundered. "You mean carried away—"

"Yes. Listen, wash that sticky juice off your face. I am going to venture out a little, see if I can get us something else to eat, maybe some proper clothes for you—if I am lucky, even a horse. I have more money the thieves did not take in a purse tied against my skin," he added, patting his flat belly. He rose lithely to his feet.

"Oh," she said, sitting up and pulling her short skirt down under his harsh glare. "But I should go with you."

"No. Just keep your eyes open here," he said, and started away.

"Darcy..." she called after him. It was the first time she had used his given name.

He spun around, still looking every bit as if he were furious with her. "Well?"

"You—you wouldn't just go off on your own, thinking that one or the other of us has a better chance getting this additional information to Mr. Franklin separately, would you?"

"No, Merry. I had thought of that, but no. Please believe me—on that."

"I do," she replied.

Her open honesty and her trust in him made him curse himself all the more as he strode across the field toward the closest house.

Merry was appalled to realize that she had fallen asleep in a shaft of sunlight through the trees. She had truly meant to keep watch. Leaping up, she darted along the fringe of the grove to assure herself that the flat, fallow fields that ringed it were deserted. Surely she had not dozed long. How she would love to wash before Darcy returned, especially in case he found her something clean to wear. The idea of her riding into fashionable Philadelphia to meet the wealthy Shippens like this appalled her!

She hurried to the pond and waded in to splash herself. The thought of her wardrobe in Hessian hands made her curse them and the British all over again. But it was a small sacrifice to make to help their new nation. Now that Darcy had confided in her, she intended to be certain he understood that she meant to help him once they arrived. After all, he had heard General Washington himself say he would value her aid!

She darted out to the leafy perimeter of the grove to check the fields again. Only a few people walked on the distant road. The

British and their looting cohorts in this area must have made folks stay close to home. She shivered in the breeze. The cool water had felt so good, but her soiled garments clung damply to her, chilling her in the shade. Surely she had time to take these things off and have a quick dip before she clothed herself again to watch for Darcy.

She ran back to the pond, peeling off her ragged-hemmed skirt, her sopping whaleboned bodice and her tattered stockings. She wet her long ash-blond tresses and even dared to splash a bit. Despite the fact that the enemy still lay between her and safety, she had never felt freer and happier. Wrapping her gown around her like an Indian blanket, she hurried out one more time to check the fields. She decided on just one more moment in the waters. She waded back in and scrubbed her face again.

Darcy Mont felt torn in more ways than one. He both desired and detested being with Merry Morgan. She was the best thing that had happened to him in years, and yet the worst. She was sheer trouble, and perhaps even bad luck. It absolutely unnerved him that she was so blond and fair of face, forcing him to recall the bad times in his life. He regretted sharing his mission with her. Then he had gambled that he might not escape the British net, but when he had bought this horse just now he had learned he should have kept his secret!

The British had vacated this area last night for the attack on New York City. Those soldiers on the bridge last night who had finally made him decide to confide in her were no doubt being summoned to join the main body of troops. He had needlessly placed the safety of his mission in Merry Morgan's hands. If she was to thoughtlessly let something out . . .

He rode the black mare slowly across the plowed field toward the grove of trees, rehearsing in his mind exactly what to tell her: that he thanked her for her trustworthiness and that France owed her a debt of gratitude for getting him away from the British. But that she must never tell a soul a thing he had shared with her, and that he would not be needing her help further. And if she was overly grateful for his thanks in a way that made him lose control of himself with her again he would simply point out to her that it was her quick mouth that had gotten him in trouble with the British in the first place. He had to take a strong, hard stand. She was beginning to get under his skin, and he could not afford that as a French agent—or as a man!

When she did not appear to greet him and admire the horse as he expected, he approached the grove slowly and quietly so as not to startle her. A moment's worry that she had run off stabbed him. Frowning, he wrapped the horse's reins around a branch and let it graze. He left the food in the single saddlebag but took the jade-green gown he had bought for her. He was tempted to call out to her the good news that they were safe, but the image of her hurtling into his arms to hug him in jubilant celebration made him stop. He edged forward. And then he saw her—entirely too much of her!

She stood, quite naked, thigh deep in the center of the small pond. She looked entranced and entrancing—a bewitching woodland nymph with sunstruck hair half covering her lush, pointed breasts. She was stunning, her tiny waist and the swell of her hips framing the golden triangle of moist, mossy hair at the apex of her ivory thighs. A fierce jab of longing for her assailed him. He felt himself swell and strain against his taut breeches. He sucked in a sharp breath.

At that, she spun around to face him, gasping. She knelt quickly in the water, her hands spread like twin seashells to hide her breasts.

"Darcy! Oh, but I just looked! There was no one walking in the fields!"

He stared like one demented. He saw her pert pink mouth form words, but he did not hear them. His self control shattered, he strode down into the pond as if it were not even there.

He expected her to squeal or run, to scramble for her clothes on the sloping bank. Too late he realized he had wet the new gown that he held draped over his arm. He did not stop. He splashed to her with giant strides and glared down at her. He had never wanted a woman so fiercely in his life! But he stopped three feet from her and stood like a statue with clenched fists and burning eyes.

To his amazement—and obviously hers, too—she stared back and stood to face him squarely, proudly, her hands at her sides. Rivulets of water rippled down her flesh; her sleek golden hair draped like a curtain over her high, proud breasts. Droplets clung to her in the most amazing, magical places, in the valley between her breasts, in her navel. He saw her clench her belly muscles; she shuddered once.

"You are so beautiful, *ma belle, ma belle*," he murmured, and moved to lift her.

She entwined her arms around his neck. Their lips met in a flowing, building kiss. Cradling her, he walked out and fell to his knees on the grass and laid her down. Warning bells clanged through him, echoes of danger, of madness, but he could not stop.

Merry's head spun; her body soared at his gaze and at his touch. She was aware of herself everywhere he touched her, yet she had never been more sensually attuned to other things—the breeze, the beads of moisture on her skin, the prickle of grass along her bare back and her bottom. She shivered in a ripple of gooseflesh everywhere he merely looked. Something both sharp and sweet sprinted up and down her spine, and she could have flown away.

She kissed him back fiercely, trustingly, totally. She had not meant for this to happen, but she could not hold back. This man was meant to be hers. He had confided in her, trusted her. This rampant desire surging through her to give him everything was only the beginning of their love! She gasped and flung her wet hair back and forth across the grass as he lowered his head to pleasure not only her sweet bruised lips, but her breasts, as well.

The triumph of her womanliness tingled to her toes. His big, warm hands were everywhere. She wanted to remember everything they shared, every motion and moment, but they rushed by faster, faster, in a building blur of need and want.

He spoke to her in a rasping blend of French and English. Compliments, endearments, punctuated by wilder kisses and tiny nibbles up and down her quaking flesh. She followed suit to see how each bold caress spurred him on. Quickly she learned to both demand and deliver more. And now his hand was working wicked wonders between her thighs, and she knew the answer to so much she had never even fathomed about what passed between two who loved.

She surrendered to it, to him. Through the stretched fabric of his breeches she felt the thrust of his desire against her bare thigh. At his encouragement, she touched him, stroked him there through the cloth, wanting to know more. She clung to his neck as he settled and positioned her under him. He separated her knees and fumbled with the buttons of his breeches. And then she looked past his shoulder and screamed.

"Darcy! Someone's here! Look!"

He tried to jump to his feet but tripped over her new gown and sprawled back to his knees. Merry yanked the gown away from him and over her. She tried to scuttle back into the trees like a crab. His heart banging against his ribs, he saw too late what she meant!

His horse had loosed its reins to follow him down to the pond to drink and now stood patiently, watching them both with liquid eyes. "It is just the damned horse...." he muttered.

"But whose? Someone must be here!"

"*Sacrebleu!* Ours!"

"What? You never said—"

He muttered a string of French words that hardly sounded like endearments, then added, "I told you I might get a horse. You should have expected it! I meant to tell you at once, but I believe I got distracted." He stood dazedly, furious with himself and with her. "Distracted intentionally by you, I have no doubt," he clipped out, his voice gone cold and sharp.

She blushed all over at his accusation. "I saw no one walking when I looked. I had no idea you were spying on my nakedness like some savage!"

"Savage? Do not shift the topic! I know all the tricks, Merry, from a virgin or not. I assume you are a virgin, despite how fast you seem to take to things!" he muttered with a freezing glare.

"Things French are very hard to take!" she retorted with a meaningful matching glare at his breeches. She was stung to the quick by his quick change of mood. She scrambled to her knees, wrapping the gown around her midriff. "As far as I can see," she went on, "things French are very selfish, arrogant—"

"That is quite enough!"

"It isn't! You could have told me about the horse. It just makes me wonder what else you have conveniently forgotten to say."

He cursed himself again for ever having been stupid enough to share anything important with a woman, even if he could have been captured and shot any minute. He turned his back to her and said, with as much patience and coldness as he could muster, "Just put on that gown I bought you. I have learned we are past the British invasion line. And this horse leaves for Philadelphia as soon as you have eaten a meat pie I selfishly, arrogantly bought for you, too. I shall be over there with the horse when you have settled yourself down enough to ride."

What insulting thing did that last cryptic comment mean, she fumed as she watched him stalk away. *Reared a gentleman through and through,* Cam had said of him—mistakenly. If Darcy Mont had possessed the least part of a gentleman, he would have simply turned his back when he had come upon her bathing stark naked like that! Yet, as she tugged her green gown, almost the color of his eyes, down over her still-damp skin, she knew she had wanted him to come to her. And she admitted she would rather her Darcy be a man through and through than a gentleman any day.

Stiff and unspeaking, they rode miles to an inn near Brunswick, where they spent the night in separate rooms that he paid for with gold coins. How much she really owed him for her care and safety began to nag at her the next day as she bounced behind him—her hands of necessity around his lean middle—on their horse toward Philadelphia. And how much she owed him for awakening her female self… But she would surely have time to teach him that when he simmered down a bit.

Past Trenton he began to thaw, though he still avoided her questions about his past. Beyond Bristol, he described the sights to her. After hours jogging up and down so close together like this she was beginning to fear her body's unfulfilled yearning for him again. Still, it was a pleasant ache. His ironclad voice showed no hint that he had almost lost his head for her twice before.

"Nervous about meeting the Shippens?" he asked when they passed one of the ten-mile road markers that he had told her were of Ben Franklin's design.

"Wouldn't you be, with scuffed shoes, a sunburned nose and only one gown to your name, and that too tight across the bosom?"

Darcy shifted in the saddle, as he had numerous other times when she'd rested her cheek on his back in exhaustion or when she'd accidentally dropped her hands against his thighs when she'd dozed off. He didn't think she realized what an exquisite torment this ride had been for him, especially at this steady gait. He had not desired a woman this desperately for years, and he could not stop his mind from picturing him riding her at his same plunging pace!

"Philadelphia down below!" he announced, sounding relieved at last. She peered around his broad shoulder to survey the distant panorama from a rise along the Schuylkill River. Set like a gem in green meadows and woodlots cradling vast private estates lay a city on a strip of land between two rivers. Church steeples merged with masts in the glittering two-mile harbor along the broad Delaware River as the sun sank, staining the city's blue-gray roofs and stone chimneys all rosy. Perfectly straight, right-angled streets of brick buildings seemed to stretch forever. It made New York look small.

"We have made it!" he declared triumphantly as he urged the horse to a quicker gait down the broad paved thoroughfare clearly labeled Market Street.

Not yet, she thought as she clung harder to his waist. You and I, Darcy Mont, not quite yet!

Chapter Five

The ruffian and the ragamuffin, the ruffian and the ragamuffin, Merry thought over and over in a rhythm to match the
beat of their horse's hooves down Market Street into the heart
of Philadelphia. That was surely what the well-dressed, busy
citizens of this town were whispering to each other at their arrival: "The ruffian and the ragamuffin." She was acutely aware
again of her torn, stained stockings and her scuffed shoes,
peeking out from under the too-short gown Darcy had pur-
chased from a shorter, thinner woman. Darcy's once elegant
traveling garb was stained with grass, mud and berries. They
were both dusty, windblown and tired. This city, by contrast,
looked proper, prosperous and polished.

Even side streets were crowded with coaches, chaises and
carts of all kinds. She marveled at the wide, tree-lined boule-
vards of the metropolis. Before the colonies had rebelled,
Philadelphia had been renowned for being the largest city in the
far-flung British colonies, second only to London itself. The
thoroughfares were laid with paving stones, not cobbles as in
New York. Public pumps with people fetching clear water stood
at almost every intersection, unlike New York's temporarily
abandoned, half-completed system of wooden pipes to haul in
drinkable water. They passed a medical college, private schools,
more than one library and numerous lecture halls among the
massive, impressive houses of state and national government.
Why, even the fruit sellers along the way, with their crimson
pyramids of apples, seemed well attired, she remarked to Darcy
to break their mutual silence.

"That is only one of many things that have impressed me about your country," he told her. "Unlike in France, even your farmers and street hawkers are well attired, independent and proud. But for the kind of cloth on their backs I can hardly tell most of them from the rich Quakers and bourgeois gentry who run this town—and but for the gentry's noses in the air," he added, illustrating with a swipe at his own lifted nose.

Merry laughed, grateful that he had soothed her trepidation. She chattered more observations to him along the way. But when he guided the horse past the lovely Commons, where fashionable ladies were "taking the air" in small, smart carriages, she fell silent again. When he headed their mount down Fourth Street, a shaded lane of large, lovely brick and stone town houses, her concern about the welcome she could expect from the Shippens left her silent again.

"It is this house, I think," he told her, and panicked her by leaving her sitting astride while he dismounted and rang the bell. A starch-aproned maid with a butterfly lace cap appeared, closely followed by another. Both gawked at Merry over Darcy's shoulders, until he spoke to them and one hurried away. Merry's face heated. She slid off the horse before Darcy could come back down the broad stone steps under the small pillared portico to assist her. She shook out her skirts and brushed her mussed tresses back, but there was nothing she could do about the way the green bodice strained across her breasts, or the shortness of the gown that flaunted her scuffed shoes as if she were a servant girl fresh off some farm.

But then Merry recalled how Darcy had praised even the simplest American workers as independent and proud. She pictured again the defiant faces of the New Jersey farmwife and her two daughters as they had argued with those Hessian marauders. And, next to Darcy, she stood straight and proud as the Shippens' front door opened and a short, stocky, elaborately bewigged man appeared, accompanied by three pretty girls in light-colored, flower-sprigged summer gowns.

"Oh, Papa, but that cannot be her!" the youngest one blurted out, much too loudly.

Although the middle girl, with spectacles on her nose and a white kitten in her arms, just stared owlishly and said nothing, the eldest, very pretty, with her hair piled and padded nearly as high as her head, remarked, "But who *is* that man with her?" But then Judge Edward Shippen stepped down to speak with Darcy and extend his hand kindly to Merry.

Still, Merry felt bereft when Darcy bade her farewell and departed hastily just a few minutes later. She had not even had the opportunity to ask him when he would call on her or where he lived. After all, she had to discuss ways she could continue to aid their common cause now that they were safely in the nation's capital and near Ben Franklin again. How she would love to sit in on Darcy's sessions with the elderly statesman who was about to become the ambassador to King Louis's court!

But the hubbub of a hundred questions from the three Shippen girls swelled around her until Judge Shippen shooed away bespectacled Polly, aged fifteen, and chatty Sarah—Sally to her family—aged thirteen. At first, Merry was grateful it was the eldest, Peggy, only two years younger than she, who was selected to escort her upstairs to wash and change for supper.

Margaret Shippen, called Peggy, was a lively, dainty girl with an obvious penchant for cascades of ruffles, bows and puffs of artificial flowers. As soon as they were out of Judge Shippen's earshot, halfway up the stairs, Peggy declared from behind her ornate fan, "What a simply marvelous adventure you must have shared with that rakish man!" The ice in her pale blue eyes cooled the warmth of the pert smile that appeared over the lace-edged flutter of fan. "I swear, but the sun or something's put such color in your face, Merry Morgan! Surely you'll tell me absolutely *all* about it after you've rested a bit! How daring to be off unchaperoned with a man one's not even betrothed to, especially when one's of the age to have to guard a reputation!"

Merry was amazed that Peggy could make apparent compliments seem so steeped in suspicion and guilt, but she agreed to tell her a bit of their adventures later. Peggy Shippen was slender and so elegant that Merry bemoaned her curves and her dowdy costume once again. Above Peggy's rouged and powdered face, more artificial flowers bloomed like a miniature garden in her cleverly coiffed pale brown hair. If the women of New York had given up their hair pads and powder as a symbol of protest in this war, the patriotic custom had certainly not reached here, Merry observed silently.

"This will be your room, right next to mine, though of course it's much smaller." Peggy swung open a door partway down a long, carpeted hall lined with doors and family portraits staring down long noses from gilded frames. "It used to be a sitting room for me. See, there's a connecting door over there, but I'd prefer we kept it closed."

"It's a lovely room," Merry murmured, surveying the flowered carpet, the blue silk testered bed and the caged birds painted on the walls. "What lovely paper hangings!"

Peggy laughed. "Wallpaper, you mean," she corrected. "And look, over here on the hearth, a bath stove that burns coal. It's quite the modern rage, you know."

Merry didn't know, but she nodded.

"Pity," Peggy plunged on, "that those nasty, dirty Hessians took your things. I rather think our British friends could fight their own wars, don't you? Meanwhile, until we can send for my favorite seamstress and milliner for you, you'll have to borrow a gown or two of Polly's, since she's rather . . . well, robust-looking, too."

"I regret the extra expense to your father. I'm certain my family will send money when they hear."

"Oh, don't fret about that," Peggy assured her with a rattle of ribboned fan. "Papa is simply swimming in money, though you'd never know it, the pinchpurse way he acts in this war. He used to be more generous and quite the patriot, but lately he's afraid things are tilting the British way, so he is, too."

"You don't mean he's actually become pro-British? A Tory?" Merry blurted, horrified. Obviously Cam and Libby hadn't known this. But she had found herself liking the slightly befuddled-looking man downstairs just now!

"Let's just say Papa's rather a fence sitter and can't make up his mind what to do," Peggy declared condescendingly, as if she were speaking to a child. "It's been building ever since Mama died, it seems."

"I'm sorry."

"Yes, well, I take her place entertaining when I can."

"But in New York there's hardly any social life right now, and no one has a seamstress and a milliner anymore. And no one wants one, anyway, if she intends to copy British styles."

Peggy's disdainful expression looked set in stone. Merry cursed her quick tongue. "I didn't mean—" she began.

"Of course not. I can see you are quite overwrought and overwhelmed. But, you see, Merry, this is Philadelphia, not New York. We set the fashions here, not mock them. And the British aren't really monsters, but absolutely the most civilized nation to ever walk the earth, don't you think?"

"Before the last few years, I would have said so," Merry retorted, her voice hardening in spite of her best efforts. She had wanted to befriend the Shippen girls so much, to learn from them, and to help them, too. But there was a fanged edge to Peggy's voice and demeanor that kept gnawing at her.

"There now, I'm sure we'll agree on simply everything," Peggy assured her, patting her arm with her fan. The silk flowers in her lofty headdress nodded, as if in agreement. "I'll send a maid who's not busy in with bathwater, a gown and some ribbons for that hair. And of course you don't know how to work those Venetian window blinds Father brought back from his grand tour," she went on, and strode to the strange thin slats across the window under the draperies. "Here, you see," she said. She pulled a cord to rattle the slats as they lifted together.

"The grand tour?" Merry asked. "Can your father speak French, then?"

"French? Of course not. No one who ever owed allegiance to England would. Latin and Greek, of course, a bit of Italian, as it's quite the thing in architecture here and at the country houses up on the Schuylkill. I'm sure you'll simply adore our country place, too, and be very happy here," Peggy declared archly, as if she meant to challenge and not to comfort.

"I'm certain I will. Thank you," Merry managed, though the words scratched her throat.

Peggy Shippen rustled out without a backward glance, and Merry heard her go into her room next door. She felt exhausted and alone—and already lonesome for Darcy, even in his worst moods. She lifted the Venetian slats farther behind the

Indian chintz draperies—no doubt all the rage here, too. She gazed out over the vast expanse of roof behind the house and wished she could climb right out this window to escape with Darcy all over again.

Peggy Shippen flounced into her room next door to Merry's and perched on her high bed, despite the wrinkling whoosh of her ruffled, ribboned skirts about her. She collapsed her fan and threw it across the room, not caring that it bounced off the painted fire screen before the unlighted hearth and smacked on the tiled floor. How absolutely horrid that her home had to be invaded by that wide-eyed blond hoyden! Some would say Merry Morgan was pretty, Peggy supposed, even in those wretched rags, but Peggy saw that untutored, country-bred little snip of a flaming patriot simply as a—a fly in the ointment around here! And who knew but that she wouldn't persuade papa to renewed patriotic emotions, after all the trouble Peggy had taken to persuade him to favor the British. And as long as the colonials held this town she'd have to keep a watch on her tongue and her heart, especially with that Morgan chit in her own house.

She bounced up and strode over to her dressing table to tilt her mirror up, then stepped back to see as much of herself in it as possible. She hugged herself for comfort. It was as if Merry Morgan had brought some chill of foreboding into this house where Peggy had always reigned supreme.

But then, as quickly as it had come, the dark, dissonant music that often swirled through Peggy Shippen's brain turned to a lively minuet. She began to pace in time, whirling in a perfect pirouette so that her fashionable, elegant skirts belled out gracefully around her. Her own hands, gripping her upper arms, became those of a handsome British officer, smartly attired in an epauleted crimson uniform. If the British would only take this town, there would be banquets and dances simply every night! She began to hum a Mozart tune, and then she began to put silent thoughts to it.

She could have just screamed when she'd seen that woman get down off that horse out there with that dashing man! And her father had accepted her so politely, so warmly! If his own supposedly beloved firstborn daughter had gone riding with a man alone, however chaperoned and proper, Papa would probably have scolded her for a week! Papa had seemed to be warming to the Tory cause lately when he'd seen how poorly things were going for the colonists—and at her and their family friend Toller's careful prompting—but she worried about that, too.

Pretty Peggy Shippen began to form words aloud to her private minuet: "I will glory in Papa becoming a Tory.... That Merry Morgan is such a hoyden.... I hated to give up my own room next door.... I am much prettier, wittier, than her.... If she gets in my way, I'll make her pay!"

Dizzy with dark feelings, but with no clear plans for putting Merry Morgan in her place as yet, Peggy spun around and around until finally she grabbed a bedpost, gasping for breath.

Those first few days, Merry tried her best to settle comfortably into the Shippen household. She found she greatly enjoyed the company of the middle daughter, Polly. The girl was quite patriotic and a great reader, much like her own sister, Libby. Polly was plain and subdued and took some encouraging to flourish. When Peggy was in the room, she simply wilted into a corner with her kitten, Rebel.

"I swear," Peggy had announced, "if I sit in another chair and get cat hair on my gown one more time I'm simply going to have that kitten drowned!"

"You had better not even jest about that!" Polly exploded. "Just sidle up to Papa to get another new gown, then, when he's worried about even keeping the country house, why don't you?"

"You wretched little snip!" Peggy flared, flouncing off with her adoring youngest sister, Sally, in her wake.

Merry found Edward Shippen very considerate, if something of an enigma. He was distinguished-looking, whichever of his wigs—the ornately curled one or the simple Quaker one—he chose to wear for the day. But his pockmarked face framed eyes that never quite seemed to settle. If Peggy could look right through one, Judge Shippen never seemed to know what to gaze upon. With a rigid schedule, he insisted on running the household "by the book," but he seldom seemed to know his own mind, especially when he came up against his eldest girl's whims.

On her way down to the dining room one day, Merry overheard Peggy scolding him shrilly, "But, Papa, Mama would surely have wanted us to keep up social standards!"

"This is wartime, my dear, or haven't you noticed?" Judge Shippen asked quietly.

"Indeed I have, thanks to your moping and the gloomy warnings from that mouthy gaffer Ben Franklin and the others who run this town! Here I am of marriageable age—poor, bookish Polly is, too, almost—and we're sequestered here like nuns while you dither about whose side you're on!" Her voice rose in volume and in pitch. "I swear, just climb out of the grave you've fallen into with Mama! Be on the side of whomever holds the town, I don't care. Just throw the best parties, so we don't dry up and die here!"

Merry jumped as a piece of china shattered. Judge Shippen ordered Peggy to her room, but she had a final salvo. "If we go on like this, Papa, like the strict Quakers we're not, I'll be a spinster forced to cavort around the countryside with strange men—just as our country guest did with that reckless Darcy Mont! And don't say I didn't warn you!"

Merry stood there, ashamed and annoyed. Another plate crashed, then Peggy rushed out and up the stairs without so much as a glance at Merry. Polly came down quietly and stood behind Merry. She put a gentle hand on her shoulder.

"Don't let Peggy's words or tantrums fret you, Merry," she said comfortingly. "Peggy always breaks things when she doesn't get her way. I think she'll break herself someday. But it does my heart good to see how jealous she is of you. She's flaunted herself for years as the pretty princess of the town, and she has poor Sally worshiping at her feet—and Papa cowering."

Merry didn't know what to say. Peggy Shippen jealous of her? But right now Peggy Shippen was the least of her worries. She had not heard from Darcy in a week. And tomorrow she was going to send for him through Ben Franklin and find out why.

* * *

"Merry, I thought you agreed to come and *listen* to this lecture," Darcy protested quietly out of the side of his mouth at her next whispered question.

"I came so we could talk."

"Later, then."

"With Peggy and the Shippens' friend Toller Devlin hanging on our every word? They said they would be back in just a few minutes. Most of what we need to say is *secret*."

"And won't be much longer if you persist in talking here."

She settled back stoically, angrily, in her seat, gripping her folded fan so tightly in her lap she could have crushed it. Darcy squirmed uncomfortably in his chair next to her in the American Philosophical Society lecture hall as the first speaker droned on about Voltaire's use of satire.

Darcy could not keep his mind on the talk—and not because these wooden seats were hard or because he'd met Voltaire himself at Versailles last year and had read his work for years. He should never have agreed to take Merry out for the evening, not even when Ben Franklin—due to Merry's note to the old statesman—had practically commanded it.

He knew she sincerely wanted to help him, but she was such a distraction he could hardly think straight. He could smell the sweet-scented gardenia in her upswept golden hair. Each time she moved a satin-covered knee he recalled how it had looked undraped and wet with pond water! And the rest of her, too! He groaned inwardly and shifted in his seat again. All he knew was that he was glad he was leaving next week for France to ready things for Ambassador Franklin. Then he could clear his head and renew his dedication to the cause with the beauteous, seductive Merry Morgan an ocean away instead of a few city blocks—or in the next damned chair!

He thought about her day and night. However busy he kept himself briefing Franklin on French policy and court decorum, thoughts of her intruded. Improving Franklin's French only made him picture Merry's bright, beautiful face as she proudly repeated the latest French word or phrase she had learned. Sleep was no escape; she invaded his dreams and his deepest midnight longings. More than once he had awakened to find himself in an actual sweat, crushing his pillow to him, longing to charge over to Shippens in the dead of night to demand that she come down to him, propriety and the past be damned!

Before the little vixen had sent Franklin her tartly worded note saying that there were "things French" she had yet to discuss with Darcy, he had decided he would not, could not, risk seeing her again. She would have to understand that if she wished to help him as she had vowed she would have to keep quiet about his work—and keep out of his way so that he could do it! Yet here he sat at a public lecture with Merry on one side. On his other, except when they left to chat to some friend, sat coy, overcurious Miss Peggy Shippen and the rich, probably Tory friend Peggy had dragged along as an escort, who could not keep his blasted eyes off Merry!

It was a warm mid-September night. The women plied their fans even harder during the intervals between lectures to ward off the tobacco smoke drifting in sweet and heavy through the open street doors of the lecture hall. Everyone was downing the crystal cups of fish house punch and the tiny bits of rye toast spread with white Philadelphia cheese sold at tables in the corner of the foyer. But Darcy, much to Merry's relief, had finally relented to take her down the street for a breath of air.

"Don't you realize I could be a tremendous help to you?" she asked him.

"It is not your risk or concern, Merry, not now that both of us are safe."

"But we're not safe! Nothing and no one is until America wins this war! You yourself said it's going to go a long, long time unless France fully lends her help."

"But it has to be secret help for a while."

"I won't even tell people you're French!"

"You don't have to! That Toller Devlin—who can't keep his eyes or his helpful hands off you—knows a French accent when he hears one!"

Merry stopped to face him on the corner by a public pump. Was he implying that she had been too stupid to recognize him as French at first? She'd show him! She was going to learn fluent French somewhere, somehow, and curse him in it soundly if it was the last thing she ever did!

But his eyes seemed to be drinking her in under the flaring street light, and little sparkles lit her insides. He had complimented her rosy-hued gown earlier, though not as effusively as the suave Toller Devlin had. Still, she cherished the slightest glance from Darcy.

"Merry, please, let me say it this way." Darcy seized her kid-gloved hands. "You will help me most right now by letting me, and me alone, do my job. Having a stunning young woman about me—even at something as proper as a lecture, with others accompanying us—will draw attention to me. I cannot afford any sort of attention right now, not even yours. Later, if I see a way you can help, I swear I will take it under advisement."

"Advisement? Yours? Mr. Franklin's? King Louis's?"

"Shh!"

She plunged on. "I can only say, the way I thought things were growing between us—I mean, the way you trusted me—meant something for our futures. I see now I was sadly, stupidly mistaken. After all, I'm only a foolish woman—" her tone was sharpening "—and you, no doubt, have to take that under advisement, too!"

She spun about and started back toward the open doors of the lecture hall. People had gone back inside, but a blue haze of tobacco smoke still hung in the air.

"Merry," he said, catching her elbow lightly to halt her stride, "please do not think I did not value our time together or that I am ungrateful. But there is just no way, with all the dangers, that we can be together now."

Her hands shot to her waist, setting her puff-hipped rose-and-cream lace skirts to bouncing. "Then I shall help your cause and erase all the dangers by bidding *you* a final farewell, Mr. Mont. If there is just no way we can be together, whatever are we doing here?"

She knew she had to flee before he saw her tears. She marched right down into the street, darting between carriages and carts. She heard him shout, "Merry!" and charge after her. On the brick footpath opposite him she lifted her skirts and hurried faster. Angered and hurt, she was around the first corner and starting toward home before she realized she was showing him that she was, indeed, the danger he had said she was.

What if someone saw them quarrelling publicly and gossiped or inquired about it? Peggy's and Toller Devlin's questions as to why she'd run home would be unending—and another concern to poor Judge Shippen. She detested the way Peggy pouted and threw tantrums to get her own way, and she was no Peggy Shippen.

She stopped so fast that Darcy nearly collided with her. He put his hands on her shoulders to steady them both.

"I'm sorry," she said as he turned her slowly around. "Even if you did care for me, which is obvious fantasy on my part, it would be wrong for me to demand you put my feelings above your duty. Not in these times. Peggy and Toller will be wondering where we are. We'd best go back in. And I'll not bother you again unless I have some sort of news that will make a difference for our...your task. Agreed?" She thrust her chin upward and looked him in the eye.

He looked so startled that despite her inward pain she almost laughed. "I—yes, certainly. Agreed."

"How silly to think one woman would matter in this mess, especially when our sex is such foul luck," she clipped out as a final protest. But her victory over her own emotions, and perhaps over him, felt empty as they hurried back across the street toward the lecture hall.

"Merry, I just want you to know that—" he began when they were just inside the door.

"Shh! Let's just listen to the lecture from back here."

As the lecture droned on, he stood dumbfounded at the way she'd turned the tables on him. Did she have something else up those lace-ruffled sleeves? She had said and done everything just now that he could have wished from her. Yet he yearned to rip that demure but ironclad control from her, to crush her to him, to carry her out of here and use not her clever brain and her patriot desires but that beautiful woman's body that set his heart afire—

He jumped at the man's voice just behind him. It was as if someone were announcing his thoughts to the entire lecture hall.

"A fire! A big fire down the next block," the man was shouting above the lecture. "Volunteers needed, and bring your buckets!"

Patrons poured out of the lecture hall, sweeping Merry and Darcy along with them. In the street others ran or pointed in the direction of the reddened sky above rooftops.

"Can you find Peggy and the carriage?" he asked Merry. Her face, lit by the reflected flames, had never looked so strong or so stunning.

"Not in this confusion! I'm coming, too!"

He thought to protest, but he knew better. Anyway, in this tightly packed town, where a fire could jump from street to street in mere minutes, every hand was needed to carry goods and pass the leather water buckets along. Even after the arrival of the short-hosed hand pumper that the city volunteer brigade would eventually roll to the scene, it sometimes took hours to quench a blaze. Darcy had gone to an earlier fire with old Franklin, who had established the city's seventy-five fire brigades and their training sessions. As in this war, one little flame could threaten to spark a massive conflagration!

Darcy ran to help, and Merry stood back to watch while the lines to pass the buckets were organized. Each deep, narrow leather bucket that appeared on the scene bore its owner's painted name and identifying symbol so that it would be returned. She marveled that the three-story building on fire seemed an inferno within while its brick facade looked untouched.

Darcy soon disappeared in the churning crowd of men, but she knew well that he could take care of himself. But when men kept tearing by her to fill their buckets at the pump until the pumper arrived, she got in a line to help pass them, too.

"Look, ma'am, no need to ruin that gown and gloves," some man beside her said.

She did not break the flow of buckets. "I want to help!"

A few other women joined her in the line, but none who were attired so finely. She slopped water down her skirts more than once, and she began to perspire. Her kid gloves were soiled. A shame, she thought to herself, but she could launder this outfit if she had to. There had to be priorities in this life!

She cheered with the others in the bucket lines when they heard the clanging bell of the hand pumper as it was rolled in at last. And then, in the chaos, Merry saw Peggy Shippen watching at a distance with a small, excited smile on her face. On one arm she had Toller Devlin, expensively attired in sky blue, and on the other, the dark-garbed Mr. Franklin. All three of them spotted her at once.

"Oh, what a sight!" Peggy scolded as they walked over to her. "That gown! Are you always so wretched to your clothing? I had wondered where you and your Mr. Mont had run off to!"

Mr. Franklin bowed and kissed the back of her wet, ruined glove. "Philadelphia could use a thousand more like you in these coming times, Mistress Morgan!"

Toller Devlin's gray eyes reflected the flames behind her. It was as if he, like the ruined building, were seething within. "The sight of you so . . . energetic and so willing here, my dear, only starts a fire in my heart," he said, his mouth in the strangest little twist.

"Toller, you goose!" Peggy protested with a nervous laugh. "Indeed, at least this is much better than that dry lecture."

"Mistress Shippen will probably also thrive on the war when it comes to Philadelphia, Devlin," Franklin put in. "For the excitement, if for nothing else. And you, Mistress Morgan...I could have used a bold experimenter like you at my side more than once in past endeavors," he said. He took her arm and guided her away from the other two, as if he wanted to view the flames from another angle. "Darcy's in this crowd somewhere, I take it," he said.

"Of course, sir. Where there's smoke, there's Darcy!"

The old man chuckled appreciatively. "I might have said that about you, Mistress Morgan. I am certainly going to miss you!"

"And I you—and that dratted French tutor of yours."

"But he'll be back and forth."

"Not to my front door, it seems."

"More fool he. Perhaps someone shall help him to see the error of his ways before he sails Wednesday next."

"So soon! I—He didn't tell me."

"I'm giving a private little supper party for him Tuesday night at eight. Perhaps Judge Shippen would allow you attend as my guest."

"The judge, perhaps, but Darcy would not care for it."

"I see. Then let me say only that his ship is called the *Brazen*, and that it departs midafternoon, downriver from Chester, a mere carriage jaunt away. As I shall be riding down by a circuitous route to bid him farewell, might I take you along for a breath of fresh air?"

"How kind, Mr. Franklin, but will he not blame you for mixing in?"

"Mixing in the business of others, my brave little patriot, is all there is left for a widower of seventy!"

Their eyes met and held. "Well, perhaps it would give the man something to think about on his way over," she said. "If Judge Shippen allows it, I shall take you up on your offer of a breath of fresh air!"

Darcy had joined Peggy and Toller as they strolled back over. He was soot-streaked and drenched, and his thick black hair had spilled out of his hair queue. He looked like a wild man. She almost imagined that she could see straw in his hair again in the darkness and that the murmurs of the crowd as the innards of the doomed building shifted and fell were the shouts of looting Hessians.

But she snapped back to the present when Darcy said only, "For all your troubles, I owe you a new gown, Mistress Morgan, but it would be entirely improper."

"Oh, yes, really!" Peggy blurted out—much too loud—before Merry could answer.

"You yourself could use a change," Merry said to Darcy. "I'm sure Mr. Devlin can take us home. Goodbye, then, Mr. Mont, and thank you for the lecture."

There, she thought smugly. She had managed to best him, but she would see him once again before he sailed, whether he liked it or not. She longed to look back at him, but she forced herself to take Toller Devlin's immaculate arm as the three of them strolled away from the seething embers.

The afternoon Darcy sailed from Chester was too lovely for goodbyes. The sun shone from a cloud-puffed sky, and birds sang, shivering the darkening leaves of the autumn trees. But the beauty of the day did not calm Merry. She had been on tenterhooks since the fire in Philadelphia. It was as though another fire burned inside her! As Ben Franklin said, Darcy would return to America, though perhaps not for months, and not necessarily to Philadelphia. Merry knew now how desperate her sister had felt in the face of separation from her beloved. At least Libby knew that the man she adored loved her in return!

Then, too, more terrible news had arrived from New York this morning. It had been bad enough when word had come that the British had captured the city. Washington had lost again, at the battle of Kip's Bay. He had successfully retreated once again, this time across the broad Delaware River. Word of that defeat had been rumbling through the capital city for days. But the most recent news was sadder still to Merry.

There had been a fire there, too, but one that had not been battled or contained. Some said the British had set it, some said the Tories, some said defiant Whigs, but one-fourth of the once-proud port city of New York had burned to the ground. And the British general—like Nero, Mr. Franklin said—had cavorted with his mistress and allowed no troops to fight the flames. Since Darcy had come down to the ship yesterday, Mr. Franklin said, he probably didn't know of the new tragedy that had befallen New York.

Merry sat nervously in Mr. Franklin's carriage while he went aboard to locate Darcy and apprise him of this new catastrophe. When Darcy told the French this, she wondered, would it spur their help or convince them that the patriot rebellion was a lost cause?

Sitting there while the driver attended to the horses, Merry studied the ship that would take Darcy on his four-to-six-week journey to France. The *Brazen* was a three-masted sloop. Mr. Franklin had told her it had eighteen six-pound guns in case it ran afoul of British cruisers. She realized then that she would even welcome the danger of that if she could only go along.

She watched the *Brazen*'s crew roll the barrels labeled Vir. Tobac. up the gangplank and into the ship's hold. But she looked away when she noted that most of them eyed her in return. She had worn a robin's-egg-blue gown, a cape of a darker blue and a feathered bonnet, and she had taken inordinate care with her hair. Yet perhaps Darcy would refuse to come down even to bid her farewell, no matter how convincing Ben Franklin was. It was no doubt getting near departure time. Dockhands were fussing with the thick mooring lines on the deck. And then she saw Darcy.

He was garbed all in raven black, the way she had first imagined him, back when she had pretended she could control him and her own life. He came quickly down the gangplank toward her; she did not see Ben Franklin. He strode straight for the carriage and looked up at her with those surprising green eyes.

"You came along to get a breath of fresh air, Mr. Franklin says. You know, you have always been that for me. Will you walk?"

He reached for her hand to help her down before she could reply. Her skirts billowed in the river breeze. Her heart beat fast. Each breath seemed suddenly distinct and painful.

"I just came to bid you best of luck in your admirable, important mission," she said, beginning the brave little speech she had been rehearsing for days.

"I did not mean what I said that time about women being bad luck on a ship," he countered in a rush, as if he, too, had a speech prepared. "Besides, you were good luck for me when we were imprisoned in New Jersey, and I shall not forget that."

That tiny bit of tenderness made her eyes fill with tears. She had been trying to memorize his face, and she looked away. He touched her elbow—it was the first time he'd touched her that day—to escort her along the edge of the dock. Both strength and longing poured through her.

"And I shall not forget you, either, Darcy Mont. You're so blessed to be able to go home like this." She fought back the urge to cry and plead. She forced herself to gaze out over the broad expanse of blue-gray river. "I miss New York. I worry about what the blasted Brits are doing to it—to the whole country. Still, I would love to see France. To go there with you."

Her fervent little speech hung suspended on the wind. He propped one foot on a low mooring post and turned his head toward her. His thick eyebrows shadowed his narrowed eyes, and the little cleft that signaled a frown set deep in his chin.

"France is not the place for you, Merry Morgan! It seems a beguiling, precious jewel, but when you reach for it—*voilà*, it is counterfeit, paste. And certainly it is no place for you with me!"

"Why not? I think we make a rather good team, and—"

"No! You do not know me, Merry! I am no *chevalier*, no knight in shining armor riding in. I am not the man for you!"

"I happen to disagree. You have sacrificed much to ride in here to our nation, which needs your nation's help."

"That is different! That has to do with winning freedom, not giving it up!"

"I don't know what you mean."

"And best you do not! Grow up, Merry. War is no time for love. Maybe peacetime is not, either. But, if you wish, you can have the men of Philadelphia, like your adoring Toller Devlin, at your feet."

"But I do not care for him, and I just know—"

"You do not know me!"

"If I don't, that's your fault, so—"

He reached around to seize her chin. In France women teased, they flirted, they seduced, but they did not pour out their minds and hearts honestly. No one did. And after Frenchwomen captured their husband, they lied and cheated and betrayed. But this woman! It actually frightened him how forthright she seemed to be, how utterly open! She wore her very beautiful heart right on her sleeve.

He tipped her face upward, and she looked unflinchingly into his harsh glare. He studied her defiant expression; her full lower lip trembled, but she did not quail under his gaze.

She had no way of knowing that his seething fury was not directed at her. He was trying to memorize her face so that when he was at sea and when he was in France, firmly mired in court intrigues, it would not blend with that other face, the one he detested. The thought that Merry would become the woman in his nightmares was his worst fear. Although, curse it, that would be his only salvation from her.

"*Adieu.* God bless you, *ma chère rebelle*," he said finally, and leaned forward for a quick, warm kiss. His fingers tightened on her arm as if he would have liked to yank her to him.

Surprise, then every other emotion, surged through Merry, sapping her strength, when he stepped back and his hands dropped away from her elbow and chin. But before she could throw her arms around him to keep him here he turned and strode aboard the ship without looking back. And, through her tears, she saw only an old man with spectacles and gray, wispy hair who helped her back into the carriage when the ship set sail.

Chapter Six

From where he sat at the foot of the long linen-covered table, Louis Philippe D'Arcy Montour, comte de Belfort, glanced out the tall window and then back inside. Beyond the panes of glittering glass, the first snow of February 1777, fell to cover the gilded gates and sprawling roofs and sooty chimneys of Versailles in cleanest white. Inside, the mirrors and polished parquet floors of the Galerie des Glaces blazed in the light of eight thousand candles, matching Queen Marie Antoinette's diamond chandelier earrings.

Outside, ice stretched a brittle white shell over fountains, ponds and canals. Inside, despite the buzz of voices and the music, D'Arcy Montour felt that same, bone-chilling cold rising from the revelers here. After his months in America, the curled and powdered wig and hat that were *de rigueur* in the presence of royalty weighed him down. His golden brocade garments, the tourmaline buttons winking from his waistcoat, felt almost feminine.

He sighed and wished for other places, other times, other people. The warm memory of one person in particular he could not shake, even amid the banquet of glittering females spread about him here, as rich as the ten-course dinner on the silver-studded table.

"Any other sort of *bonbon* you would like, *mon cher comte*?" the red-haired Jeannette de la Senart asked with a meaningful pout. She leaned over so far to offer him a piece of marzipan that she might as well have popped her powdered breasts out of her low-cut bodice onto his plate. But he knew she had been offering him much more than that throughout the meal, with her slanted smiles and her knee pressed tightly to his under the tablecloth. It mattered not one bit to the marquise de la Senart that she had been married but four months. Of course, her husband the marquis was drooling over a plump blonde of the influential Noailles family across the table.

"I believe I have had quite enough of everything, *marquise*," Darcy said, and scooted back a bit from the table and her reach. He could not keep himself from thinking even now, while partaking of this bounty, that the price of one of the queen's weekly supper parties would feed Washington's entire army for a day. But whatever would those stalwart, plain-fare American souls make of pickled eels and pheasants stuffed with oysters and burgundy-soaked cherries, he mused grimly.

"By the Virgin, you're even gloomier than before you left us last!" Jeannette protested. She was a petite woman, but with her foot-high pomaded coiffure, with its swinging birdcage and its live songbird—which refused to sing—she dwarfed many of the other female courtiers. "While you were over in those American colonies," she asked with wide hazel eyes, "did you see any of those dreadful savages?"

He was tempted to tell her that in his thirty years he'd learned there were different definitions of the word *savage*, and that some applied to members of this most civilized court, but he held his tongue. "A goodly number. And I'm afraid most of them were British."

She laughed throatily and retorted in a stage whisper, "We'd best not tell the British ambassador, Lord Stormont, you said that. Or the queen, since she favors all things British. Both of them are out of sorts at that Franklin arriving as ambassador, anyway. And Lord Stormont's probably got his little spies out watching you, too, you naughty boy. But he's never been in my bed, if you'd like a good place to hide. I adore adventure! I'd like to know all about your travels in intimate detail. Especially how the rebel women over there are to your taste. You know—"

"Excuse me, *madame la marquise*. I see someone I must speak with." Darcy untied the huge napkin from his neck before his footman could. He rose, bowed once, ignoring her cloudy countenance, and went across the room. The man he sought had just come in. Darcy was weary to the hilt of women trying to bed him just because of his American adventures and his dark reputation.

Just inside the massive gilded and festooned door, Darcy saw the gangly Gilbert du Motier, marquis de Lafayette, jerk to a halt and scan the vast room with a frown. Though he was barely nineteen, the wellborn young man's red hair was already thinning under his high-fronted white wig. He was probably not late, Darcy thought. He had probably been invited only for the dancing after dinner. The young nobleman was temporarily out of Marie Antoinette's good graces for having stepped on her foot while dancing with her. To punish him for that, she refused to feed him, but she commanded him to dance anyway, while she and her intimates snickered and gossiped behind their fans. It was a plight Darcy sympathized with totally, though, unlike him, Lafayette had suffered merely from committing a faux pas.

But it was hardly because they both shared sullied reputations here at court that Darcy wished to speak with Lafayette. His own informants had told him earlier in the week that, despite the fury of his family and the king, Lafayette intended to volunteer to fight at his own expense for Washington in the American war. If someone from such a lofty family as Lafayette did that, it would be hard to convince the British it was not with King Louis's approval. Yet Darcy greatly admired the young man's dedication and daring, so he had arranged secret meetings with both Foreign Minister Vergennes and the new American Ambassador Franklin to help with arrangements. But he had not heard how things had gone.

Darcy greeted him with a stiff bow. "*Mon cher marquis.* Your servant, sir."

"*Monsieur le Comte.* Your servant."

After the proper greetings and inquiries were exchanged, they spoke more informally. Lafayette was buoyed by Franklin's encouragement and wanted to do anything he could to help the rebels. "Like you, sir," he said, his eyes aglow, "I do this for the great cause of *liberté*!" He confided in Darcy that he would sail over this spring on his own ship and report to Washington for whatever duty he would give him, despite the French king's disapproval. "And I'd like you to sail back with me, sir," he added. "Of course, since I'm going with no one's permission, we'll have to give some other sort of destination until we're out of port here."

Darcy noted well how fervent and inspired this often-awkward young man was when he spoke on military subjects. Darcy recalled that when it came to polite chatter or speaking to women other than his young wife, Adrienne, the young nobleman froze as stiff and still as the ponds outside.

"I'll take it under consideration, *mon cher marquis*," he told Lafayette. "I have done about as much as I can here until the British ambassador, Lord Stormont, loses some of his cachet or the rebels win enough of a battle to give King Louis's ministers more nerve."

"Forgive me, sir," Lafayette said, blushing hotly, "but I take it there's another reason you'll go back, since I'm to tell you of—well, the letter Ambassador Franklin just received for you." He was floundering pathetically. "From, you know, a certain pretty young lady in Philadelphia, I believe he said."

Darcy's insides flopped. He had tried to wall off thoughts of Merry Morgan, had tried to like several of the young, single women newly come to court, but they had bored him. Even the proper things they did made him furious at them and at himself. Just last week Alexandrine Troyennes, whom half the court would have liked to bed, had turned him to a hermit again with just one little slip: she had scolded him for kissing her lips when they were rouged.

"Not on my painted lips or cheeks, my pet! Have you quite misplaced your manners over there in that heathen land? On the neck only, and watch my hair . . ."

He had simply turned and stalked away. It had only fed his outrageous reputation when word of that incident had gotten around. Even now, standing here with Lafayette, who was often the butt of alcove gossip for adoring his young wife and dancing poorly, he flinched when he thought of the buzz of bitter accusations aimed at himself. After all, the boy Lafayette's bumbling indiscretions were hardly on a level with his own dark scandal and tragedy.

"Perhaps I should go to see Mr. Franklin instead of staying here for the queen's so-charming dancing, then," Darcy told Lafayette, with a quick elbow to the arm to let the serious young man know he was jesting.

"But, well...you'll be noticed and missed. Haven't you been commanded?" the young man protested, evidently missing the gibe.

"As you have been commanded not to fight for America, eh?" Darcy replied with a tight grin. He patted Lafayette's smartly uniformed back. "When you've been to America, my friend, you will revel in walking out when commanded to stay. Besides, I believe that until our king beds our queen she and Lord Stormont may have their tête-à-têtes, and I shall only obey her when she comes to favor the Americans."

Lafayette smiled broadly and stood a bit straighter as he prepared to make a sortie into the fray alone. His admiration for this enigmatic man they said such strange things about shone clearly on his ruddy face. "Then I shall be in touch soon. *Vive les américains!*" Lafayette called after him with a bold grin.

Darcy smiled and walked out just as the others rose for their well-appointed places in the English country dance Lord Stormont had taught the queen.

When Ben Franklin stopped chatting and drinking his wine long enough later that night to get up to seek the chamber pot in the other room, Darcy whipped out the letter from Merry to read it again.

"My dear sir," it began, entirely properly, but it made him smile. Had she agonized over how to address him after the four months they had been parted? Had she decided this would surely put him in his place? *Sacrebleu,* even the vellum she had written it on almost burned his fingers with its genuine emotion, especially compared to what he'd seen from Frenchwomen lately. Yes, he was going back to the colonies soon, but if he knew what was good for him—and for Merry Morgan, too—he would not be seeing her again!

I hope you and my dear friend, Ambassador Franklin, have heard by now of our commander-in-chief's first great victory. We hear Lord Howe is refusing to call it such, for he will not credit a surprise attack as a fair and noble fight. Having once suffered a surprise attack myself during the battle of Long Island, when I was but trying to help a poor, wounded soldier, I can even sympathize with poor Howe. But, unlike him, I can admit when I am properly chastised. If he cannot learn from his mistakes, as some of us do, God only can help him.

Darcy smiled broadly. Merry might imply all she liked that he had conquered her in some way, but he knew better. Yet her innate wit teased him, making him want her all the more. Damn her, how the little vixen aroused him, and with nothing more than a piece of paper and some ink!

He read more:

The best news of our army's Christmas night attack across the Delaware River, I believe you will agree, is that Washington took a large band of Hessians captive there. I am not ashamed to say that, for personal reasons, it warmed my heart. Please tell your king and his ministers—not his queen, as women, even royal ones, are, of course, of no account—that our men have also won skirmishes in and around Princeton . . . and more victories are to come!

I myself have personal battles to wage, also, that I shall continue to fight upon sighting the enemy again. Meanwhile, I am in continual skirmishes with a certain Toller Devlin. I believe he should have been named Toller Devil! The man is some sort of wealthy Tory I keep about me because he may be of inestimable informative aid later, if you take my meaning. He collects all things. Indeed, lately he has wanted to collect me.

That poor attempt at wit annoyed Darcy. She was trying to pique him, to make him jealous, but he was having none of that. It would not matter a fig to him if she married that son-of-a-bitch prig Devlin, damn them both!

"Sacrebleu!" he cursed aloud just as Franklin came back in.

"What's that, Darcy? I thought the letter would be quite good news, considering the secret dispatches that came with it. I cannot wait for both of us to tell Vergennes tomorrow so that he can inform the king that we Americans may bend but will not break! And then I cannot wait for that blasted British toady Lord Stormont to hear!" Franklin declared, downing another goblet of burgundy.

"Interesting that this note from Mistress Morgan was in with your secret dispatches," Darcy observed. The thought had only now struck him.

"I told her she could write to either of us if she so desired," Franklin retorted, with a twinkle in his eye that his spectacles only magnified.

"You are quite the meddling matchmaker, Mr. Ambassador. Best keep to international affairs of the other sort," Darcy declared, frowning, as he stuffed the letter back inside his waistcoat without rereading any more of it.

Franklin shrugged his shoulders innocently. "It is my firm belief that closer French-American ties are needed," he said. He could not even stop his chuckling when Darcy bade him a stiff, stubborn good-night and went back out into the snow.

The nine months since Merry Morgan had last seen Darcy Mont had passed in a blur of new people, places and pursuits. With the Shippen girls she learned to tat lace and to paint flowers and birds on glass. Yet, even with busy hands, her busy brain never forgot her enigmatic Frenchman. Although Merry was not half so adept as Peggy at it, she had learned to play the latest keyboard instrument, called the pianoforte, and she lent her sweet soprano to the town's drawing room society with hymns and country songs. Still, she felt a dull ache of loss deep inside every time she thought of Darcy Mont.

With the shining Peggy and the shy Polly, she took dance classes twice weekly. She paid far more attention to the French *menuets* and the quick allemandes than to the Virginia reel and the colonial dances. She dreamed of the day she might dance at the French court with Darcy—if he ever came back. And, unbeknownst to the others—except her friend, the middle

Shippen daughter, Polly—she was trying to teach herself French from a book she found in Judge Shippen's library, though she had no idea if her pronunciation was worth a whit.

Merry attended numerous lectures and town meetings, most with the avid-eyed Toller Devlin as her escort. And in June and July she summered with the Shippens at their pleasant country home, the Oaks, on the Schuylkill River, adjacent to Devlin's sprawling Italianate mansion, Devlinton.

Merry stood, temporarily alone with her thoughts, on the half-moon portico at Devlinton Manor on the last day of July. Her hands on the white marble balustrade, she surveyed the grand view of gardens, grape arbors, artificial lakes and fine Pennsylvania oaks and white pines beyond. A deep sigh lifted, then slumped, her shoulders.

"You adore it here, I can tell." Toller's voice broke into her musings as he came up behind her with a chilled crystal cup of punch extended in his bejeweled fingers.

"Yes, I do," she admitted, still gazing off at the blue-green vista. "It makes the war seem so far away. But I feel guilty about that sometimes, as if I should be helping win it."

"Life's too short to feel guilty, dearest Meredith! Guilt is such a blasted bore!"

Toller was always immaculately attired—today in gunmetal-gray satin—even in the country, where the Shippen girls clung reasonably to cool sprigged cotton. She edged slightly away so that his legs would not brush her skirts. She accepted the cup he offered, though.

"Ah, but you are a passionate, provocative little patriot!" he teased, stepping smoothly between her and the balustrade to lean back against it.

"And proud of it!" she declared, purposely ignoring his choice of words and his leer. She fancied she was becoming quite adept at deflecting Toller's innuendos by now, and she knew that rankled.

Toller Devlin was exactly Merry's height, and he was sinewy, and quite handsome in an overly polished way. He reeked of the snuff he used so frequently from one of his collection of European snuffboxes. And, Merry had been told by the Shippens and by every other Philadelphia matron or maid she had met, he was one of the richest and most sought-after bachelors in all of Pennsylvania. But, Peggy had informed her archly, he was just an older family friend to her. She was hardly interested in a man as old as Toller for herself. He was thirty-two, after all. As if, Merry thought, that would make a difference when one really loved. Why, Darcy was thirty to her twenty, and she deemed that perfect.

Now, as Toller's eyes moved thoroughly over her, Merry regretted not having gone out riding with the others this afternoon. She had mistakenly thought that Toller, as host, would go along to give her some time to herself here. But he hadn't, and he'd ruined her daydream, too, so, as usual, she decided her best defense against him was an attack.

"And does it not give you even a twinge of guilt that you have not volunteered to fight for your country's freedom?" she asked as he sidled closer.

His sleek eyebrows lifted. "What is my country? That's the question."

"What is your country? This one where you've made your home, your life, your fortune, of course," she insisted, her voice taking on a sharper edge.

"Now, now, my dearest Meredith. First of all, it was my father who made my fortune. I've only tended it since he died. Then, too, when one has placed loyalty and loving allegiance elsewhere, it is hard to change, is it not?" He pried her punch cup from her stubborn grip and set it on the balustrade next to his. He moved closer yet, keeping a hand on her wrist so that she wouldn't move away again.

But already her eyes and her thoughts were distant. She realized that she felt loyalty and loving allegiance elsewhere, too—for another man. Even though Darcy had not answered the letter she'd sent via Mr. Franklin months ago and had probably not given her one thought while he'd been cavorting with the fine ladies of France, she still cared deeply for Darcy Mont.

When Toller had interrupted her, she had been thinking that perhaps this grand country estate looked a bit like King Louis's Versailles. Darcy had said Versailles had lakes and gardens and woodlands, too. She had been picturing how she and Darcy would look together, strolling the gardens, dancing the new dances she had learned, chatting in French, kissing under the grape arbors—

"Meredith Morgan, damn you for a dreamy, teasing jade!" Toller's voice slashed through her thoughts. Her eyes jerked up to meet his seething gray ones. "Here I am, *the* Toller Devlin of Philadelphia and Devlinton, finally smitten!" he muttered, more to himself than her. "And the lady in question is a rabid rebel who never listens to one blessed thing I say!"

"Toller, that's not true, and I—"

"You do realize there are young ladies of fine breeding standing in line for my attentions, do you not?" he asked.

She had never seen him so riled; his usual suave, sleek looks and demeanor had cracked, and she could see the man beneath. She watched him pat his high forehead under his immaculately curled wig with a lace-encrusted handkerchief before he went on. "You know, my father was right about life. 'It's not the pence and pounds that matter, but the power they provide,' he used to say. He made a fortune with that motto!"

"And what is *your* motto, Toller?" she asked, not flinching under his angry scrutiny. "Protect your papa's pence and pounds, and above all don't fight for the country that allowed him to earn your fortune?"

"Judas Priest, you don't know a thing about what you're talking of!" He had lost his temper with her at last.

Thank heavens, he fumed silently, he'd had the sense never to become emotionally entangled with women, despite the string of mistresses he'd kept discreetly over the years and the bastard children he'd farmed out surreptitiously here and there. Here he'd spent all this morning showing Merry his impressive, imported European collections. But she was obviously bothered by the display of his wealth. She'd dared say something ridiculous about many of Washington's soldier boys still running around barefoot! At least she had shown some interest in his French collections: Limoges and Sevres porcelain and Gobelin tapestries.

He fought to rein in his temper. There would be time enough later to treat her as she deserved to be treated. There would be time enough later to tame her. "Now let me explain, my dear," he said, more quietly this time, with a sweep of arm that encompassed grounds and the house. "The Devlins made their fortune through several generations, trading with our *home* country, Britain. Britain! The motherland! Have we any right just to abandon her in a little family squabble?"

"It's a war, not a squabble, Toller," Merry replied. "The motherland will not let her adult child grow up or think for itself. Mother Britain wants to punish us at her whim, keep us under her thumb and never let us inherit a thing, the way your father obviously let you inherit!" she concluded with a circular sweep of her arm.

Toller was afraid he was actually going to strike her. His ringed hands clenched and unclenched. But he could not help wanting this passionate, stunning woman for his own. He wanted her desperately, right now, in bed, thrashing under him until that defiant spirit was broken. He wanted to own her, just as he did his silver-and-gilt rococo mirrors, his silver ewers, his Chinese ivory miniatures. But she was strong enough that she would have to be bought by subterfuge, or possessed by wooing and coddling, until he had her right where he wanted her. He would prefer her as his mistress, but if she would not acquiesce, well—he supposed he had to marry one day. He would win her in the sure and steady way the British were going to capture the rebels she was so damned fond of—and he'd break her soon enough of that passion, too!

He closed the space between them. "I apologize for my hasty words for now, dearest," he said.

"For now?"

"Later, when you come to understand me better, there will be no need. But for now let us kiss and forgive. I couldn't bear it if you were vexed at me. A kiss to seal our truce, hmm?" he wheedled in his silkiest tone.

He knew she was going to deny him even that again, and it infuriated him. But right now he had no choice but to seize Meredith Morgan, to show her how good it could be between them.

"I hear the riders returning!" she cried, relief all too obvious on her face. She backed away from him in a sudden swish of pink flowered skirts and stiff petticoats. "Oh, look, Toller, it's not the girls at all, but a man. A soldier, I think, in blue and buff. I wonder—"

To his chagrin, she turned her back on him and ran along the portico and down the broad steps to the graveled path. He hurried along behind, hoping the news this messenger brought was good for his Tory friends and British allies. Indeed, he *had* volunteered to help the army—the British, for he had several friends and close contacts there. Fortunately, the news had been quite glum for the rebels lately.

She was jumping and waving now, most fervently, but it still made him want her when she acted like that. He informed whatever gods there were that he had to have Meredith Morgan, and the sooner the better, after these nine months he'd been dragging the other Shippen girls around and flattering proud Peggy just to be near Merry! He knew Peggy didn't like her, so perhaps he and that pretty, pompous Shippen chit could join forces to bring her to heel. If he, Toller Devlin, couldn't have her, he'd see no one else ever did, either. Damn her, she was actually screaming out the stranger's name!

"Cam! Cam!" Merry launched herself into the tall, handsome blond man's arms as he dismounted. Just then the Shippen girls and their escorts cantered back in.

"Everyone," Merry said, beaming as the riders dismounted and strode closer, "I'd like you to meet my brother-in-law, Lieutenant Cameron Gant. Cam, however did you find me?"

"I went to the Shippens' town house, and then to their country home, where they told me you were all here visiting!" he admitted with a grin. Peggy strolled closer, dragging her winded horse. She hung on Cam's every word as he told Merry that Libby was fine.

"Washington's making camp right outside the city to defend it in case General Howe comes calling here as he did in New York," Cam announced after formal introductions had been made all around. Merry and Polly applauded, but the others looked as if they'd heard the tolling bell of doom. "And I've already asked your guardian, Judge Shippen, and he's agreed," he told her in a rush. "There's to be a welcoming party for some of Washington's new officers two days hence, and I've been requested to invite you.''

"Oh, how simply wonderful!" Peggy squealed. "A party with officers!" She jerked her horse hard by the reins to follow Cam as he pulled Merry a few steps away for a private word. "And all of us are going!"

"I'm sorry, no, Mistress Shippen," Cam admitted sheepishly. "Just a few ladies General Washington had known before, so—"

"Then damn your General Washington!" She smacked her horse so hard with her riding crop it would have shied into Merry if Cam hadn't grabbed the reins.

"Now, Peggy..." Toller said as Cam escorted Merry a few steps farther away and bent to her ear.

"It's actually a party to present a young French officer named Lafayette to Congress," Cam explained in a lowered voice. "He's to have an honorary major general's commission and work with Washington. He's a friend of Darcy's, I take it, and—"

Merry's insides cartwheeled. "Darcy's friend? Darcy's here?"

"I didn't say that. I don't think so, but who knows where he'll pop up next? This Lafayette evidently knows him."

"Then I should like to know Lafayette, too. No matter what," Merry added with a nervous glance over Cam's epauleted shoulder at the fuming Peggy and the frowning Toller, who were whispering furtively together.

General Washington's dinner for his officers and the newly arrived marquis de Lafayette was held in Daniel Smith's elegant City Tavern in Philadelphia on August 2, 1777. Members of Congress and the leading Whig citizens of Philadelphia and their ladies sat interspersed with the general's staff and guests at a T-shaped table, partaking of turtle soup, sirloin of beef, leg of pork with turnips and salad.

Conversations buzzed up and down the table about the two American generals, Gates and Arnold, who were facing General Burgoyne's army in the New York State campaign. People whispered that Washington put little faith in Congress's appointed "Granny" Gates but thought Benedict Arnold, nicknamed "the Dark Eagle," a bold military leader. And everyone was hoping that distant military action would keep the British commander, "Sir Billy" Howe, sitting tight in New York City and away from a possible attack on this city he was said to covet as the "prized rebel capital."

Soon everyone rose for numerous toasts with Washington's favorite Madeira. Merry strained forward, all ears, around Cam's shoulder to hear Lafayette's aide address the crowd. The aide introduced the man they'd all come to meet.

"Ladies and gentlemen. The marquis de Lafayette, the honorable Gilbert du Motier, thanks you all for this great honor. He is striving to learn your English. I give you the marquis."

The red-haired young Lafayette stood and raised his glass of Madeira to them all. Merry thought how different he looked from the way she remembered Darcy: almost pudgy compared to Darcy's lean angularity, open and affectionate, instead of wary and austere. He even blushed slightly, and his speech was painfully halting.

"I thank you so much. The general especially. Ah, I did tell him, Lafayette comes to help, to learn. From him. From all of you. Ah... I give to your great cause my funds. My life. And I shall say, I am charmed by everything here in your country, but not for those, ah...mos—the mosquitoes! *Vive la France!* Long live America!"

Everyone laughed and drank, cheered and applauded. Again, though she'd done it several times before, Merry squinted into the glow of the candlelight to scan the faces. Darcy wasn't here, but she kept hoping, praying, like the dreamer she was. Why couldn't he be sitting here with her and Cam—and dear Libby, whom she missed dreadfully, too?

Afterward, folks chatted and mingled over more Madeira or cups of punch from a large glass bowl filled with chunks of ice—ice in August!—that some rich Whig had brought into town from his ice-house in the country. A rolling wooden trolley table laden with trifles and rich, thick syllabub in dessert dishes sat next to the punch. Finally Merry had her turn to speak briefly with the Frenchman who meant so much to Washington as a symbol of future French aid.

"Mademoiselle Morgan. Charmed. Charmed," Lafayette told her with a shy assessing smile as he lightly kissed the backs of her gloved fingers. Now why couldn't that dratted Darcy be as gallant and polite as that? Merry thought wistfully.

"I believe we have an acquaintance in common in France," she told Lafayette from behind her ribboned fan.

"Ambassador Franklin, *mademoiselle*?"

She lowered her voice even more. "A man named Darcy Mont."

"Of course. D'Arcy Mon*tour*. I ask him to sail here with me, but, ah...the last moment he could not. Personal family problems, no? *Quel dommage!*"

"*Quel dommage,*" she repeated, matching his pronunciation, proud that she knew what he meant. Just then Cam appeared to whisk her away to meet some others. The little exchange had set her teeth on edge. Darcy Mont evidently wasn't Darcy Mont at all, but Darcy Montour!

"Cam, I supposed you know a great deal more about Darcy Mont, or whatever his real name is, than you ever told me before!" Merry scolded as he escorted her across the room.

"I had no idea you two were destined to rescue each other and spend two days together, Merry," he said without meeting her eyes. "Dare I hope you feel warmer toward him than you did the day Libby and I put you on that coach?"

"Hardly! Not until you tell me more about all this secretive, underhand—"

"Not I," Cam replied with a cryptic smile, "but there's someone else who would like a word with you about such."

To her surprise, Cam led her out of the common room into the hall and then into another, smaller room. General Washington sat there, his Madeira at his elbow, signing papers before a bright double bull's-eye lantern that cast his big features in sharp relief.

"Oh, General Washington," Merry blurted out. She was touched when he rose to extend his hand to her. Cam stood momentarily at her side, then moved against the side wall, as if to let her have the general's attention to herself.

"I must make this quick before I'm missed, Mistress Morgan," he said, sitting again. "And then it's back to the troops camped at the Falls of Schuylkill, and I'm taking our *new* French friend with us.''

Was he implying that Darcy was their *old* French friend? She wasn't about to rise to the bait. She suddenly became convinced that Darcy was never coming back. His own family problems, his own desire for France—or dislike for her—she did not know why it should be, but it hurt terribly all the same.

''Mistress Morgan,'' General Washington began, gazing intently up at her, ''I have reason to fear that General Howe will try to take this city in the future. We will endeavor to repulse such an attack, of course, but we must have contingencies.''

Her heart began to thud. ''Contingencies?''

''You vowed, I recall, to do what you could for the cause of freedom here in Philadelphia when last we met.''

''I did, sir. And meant it, too.''

''Then you are the one I want for this task, and I see we've chosen the right code name, too, haven't we, Lieutenant Gant?''

''Yes, sir.''

''I am asking you, Merry Morgan, if the British should take this town—or even if they do not and you hear aught that might be of use to our side—to get that information to a certain liaison who will be riding back and forth to my camp. You will sign your messages only as Flame, and your contact will be called Torch.''

She stood stunned, but thrilled. She could feel her heart pounding; she clasped her hands so tightly at her waist that they began to go numb.

''Freedom Flame, what do you say?'' Cam asked.

''Yes! Oh, yes! I want to help!''

''It means secrecy, some risks,'' Washington added.

''I understand.''

''It also means learning secret codes, passwords. . . .'' Cam put in. ''And a certain, well. . .self-disciplined sacrifice.'' At last Merry spun to face her tall brother-in-law. He seemed to be having trouble forming his words. ''I mean,'' Cam went on, ''putting aside personal prejudices to work closely with people you may not like yet have to take orders from—''

"You'd best show her what you mean, Lieutenant," Washington said. "But I am relying on her to be of greatest help to us."

"Yes, I shall. I'll learn whatever I have to. You'll be hearing from me, General—from Flame."

No sooner had polite goodbyes been said than Cam hustled her out in the hall again, then back into the crowded common room. "Cam, what—?"

"I have to tell you, there was another reason you were invited tonight besides Washington himself wanting to ask you to help," he said, not breaking stride as he steered her around the edge of the still-crowded room toward the alcove with the punch bowl and the desserts. "It's nice that you've been studying French, Merry, because maybe it will help you with your liaison."

He took her straight to the group Lafayette was addressing. Everything fell into place for her. So that's it, Merry thought. One of the first things Washington will have Lafayette do is coordinate spying in Philadelphia. She said as much to Cam, who only grunted, as they waited for the others to move away from Lafayette in the dim, curtained alcove. Now he stood bent in intimate conversation with only one man. Cam pressed her forward.

The two men turned toward her at once. Merry gasped. Her hands shot to her mouth. Lafayette might as well not have come to town at all.

"You!" she gasped to Darcy. "But you weren't here." The floor seemed to tilt out from under her. She felt she was on wheels, like the tables laden with punch and food behind her.

Darcy's green eyes glittered over her, but he bowed stiffly. "Just arrived, Mistress Morgan." He greeted Cam brusquely with a nod. "Gant." His face looked carved from stone. He was evidently as unhappy to see her as she was thrilled to see him.

"The answer again is no, my friend," Darcy told Lafayette. "It would never work. Mistress Morgan will tell you the same."

"The same? What won't work?" Merry demanded.

"I regret it is too late, Darcy." Lafayette drew himself up to his full height. Darcy still towered over him. "I shall not fail

General Washington in my first task. Nor shall you in any of yours!''

Merry was amazed at how forcefully Lafayette could speak when he had to. But whatever were they arguing about?

"Mistress Morgan—" Lafayette lowered his voice and scanned the room "—it is well you know this man. He is your liaison. The Torch. Ah, under him, you must do what he says. Work closely. Then he reports to me in the army's camp."

Merry's lower lip dropped in shock, then set hard. Darcy was glaring at her. This was her big chance to help, and he was ruining it all! He didn't trust her enough to want to be around her, not even for the cause of helping both their countries. Drat him! He'd been gone for months and he wasn't one bit glad to see her. He'd confided everything to her once, when they'd been in dire straits, and now he couldn't bear to meet her eyes.

"Look, Merry," Darcy began, reaching for her arm, "for personal reasons, this will not work, so—"

"Don't touch me!" she snapped. "I am helping, so you play the coward if you will!" Furious and hurt, she shoved him away. He lost his balance on the polished wooden floor and skidded a step back, bumping the trolley with the syllabub and the trifles. Glass skidded, then crashed, as the trolley bumped the table with the punch bowl. Ice swayed and rattled against crystal. Then the bowl slid right off and shattered on the floor in an upward shower of reddish punch and ice, spraying them all.

People gasped. Heads turned. Cam pulled Merry away from Darcy and Lafayette, who stood mopping at themselves with handkerchiefs and quickly proffered towels.

"You see, my friend!" Darcy's words were as cold as the ice at his feet. "I cannot! It just will not do!"

Embarrassed, and crushed by his hatred and her foolishness—not in shoving him, but in loving him—Merry let Cam lead her out the door.

Chapter Seven

Merry knocked on Peggy's door just after dawn on a crisp early-September morning.

"It's Merry, Peggy. Are you ready yet?" she called. "The British may be coming, but the Americans are here! Hurry, or we'll miss the parade!"

Cynthia, the housemaid who coiffed Peggy's hair, opened the door. Merry could see Peggy, still in her ribboned dressing gown, sitting bleary-eyed before her mirror having a saucer of coffee.

"I'm not going till Toller calls for us, and best you'd not either, the simply wretched way you've been treating him!" Peggy called out, her tone both morning-raspy and scolding.

"I'll see you later, then," Merry called over Cynthia's shoulder, and hurried away before the conversation could go any further.

In the ten months she had lived with the Shippens, Merry had never crossed the threshold of Peggy's sacred boudoir. Nor had she ever stepped into the realm of her friendship, though at times Peggy seemed overly ingratiating, as if to make up for her outbursts. By the time she was halfway down the stairs, Merry had already decided that she was not going to miss the parade of American military strength this morning, not even if Peggy threw her finest raving fit later. And she was certainly not going to linger just to be escorted by Toller Devlin. He had been both too possessive and too presumptuous of late, and in any case, all she wanted was to be with that dratted Darcy Mont, or Montour—whoever and wherever he was.

She took her bottle-green cloak, which was lined up with the others on the settee in the hall, and peered into the drawing room, then the dining room. She heard much bustle upstairs, but there seemed to be no one down here yet, not even Judge Shippen, who often rose early. The opportunity to be alone, even amid the crowds, was too alluring to ignore. She popped her head in the kitchen to tell the servants she was going toward the Commons and would meet the Shippens there. She swirled the width of cloak over her dark blue walking gown and pulled up the large hood as she closed the front door behind her.

Suddenly the bright September day seemed to blossom with the promise of high adventure. She was free for a little while, as free as she wanted her new country to be. She nearly skipped as she walked down the steps and moved briskly in the direction other folk were heading. The parade was to enter the city down Front Street, then turn up Chestnut to the Commons. Her heart beat to match her steps. It was as if she could already hear the rattle of drums. General Washington would lead the parade, and word was that he would have his new French major general, the marquis de Lafayette, at his side. How she would love to find a way to have a word with either of them. After all, it had been four weeks since she had accepted their assignment as Freedom Flame, and no one had contacted her since.

Worse, she had not seen Darcy again, and she was tormented by the thought that he had somehow talked Washington, Lafayette and her own brother-in-law out of letting her help inform on the British. Had Darcy demanded that Washington and Lafayette assign the task to someone else? The scene she'd inadvertently caused at the banquet could have been ammunition for him if he told them that she couldn't be trusted to work unobtrusively. Or was she only to be contacted later, if the catastrophe occurred and the British pushed past the American defenders to take the rebel capital?

But it was her relationship with Darcy himself—or the lack thereof—that really made her furious. He must surely detest her now. But, the more she tried to detest him, the more she cared for him. Her dreams and her waking fantasies were no longer of an adoring, humbled mystery man she conjured up and could control. The face, the body, the voice, the touch . . . now it was always that aloof, hostile malcontent Darcy Mont! Yet she yearned for him with every element of her being.

Distant music floated to her before she heard shuffling feet and wild cheering. Down the way, the ranks of mingled, many-hued uniforms swung onto Chestnut Street and plunged north toward Merry and the Commons. She hurried along the brick footpath to find a clear spot where she might await their approach. All Philadelphia seemed to have turned out to cheer Washington's boys on. Let General Howe and the hated Hessian commander, General Knyphausen do their worst. Let their ships enter the Chesapeake and spew out their soldiers. Philadelphia was surely safe with these fine, proud, smiling American troops to defend it.

She was so excited that she left the Commons to run toward the approaching regiments. Drums and feet beat a muted music; fifes shrilled. The new flag, red, white and deep blue with stars and stripes, flapped above their heads. It had been commissioned, she knew, by General Washington from a widowed upholsterer named Betsy Ross, right here in town.

Then there was the stern-faced general himself, mounted on a sidestepping white charger at the head of his troops. Wide-eyed and stiff-backed, Lafayette rode a coal-black mount right behind him. Merry squinted in the morning sun, but she did not see Darcy anywhere in the army's ranks. But how foolish of her. Lafayette was here openly to help, but Darcy's duty was of a secret sort. When Cam rode by later at the head of the Second New York with a nod her way, she cheered and huzzahed until she was hoarse. How grand and glorious they looked! It was as if victory were already theirs!

She followed alongside the parade, back toward the Commons, where she saw Judge Shippen with his two younger daughters. She waved and smiled, but they did not see or hear her. Just beyond them stood Peggy, in a salmon velvet cloak, with her arm linked through the immaculately attired Toller Devlin's. As usual, Merry thought, those two looked as much conspirators as friends.

The raucous noise swelled when the American ranks cut right across the grassy Commons, whose trees were just beginning to flaunt their autumn colors. And then, behind her, she heard that one voice she always sought. She nearly jumped out of her skin.

"Good day, rebel Merry Morgan."

She whirled to face Darcy, standing just behind her. Her hood fell back from her hastily curled and upswept hair, but she did not think to reposition it. She could not think of anything at first. He was all in black, from bicorne to boots. He looked grim, but so...so splendid. And, just perhaps, not too angry with her for having shoved him in the punch last month. His eyes assessed her boldly. She steeled herself to treat him as coldly as he deserved for not having come to see her, but she felt a hot blush creeping to her cheeks nonetheless.

"A good day to you, Mr. Mont," she managed. She almost blurted a hundred questions, but she had to show him she could bridle her tongue! Still, her heart was pounding harder than the ranks of marching feet, and the blood blaring in her veins was drowning out the drums.

He moved to stand beside her as they faced the parade together. "What do you think of this fine display?" he asked, as though he had been with her all along and was simply making more polite conversation.

"It's glorious!"

"Look again," he said. "Look closer. And tell me the truth."

She frowned and squinted again at the marching display. How dare Darcy just appear like this and demand answers to some test! She ought to turn her back and walk away. But perhaps he had come to apologize, to ask her to help. Perhaps Lafayette and Washington had taken him to task for ignoring her. That would make her so happy! To calm herself, she continued to study the troops. She forced herself to think clearly. Now, beneath the flash and the bravado, she saw the ragged ranks, the tattered clothes, the ambling steps, the youth and inexperience of men who had not yet had a real victory beyond quick retreats and surprise attack-and-runs. Their spirit was jaunty, yes, but in truth they looked haphazard and ragged. She shuddered involuntarily, but focused on the most hopeful thing she saw.

"I see that Washington is flaunting Lafayette, and thus the tacit French approval of our cause. It's been bucking the town up for weeks to think that a nobleman has chosen to give up a luxurious, peaceful life at Versailles for a harsh war experience here."

Darcy's frown deepened at her distorted view of life at the French court, but he said only, "Good. Go on."

"I see sprigs of green stuck in every man's hat to show that the cause is yet young and flourishing."

"Washington wanted every man to have something in common, despite this motley array of uniforms. He has had to work day and night to make these troops look like an army and not a mob. But do you see the troops that can withstand a British assault?"

She spun around to look at him. His face seemed carved from stone. His skin was burnished from the sun, making his eyes and cravat look stark white. He had been spending a great deal of time outdoors since she'd seen him last, probably with these troops, so how dare he disparage them! But as to his question about these soldiers, with their clean new flag and their bright sprigs of green, holding off the brutal British and Hessians she'd seen at far too close range several times already—

She frowned back at him. "You've turned defeatist."

"Ever the realist," he countered. "And so I've come to ask you if you will take a walk with me. I've already asked Judge Shippen for permission, though I'm afraid my request set both pretty Peggy and your friend Toller Devil to whispering again."

She could not keep the smile from her face. Even with the dangers to come, even with Toller and Peggy skewering them with barbed glares across the sea of bobbing heads, even with her own past defeats with this elusive man, her heart soared.

"Then, to the devil with pretty Peggy. The merry Merry accepts the kind invitation of dreary Darcy," she quipped sharply, and was rewarded with at least a twitch of one side of his lips.

"The only woman I ever knew whose plucky wit could rival Ben Franklin's. Come on, then," he said, and escorted her away from the Commons and its cavorting crowds.

Though Merry and Darcy did not turn back as they started away, Peggy Shippen's hate-filled gaze stabbed them in the back. She fumed silently over Darcy's seeking Merry out again—and with Papa's permission. Why, the only man she had about to act as her escort was Toller, who was simply years older and, despite his vast wealth and Tory ties, not exciting—in that way—at all! Absolutely the first chance she got to be alone with a dangerous, delicious man like that Darcy, she'd take it, no matter what Papa said or did!

"That storm cloud of an expression predicts more harsh weather," Toller said lightly. He realized instantly when she swung her narrowed, glittering gaze on him that he had overstepped. Damn, he, too, was furious to see that Frenchman walk off with Merry Morgan, but he wasn't going to throw a public tantrum such as he sensed was coming from Peggy.

"It's only that I don't trust the likes of Darcy," Peggy told him. "Or her, for that matter," she added, as if she didn't deign even to call Merry by name.

"Patriotic to her pretty little toes," Toller put in above the roll of drums, "but hardly dangerous. You don't really think she's going to go fight with Washington's raggedy boys, do you?"

"I think she's out to make a fool of you and disrupt my family. At the very least," Peggy spat, and turned away so fast that Toller had to lope along to catch up with her. "Sometimes she makes Papa think twice about where his political loyalties really lie!"

"Mmm... Fool that I am, I can sympathize with that," Toller said, trying to lighten her mood. "She argues like a lawyer, but she looks like a goddess, and—"

Peggy's fan cracked down hard on his arm, and he actually yelped aloud. Why Judge Shippen had never taken a strap to this willful woman was beyond his understanding, Toller raged silently, except that she was perhaps the only one the old man had had left to talk to after his wife's death. But, looking at her now, Toller admitted that he'd underestimated the depths of Peggy's capacity for jealousy and even vengeance. Petty her passions might be, but they seemed also to be precariously balanced. Or was it merely deep frustration at not having a suitor in these terrible times? If only he could find her one to calm her down and get her under his control. Perhaps, when and if the British took the city—

"Toller, I'm sorry," she was saying, now with a mere flirtatious tapping on his arm with her fan. Her lips softened from their hard line of rage to a mere pout. "I know you and my sister Sarah are my only allies since that woman's come to town and turned everything upside down!"

Cautiously Toller tucked Peggy's arm in his, and they made their way through the crowd on the fringe of the Commons. Yes, he mused, he had to agree with Peggy there. Merry Morgan had turned him upside down since she'd come to town, and he meant to possess her, whatever it took. But he'd never tell Peggy that now. He'd just glimpsed the depths of Peggy's dark hatred of Merry. Perhaps, he thought smugly, he'd soon enough find a way to use that new knowledge for his—and, of course, the Tory—cause.

"Come on, my dear," he coaxed. "You're the most beautiful woman here today, so let's see if we can turn a few of those crudely cropped rebel heads under those dirty wigs, eh?" That almost put a smile on her face. Luckily, he hadn't added that she was the most beautiful here only because Merry Morgan had left the area. Or no doubt these soldiers would have seen a public display the likes of which they'd never see again, even if they staged an actual battle right here on the Commons!

Darcy took Merry west on Tenth, then toward South East Square, a smaller, treed version of the Commons. Yes, he admitted to her as he hurried her along, he'd been at the American camp along the Schuylkill, when he hadn't been riding back and forth to arrange some things. And, yes, if the British took the town, he would need her help.

She sighed heavily and shook her head. "They won't take Philadelphia. We just will *not* allow that!"

He did not break the quick pace he'd set for them. "That is your heart talking, Merry Morgan, not your head. And, if you intend to work with me to become Flame, such emotions could be deadly."

"Yes. All right. I see," she said, pushing herself harder to match his stride. She understood far too well what he meant. It sobered and frightened her the way her emotions concerning not only her country but also this man churned inside her. She was both hurt and angry that he had not been near her for nearly a month, but she had to muzzle that if she was to work with him for the cause. This man stirred such passions in her that she was often torn between pounding him with her fists and wrapping those same fists around him and sobbing for pure joy at his merest glance. But she grasped that he was telling her that they could work together only if she could put her emotions aside. Could she do that, just as he did? She could not help the way she felt about him.

"Do you know where we are?" His question interrupted her jumbled thoughts. "It is called Ravine Road, though there's no marker. Could you find it again?"

She looked around. They were on a narrow cobbled street on the eastern fringe of the city. It seemed almost rural here, with small wooded valleys and houses set farther apart then in nearby neighborhoods. She nodded solemnly.

"And do you trust me enough to come along and do what I say?"

Her eyes collided with his challenging stare. "For my country, yes."

"What else?" he asked. There was a glimmer in his sharp gaze that she could not read. He led her off the gravel footpath and past a small brick house. Behind it, a makeshift rope-and-wood footbridge, just wide enough for one person, straddled a wooded ravine. Darcy loosed her arm and walked across it, holding to the rope handrail. She followed him as readily as she had the night they'd fled the Hessians in New Jersey. Whatever would the Shippens say if they could see her now? she mused. But on the other side of the swaying bridge she halted.

"A chicken coop?" she asked as a clapboard, shingled building appeared, still half hidden by the thicker foliage of the ravine.

"It used to be. You could call it a pigeon coop now. The family who owns this—" he pointed back toward the house they'd passed "—believes that I have leased and refurbished it for an *affaire de coeur* I am having with a certain lady. If you have any problems with that story, say so now."

"As long as it's strictly a story," she replied, amazed at her own aplomb. She fought to keep her voice steady. Did this man think she would beg for his favors, his smile? Let him be snide and grim and secretive. She was in this for her country, not for him!

"Then I shall trust you," he said simply, but his own thoughts snagged on his words as he fumbled with the lock.

He was fighting his own urge to know everything about her doings in the months they had been apart. But he was desperate to keep this strictly impersonal. If not, he—and perhaps his mission—might be doomed. Obviously, she had flourished. She looked as beautiful and as beguiling and as bold as ever, and that rattled him to the soles of his feet. He had done entirely too much thinking about her. He realized, as Lafayette had said, that his vehement arguments that he could not work with her showed his own weakness for her. He was trapped now, and he would make the best of it. But he was worried that when— when, damn it not if—the British took this town, he would be forced to operate completely in secret and would need this alluring, alarming woman even more than he did now to fulfill his assignment.

He ducked his head to lead her in the door. "*Voilà*, one of my headquarters," he told her with a sweep of his arm that encompassed the small single room.

"*C'est charmant,*" she threw back at him, hoping the French she'd tried to learn from Judge Shippen's book was pronounced so that he could recognize it. Embarrassed, she scanned the slant-roofed room, and missed the startled look that softened to an admiring glance.

Eight gray-and-white pigeons with bands on their legs cooed and pecked at grain in wood-slatted cages. There was a tiny,

unlit stove with a shovel leaning against it, a long worktable
with a high plank bench, a narrow, if long, straw mattress and
quilt on a cot, shelves with books, paper and bottles and not
much else.

"Let me take your cloak, and then come over here and sit,"
he said, a bit too gruffly. "We have a great deal to do in a short
time."

He was thrilled, as he had been once before, when he had
shared his mission with her in the wilds of a New Jersey wood,
to see how quickly her mind worked. His explanation of the
homing pigeons to carry messages to Lafayette at the American camp took only a few moments. She easily grasped the
number codes they would share by each using a copy of John
Bunyan's *Pilgrim's Progress*. The message to be sent would be
indicated, word by word, by numbers for the page, line and
word from the book. He told her he had picked this location
partly because, if the British ever put up sentries around the
city, this ravine led to a hidden way out. He explained the use
of couriers and passwords and safe spots in town to leave messages if she could not get them here. He told her that old
Widow Windham's house, on the very next street to the Shippens', would be a safe drop spot for her, and he told how to
leave messages in code in the widow's window box on a mere
walk around the block for air. There was also a hollow knot in
a tree near her she could use. He described the boy, to be called
only the Lad, who might toss gravel at her window at night if
there was some emergency task to be accomplished.

"If you hear the gravel, open your chamber window wide,
and he'll throw a rock in with a note tied to it."

"Well, then, I guess I should tell you my window is around
in back on the north side, and—"

"I know. Just get out of the way of the missile and do not try
to catch it!" he added, his voice still entirely too harsh, considering how calmly they were getting on.

"And hope he doesn't break the panes and arouse the Shippens, you mean. As you probably know, Peggy's window is
right next to mine."

He ignored her sudden testiness. "If any glass breaks, just get the message off the rock and make up some tale about vandals tossing stones. I'm sorry, Merry, but this sort of task will probably call for a quick, sound falsehood now and then, and I realize that is not in your nature."

As close as they sat together on the plank bench at the table where he'd been demonstrating the codes, she turned to look at him. The slightest softening of his voice shook her. "Are you so skilled at falsehoods, then?" she asked.

A frown crushed his high brow and brought back that little warning cleft in his chin. "I have learned to recognize that deceits are, unfortunately, the worst part of life. Now, before I take you back," he went on, "you must learn to interline a message."

He grabbed a piece of paper with a letter written on it. Merry sensed that he had almost shared something of his past with her. Someone he cared for must have betrayed him somehow. She longed to ask him, to smooth those lines away from his furrowed brow. Instead, to show him she could be everything he needed for this important task, she forced herself to concentrate on the page.

"You see, a normal letter," he began. His voice seemed rough and raspy again. His shoulder bumped her arm as he reached for a stoppered bottle of ink, but the ink was not black. It swayed in its bottle—a pale, milky-green hue.

"That's not ink, is it?"

"Invisible ink when it dries. Lemon juice, milk, antimony. From France. You write a second, small lettered message with this between these visible lines. To read the hidden message, the receiver must heat it on a hot surface—I use a shovel that has been in the coals. But before you begin to write your invisible letter you always underline in the other letter either the first *H*, which means to read it with heat, or the first *A*, which means to soak it in acid. See, this ink bottle is marked with an *H*. I will give you some to take back with you."

Merry was awed by the complexity and ingenuity of what she had stumbled into. Curious, she leaned closer to him as he took a normal quill pen and dipped it in the strange ink to write a line. As soon as each faint word dried it disappeared.

"But you can't tell if you've made a mistake with this," she observed.

"If you bend closer, you will see the words just before they dry, especially in the lamplight," he said, pulling the bull's-eye lamp closer.

He let her try the next line. She leaned closer to write; he leaned closer to watch. As he dictated the message to her, his deep, quiet voice vibrated clear through her. She could feel his body warmth. His breath brushed her cheek. She scented the rich, masculine tang he always had about his person. A curly tendril strayed from her upswept coif; her petticoat rustled when he shifted his knee closer. The heat of his hip and thigh seemed to soak through the fabric to swamp her senses.

Her hand began to shake. Did he have to lean so close? His right arm curved around the letter she was laboring over. His other leaned on the wall just behind her, as if she sat in his embrace. Her concentration on her task wavered. She bit her lower lip to steady herself. Little wanton flutters feathered the skin along her stomach, making her clench the muscles there. She clamped her soft thighs tighter together. She was drowning in his nearness, though he was not touching her at all.

Darcy couldn't keep himself from shifting his weight beside her on the plank bench. It bounced to jar her hand.

"Drat!" she snapped, but she went gamely on until he stopped dictating the sample message to her.

"I'm ready," she told him, afraid to look up. "Go on."

He repeated the last phrase, but his mind was no longer on his work. He was the one who was not ready for what she did to his poise, his need for isolation, even when they were not together. She haunted even his dreams, and it panicked and infuriated him. Amélie was the only female he had allowed to find a place in his heart, and he wanted even her out.

As for Merry Morgan, he could only hope they could communicate over the months by invisible letters and codes and ruses, not in person. She had not even blinked at the story he had told the woman who owned this place—that if there was a young female here it was to be kept most discreet so that her family would not find out. Damn, but he almost wished this were a place for romantic *tête-à-têtes* and a wild *affaire de coeur*! It was hard as hell to keep his hands off her when they were this close and he breathed in her sweet scent like this. And with that little bed over there just beckoning—

"Well, *monsieur*?" She broke into his rattled, guilty thoughts with another stab at French. Her efforts at that both pleased and provoked him. "Do I meet with your approval? I know you didn't want to work with me because I'm just a woman and you think I'm always getting in your way—"

"Yes, you are," he muttered, and took the quill pen from her and stoppered the precious bottle.

She stood up so quickly that she almost tipped them both off their plank seats. Her voice was even more on edge. "I realize you don't like me, but I can do whatever you need for—for all this."

"Merry, let us just—how do you say it?—wash the air here."

"Clear the air. And I'll prove to you that you were wrong about me!"

"Keep your voice down."

"I do apologize for shoving you into the punch the other night," she said, more quietly. "I'll not be a bit of a problem to you anymore—"

He reached for her wrists to pull her back down. The plank bowed, then bounced them together. "But you are a problem to me! And I know only one way to make it better!"

He could not stop himself. These feelings had been crashing through him since he had carried her naked from the pond months ago, maybe since the day he had bound and blind-folded her on that bed in Manhattan. His big hand clasped her chin to still all protests before he realized that there were none. His other hand fastened in her thick, sunlit hair to tug her toward him. He slanted his head as his mouth covered hers.

Everything between them exploded. Her hands clung to his shoulders, then moved to grasp his powerful arms to stop the spinning of the room. Battle drums muted; the quick-time march in her head and heart began.

"Mmm," was all she managed as he deepened the kiss and her mouth softened, then opened, under his fervid assault. His tongue foraged inside the warm, wet cavern of her mouth. He plundered even more boldly, and she responded. He tasted of

tartness and tenderness and temptation. He smelled of fresh air
and leather and the most delicious danger, and it all sent her
head spinning.

His hands raced over her back and hips. He lifted her; she
soared high, still not letting him break the frenzied kiss. Her
arms wrapped around his neck; her tongue sparred with his in
a furious duel. He shuffled out from between the bench and
table, and laid her carefully down on the narrow, prickly straw
cot, where he leaned over her, caressing her, still kissing her,
until they could not breathe. Then he lay, carefully if heavily,
beside her, as if to pin her to the mattress.

His hands explored her, more leisurely now, molding, clasping, her eager flesh right through her gown and petticoats. She
grasped him, too, held him to her, even pressed herself closer
with her fingers splayed across his back. With her hands, shyly
at first and then more deliberately, she learned the hard muscles of his shoulder, back and waist. He was angled and taut
everywhere she was rounded and soft. She could feel the blatant thrust of him against her lower belly, even through her
bunched-up skirts and petticoats. Not only did she not protest
when his hand marauded under her skirts and slid heavily up
her stockinged leg, she leaned back slightly so that he could
ruffle the material higher.

"Oh, Darcy," she moaned as his hot kisses sprinkled her
eyelids, cheeks and throat. She arched back in sheer delight.
She was out of breath, as if she had run miles. Even breathing
this fast didn't help her dizziness when his hand crept up her
bare thigh, above her ribboned garter, and he kissed her peaked
nipples right through her stretched bodice.

"*Ma belle*, I want so to finish what we started that other
time. I know it is so fast, but I need you desperately—" His
words came raggedly as his skilled fingers found and fondled
the damp juncture of her passions.

She knew that what he was doing to her was sapping her
strength, her reason, everything but the desperate desire to lie
even closer to his big, hard body, with no barriers between. But
then, then, what would he think of her? He had been away for
months; he had stayed away for weeks. He didn't really want

her around him. He distrusted all women. So why, why, was he doing this? And why must she love and want him so?

"Darcy," she gasped. "We...I can't yet. Not like this...here...so fast. But when we have proved...how we really feel about each other, then..."

He lifted his big, tousled head. She had pulled his queue awry, and his black hair spilled out, spiky and loose, like a wild man's. His features looked stretched taut; his eyes were glazed. He looked in pain, and he pressed his loins so close against hers that she was afraid at first he would not let her up. His eyes narrowed. He shook his head as if to clear it.

Then he sat up abruptly and ran a hand through his hair. He rustled her skirts down over where his hot, insistent fingers had just been. She leaned her head back against the wall, both relieved and bereaved that they had stopped the madness. She still tingled everywhere he had touched or kissed her. She still felt his rhythmic, demanding strokes between her legs, as if he had invaded far inside her, yet there was not the fulfillment or the release that she now found she craved more than ever.

"*Sacrebleu,*" he gritted out, not looking at her. "I knew this would happen! And now it is too late, since you know everything."

Her voice came shakily as she fought back confused tears. "That's one of your falsehoods. I know almost nothing of you, Darcy Montour, the man."

He frowned and stood. He brushed himself off as if to rid himself of any touch of her. She glared at his broad back, wishing she had that shovel by the stove so that she could knock him over his hard head.

"The way we will be working together, there will be no need...for that...for more mistakes," he clipped out. "Come on, then. I must get you back, or they will all wonder."

She stood on shaky legs and flounced out her skirts. When she spoke, her voice suddenly sounded so bitter that it surprised even her. "Will they? Well, if they ask, I'll assure them that your kisses shake the universe and your touch makes a maiden swoon!"

"Merry—"

"That your godlike French skills at seduction make us mere mortals mourn when you stop your heavenly touch. You see, I'm quite good at falsehoods, too, *Monsieur* Montour. And don't bother walking me back. I'll do my part for this war quite apart from you, just the way you want!"

She tossed her cloak around her shoulders and hoped he hadn't noted her trembling or her tears. She yanked her hood up over her head and grabbed her copy of *Pilgrim's Progress* and the bottle of pale-green ink. She spun away. "Torch and Flame—what silly, stupid names!" she spat before the door banged hard behind her.

He dropped his face in his hands. Just like the door, the little window he had opened to her was slamming shut again. He cursed himself for touching her, and he cursed himself for having stopped touching her.

He raked his thick hair back and hastily retied it. He grabbed his bicorne and fumbled to lock the shed as he went out. He hurried across the trembling ravine bridge and followed her at a distance to be certain she got back safely. After what they had just shared, he didn't feel safe himself, and the war had nothing to do with it. She **had** fired her salvos, stormed his defenses and dictated her own terms. And, he feared, even as hurt and furious as she was, it was he who had lost this battle.

But, *sacrebleu*, just look at her up ahead! The woman would make a terrible spy! She was moving much too fast to look nonchalant, and she had not once looked back to see if she was being followed! And if he couldn't keep his eyes and hands and thoughts off her, perhaps others couldn't, either, and that would draw too much attention! He fumed with repressed frustration each step he took. He still felt this fire in his belly for her that nothing seemed able to extinguish. He almost hoped she would fail miserably at her first task so that he could tell Lafayette and reject her and not have to feel at all responsible for her anymore.

A week later Merry lay awake in her bed at the Shippens' house. It was but a few short hours from dawn, and she had not slept a wink all night. She had tossed and turned until her once crisp linen sheets were a rumpled sea of wrinkles. Boom-ba-boom, the distant cannon had sounded again and again, all day and most of the night. Boom-ba-boom, like distant thunder that neither came closer nor rolled away.

She could not bear the waiting. She could not bear that Darcy and Cam, Washington and Lafayette and those jaunty, ragged troops were out there somewhere making a desperate stand for Philadelphia's freedom against crack British and Hessian troops.

If word came that the Americans had lost, the Philadelphians were prepared to sweep into action and move various things to other Pennsylvania towns. Congress would move to York, the state government to Lancaster, and staunch Whigs and peaceful Quakers would send their goods and their daughters away to Lebanon. Ever since the enemy had begun plundering and foraging their way across the state, there had been rumors of their raping more than the land. But not even that terror had kept Merry up all night, as this nightmare battle had.

And then, just after midnight, silence had come. And still she could not sleep.

Her mind kept repeating some of General Washington's speech the day of the parade, which the local papers had all printed: "Now is the time of our most strenuous exertions...we must free the land from devastation and burning and female innocence from brutal lust and violence..."

Her mind drifted, but she did not doze. Through her most strenuous exertions she had fought to free herself from longing for, from loving, Darcy Mont. Yet she felt devastation and burning inside for him. She knew next to nothing of his life in France, of what made him angry or dedicated or brave or mocking, of why he was the way he was inside, nothing. And all her own strenuous exertions had not freed her from wanting to please him, to comfort him, to share everything with him. Her once carefully tended female innocence would never again be free from her love—or, yes, her lust—for him. She knew the violence of her desires, but he seemed not to need her at all, except in great flashes of explosive need. His green eyes, his kisses, his hands on her flesh, the sound of his whispered voice—

She gasped and sat bolt upright in bed. She grasped the sheets and quilts to her throat. Had she dozed? What had startled her? It was quiet now.

But then she heard the rattle again, the thudding that shook the window glass. More distant gunfire? No—gravel on the window, just as Darcy had said!

She leaped from the bed and pulled her dressing gown around her. Outside, the stars still shone, but all was in shadow under her window. Shaking, she did as Darcy had told her last week. She pushed both windows wide, despite the rush of cool night air. She pressed herself against the wall next to the draperies and held her breath. A rock sailed cleanly into the room and bounced twice on the carpet before rolling under the bed.

Grunting, she felt for it in the dark on her hands and knees. Yes, a note! She fumbled to light the candle by her bed with her flint-and-steel kit. Twice the breeze from the window blew it out. She knelt on the floor to light it and managed to read the crumpled note, written in a shaky hand but very visible ink: "Flame: Torch needs you. Wounded. I have a ladder and a horse waiting. The Lad."

Though she shook like the leaves rattling on the tree outside her window, she yanked on her dark blue day gown and jammed her feet in shoes with no stockings. Darcy wounded? How badly? But he needed her. He needed her! Neither the possibility of discovery nor the danger mattered beside that.

As an afterthought she shoved her extra quilt and a bolster under the covers so that it would look as if she still slept there if someone peeked in. She did not hesitate for an instant when the rungs of a wooden ladder thumped against her windowsill.

The Lad and his horse took her in the black of night to the narrow, cobbled street Darcy had called Ravine Road. "A bad defeat for Washington's boys, and your friend got hisself shot in the arm" was all the thin, lanky boy could tell her.

Her fears shook her harder than the bouncing horse or the swaying bridge as she followed him across the ravine. She prayed Darcy was not badly hurt. Just a bullet in the arm, she kept telling herself. With all those big guns she'd been hearing out there, surely just a bullet in the arm was not too bad, even if the army had been defeated.

The Lad left her at the door and told her that he'd be across the bridge with the horse and that he had to get her back before dawn. She put her hand to the latch; the door creaked inward.

Darcy was not on the cot, where she'd expected him to be. He sat, his profile etched by a single thick candle, hunched over the worktable.

"Darcy!" was all she managed before her voice caught in her throat. She ran to him. He looked grim, almost demonic, his craggy, smoke-smudged features elongated by the wavering light.

"Thank God you came!" he muttered. Then the words spilled from him. "I regret getting you out at night like this. But this letter has to go in dispatches to France on a ship leaving today, before the British take this place."

"Oh, no! They're really coming here?"

He plunged on. "We must write a letter to counteract whatever else King Louis and his ministers will hear about the battle at Brandywine! My right arm is useless, and I cannot write so small with my left. Sit down next to me and write it. Then you will have to get it to Ben Franklin's house by noon to go by packet with his family letters. See, we've got to interline it on this epistle from his daughter, in case it is taken."

She heard his words, but she was gaping at his right arm. In the feeble light, his white shirt looked as if it were soaked with shiny, black tar, but she knew it was blood. She bit her lower lip to fight back tears.

"We've got to bind you up. We've got to get a surgeon, Darcy."

"I had one before I rode back those damned long twenty-five miles from Brandywine Creek," he told her, his voice harsh with exhaustion and pain. "The bastards broke through our lines—but not before we put up one hell of a fierce stand against Hessians and British regulars in an open fight! 'That colonial rabble' gave them shot for shot before we were outfoxed again, Merry. The American spirit is not broken! Even when the enemy takes this town, and they will soon, the Americans will fight, again and again! And that's what Franklin's got to tell them at Versailles, or any hope for real French aid may be lost before it is even begun! Damn my arm! Just do as I ask for once, and sit down here and write!''

She did exactly that, since he'd claimed he'd seen a surgeon, but she sensed that he was bleeding again. Sometimes she was certain she was, too. She copied the message out with the invisible ink, but her mind was on his wound and not his words. His voice wavered, growing faint and rough at times.

''Just write, damn it!'' he repeated harshly once again when she squinted at his arm. ''Lafayette took a ball in the leg, and he kept fighting right beside me until blood ran out the top of his boot. Now write!''

She hadn't known that Darcy would be in battle—and right next to Lafayette, too. She fought to keep tears of fear and pride from splashing on her carefully scripted words and the ones Franklin's daughter Sally had already written. She fought to beat back her emotions and do her duty, just as soldiers did. But when the letter was sealed and he tried to hurry her away, she whirled around to face him.

''Not until I know you'll be tended to again. You're still bleeding, and you're in pain—and, therefore, so am I!''

He looked abashed at that, and moved, despite the mask of brusqueness and self-control he hid behind. He took her free hand with his left one and squeezed it hard.

''Merry, I have been through worse,'' he whispered. ''And not with someone so special at my side. The wound is nothing. Besides, there is a lot of pain and bleeding yet to come. But I—I cherish your personal concern.'' He lifted his hand from hers to cup her damp cheek and rub away the tracks of her tears. ''And I am grateful. *Merci,*'' he said, his voice very soft.

His sudden shift touched her deepest reserve of emotion. ''It's more than personal concern, Darcy. God help me, you are the most frustrating, infuriating man, and yet it's more than that! I love my country, yes, of course I do, but I also can't help that I lo—''

''Do not say that! Not in times like these!'' he muttered, but he pulled her to him hard with his good arm. She clung, her cheek pressed to his thudding heart, careful not to bump his right arm. She inhaled the heady scent of him—horses, sweat, battle, gunpowder, even bravery mingled with fear. And then she lifted her face to his and kissed him hard, full on the lips. She knew she had to get back before dawn. She knew they both had much to do. But it took every shred of strength she possessed to pull back when she felt him respond with a fierce need of his own.

"Just promise me you'll be safe." She stepped back. "And promise me you will not just disappear again with no word!"

He shook his big head. His eyes were still in shadow. "I cannot help all that. But when the British take this town, just be careful they do not take you, too, my Merry Morgan. I will need you even more then, as I will have to stay out of sight."

"Yes. Just send for me. I will need you, too!"

And before he could deny anything either of them had said, she bounced another lightning kiss off him that barely missed his mouth. Clasping the letter, she whirled and went out. And, despite her personal danger and the hovering horror of a British occupation, her heart sang all the way back that Freedom Flame could prove herself to Darcy Mont and her new country at last. And, the entire British army and the Hessian hordes be damned, he had called her "*my* Merry Morgan!"

Chapter Eight

It's going to be today or tomorrow! I just know it!'' Peggy practically sang at the breakfast table ten days after the American defeat at Brandywine Creek. The entire Shippen family was assembled, along with Merry. "The British are finally coming to town, and then we'll see some fine uniforms and not all those mismatched smocks and dirty homespun hunting shirts, for heaven's sake. Shiny brass and pristine gaiters and crimson coats—that will be *my* kind of parade!''

"Daughter, I insist you keep your voice down!'' Judge Shippen said. He wore his severely cut Quaker wig today, but Merry wouldn't be surprised to see him switch to his British style periwig soon. "These days,'' he pronounced, his voice low and jerky, "even the walls might have ears.'' He glanced around the table at each young woman in turn, and Merry had to force herself to meet his eyes. "And Peggy, if the rumors are true, we just might have to billet British soldiers here, and I won't have—''

"You won't have me misbehaving, I suppose,'' Peggy put in tartly, taking another slice of buttered toast. "All I can say is, this stodgy town can't help but be livelier than it's been under this dreadful rebel government. Washington's allowed so few of his absolutely stern-faced officers in town at all. I, for one, am ready to have a few smartly attired and wellborn men about. And if we all know what's good for us—including you, Father—we'll toe the British line with a smile. I know I intend to.''

"You'd like to have the entire British officer corps toeing *your* line,'' shy Polly dared. "You've been a dyed-in-the-wool

Tory from the first. And you're angling for a rich London marriage just to escape from here. I've seen you flaunting your bait and hiding the hook."

"You'd best mind your mouth, sister dear." Peggy spoke with her mouth half full, despite the fact that she'd scolded Polly for the same faux pas earlier. Even Polly's cuts couldn't dampen Peggy's ebullient mood today. "As Father says, this town abounds with tattletales who just might tell Toller and his friends that you—and our frowning guest, Mistress Morgan here—are all for the rebel cause." Peggy rolled her eyes dramatically and smirked. "Of course, if you'd both unbend and have a bit of fun in this dreary place, perhaps we could all be friends again."

Merry held her tongue. Darcy had warned her not to alienate the Shippens, even in the face of the judge's wavering loyalties and Peggy's spoiled antics. She was not to cut any ties that might mean useful information for Freedom Flame. For the most part Merry agreed, but she intended to draw the line when it came to cuddling up to Toller Devlin.

"I think," Merry said calmly now, fighting her desire to toss her coffee in Peggy's smug face, "we'll just have to learn to judge the British as individuals and give them their due."

"Bravo!" Peggy exclaimed with a patter of applause. "I'm sure we'll all get on simply beautifully with them. And," she added with a ruffle of ribbons in her high teased and padded coif, "whatever have we been taking those dancing lessons for if not to put them to good use?"

In the hall after breakfast, Merry prepared to take the daily constitutional she had begun when she had needed to get Darcy's letter about the battle of Brandywine to Ben Franklin's house. As she tied her cloak, her friend and ally, Polly, sidled up to her.

"I declare, it went sailing right over Peggy's high head what 'giving the British their due' might mean," she said, grinning at Merry. "I wish I could be as clever as you!"

Polly's words at breakfast taunted Merry as she strolled around the block toward the Widow Windham's house. How often she dealt in double meanings these days, saying one thing and thinking another since she'd become Freedom Flame. Her concern for Darcy's safety burdened her daily, but she pretended to care not a whit for him around the Shippens. And she still could not stomach Toller Devlin's visits to her and Peggy, but now she pretended she enjoyed his company. The British hovered just across the Schuylkill and would be in town by tomorrow with no troops to stop them from taking what they wanted in Philadelphia. Once they got here, she would have to be more than civil to them so that she could help ruin them. Double meanings, double thoughts, double actions. Duplicity, in fact. She glanced furtively at the Widow Windham's flower box, where she could leave a message if the need ever arose. Then she walked right by as if she hadn't a care in the world but for taking her daily walk.

The next morning, Philadelphia lay open and waiting for its British and Hessian conquerors. The Continental Army was out there somewhere, no doubt planning another attack. Both the national and the state governments had fled; many staunch Whigs had, too. General Howe's advance patrols had told citizens that the British would take the town today. Right on schedule, in they came, playing ''God Save the King'' on bagpipes and daring to shake hands with grateful Tories as if they were liberators.

But they found a town stripped of most supplies. All lead pipes, weights from window sashes and bells, including the Liberty Bell, had been carted off to keep them from becoming British bullets. Wagons, cattle and horses had been driven off. Dikes had been cut to flood grassy meadows that might serve for grazing, drilling grounds or tent sites. Many storekeepers had hidden their stock.

In retaliation, the conquerors looted more farmland, sacked some shops and billeted the majority of their troops in the little village of Germantown, ten miles away. However, some of Lord Cornwallis's redcoats and the mustached, green-coated Hessians under Knyphausen took possession of Philadelphia, while Commander Howe requisitioned a pleasant country house for himself and his married mistress five miles out. And Howe's long arm reached out to tighten his hold on the city from his office in John Penn's House on Market Street.

Barriers and pickets went up at the city's outskirts, and passes were required to get in or out. The remaining shops were closed until the army "requisitioned" all they wanted from the Whig-owned ones. Tory informers seemed to crawl from the gutters to point out those of rebel bent. The jail on Walnut Street, across from the statehouse, was soon jammed with "suspicious" persons. Houses were ransacked, gardens stripped of autumn bounty, a loyalty oath demanded. Troops were forcibly quartered in many homes, but—evidently thanks to Toller Devlin—not at the Shippens'.

"You have me to thank you aren't being tossed out of your cozy bedchamber, my dearest Meredith," Toller whispered hotly in her ear the day he brought a British officer friend to the Shippen house for a visit. "Though, if that ever happens, I'd be more than delighted to take you in, hmm?"

Merry forced herself not to claw that smug look from his face. As much as she loathed him, she had decided her duplicity would have to extend to Toller now. Any news she could glean from him—or from this lobsterback, Major John André of His Majesty's Seventh Dragoons, whom Peggy was all eyes for—might help the American cause. Still, Merry fluffed her skirts out wide on the drawing room settee so that Toller would not crowd her. And when Judge Shippen and the younger girls took their leave to allow Peggy and her to entertain the two men, Merry covertly studied the British officer who leaned so close to the sparkling-eyed Peggy across the way.

"Toller, you rascal," John André was saying, his gray eyes, eyes that were nearly the same shade as Toller's, never leaving Peggy's face. "I say, but I was misinformed when I was told that this rebel capital had been stripped of all its treasures! Here I find the loveliest treasures of all! I simply cannot have you lying to General Howe's chief of intelligence like that, my friend!"

Peggy laughed and fluttered her ribboned fan, but Merry, watching her closely, was surprised. As many men as had hovered around Peggy since she had known her, she'd never seen the young woman speechless and downright giddy before. And blushing, just as she herself did when Darcy looked at her like that. Despite Toller's intimate whispers, Merry's gaze took in

John André again, just as her ears had taken in that he was
General Howe's chief of intelligence and that Tory Toller himself had been feeding him information.

Blond, with gray eyes, worldly and handsome, the twenty-
five-year-old Major André appeared to radiate from within. His
appearance and manners seemed shiny, glossy. Even his clever
repartee was gilded with a sheen, as if he'd selected and polished each remark like a crimson apple. Yet at times his face
seemed to ice over with a cool, calm, detached look. It was very
different from any of Darcy's attempts to hide himself. Yes,
Merry thought, as André slanted an assessing stare her way that
made her drop her gaze, his eyes not only glittered but seethed.
He was like that burning building that had been an inferno inside while its brick-and-stone facade had stood quite untouched for all to see.

"And I vow to both you beauteous ladies," Major André
promised, "there will be dances and theatricals and many,
many more pleasantries. I, for one, look forward to a charming winter season here to rival even London's."

"Our very own *beau monde*?" Merry put in tartly before she
realized one of Darcy's French phrases had just slipped out.

"Ah, indeed." André lifted his goblet of Madeira from the
table beside him. His smile was dazzling as he handed Peggy
hers. Her hand actually trembled, Merry noted, when their
fingers brushed. "To a peaceful and prosperous winter respite
in the British colony of Pennsylvania," André said, leading the
toast. "Surely the next best thing to London, thanks to the
present company, and more of it, eh, friend Toller?"

"Just so, Major André." Toller handed Merry a glass for the
toast. To Merry's chagrin, Toller dared to slide his unseen hand
under her thigh on the settee as he smiled at the couple across
from them and hefted his glass.

Merry chose not to protest Toller's audacious move aloud
before the avid-eyed André and the obviously smitten Peggy.
After all, she had to get along with Toller, especially since he
had asked the other day where her "friend" Darcy had been
keeping himself lately.

"But don't you fear the rebels will attack again?" Merry inquired of André.

"We were amazed by their ferocity at Brandywine, but we feel it was from panic and desperation—a last hurrah. Indeed, we'll see naught organized from that rabble until spring thaw," André declared. "But, I say, how charming to find so stunning a lady with military and political interests, Mistress Morgan," he remarked condescendingly, his sleek eyebrows lifted challengingly along with his glass.

"Hardly charming! Pure foolishness," Peggy protested, annoyed even by André's brief attention to Merry. "As for me, I simply cheer the British victors!"

André's smile bathed Peggy with a warmth that did not reach his eyes. "Then cheers to His Majesty and his coming victory in this war of rebellion," André intoned with a blinding flash of smile.

Merry silently made her own toast. To His Majesty's coming defeat in this war of independence. But she managed to lift her glass and touch it to her mouth. The sweet Madeira burned her lips like acid; she did not swallow one drop.

But when Toller forced his hot hand higher up her thigh, she did take advantage of an old trick. She spilled Madeira on his thigh and jumped up with flustered apologies.

"Judas Priest, my dear!" he clipped out. "You'll find it will take far more than that to douse my ardor!"

André laughed, and Peggy fanned herself harder. But Merry just wished desperately it was Darcy sitting here, touching, flirting—yes, drat him, courting her—instead of this demon Devlin and his angelic-looking friend André!

Four days later a note appeared in the drop nearest the Shippen house. Merry found it nestled snugly in the knot of the old chestnut tree she checked often just down the street. Her daily walks were briefer now; sometimes she had to sneak away, since Judge Shippen insisted on maids escorting them with all the soldiers in town now. Merry's heart beat even harder as she unfolded the small missive in her room and saw that it was blank. Invisible ink! Since Darcy had never given her acid to develop a letter, she assumed it would be done by heat. Her hands trembling in her eagerness, she picked up several coals with tongs from the bathwater heater in her room and dropped them in her bed warmer. She pressed the note to the heated brass and watched the words drift into view:

FF: Must know all Br. shipment of supplies to stop them. Use the window box. Reply by 1 October. In haste. Best wishes. T.

The first of October! But that was today! Why the rush? Drat! She couldn't bear not knowing things! Was Darcy going somewhere? Off to stay with the army again—or, worse, back to France?

She pressed the note to her cheek for a moment, then sniffed at it, as if it might give her the essence of the man she missed so every hour they were apart. But it just smelled like wood and wind after being in the tree. Her quick mind raced to absorb all the little note conveyed before she tore it to shreds and burned them against the silver coals in the brass bed warmer.

So Washington's troops, just waiting for the right time to attack the British again, were hoping to starve the British out, she surmised. Why, only yesterday she'd heard John André tell Peggy of ships coming down from New York with supplies from which he hoped to requisition some things for a banquet he was arranging for General Howe. But the ships weren't expected until next week, and she hadn't realized Darcy would be interested in food shipments, as well those of troops and ammunition.

She dug out her bottle of invisible ink from the bottom of the single chest in her room and wrote Darcy all she'd heard. "Best wishes to you, too, and please keep safe and well," she concluded. She would have liked to sign it "With my love," but she didn't dare, however true it was. More double thoughts and double meanings for the cause, she told herself sadly. Sometimes all this underhanded maneuvering made her feel almost sordid.

She folded the now-blank paper and waited for a moment when Judge Shippen was out and the girls were resting. She met no one going down the back steps and was out into the crisp autumn sun in a flash. She forced herself to take her usual leisurely stroll around the block. How she wished she had the time to ride clear over to Darcy's shed hidden in the ravine to deliver this to him in person!

Her mind sped ahead of her feet. He would be so happy to see her there. Her message would be invaluable; he would tell her—exactly what they needed to know. Now they could stop the British shipments and take all the food for Washington's hungry boys and run the British out of Philadelphia. And then Darcy would draw her down beside him on the little straw cot. She would have to be careful not to hurt his right arm; surely he still had it in a sling. She would offer to change his bandages, and he would be so grateful. He would gaze adoringly and humbly at her. But even while she bound him up his good hand would caress her, again and again. He would draw her gently, then fervently, into his arms, and then she would open herself to him to love him and—

She jerked to a halt, stunned to find she was already at the Widow Windham's house. The elderly widow had been an invalid for years and was cared for by a nephew who also lived in the small house. Merry assumed that it was the nephew who was Darcy's contact here. Looking casually both ways, she saw no one, so she strode up the walk, then around to the side flower box, which was still bright with yellow-and-red marigold blooms the early frost had spared.

Unlike most of the windows, the one above the box was not shuttered, but the blue brocade draperies were drawn. With another quick glance around, she pushed the note down into the cool soil of the window box. She couldn't resist snapping off just one flower to take back as a memento. After all, Darcy's hand would be here among these flowers soon, and it would be a little reminder—

She gasped and jumped back as the draperies moved. She stepped back to run, but the face at the window was Darcy's! Her blood pounded in her ears as she gazed up to see her reflection superimposed over him. A little voice told her she should move away, walk back, return to the Shippens'. But she hadn't seen him since the night he'd been wounded. There was so much more she could tell him in person. And he seemed to be gazing down at her with more than a command to be on her way!

She turned and strode for the back door. She had knocked only once before it opened and his voice said, "Quick. In, now that you are here." Thrilled, she darted inside.

"Darcy! I'm so happy to—"

"Are you crazy?" he demanded. He closed the door behind her and leaned his left hand against it, as if she might flee. His eyes raked her greedily from bonnet to shoes, as if he wanted to assure himself she was all in one piece. He knew he was in a terrible mood, and he tried to stem it. France might not budge to send aid unless there was a big American victory soon, and that possibility seemed remote. Dedicated men the caliber of Washington were being slandered by Congress and fair-weather patriots just because of a few lost battles. Considering what Washington had to work with and who he faced in the field, those hard-fought battles and strategic retreats were really victories! And there was another battle looming tomorrow, and Darcy wanted to be out there fighting to take Germantown when he had been ordered to stay in the city!

In the tiny, tense lull between them, Merry took Darcy in, too, her gaze hopeful and eager. His wounded arm wasn't in a sling. And he looked neither adoring nor humble.

"Did you bring the note, Merry?"

"Didn't you see me put it in the window box? You said—"

"I know what I said. Sometimes I cannot help what I say," he muttered, and tugged her into his arms.

Her feet could have flown. She hugged him back hard until he cleared his throat and stood her away from him, his hands on her blue-cloaked shoulders, steadying them both.

"I—I thought this house was just a place to leave messages," she managed, though her head still spun. "Why are you here?"

"I cannot actually spend the winter in that shed. They would begin to wonder. I stay up under the eaves here while I am in town."

"Oh," she said, hurt. "So close to me at the Shippens', and I didn't know—"

"The less each individual knows, the better," he insisted, his tone even more brusque than before. "You know now. Is there anything else you have to tell me?"

She explained that Major John André came calling on Peggy every day. And that Judge Shippen trusted her and Toller as chaperons but André had to be drawn out to get him to talk about military matters. He was quite talented at poetry and sketching and loved the theater. He was going to put on amateur theatricals, and she and Peggy would take part if Judge Shippen ever decided to give him permission, she rushed on.

"How touching. So now you are *très intime*—all cozy—with Sir Billy Howe's chief of intelligence whose duty it is to betray and arrest spies like us!"

"I'm hardly intimate," she retorted, hands on hips under her bulky cloak. "And can you think of a better contact? I told you, he comes to see Peggy, not me!"

"And brings Devlin with him, so you are forced to be sweeter than ever to him." He knew his voice cut like a lash, but he was furious. And it was himself he was furious with, for having to urge her on to such things.

"I cannot believe you're saying all this to me! And in such a tone! What do you want, anyway?"

He silently cursed both himself and her. He dared not tell her what he really wanted from her! It would be just like her to give it! He had been going crazy worrying about her, yet he was forced to send her out to get information from that Tory bastard Devlin and General Howe's witch's familiar, John André. André's talents for terror and brutality were already as legendary among American officers as were his cultured tastes in polite society. If Merry's brother-in-law, Cam Gant, knew who she was playing cat and mouse with, he'd challenge Darcy Mont to a damned duel!

Darcy's desire for Merry warred with his need to be rid of her right now. Here stood temptation in the flesh, temptation that could make him lose control and forsake his duty and his vows! Merry Morgan, right in his grasp, in a house temporarily deserted but for a nurse and an old woman in one of the beds upstairs. Only because his contacts had spread the word that Widow Windham was demented, as well as ill, had they escaped having troops quartered here. He knew that if he did not cherish freedom so much he would demand a new assignment.

He felt trapped by this backstairs existence, and by his frightening need for this woman.

"Merry, you must go now. Our being together is entirely too risky."

"Everything we're doing lately is. Flame and Torch. This whole struggle for national freedom. But I believe in it, and so do you. And we have to believe in each other. I think we're a good team."

"I just will not have you caught—or worse."

"That's as good an excuse as any for not wanting me around. And when the war's over you'll find another." Her bitter words amazed her as much as they did him, but she couldn't take them back now. She thought how shocked her mother would have been to hear her address a man like that. My, my, like some brazen hussy. You'll never get a husband that way, my girl, she would have scolded.

Darcy studied the frown on Merry's face and felt himself crumbling inside. He wanted to kiss her, caress her. But he knew what that would lead to. Merry Morgan was not a woman to bed and leave like those of the French court. She was open and honest, and he cared for her deeply. Yet he felt he had no choice but to send her back to Toller and André—and without that teary-eyed look for him. There were some things, unfortunately, bigger than their need for each other. He had to be sure she did not want to see him, that she did not come rushing to him unless he summoned her.

"I just want you to know," she was saying, "I don't let Toller really touch me, so don't you be so touchy about it, and—"

He forced himself to laugh at her naïveté when he would have liked to admit how endearing it was. It touched him that she confessed this, rather than trying to make him jealous, as a court-schooled woman would have. But this was his Merry Morgan, not that other woman he had once so truly trusted and deeply desired.

"Me, touchy?" he blustered, hoping his callous look and tone hurt her at least as much as it did him. "I think it is about time you finally got close to Devlin. You had best give him a few more crumbs of your affections than you have given me."

He forced a smirk, though the words felt like acid on his tongue. "But I suggest you guard your little-girl heart. You always did wear your feelings too much on your sleeve."

She stepped back against the door, which bumped her bonnet forward over her face. She shoved it back. "Really? Is that what you think?" she sputtered. "So I should really cuddle up to Toller, is that right? André, too, perhaps, except that Peggy would hate me even more than she does now. You know, she's vowed to sneak out to meet him if her father denies her André's visits. It pains me to think my sneaking out to see you puts me in the same category with her. I see now you want me to seduce Toller and his Tory friends for any scrap of news to help *you* make *your* fine French hero's name with Lafayette and Washington and King Louis. I must admit, I've seen how shallow, heartless seduction is done in my sordid association with the likes of you!"

He hated himself for pushing her to this. And he almost hated her for making him want to throw everything he'd worked for away just to have her for himself. At least they were arguing again, because this way he could resist the temptation to sweep her up and carry her to his little mattress in the loft upstairs to lose himself in her. And then he might be lost to his duty.

It took all the self-control he had to reach around behind her without touching her and pull open the door. He darted a glance outside and took her arm. But she flinched away and stepped out herself. Her beautiful face seethed with anger, and her eyes flashed with a pain that ripped his insides and made him bleed regret.

"The things I stomach for freedom, and I don't mean putting up with Toller Devlin!" she shot at him.

"I tell you what, Merry. Come back to see me only when your countrymen have a glorious victory that we can celebrate together! I will be safe for years to come that way. And try to follow orders next time!"

"You—you froggie bastard! That's what the British call you, so write it down in your ink. And you can go to hell—or back to your precious France—for all I care!"

She stormed away, and she had turned the corner before she forced herself to breathe more evenly, to slow her frenzied steps. That was it, the end! She was absolutely done with Darcy Montour, except as a contact, and then only because she loved her country. She loathed the way he treated her. She loved...she loathed...she loved...she loathed.... The footsteps she scuffed on the brick footpath seemed to taunt her all the way back to Shippens'. She loathed...she loved...Darcy...Montour....

The next day, October 2, 1777, the Americans struck at night to surprise the sleeping Hessians and British at Germantown, ten miles outside Philadelphia. The British called it another bloody defeat for the Americans, but by now Merry knew how to read the signs, and she could see that this was really the best American victory that could be hoped for at this stage of the war. Despite her anger at Darcy—and her fury was compounded by the realization that he must have known of this coming battle and had not trusted her enough to share one word of it—she wrote to him in invisible ink and hid it in the tree down the street:

T: P.'s adoring Major A. admits that the Battle for Ger. was so fierce the Br. almost retreated. I overheard that the Am. fought the Br. to a standstill for 5 hours—surely that will go far in B.F.'s skilled hands to boost the Am. cause in Fr. And, after all, the Am. dared attack the Br. Still, I recognize this is not the "great Am. victory" you told me I can come see you to celebrate, nor would I. Henceforth, you shall see naught of me but notes.

My only joy in this Battle at Ger. is that Major A., boasting as he did that G.W.'s rabble would not dare attack 'til spring thaw, was proved wrong and made to look the fool with his superiors. But then, he has also predicted Tol. will ask to wed me soon. Perhaps Major A.'s predictions will not be wrong twice. Since you are my superior, I shall take your advice to give Tol. more than a few crumbs of my affections. F.

* * *

The note showed Darcy that his handling of Merry Morgan had achieved the exact effect he'd wanted. She detested him, she was staying away, she was doing her job.

Yet he shredded the note with more fury than he knew he possessed and slammed his fist again and again into the wooden wall until the pigeons' cages rocked and the cooing birds flapped their wings in protest.

Two weeks later, word came from New York State that the first great victory the new nation had sought had indeed come to pass. At a place called Saratoga, the British general Burgoyne had been soundly defeated and had surrendered to the Americans under General Gates. Word was that the much-admired American hero General Benedict Arnold had really won the day by rallying the men. And all that despite a leg wound, and after Gates had removed him from his command for insubordination. But the victory was officially Gates's. In a way, Washington deserved much of the credit, for if his troops had not held Cornwallis and Howe in Philadelphia by the attack on Germantown fresh British troops would have been sent north to save Burgoyne.

In Philadelphia, Whigs dared to dance in the street at the news of Saratoga. At first, Merry managed to conceal her joy, but Peggy caught her laughing with Polly over it and threatened to tell Toller and André. Merry forced herself to bend over her embroidery that afternoon, only whispering to Polly. But she was on pins and needles of another kind, wondering whether Darcy was in town, whether he knew about Saratoga and how shocked the British command was by it. When she saw Peggy sneak out to meet Major André at the corner for a forbidden carriage ride, she decided to walk just as far as the Widow Windham's house to leave a note.

It was a windy mid-October day, and gusts of crisp wind buffeted her skirts and her bright blue cloak. If she accidentally saw Darcy today, she thought, she'd be tempted to toss the note in his face and stalk off to show him she did not favor seeing him, victory or no victory. Perhaps she should have brought a truly blank piece of paper and let him try to develop it with his heat or his acid. It was his heated stares and his acid tongue that didn't allow them to really trust each other.

She looked all around, then sauntered up the walk to the Widow Windham's. Suddenly just leaving this message in the flower box, as that insufferable Darcy preferred, was not enough. After all, he had mockingly told her she could come to see him at the first big American win! It had been decided at the beginning that she would answer any questions the Shippens might have by saying she was visiting the ailing widow, so perhaps she should.

Suddenly angry at Darcy's urging her to sweeten up Toller Devlin no matter how she really felt, she walked right up to the front door and banged the knocker. If Darcy was not in, that was fine, she tried to tell herself as her gloved fingers twisted the knitted chain of her equipage in knots tighter than her stomach. How she'd love to leave this note right on Darcy's table or bed upstairs. Let the all-knowing, invincible Darcy Montour wonder at her daring to get the note there!

To her amazement, when she knocked the second time the front door swung inward against the press of her hand. She shoved it a bit farther and squinted inside. "Hello? Just a neighbor come to call on Widow Windham. Hello?"

She stepped in and closed the door behind her. She walked in a few steps and stood near the open drawing room door to peer nervously up the stairs. The house stood shadowy and chill. "Is anyone there?" was all she got out before it happened.

A big pair of hands clapped over her mouth and body to hold her prisoner, just like that day last year at the Gant town house.

"It never ceases to amaze me how much you have to learn!" Darcy whispered. He dragged her backward while he closed and bolted the front door. "It is time someone taught you to do as you are told!"

He lifted her as if she weighed no more than the note clasped in her glove. The house spun around her. It seemed deserted. There were no signs of life. One hand still pressed to her trembling lips, he carried her up the main stairs and then up creaking attic steps to the little hidden loft above.

Suddenly she was very afraid. Not of him, really, so much as of herself. Had she come for this? The message she had written on the paper she clasped might be invisible, but she knew her feelings for this man had never been. In all her feverish dreams of him, she could not have imagined so ravishing a moment, so complete a fulfillment of her deepest desires. He bumped his head on the last step into the attic, but he only held her tighter to him as he strode across the floor. He put her down on the oval rag rug next to a big bed and untied her cloak and her bonnet ribbons.

"Are you so sure I won't scream? I only came with a note," she said. Her voice was raspy and not her own.

"Another note to make me half-crazy thinking you'll wed Toller Devlin?" he demanded. "To drive me to this, thinking you'd do this with him!"

"To tell you what a great victory at Saratoga—"

"I know. I was afraid you would come! I prayed you would come! We will have our own celebration for the victory together, just as I said—"

His hot breath, his quick, sure hands on her, were madness. Months of pent-up longing for this man, a lifetime of waiting, poured through her as his hands tugged her gown off her arms and down over her hips. And then she began to help him.

"Darcy, Darcy, I didn't want to be with them...Toller *or* André! I worried about what you were doing, and I wanted to be with you, so—"

"Shh! This is what I am doing, and this is what we both want now!"

The fierceness of his hands and his kisses stunned her. Yet she untied his cravat and shoved off his black coat and his dark blue waistcoat. Then her hands were tangled at her sides in lace straps as he tugged her corset and chemise down to free her full breasts and her rib cage.

She sighed, entirely surprised by the roar of sensation shooting through her as his hot mouth spangled wet kisses down her throat to capture a dusky-rose nipple. He teased, then sweetly tormented, first one and then the other with pouted lips and darting tongue. His hands cupped her bottom through her clinging petticoats before they, too, slid to her feet. She held hard to his shoulders to keep from toppling as he sampled, then suckled, her full, tingling breasts.

"Oh, that feels . . . so strange . . . so wonderful!"

"Mmm! Tell me more how you feel, *ma belle*. Tell me what you want!"

But all she wanted was him. Now and always, their differences be damned! She began to tremble from deep within; she stood there all wobbly-legged in shoes and half-ungartered stockings and nothing else. He knelt before her to press velvet kisses to her belly as he skimmed her stockings down to her ankles.

She raked her fingers through the thick, dark hair that rasped against the sensitive skin of her belly. Was this really, really happening at last? Her garments puddled around her, and she remembered the day he'd caught her bathing and she had boldly stood nude before him, longing for his touch. She loved him so, and she had almost from the first—and perhaps even longer than that. She had teased and taunted, and she had fought him and herself. And now all restraint was being swept away by this demanding possession that she wanted with all her heart.

Again and again he feathered caresses over her satin skin, kissing her everywhere. Darcy Montour on his knees before her like the humblest suitor, she thought dazedly. She shook with silent laughter in sheer joy. But she caught her lower lip between her teeth to keep from crying out her need for him, her desire for complete surrender in this intimate war that they had waged for so long. Her hair spilled loose to cascade over him, a golden curtain, as he stroked between her warm thighs. Then, just before her legs gave way, he stood to sweep her up and whirl her once around, sending her shoes and stockings flying. And then he laid her on the bed and stared down at her with burning eyes as he tore the rest of his own garments off and flung them away.

Despite the dizzy rush of blood behind her eyes, she gasped at his magnificence. Broader shoulders framed a broad chest with a curly mat of midnight hair and tiny male nipples that were peaked like her own. A flat, fluted belly tapered to his breeches before he tugged them off and yanked down his stockings to flaunt powerfully muscled, hair-flecked legs. He was so aroused, so ready; she started at this sight she had only wondered about before. The marriage bed she had thought of for years . . . surely she would learn all its secrets now.

His big form blocked her view of shadowed rafters and stark sun slanting through the high half-moon window. "I tried to smother this for so long!" he said, perhaps more to himself than her. "I told myself, next time I get the chance—and *ma rebelle américaine* is still willing—I will just give in and try it the other way."

Merry was amazed to find that she could form words. "What other way?"

"This way. Taking you. Loving you. Conquering you, as you have me . . ." he rasped, and his big, hard body descended to press her down into the softness of the sagging mattress.

His endearments buzzed through her head. Loving, he had said. Taking you. Conquering you. Yes, yes, she was still willing, always, to have him and love him! She meant to tell him that, but his mouth was pulling at hers, pulling all rational thought away.

Everything merged in the rush of his hands, and hers answering them. And then that blurred into the hot command in her ear: "Spread those sweet legs for me, *ma chérie*. Let me in. Please let me in. . . ."

She moved her hands and lips to meet the challenge of his. She matched him kiss for searing kiss, deep, demanding, devouring ones that somehow gave all as much as they took. Her tongue plundered his ear and flicked down his throat. She nuzzled his neck and nipped the thick sinew there. She moved her hips in little circles that she could not control, answering the blatant, ceaseless stroking of his hand between her thighs. At the first slick invasion of his fingers inside her, she thrust upward to meet him. And then, reveling in her victory as well as his, she obeyed him and spread her legs.

He knelt between them and widened his knees to open her even more to him. It seemed so natural; she had always felt this way, had always wanted to be his, completely open to him, wanting him, trusting him. He hovered closer, kissing her. He positioned himself against her and nudged in. She met him boldly until he leaned heavier, closer, and she felt the barrier inside herself between them.

"Oh!" She gazed up, surprised, into his glittering green gaze. He was so close over her that she could count every lash that lay against his bronze skin.

"It is all right. *Sacrebleu, ma belle*, it is so wonderful! In these terrible times I do not know what I can promise you, but that you have always done this to me and always will—"

He covered her mouth with his to still her cry and thrust deeper. The sharp tear seared through her and then dissolved in a hot rush of sensation. He held still over her, kissing her, murmuring compliments and encouragements that she knew she would always treasure. And then, when she felt her breathing quiet and thought perhaps it was over, he began to press and pull inside her.

The ache for him there built and built, until passion swelled and threatened to swamp her. So it wasn't over, she marveled. It only led to this, to more. She tried to shift her hips away, sideways, then rose to meet him. He groaned.

"You always did learn fast . . . always. . . ." he muttered, and increased his pounding pace.

It was as if he were riding her now, pushing her on, waiting for her, then pulling her farther, farther. His hands and his lips were everywhere again, even when they were joined so fiercely to her. Her thighs lifted to grasp his ribs. She could not control her breathing. And something dark and daring and delicious unwound itself deep inside her loins and then exploded in bright stars everywhere just as he pushed hard into her. He murmured her name again and again as his big body convulsed, and then he lay still at last.

He held her lazily as their bodies cooled. "Dangerous insanity," he whispered against the tumbled curls at her temple. "You must get back."

"I know," she sighed, but she cuddled closer. He moaned, and she felt the thrust of him against her hip again. She froze in his arms a moment. He could repeat all this so soon? She might not tell him, but she was certain she could, too, as weak and floaty as she felt. "At least," she ventured, her voice suddenly shy and small, "we can really trust each other now."

"And be lovers—careful lovers—when we can manage it," he said, and kissed the side of her throat.

She nodded, ecstatic. Lovers, careful lovers. But she wanted so much more! At least, now that they had come this far and there was a truce—no, a permanent peace—between them, surely she could convince him that he could not do without her. That he would want to wed her, take her to France someday, perhaps come back here to live after the war. "After all this ends here in America," she whispered, "I would love to see France with you, to meet your family and friends there."

He sat up abruptly and pulled her up. "With everything else, I just cannot think about that now," he said, a new edge to his voice. He scooted by her to gather her garments from the floor and toss them on the foot of the rumpled bed.

She lamented the fact that his eyes seemed shuttered to her again. It struck her once more how little she knew of this man's other life, in France. Perhaps he had a woman there that he loved. The thought made her scramble for her clothes.

She stood stock-still under his ministrations as he hurriedly hooked her corset and gathered the jumbled garter ribbons he had tugged off earlier. Even on a woman's undergarments his hands seemed so swift and sure, she thought sadly. Her heart fell farther; suddenly this little love nest they had shared felt very cold. She wanted to convince him there was some sunlit future for them together, out there in the world, as well as in here! But she held her tongue, her feelings and her fears knotting and tangling tighter than the ravaged garter ribbons he held out to her in his big hand.

Chapter Nine

Bells on the horses' harness jingled, masking the crunch of snow beneath the runners of the sleigh. The biting breeze and the reflected glare of the sun made Merry's eyes water. But even as Toller helped her down ahead of John André and Peggy from the four-person sleigh at their little picnic spot along the frozen Delaware, her thoughts were not there.

She squinted into the wind toward the northwest. Sixteen miles away in that direction the American army survived in their winter camp at Valley Forge while the British reveled and feasted in Philadelphia, waiting for spring and the next campaign of the war. Then these well-fed, well-armed, well-clothed British would attack the tattered army Washington was trying desperately to hold together.

Eight soldiers from André's staff, crimson as cardinals in their warm wool garments, had prepared a party for them. Spitted smoked sausages crackled over a fire; hand-warming, belly-warming pewter mugs of hot chocolate were handed around. Sleighing and skating parties, the theater, the weekly dances at Smith's City Tavern, and the lively officers' dinners at the Bunch of Grapes—all that delighted Peggy saddened and shamed Merry. It made her feel quite the traitor, despite her covert contributions to bringing the British down.

"I say, I'll never know how those rotters out there at Valley Forge knew to take that shipment of wine I ordered for General Howe from New York," John André was telling Toller. "But this hot chocolate we took from Ben Franklin's well-stocked pantry almost makes up for that affront now. Let the old goat run about Paris as a so-called ambassador begging for money and ships. When we're done with this town and his house, he won't have a pot left to pee in.''

As the two men chortled, Merry turned away as if to watch the distant skaters so that the men would not see her expression. She hated the way they laughed at dear Mr. Franklin, but she could not help her triumphant smile at the thought of one of her small victories of the past month. There had been few enough of them, so her tip to Darcy about a wine shipment had to count for something. But recently the British had taken several American forts farther down this river, and supplies came in almost unchecked now.

''Judas Priest, at least the flea-bitten Yankees didn't halt the ship with the 300 women to warm the troops this winter,'' Toller whispered, slyly elbowing André. He evidently didn't want the women to hear, but the wind took his words straight to Merry. She turned to see if Peggy had noticed, but it would not have mattered if she did. Peggy Shippen was entirely smitten with John André, and he could do no wrong in her eyes. Merry detested the object of Peggy's affections, but she sympathized deeply with her fervent love for a man she might never keep.

For weeks now Peggy had hung on every word John André uttered. She always carried a lock of his blond hair hidden in a locket that she had never shown her father. She cherished what Merry thought was a none-too-flattering sketch André had done of her. She disobeyed Judge Shippen by going out privately in André's carriage. And she'd risked the judge's righteous wrath by coming in very late last week to the scolding of her life. She'd shattered her boudoir mirror in a raving protest. Merry knew that if she had not agreed to come along today with Toller on this sleighing party Peggy would have been forbidden it. At least since Peggy realized it, too, she was warmer to her than usual. She smiled now at Merry as she swished over to her side, her gloved hands thrust in a fox-fur muff.

''Dear Merry,'' Peggy began with a roll of her pale blue eyes before she could say a word, ''I would appreciate a little, tiny favor.''

That was a surprise, Merry thought. Peggy had never admitted she needed anything from her. Nor had she ever called her "dear" before. Merry had been quite convinced that Peggy distrusted her lately; perhaps André, who always had her ear, had asked Peggy to watch her.

"If I can help," Merry said, her words puffing clouds in the air. "I owe you and your father a great deal."

"Well, you know, my father has been most unreasonable of late."

Drat, Merry thought. She's going to ask me to lie and cover up for her when she sees André secretly, and I cannot do that!

"He only wants what's best for you, Peggy. He loves you very much, and—"

"It's John's love I want above all else!" she cried with a lightning glance back at the men to be certain they could not hear. Her fingers gripped Merry's arm hard, the comfort of the muff forgotten. "And Father's ever in the way! Now I must give my answer to John today about this, so—"

"Answer? He's not asked you to elope with him or some such?"

"Not yet. But he will," Peggy declared, pounding her gloved fist against the muff as if she were trying to convince herself instead of Merry. "He's asked me to dinner to Ben Franklin's house, a private dinner, and I need you and Toller to go out with us from home and then go off yourselves somewhere.... You understand. And I will not tell Father a thing about where you are, either."

Merry froze as stiff as if she were one of the snowmen the British soldiers had made down the hill. In the first place, it irked her that Major André had dared to quarter himself and his staff in Mr. Franklin's fine home and use its goods as if they were his own. And it riled her that Peggy expected her to betray Judge Shippen and then to go off somewhere on the sly alone with Toller Devlin, whom she still strove assiduously to avoid in compromising situations.

"Peggy, I don't know how to say this, but—"

"Just say yes!"

"Your father's been so kind to me. He trusts me, and you don't want to risk his trust, either, I'm sure, so—"

"As a friend," Peggy gritted out through clenched teeth, "I am asking for your help, Merry Morgan. But I am telling you not to make an enemy of me. Do you think I don't know why you play Toller for a fool?"

Merry's startled gaze slammed into Peggy's ice-blue one. Could she know about the spying? Then she—and Darcy, too—might be doomed, since Peggy held nothing back from André!

"Meaning?" Merry ventured.

"Meaning someone of your background would not pass up someone with Toller's flair and fortune unless there was a reason! So your heart must still be set on that rakish Frenchman, who's probably out there with that froggie Lafayette and the rest of them, hiding at Valley Forge! I've seen your face when anyone talks about him, I don't care if he hasn't been around in ages. And I heard about that party for Lafayette, when you had a lovers' quarrel with Darcy and threw some punch all over him—no doubt just to make up later in private."

"That's—that's not so!"

"You forget, friend Merry," Peggy insisted, "I know all the signs of deep, abiding love now, unrequited or not!"

"Female talk?" John André interrupted, drawn over by the heated tenor of their conversation. He swooped an arm around Peggy's shoulders. Peggy's cold frown melted into a charming smile.

Peggy had no chance to continue the conversation, but after that, Merry felt as if she'd been punched in the stomach. Peggy had struck her a terrible blow by using her love for Darcy as a weapon and a threat. If she didn't agree to help Peggy next time she asked, who knew to what lengths she would go? Merry could not risk alienating her and thus André and Toller, yet she couldn't bring herself to betray Judge Shippen's trust, either, no matter what.

Luckily, it turned out that Peggy knew better than to ask Merry to help her deceive Judge Shippen again, and Toller evidently covered for her and André on his own. But Merry still regretted that it must be written as clearly on her face she loved Darcy Montour as it was on Peggy's that she adored John André. A sobering thought struck Merry. Perhaps there could be no double meanings when it came to love.

* * *

Two days before Christmas, Merry headed back to the Shippens' after checking the widow's window box and the nearby tree for notes from Darcy. She had found nothing, had not done so for over a week now. A huge, cold lump of despair settled in her stomach. Surely nothing dire had happened to him. She would assume he was simply not in town. But she felt wretchedly alone, despite the fact that she was to join the Shippens tomorrow for a holiday celebration at their country house.

Everyone else had gone on ahead, but she and Peggy had both stayed on in town to recover from winter colds. Every time Merry had tried to amuse or reach out to Peggy, she had been rebuffed furiously. After Merry had refused to lie to Judge Shippen to cover Peggy's blossoming *affaire de coeur* with John André, Peggy had turned openly hostile. Still, it seemed from the way Toller had come calling on Merry, that Peggy had said nothing to him about her and Darcy. Merry could only pray that the reason was that Peggy could not prove there was anything still between her and the Frenchman, not that she was waiting for the best moment for revenge. Polly Shippen had always predicted that Peggy's temper would ruin her someday, and Merry didn't intend to fall victim to it.

Merry hurried along the back alley past the carriage house toward the servants' door. Only a skeleton staff was here; most had gone out to the country house with the family. Merry scuffed a bit of snow from her path and thought of Darcy again. If he had meant to rid himself of wanting her with one bout in bed, perhaps he had succeeded. As for her, she would never be the same again.

Now she knew, *really* knew, how things could be between them in a blaze of wanting and fulfilling. No more the dreamy fantasies of his simply holding and caressing her and then...nothing. Now her desires were fed by memories of how he had touched her, kissed her, loved her—drat him, if it was love at all on his part! She could recall each sensation in the attic with him that day. All the time she'd spent in her own bed this past week with her eyes and nose running like a pump she had played back little scenes of their moments together. Those scenes were finer than anything John André's little South Street Theater could offer. Darcy's fervent words to her, that soft, seductive tone she could almost hear right now— No, it was John André's voice she heard!

"Peggy, my darling, I cannot risk leaving you with child. Your father would kill us both, my sweet, and I'll not have one hair on your beautiful head hurt!"

Merry jerked to a halt on the other side of the fence and peered through the tall slats and ivy vines. John André was standing with Peggy at the servants' door and was holding both her hands to his lips. Peggy's cheeks were glazed with tears. It was obvious both thought they would be undiscovered here. Despite how things stood between her and Peggy, Merry again felt deep sympathy for her plight.

"But if General Howe is going back to England, promise me you shan't go with him," Peggy pleaded. "I simply couldn't bear it if you left me here!"

"My duty is here, my darling, you know that. I won't be leaving. All I am going to do is plan a farewell festival for Howe's departure and make you the centerpiece of it—the most wonderful woman in all of Philadelphia!"

Merry pressed both hands to her mouth. She had been so astounded to come upon them like this that what she had just overheard had not sunk in at first. A bombshell! The British commander, Sir William Howe, was going back to England. That would make the Americans rejoice! It would give Washington and his army the lift they needed to get through the winter. And if she could learn exactly when Howe was departing, perhaps they could take his ship on the Delaware, the way they had that wine shipment!

Peggy's passionate, pleading words tugged her mind back to the present. "I need you, John. I love you so. You know I'd do anything to please you, anything at all, my dearest, if you'd but ask." She trembled visibly in his embrace as he kissed her and then set her back a step. Despite his next words, the chill that Peggy seemed never to sense about the man froze Merry more sharply than the cold December day.

"Of course . . . I need you, too, my sweet. I have plans for you—for us, believe me. And perhaps there will be the chance soon for us to prove our love again. Inside, now, my darling. I can't have you catching another chill out here, any more than I can risk leaving you with child. Indeed, I cannot bear to do without you again, but our first time together was so wonderful, we shall both just have to wait.''

Merry thought she would be ill as she beat a quiet retreat. Her stomach twisted with excitement at the thought of telling Darcy of Howe's departure, but more than that she was sickened by poor, pretty Peggy's predicament. She and André had evidently consummated their relationship once, and now, perhaps, André wanted no part of such a risk again. But Merry sensed what Peggy did not—that he was only using her to advance his own ambitions. And it terrified her, as she hurried in the front door and up to her room before Peggy could discover she had been out, too, that Darcy might feel the same way toward her.

In the next few hours, Merry beat back her fears and put her plan in action. She told both Peggy and the two remaining housemaids that she still felt ill—no untruth at the time—and preferred to stay here over the holidays. She sighed with relief as Peggy, her face muffled to ward off the wind and perhaps hide her tears, was driven away in the family sleigh. Though it was just midmorning, Merry told the maids she was going back to bed and did not wish to be disturbed until she summoned them. When she bundled up to go back outside and tiptoed downstairs, she heard the two girls having tea in the drawing room with the stable boy. She silently wished them a happy holiday as she hurried out the back.

In the depleted Shippen mews, she saddled one of the two remaining horses and led the mare down the alley before mounting. This was too important to leave in Widow Windham's window box. It should not take her long to ride to Darcy's shed on Ravine Street and leave the message there. And if he just happened to be there, perhaps they could at least share a holiday toddy together. Beyond that, what she would say and do next time she was alone with him— But her thoughts went no further.

She shivered in the cold, but the horse and her excitement soon warmed her. The day was suddenly lovely, and there was the hope of serving America and seeing Darcy. A dusting of new snow etched the branches of the trees; ropes of smoke twisted from chimneys into a cloudless blue sky. Hoping Darcy's landlords would not think a thing amiss if they glanced out to see her, she dismounted and led the mare behind the house.

She tied her reins to a tree and walked across the creaky little footbridge. Her heart fell when she saw that the shed door was locked. Even trying to peer in the single shuttered window was to no avail, though she heard the gentle cooing of pigeons inside. She knocked. Still nothing. And then she heard the clatter of horses back on the street.

Uncertain what to do, she stood frozen for a moment. Then, stooping, she saw a blur of bright red through the trees by the house. Lobsterbacks, eight or ten of them! Had she been followed somehow? Had a woman on a horse seemed so suspicious, or had someone reported the shed being used back here? Surely Peggy would not have had her watched! Pulse pounding, she raced for her horse.

The soldiers did not seem to be coming back here. She heard a knock on the front door of the house. Could they be looking for Darcy? And then she recalled that the reason he had chosen this site was that the ravine was an escape route leading to a wood outside of town. She knew there were pickets on the main roads who demanded passes and searched travelers. But if she followed the ravine she could ride back around another way.

She untied the mare with shaky fingers and led her down into the snowy ravine. The going was hard, with bushes and haphazardly bent saplings in the way; the mare snorted in protest as her feet crunched across a frozen rivulet. Perhaps, Merry told herself, she had just panicked. Perhaps she should go back. But she went on, around trees, past the ice-glazed rocks of the ravine wall. The sun did not reach down here this early. She shuddered with cold and foreboding. Then, with another twist, the ravine opened onto a woodlot, just as Darcy had said.

When she rode out past the stand of barren trees she saw that she had indeed bypassed the guarded city boundaries. She sat mounted, chilled and nervous, on a narrow, desolate farm road and glanced back at the spires and roofs of the captive city. She thought again of how the message she had overheard would warm the American troops at Valley Forge. Perhaps Darcy would be there and she could warn him that there were redcoats near his shed. It was barely noon, and with luck she would not be missed at the Shippens' for hours. Even with this snow and the rutted, frozen roads, the American camp could not be more than a two-hour ride from here—if she could avoid the British. But most of them were celebrating the holidays in their own ways, all toasty and sated and warm. With a little shout, she turned the mare's head toward the windy northwest and Valley Forge.

The cold weather, the holiday season and the war had evidently kept most travelers from the roads. How strange, Merry thought as she jogged along the rutted lanes, that in a brutal war the British evidently stuck to some gentleman's agreement that decreed no more battles until the spring. It seemed to her that war was war all the time, and that civilized rules in it were a contradiction.

Soon she left behind the stripped, burned houses of the no-man's land around Philadelphia where the British had foraged to punish the Pennsylvanians. The closer she got to Valley Forge, after twice asking directions at farmhouses beyond the denuded zone, the harder the riding got. Iron spikes that had been scattered on the roadways to obstruct enemy horses slowed her down. Finally, over two and half hours out of the city, a detachment of four mounted American pickets rode out from a stand of snow-cloaked pines and escorted her the rest of the way in.

Her spirits fell as they crossed a frozen creek on a narrow, guarded wooden bridge and headed into camp. Stump-studded snowfields swept in all directions. Horses, men and cannons had churned the roads to mire. Crude cabins half sunk in the earth in clusters like villages stretched as far as the eye could see, each flying a bright battalion flag. It broke her heart to hear her guides proudly point out Washington's frayed blue banner flying on the hill they called Mount Joy.

"Lived in a tent jest like all of us, he did, till we got these cabins built," one man in ragged homespun boasted of their general. "Only then he moved hisself an' his top staff in that stone house there over yonder. An' it's a danged site colder than them huts, I tell you, 'cause it's jest a summer house. You got a message for the general then, ma'am, come on. An' don't mind the look on the boys' faces at the sight o' you—I mean, since you're bundled up real nice 'gainst the chill, an' lookin' fed good, too."

As they led her through the muddy lanes of the camp, her wide eyes took it all in. A sentinel on watch duty in a knit cap with strips of blankets around his feet stood in someone else's cap to protect his feet from frostbite. She waved to men with hollow cheeks and hands that were red and knotted. Her guides pointed out cabins with twelve men packed in each. They were proud of the way they were constructed, with clay between the logs, roofs of poles and earth and oiled paper windows. She saw the blacksmith's shop, too, and many hospital cabins and other utilitarian buildings.

"Food . . . it's hard to come by?" she asked.

"No, ma'am!" the youngest of the group boasted, his eyes twinkling with the "freedom flame," despite his gaunt look. "One day we have us a feast of water and firecake. And the next day, for vari'ty, it's firecake and water, eh, boys!"

They laughed at their barracks humor, though she could not bear to. She had sensed it must be bad out here, but this was dreadful—and with the worst of winter yet to come. Would there even be a Continental Army left to fight the British come spring? She thought of how the British lolled about in town, indolent and gluttonous, and guilt stabbed her again for being a part of that. After this, could she still pretend?

She longed to ask them if they knew whether a Frenchman named Darcy Mont was in camp, but then, she wasn't certain he wasn't secretive with the American army, too. After all, fifteen or so deserters from Valley Forge showed up every day in Philadelphia, and who knew what they would tell? The Americans were lucky that the British hadn't yet realized the wretched state of things out here. But then, "gentlemen" that the bloody Brits were, they would not break their code and attack in wintertime. Yet, to make sure some would-be deserter didn't spot her who later ended up feeding information to Major André, she pulled her hood even closer about her face.

She was relieved to see the other Frenchman she knew, striding with a group of men toward Washington's headquarters. She waved to Lafayette and greeted him in French. He looked surprised when he recognized her, and he came directly over to help her dismount.

"Is there trouble in the city, Mistress Morgan?"

"Always trouble, *monsieur le Marquis*, but good news today I just had to share with you all. But I'll have to tell General Washington first. You understand."

"May I have the pleasure to escort you inside, then? The general, he will be pleased you be safe and hearty. And others you would like to see, too, yes?" he told her with a shy smile. She complimented him on the improvement in his English. But she did not tell him that that distinctive lilt to his words made her long for Darcy as if she were homesick.

"Then Darcy is here?" was all she allowed herself to ask as Lafayette took her inside the gray stone house with a nod at the blue-coated Virginia sentries.

"He is upstairs in a meeting, I believe. Do not fret," he said comfortingly, his pale cheeks blushing even ruddier than the nip of wind had made them.

Though General Washington was upstairs in the meeting, too, Lafayette proudly introduced her all around. She felt so happy, honored and proud to be with these heroes and to be able to truly smile instead of pretending. The marquis introduced her to the short, swarthy Benedict Arnold, who had just recently arrived. He could only half rise to greet her, for his bandage-swathed leg was propped up on a stool and a cane leaned against his chair. Still energy and power seemed to emanate from the man.

"We heard of your heroics at Saratoga, sir," she told him.

"My thanks for those words, my dear. Would that the stubborn, myopic Congress had your good sense," he replied sourly.

"General Arnold, he will be commander of Philadelphia when we take it back next spring," Lafayette put in as if to change a volatile subject while he steered her away.

"Poor man," Merry observed. "He's bitter, isn't he? Perhaps the leg wound..."

"Wounds to his pride, I fear, for being publicly reprimanded and not promoted with some others. But General Washington, he thinks the earth of him!"

That bit of fractured English brought a smile to Merry's lips as Lafayette introduced her to the Prussian general Baron von Steuben. He wore a flashy scarlet-and-blue uniform studded with medals and ribbons. "The baron, he does teach the army maneuvers before the spring," Lafayette told her as he escorted her over to a bench by a narrow fireplace. "The baron, he is here on his own funding, just as Darcy and I. Von Steuben, he even gives dinners for the troops from his own pocket and admits no one who does not have ragged breeches," Lafayette confided with a look that was somewhere between a grimace and a grin.

But her mind had been caught by Darcy's name and that first bit of information. Her eyes were searching for him each time another officer came down the stairs. "But you are a marquis," she said to Lafayette. "You mean Darcy, as a French citizen, must support himself here, too?"

"Dear Mistress Morgan, livre for livre, my friend D'Arcy Montour, comte de Belfort, he could outspend me! His Paris home, his fifteenth-century château at Belfort, his ancestral lands, and his fine lineage rank him with the French sovereign as dearly as my meager credentials," he concluded, his voice almost humble.

But she wasn't interested in Lafayette's pedigree. "*Comte*...that means count. That isn't...royalty?" She was stunned to realize that the man she had been so intimate with was one she evidently knew even less of than she had thought.

"No, Mistress Morgan, not royalty," he told her. "But he is of the highest nobility of the land. An intimate and yet a servant of the great King Louis, even as I am, so..."

She heard no more. She trembled. She stood to flee. Her Darcy...a count. Titled nobility. Huge homes. Ancestral lands. A fortune. A friend to the king, not just someone who had visited the court. And she had cherished in her heart thoughts that she could convince him to declare his love and perhaps wed her. Her—Merry Morgan, a tradesman's girl from a cottage on Staten Island whose mother had kept beehives out back so they'd have spending money. Merry Morgan, who did not even recognize a French accent when first she heard it, who stupidly tried to learn French from a book and took four months of dancing lessons for two precious pounds so that she could impress him. And here he was used to dancing with royalty at Versailles! She had dared to dream of being taken to France. And with the count of Belfort!

At that moment, Washington and Darcy came down the stairs together, with some officers clattering behind them. And so she did not flee at all. Surprised, they surrounded her, and she managed to tell them the good news that had brought her out here and warn Darcy that redcoats had been near his shed. But even when huzzahs split the air at the news of Howe's departure and Washington led a toast to Merry with some of the very bottles of wine they had taken from John André's precious shipment for Lord Howe, her emotions felt like brittle ice. And even when Darcy smiled warmly and bent to kiss her hand, she pictured John André leaning over Peggy's and felt colder than the ride and the outside air ever could have made her.

"We cannot thank you enough for your cheery news!" General Washington said as he bade her and Darcy farewell in front of his headquarters. Still, she thought, the general's face was grim and hardly cheery. She and Darcy sat mounted, gazing down at the tall man. "Now, sir, get her back safely that secret way you both got out of our captive capital, if those redcoats lurking about your hiding place are gone," he said. "And may Providence, in whose mercy we all must trust, keep you both safe until we meet again." He smacked the rump of Darcy's horse, and they rode away in the waning afternoon light.

Merry shivered again. Even the hastily assembled celebration dinner of looted wine, stringy roast mutton and local river clams had not warmed her. Not after what Lafayette had told her, though she'd shared none of that with Darcy yet.

Throwing caution to the winds, not caring that some disgruntled soldier in camp might desert and tell the British of her trip out here, she waved as they departed in response to shouts and goodbyes along the way. The warmth of the soldiers' farewell made her feel she had supped with every man there, not just the top officers and Darcy. She realized that the bold spirit of the camp might be all that would get this army through the hard times to come; she wished her own spirits were as high.

She still felt unstrung to her soul by Lafayette's revelations. No wonder Darcy had never seen fit to share with her his mysterious past. He probably saw her as a peasant, a necessary bother in his honorable quest to do his aristocratic duty. Or perhaps she was simply a pleasant diversion for him until he could go back to the noble, stunning and sophisticated women of his country and his court. And here she had dared to desire him for her own!

Yet she squared her shoulders and lifted her chin higher as they left the boundaries of Valley Forge behind. After all, she reminded herself, she was a proud, free American, and there was no shame in that! She had perhaps saved Darcy's life once; she had helped her country and his! At least he must care deeply for this land and American freedom. Perhaps, even now, he still cared a bit for her, too.

"You are so sad, Merry," he observed as he rode his larger horse beside her, gazing slightly down at her. "Even in the celebrations and gratitude to you back there, you were sad. I know it has all been hard for you. There is a long struggle ahead yet, but we will prevail."

"Will *we*?" she asked more bitterly than she intended. "All of us peasant Americans working with you noble French will prevail?"

His concern crumpled to a frown. "What in damnation are you saying?"

"Just that I've learned some of what you haven't been saying, *monsieur le comte de Belfort*!"

"I see."

She realized his quiet calm made her sound like a New York docks fishwife by comparison. It burned deeper, as if he were condescending when he answered her.

"But you must understand, Merry, it just would not do for me to flaunt an inherited title in a land where, blessedly, there are no such burdens."

"Blessedly? Burdens? Am I to believe that? Fine homes, a family name and fortune just awaiting your return to France, and—"

"If I do not flaunt all that here, why do you?" His voice lashed her. He reached over to seize her hands on her reins with one big hand and halt her horse. "Well? Does all that make such a difference to you?"

"Yes! Well, no... only that you did not see fit to tell me!"

"I am here as a secret agent and will not bare my soul to anyone! Besides, I thought you Americans were beyond being swayed by such things as titles and fortunes and lands! In a country where each man is supposedly valued equally, what is the difference?"

"The difference? Don't you see that we're from different worlds?"

"Would it really have mattered to you, when we argued and yet desired each other from the beginning? Would you have lost your spunk and spirit and curtsied and said, 'Yes, my lord, your excellency the count?' Would it have made a difference to you when we fled the Hessians together? When we worked together and went to bed together in Philadelphia? Or when we yet touch like this?" He pulled her toward him so suddenly that she almost slipped off her horse. But his thigh, pressed hard to hers, and his hand on the back of her neck steadied her as he took one fierce, demanding kiss and then released her. He urged her horse on, and she had to grab the saddle to keep from pitching off. He jogged along faster at her side.

"But I am sick to death," she went on, refusing to let such tactics settle it all, "of double meanings and duplicity in Philadelphia with those dratted British! I may pretend things to myself sometimes, but I know the difference. I hate to lie, especially to those I care for! You obviously did not want me to know the real Darcy. I thought we were beginning to be close—to trust each other. I was deluded. I tried to ignore the fact that whenever I asked you to share your past with me there was nothing but a stone wall. I dared to hope there would be more for us . . . together . . . someday. . . .''

He sighed deeply and looked away and then back at her. His eyes were glittering green slits. ''I shall never wed again, never! Not even you, Merry,'' he said, so determinedly yet so quietly that she could not believe at first she had heard a flat denial.

She spun to face him, ignoring the tears that iced her cheeks. ''Again? Then—''

''It was a most . . . unfortunate situation. A grave mistake. Do not love me, and do not think I will marry you. But believe me, Merry, I would never have taken you to bed, nor would dream I could again, if I believed I would leave you with child when I returned to France. In these tenuous times— *Sacrebleu!*'' He smacked his thigh with his fist as they halted their horses again, ''I just never would have done that. You see, there was—'' his voice caught in his throat ''—no child from my marriage. The fault was mine . . . and the woman to whom I was once wed is gone too. . . .''

''You are a widower and regret you have no child,'' Merry said, almost before she knew she would speak. That was it, she thought, the cause of his deep-seated grief.

He nodded and looked away, his austere face closed, as if the subject were, too. But for Merry it could not be. Her heart went out to him. She loved him. He cared for her. He had even hoped their relationship would continue, her heart sang. He had suffered through the loss of a wife, through the pain of being unable to father an heir, and he felt he could not risk such unhappiness again. But she had to convince him, whether or not he could ever have a child, that he could have her! She could love him enough that any tragedies in his past could be soothed by their days together. Her heart was bursting as she urged her horse closer to his.

''I am sorry for your losses, Darcy. I would love you and want to be with you always, even if you were King Louis himself in disguise or the lowest streetsweeper. This way I have come to want and care for the man and not the count, so I just hope you will agree—''

''No agreements. I would hate myself later if I did not make myself perfectly clear, Merry. I do not want to hurt you. Yet,

God help me, I cannot resist you. But there is no hope for our future. I will never take you to France as my wife. Unless you can accept that our relationship must, of necessity beyond even my control, end some day, then it is better to end it now. Come on. Let's set a fast pace, or that ravine will be pitch-black and difficult to traverse.''

They urged their horses to a canter. The entire path of her life suddenly loomed ahead, pitch-black and difficult to traverse. Darcy himself, and her love for him, had become her worst enemies. Without the hope of having him but in a temporary love affair, everything seemed dark and dangerous ahead. She kept up, but she left her hopes trampled back on the frozen, muddy road from Valley Forge. And however much she loved Darcy Montour, no matter who he really was, she feared that the victorious spring of newly won battles might never come.

Chapter Ten

The first four months of 1778 brought a resurgence of Merry's spirits and hopes for victory in both her little war with Darcy Montour and the big war. While John André prepared to stage a farewell fete for General Howe, she picked up signs that the British might evacuate Philadelphia completely in the near future. More troop transports lined the harbor, just waiting to be filled. Officers like André seemed restless, champing at the bit for battle somewhere else. People whispered that Sir Henry Clinton, who was to replace Howe, was not as enamored of holding Philadelphia as Howe had been. Rumors drifted into town that the Americans were conducting drills and maneuvers under the eagle eye of Baron von Steuben. Occasional rockets or bombshells lit up the sky outside the city, as if to say, "We are waiting out here for your next move, you bloody British bastards!"

Though Merry seldom saw Darcy, and then only briefly, they passed frequent notes as she gleaned information or he passed common concerns and questions on to her. She wondered if he would take her suggestion that the Americans make a sortie the night of André's so-called *Mischianza* celebration on May 18. After all, the redcoat officers would be all in one place and off their guard that night; the British troops would be lined up en masse along the river to salute Lord Howe.

She kept her notes to Darcy succinct but friendly and always signed them, "With deep concern and abiding care. FF." That would at least tell him she had not changed one whit of how she felt toward him but at the same time let him know she was not throwing herself at him—at least not until the next time she got the chance!

The best news of all, however, came in April when word arrived in the new United States that the French were now at war with England, too. All of Darcy's and Ben Franklin's efforts had finally paid off, and there was a formal treaty of alliance between France and America. King Louis had signed it in February, and it promised better French-American relations and more aid. Now, Merry sighed inwardly as she heard Peggy's door slam in the hall, if it could only mean better French-American relations between herself and the elusive count of Belfort!

Rapid knocks rattled her door, and out of habit she thrust the note she had been writing under a book. Surprisingly, it was Peggy. The eldest Shippen daughter had hardly spoken to her for months. Merry regretted this, for it had made the Shippen house feel like an armed camp, with Polly on Merry's side, Sally on Peggy's, and poor Judge Shippen more than ever in the undecided middle. But right now Peggy looked radiant, if slightly disheveled. Her light brown tresses lay loose, caught back only by a single ribbon in her haste. The eyes that had been dulled just last week by the news of the French alliance glowed now with joy.

"John's downstairs with a surprise for you and me! Come down now," she cried, and tugged at Merry's arm to drag her into the hall and down the stairs.

At least they were both properly attired to greet visitors, Merry thought as she let Peggy pull her along. She knew any surprise from John André would thrill Peggy; she hoped it was something she could share in without compromising herself. Though pretending to care for both Toller and André had strained her to the breaking point since her Valley Forge experience, Merry forced a smile when she saw them and two of André's aides standing in the drawing room, their arms heaped with sumptuous materials and vibrant feathers.

"Ah, here you are," André said, his face more glowing than Peggy's. "No questions yet, you two, for I shall explain. I have chosen you to play the Queen of American Beauty—Merry...and the Queen of English Beauty—my dear Peggy—

for Howe's fete two weeks hence, and we've come to talk about costumes. There will be a water parade, music, a triumphal arch, jousting, and dancing till dawn! Now, I have done just a few sketches for the costumes here—''

"Oh, John, how splendid!" Peggy cried, and forgot her poise to clap her hands and jump up and down.

Laughing, André unwound a length of azure-blue satin from the bolt he held, draping it over her hands so that the two of them were bound together by a shimmering, silky rope.

But for Merry it was the final straw. To be paraded before all the British bigwigs as participants in their triumphal revels when the Americans were still out there struggling— No! Those men's faces at Valley Forge, their bravery in the face of cold and hunger, their courage for what was to come— No! Even if Darcy would insist she must do it to maintain her place in Tory hearts, she could not stomach this final shame.

"I regret to say I just could not, John," Merry told him, facing him over the pile of shimmering piece goods, the likes of which she had never seen. Did the ladies of the French court dress in such luxurious finery? she wondered suddenly.

"You can't be serious!" Peggy wailed. "The chance to be at the very center of things—in John's marvelous production! You're just trying to get Father to tell me I can't be in it, too!"

"That's not true, Peggy," Merry protested, trying to keep calm. "I hope your father permits you to, as I know how much you would enjoy it all. I'm speaking for myself, that's all."

"And may I ask why the blunt rejection?" John André demanded before Toller could ask.

They all stared narrow-eyed at her. She chose her words carefully. "In wartime, with so much in upheaval and so many lives disrupted, I think it's wrong for either side to celebrate with such extravagance."

Toller leapt into the fray. "Judas Priest! *Either* side? Are we to believe that? I know where your heart lies, sure enough! You mean you'd refuse if this were Washington's little party, too?"

She tried to face Toller down, but he was furious. She feared she had finally overstepped his patience and feared she might pay a price there, too. "Yes, Toller. But I doubt if a country-bred squire like the American general would abide such a show when the war is not over and it's no one's triumph yet, triumphal arch or not."

"I say, you do not mean you actually believe those rebel rotters could *win*?" John André demanded, his voice cracking.

"Just let me talk to her in private, Major," Toller said, but Peggy stepped in before he could reach for her arm.

"You've been waiting for the chance to completely ruin my happiness, haven't you?" she cried, hands on hips. "You're a sour, bitter loser, Merry Morgan, and I'm going to do my best to see you are not here in my house one more day! And I'm going to be certain that I treat you every bit the way you have—"

"Peggy!" Judge Shippen's voice cracked out behind them. Everyone jumped and turned. Polly, her eyes wide behind her owlish glasses, stood at her father's side. "You will apologize to our guest, daughter. She is living here at my invitation, and I'll not have you addressing her thus. Or putting on such a passionate, unseemly display for these gentlemen. Nor will you be prancing about amid the officer corps at this British feast gowned in what I have heard will be quite pagan garments."

"The ladies will be completely covered by Turkish veils and caftans, sir," Major André put in.

"Entirely unsuitable," Judge Shippen declared. "Peggy, to your room, and please see your hair is done properly before you greet guests next time, though there have evidently been far too many visitors of late."

"Father, I—" she began to protest, her face livid. The cords in her slender neck stood out. Her fists clenched, then unclenched, around the azure satin that she and André both still held.

Merry felt embarrassed and trapped in the center of the maelstrom, but proud and relieved, too. She would not have to be part of André's plans for an early British victory party. And, however much she had alienated Peggy, André and Toller, it had been worth it.

May 18, the night of the British *Mischianza* celebration, the fuming Peggy kept to her room. Next door, in hers, Merry had begun a letter to her sister in New Haven, a letter that would have to go to Darcy and then to Cam and then slowly on. But it had been so long since Merry and Libby had exchanged their news and their love. Even those warm feelings felt chilled by this house tonight; Merry felt Peggy's hatred seeping through the wall they shared. If Peggy's ice-blue eyes could have stabbed through the wood and plaster and wallpaper, Merry was certain, she'd be dead.

Polly came for a visit, and when she left Merry heard the faint strains of "God Save the King" from the river. The water parade was to row to Toller's country manor at Devlinton and stop there for a feast before proceeding to dancing at another house. Drat! If Peggy heard the music, also, she would hate her even more.

And then, as darkness fell, Merry heard much more than the faint strains of trumpets and drums. There was a series of explosions followed by the fierce rattle of musketry. Merry leaned out her window in the soft May night to scan the sky for points of light. Could it be that the Americans had decided to ruin André's party, as she had suggested weeks ago, or was the noise part of some planned British salute? When it all ended, she left her windows barely ajar to catch the air but still keep the bugs out. She dawdled around a while longer, then undressed without summoning a maid. The night was warm; she wore only her flower-sprigged cotton dressing gown, not having donned her night rail yet. But as soon as she blew out the candle she heard another sound and jumped.

The rattle of gravel on the window! It had been months since Darcy had sent her a letter that way! As she had been instructed, she pushed both panes wide open and stood against the wall beside the draperies, waiting for the Lad to toss the rock with the note in. Nothing. Then a scrape and a bump. And then a big, dark form climbed right through her window, crouched, then stood.

She gasped. The form turned. He wore only black, and he blended with the night.

"Darcy?" she croaked. "Darcy!"

"Shh!" he said, and stepped forward to gently cover her lips for an instant with a big, warm hand. He was breathing hard;

his breath, warm and redolent of wine, mingled with the breeze from the window. But he smelled of gunsmoke, too. Up this close, she could see that his face was smudged and his green eyes were glittering.

"I had to come, despite the risk," he whispered, his hands barely cupping her shoulders. "You deserved to know that your suggestion we disrupt André's little amusement tonight was a success! A small detachment of Washington's men slipped in to visit the big ammunition store in Germantown and blew it up. So very impolite! How sad," he said mockingly as a smile lit her face, "that the blasts rocked the hall where the revelers were cavorting and the few who chased us were in ridiculous costumes! We laughed at their antics even as our musket fire drove them back!"

She laughed silently and hugged him. He hugged her back at first, his shoulders shaking with silent laughter, too, until he realized she wore nothing under the thin fabric, which had parted when she had pressed herself to him.

"Merry...I cannot stay...." he gasped, instantly sober, and more breathless than when he had come in. But he could not stop himself from looking, or from touching, either, when she did not protest. Under the gown, his hands clasped her small waist and his thumbs stroked the soft skin of her stomach. He stared down, awestruck at the beauty of her shimmering white body in the dimly lit room. He had been without her for so long that he could not bear it. He had tried everything to shut her out, to keep from caring. But her laughter, the bold light in her eyes that heated his blood so, had haunted him day and night. He had been so afraid he would hurt her when he had to go. She deserved so much more than to get tangled up with him the way his hands were now tangled in the loosed bounty of her hair and the wispy material of her robe.

"Merry, I did not know you would be . . . like this," he managed, but when her arms clung to his neck he buried his face in her fragrant hair and pressed her closer to the wall.

"Invading a lady's bedroom, just as you've invaded her heart and life," she whispered in his ear, her voice raspy. "I've thought so long about all the things between us, and I still want you all the time...."

He moaned deep in his throat as he stepped back to part her robe again. He stared down at the alabaster perfection of her flesh. "My Merry, I swear, I did not come for this, but I need you—"

"That's enough for now. And I love you—" was all she got out before his mouth descended to devour her lips and then dance down her throat to her bud-tipped breasts.

She propped herself—both of them—against the wall. Her head spun. This could be one of her old dreams—her mystery man who came to her at night. And yet it was real, so real. She should stop him, but she couldn't. Everything spun faster, faster. This was madness, with Peggy next door, and Polly, who was in the habit of just knocking and stepping right in . . .

But all rational thought tumbled into some black abyss. Protests died on her parted lips as her breathing quickened. She held his big head to her while he plundered her breasts and ran his hands up and down her trembling flesh. He recited her name in a frenzied litany of whispers, "Merry, Merry, my beautiful Merry," as he caressed between her soft thighs with a marauding hand.

"We can't do this here," he murmured. She felt the words burn the sleek skin of her belly as he explored lower. But he showed no signs of stopping. He knelt and, pulling her down, clamped her hard against him, knees to chest, with both hands holding her buttocks to clamp her to him. She felt him there, against her middle, demanding freedom, wanting her, ready for her. Mindlessly she separated her thighs and shifted closer as if to ride him.

And then the soft, whirling night was shattered by a crashing of glass. She drew in a quick breath; his big body tensed. He threw her flat on the floor next to the bed on the rug and lay still over her.

"Peggy's room, I th-think," she stammered. "She breaks things sometimes—"

He rattled off something in angry French; she knew he was cursing the situation and his own impulsiveness. Reality and danger crashed back over her heated skin in one cold slap. She hated herself for the words, but she said them.

"You'll have to go. Polly might come in. This is insane—"

He lifted them both to a sitting position. He grasped her chin in one big hand. "I have been insane since I met you. I will go. But if you are willing, like this . . . we will find a way."

He bounced a kiss off her nose and pulled her rumpled cotton robe closed in front of her. Then he was on his feet and out the window and down the ladder before she knew he would really leave. She shoved her rampant tresses back and tied her robe with shaky hands. She was perspiring all over, and she shuddered as the breeze from the open window licked at her limbs. Another crash echoed from Peggy's room, and she heard Judge Shippen's stern tones raised in rebuke as she got to her feet. She hurried to the window and leaned out to whisper goodbye to Darcy. But he had been so quick! She saw naught but the shadows of the night, as if she had dreamed him after all.

The raw fury Peggy had first felt at being denied the central role in the *Mischianza* was nothing compared to the killing grief that now made her pick her powder and pomade jars one by one from her dressing table and hurl them against the wall. And when her sisters and her father appeared at her locked door, she ordered them to go away, promising through the door, "I'm through now."

She was through, indeed, she vowed as their footsteps went away and she lay back and stared bleary-eyed at the underside of her canopied bed. She would never trust anyone, not even John André, ever again. And she would have her revenge on all of them, whatever it took!

She kept hearing the interview she had had today with John and Toller in John's carriage. She could hear their voices yet, urging her to be a part of their plan. In the end she had agreed; she could not deny John André anything, not even her favors. She had not denied him her eternal love, even though he did not deserve it. And yet he would pay for not wanting to wed her. When she was married to another at his bidding, he would long to have her lying next to him in bed like this. She rolled over and stifled a hysterical, racking sob with her pillow as the tears coursed down her face.

"But, John," she could hear herself stammer to him in the carriage, "I thought you had said—hinted—that you would send me to New York to wait there for you if you were recalled from here. Everyone who saw us about—all our friends—surely thought so!"

"But we will be united there later, my darling. All of us must make sacrifices in the war," he had said. She wished she could block out his voice now, but it rolled over her again to torment her. "You see," he said, "we have learned from a rebel deserter that General Benedict Arnold, who did so brilliantly at Saratoga, is at Valley Forge. And, when we withdraw from here, Washington's going to name him military commander of Philadelphia. He's a bit older than you, but that is one other reason he will be besotted by you, my sweet, just as I have been."

She heard her own shaky protest. "Besotted?" She had felt stunned; it was not the carriage ride that was making her stomach churn. "I thought you loved me!"

"Indeed I do. But, you see, together you and I shall overturn the rebel cause. With your help, we can sway Benedict Arnold to turn traitor. He is already disgruntled with the way their Congress has treated him. He has already made a few careful overtures to us. And, with you at his side, urging him on, becoming a turncoat is only a step away. It will be our biggest triumph together, you and I, my sweet. When Benedict Arnold falls for the most beautiful Tory woman in Philadelphia, then we will have him!"

"Have him?" she had protested. "But I want only you—"

"And you shall have me! He will have to go to New York when he turns, and you will be with him! And that is where I shall be, waiting for you, after we pull out of here next month."

"I simply cannot live without you, John. You said you had plans for us . . . for us together, and . . ."

He had shaken her then. She had felt so weak that her head had bobbed like a flower on a wilted stalk. "I do have plans for us together!" His voice had become harsh and thickly menacing. "I want you to have the best. Benedict Arnold will be rich and acclaimed when he changes sides! We will be rewarded for having brought him over. He will be feted in London—with you at his side, and me standing just behind you. And before that, you will rule this rebel city when he is commander here. And all the time you will write in secret to me and we will count the days before we can be back together as lovers forever!''

"And John will wed you as soon as you're finally rid of Arnold, one way or the other," Toller had dared to put in at that point. She had turned her teary eyes to her old family friend and confidant. She had forgotten he was even there.

"Toller," she had said, her voice dull and muted. "You agree to all this?"

"It's a brilliant idea, Peggy, to be carried out by a brilliant woman! Seize the chance!"

And so she had nodded mutely, and had sat quietly as John and Toller excitedly outlined what her role in the plot would be. Something must have died in her then, for her mind and her heart had felt far separate from the outside of her. Only one thing had seemed to stand out clearly. If Toller Devlin, whom she had trusted once, could betray her like this, could abet John in this plan that was killing her heart, then he deserved to be punished. If she couldn't have John, then Toller wouldn't get Merry Morgan. She, Peggy Shippen, would find a way to put Merry far beyond Toller's reach as John would be beyond her own. There was nothing she could do to John, other than hoping he would regret his loss when he saw her as Arnold's wife. But there were two people she could hurt—Toller and that lying bitch Merry Morgan, who had dared to intrude on her house and her life.

Peggy sat up in her rumpled bed and put her head in her hands. Her disheveled hair covered her bent knees. She had meant to hurt Merry by having her wed Toller, whom she obviously detested, but now she'd have to find another way. If she could only be certain she still loved that rakish Frenchman, Darcy Mont, perhaps she could hire someone to force Darcy back to France for good. Perhaps once she had snagged the widower Benedict Arnold and had turned him from the American cause, gotten him to jump and do her bidding, perhaps then she'd get her vengeance. She'd force Merry to wed someone she hated—or someone who would hate her. Yes, somehow she'd find a way to ruin the happiness of those who had crossed her, and especially Merry Morgan.

She clasped her fingers around the locket with the lock of John André's hair, then pressed it close to her breast until it left an imprint in her soft flesh. The tears had started again, the last ones she would allow herself before she went to work on her plans.

The next day, when Peggy knew Merry had gone out for a stroll, Peggy slipped through the seldom-used door that connected their rooms. She gazed around; she had to find something to help her ruin Merry Morgan. She knew Merry was sickeningly sympathetic to the rebel cause, but even if she was a spy, just having André expose her or arrest her would not be enough. Even if the British executed captured female spies and traitors as they did the men, it would not be enough! She wanted Merry to suffer for years.

She searched through Merry's tallboy but found only clothes. She rifled the chest at the foot of her bed until she realized she was disturbing things and went about the task more carefully. Nothing strange there but a bottle of milky-green something. Probably a mixture to treat freckles; women all had their own secret herbal remedies if they were fair-skinned. She slammed the lid of the trunk a bit too hard. And then she saw a half-finished letter that had been shoved under a book called *Pilgrim's Progress* on the table.

Peggy lifted the book and bent to read the letter where it was. Ah, to Merry's sister Libby in New Haven. She skimmed it quickly, then read it slowly once again with a smile curving the harsh set of her lips. Yes, she had been correct about Merry's feelings for that Frenchman! When the time was right, how very simple it would be to ruin them both. And, best of all, Merry Morgan would be shattered by the same fate Peggy had to face!

The section of the letter Peggy studied for the third time read:

And as for D.M., I still fear our future is hopeless. He has been honest at last, I will say that. Dearest Lib, he has said very bluntly he will never wed again and will not take me to France with him, as I have both hinted and asked out-right. In my wildest dreams I hope he does not mean it, and even think of stowing away with him when he returns to France, but he would then detest and mistrust me for-ever. I fear he would believe I was only after his fortune or his title. And if ever I could convince him to wed me, I fear he would turn on me with hot hatred instead of hot de-sire.

It terrifies me to think what a pair we would make at the king's court. I, with my broken schoolgirl French and rustic ways, the countess of Belfort! He, among the lovely, sophisticated ladies of the realm, with Merry Morgan on his arm. In my wildest fantasies I long for the chance, but, especially with his vow to never wed again, I fear it would end in catastrophe for me and the love I bear him....

"As indeed it shall, Merry Morgan!" Peggy whispered aloud as she covered the letter and left the room. "As indeed it shall!"

That spring the British finally evacuated Philadelphia. The American army returned, and their first act was to hold a cel-ebration in honor of the French-American alliance, which the French ambassador, Beaumarchais, had signed right here in town. This festive occasion suited Peggy's purpose well enough, though she was Tory to her bones, for she attended it on Ben-edict Arnold's arm. And then it turned out that Darcy Mont knew Beaumarchais. Now that the Americans were back in charge in Philadelphia, Darcy had returned, too...with Merry Morgan on his arm, though not for long, if Peggy had her way. Yes, Peggy thought, settling with both that traitor Toller Dev-lin and that tricky bitch Meredith Morgan all in one fell swoop was first on her social agenda.

Peggy glared over the top of her goblet at Merry and Darcy, who were dancing the minuet together. Suddenly the fine white wine Benedict Arnold had ordered to fulfill her whim tasted like vinegar on her tongue. Well, she thought, let them be happy. It would make Merry's fall that much harder when Darcy turned from her.

"That's better. I want always to see you smiling, my beautiful girl."

Benedict Arnold's voice snapped Peggy back to reality. "I regret that this bum leg of mine keeps me from dancing with you when you love it so."

"Ah," she said, hoping she managed the dewy-eyed look she had always reserved for John before he had left her in pieces, "but there are other things I love more than dancing, and one is being with the hero of Saratoga. I can't say that I think much of a Congress and a nation that cannot see who should be leading this whole war, but I'm only too happy you are here with me now."

She rested her gloved hand on his broad shoulder as he beamed up at her. At least, she thought, he was a robust, sturdy man—not flaccid and old, as she had pictured him once. He had already hinted at wanting children if he wedded again, and she fully intended to get him around to proposing to her eventually. For she meant to have Benedict Arnold. Let John André see what a mistake he had made when he had put the British cause above her love.

She stopped listening to Benedict's boring account of his part in the battle of Saratoga as he told it yet again to another of his aides, who had intentionally asked a leading question to get him into it. She admired his aides' cleverness, though. One especially, the red-haired, darting-eyed Captain Stephen Michaelson, reminded her of André in the worst sense. Yes, perhaps she'd have use for Stephen later in her own little schemes.

Merry took Darcy's arm and paraded off the dance floor with him at the end of the minuet. She had never been happier. They were secret lovers again, and she was certain she was making progress with him about their future. Not that she ever mentioned marriage or going to France with him directly, but he had told her many things about the French court when she had asked. And they were working together more openly now that the Americans were back in control.

"Your friend Peggy reminds me of a serpent waiting to strike tonight," Darcy told her, and turned his back to block Peggy's scrutiny of them from across the room.

"I believe she's still mourning losing André. She flirts with General Arnold, but I don't think she loves him. I feel for her," Merry admitted, recalling how deeply she had missed Darcy when he had "deserted" her. She had seen and understood full well the depth of Peggy's passion. "But tonight, not even Peggy can mar my joy!" she assured him, though she could tell he was still preoccupied with worries.

"I hope things are well with our army, now that they're harassing Lord Clinton's flanks as he heads north. Too bad Howe escaped to England."

"And now that the Americans toast King Louis every night, as well as Washington, perhaps some French aid will come soon," she said, trying to buck him up.

Darcy's serious expression deepened to a frown. "I have been thinking I had best go back home soon to help Franklin get more weapons—and maybe a fleet, too. But I will wait a little while yet."

He saw her face fall. But he had decided to be as honest with her as he could. He knew she wanted to visit France with him, but that would mean marriage, and he would not allow that. Besides, the licentious French court would chew up an open, trusting, natural beauty like this and spit her out in pieces, and he would not permit that, either. And yet, for all that, he had to keep steeling himself to prepare for the time when he would have to leave her. The lovemaking—she insisted on calling it that—was wild and wonderful. It would be easier than ever to forego French women when he went home. No one would ever measure up to Merry Morgan.

"I wonder if Peggy Shippen sees anything in General Arnold beyond prestige and power," he mused with a sideways glance in their direction again.

"I think it's mostly that John André used her and then broke her heart when he left, so she's just bounced to the next man who shows her his favor," Merry offered. "Perhaps she's trying to save face by going after Washington's top man here—since everyone thought André would propose and send her to New York."

Darcy frowned again but said only, "Let's sport a toe with this new dance."

The playing from the string quartet was much more raucous now, and Merry was surprised that he wanted to try it. Or had he not wanted the discussion about leaving and breaking a woman's heart to go any further? But she thrust that thought aside in her excitement to tug his hand to take him out on the dance floor.

"You will have to teach me this," he teased. "Living in attics and hiding in sheds too long has made me quite the country clod."

Her eyes lit at the challenge. "You a country clod, *monsieur le comte? Quel dommage!*" she teased back in such lovely French, he almost forgot where he was. "The dance is called Burgoyne's Surrender and commemorates the victory at Saratoga. Look, slide to the left and then hop."

"If I ever dance again, that's the one I'll do," Benedict Arnold told Peggy Shippen, tugging her down into the chair beside his, from which he surveyed his new realm as military commander of Philadelphia. Damnation, but he adored this little beauty, even though she was of Tory persuasion. And besides, with what he had begun pondering of late, a loyalist wife might be a distinct advantage to him, if he could ever persuade such a young beauty to be his bride. A new life for him with her at his side as consort and queen of his heart, he thought. He felt twenty years younger than his thirty-seven at the thought of possessing Peggy Shippen. Why, if he ever managed to convince her to be Mrs. Arnold, he would buy her a country home out on the river, and that would take capital he didn't have. But he had a very good idea where to get it, right along with the respect and promotions he had overlong deserved, too!

Peggy leaned over to whisper in his ear. "Benedict, you know I told you how I simply don't get on with our little houseguest, Mistress Morgan. Frankly, I'm afraid she'll think you and I are unsuited. She's so spoiled she's quite likely to upset Papa about us. She has such a lot of influence with him, it worries me. But you see that man she's dancing with?"

"The Frenchman, Darcy Mont. A friend of Washington's and Lafayette's."

"Is that right? Well, anyway, they love each other and want to elope, and I thought I could make them both happy by helping to arrange it. And that way she would be out of the house if you come calling. If you would just give me a few of your best men for a night . . ."

"What?" He lowered his voice. "Whatever do you mean?"

She swallowed hard. She had not chosen her words quite carefully enough. This man was not one to allow the wool to be pulled easily over his eyes. "I mean, I want to get that woman out of the house so that she won't come between us. And I know how to make her happy at the same time. But I'll tell you the rest later—in the privacy of your carriage." She licked her lips provocatively before she lowered her lashes and looked at the dancers again.

She almost giggled behind her fan when she saw that her dear Benedict had to cross his legs and drape a hand across his lap to keep from flaunting his desire for her in those tight white breeches. She hoped she seemed naive to him—quite the virgin—despite the tricks John had taught her. She planned to put those tricks to good use to get exactly what she wanted from this man in the carriage on the way home tonight. And that would get her the aid of Captain Stephen Michaelson in her plan to ruin Merry Morgan's happiness for good. Peggy Shippen licked her lips again, this time in hungry anticipation, when she thought of Darcy betraying Merry as brutally as John André had her.

It was just after dark three weeks later when a boy from the docks delivered the message to the house for Merry. Peggy brought it up herself, saying she hadn't let anyone else see it because she thought it might be a love letter.

Merry's hands shook as she opened the note after Peggy left the room. Who else could it be from but Darcy, and yet he'd never communicated with her this way. Still, she chided herself, times were different now. There was not the same need for secrecy.

Merry,

I need your help. Come to the Market Street Wharf alone at eight. Do not fail me.

Darcy

Drat, what was amiss? But at least Judge Shippen was out tonight and had taken both Polly and Sally with him to a lecture. Only Peggy was in, probably expecting her suitor, General Arnold, who would keep her occupied tonight.

Just before eight, Merry put on a cloak and sneaked out the back door, just as she had in the old days, when the British had held the town. She was slightly miffed, however, that Darcy would call her out in the evening. Even with the Americans in town, the streets were not that safe after dark. Still, anything for Darcy, and he'd no doubt escort her back. She only prayed this sudden summons was not the precursor to a farewell. The French-bound packet ships always left from the Market Street Wharf now.

The moment Merry was out the back door, Peggy summoned the five soldiers, led by Captain Stephen Michaelson. They hardly looked like General Arnold's men tonight; their uniforms had been replaced by dark breeches and tunics, and, as she'd asked, not one wore a powdered wig. They looked quite the part of dockside ruffians. She shivered at the thought of what was to come for Merry Morgan and that Frenchman.

"I've thrown all her things together in two satchels and this one trunk. Be sure it all gets aboard. And the man's clothes?"

"He got his note an hour ago and went right out," Stephen told her. "His gear's all stowed aboard already."

"Good. And you have your pistols? Remember, I told you the man's quite dangerous, and you might have to force both of them to it in the end. He won't recognize any of you, will he?"

"No, ma'am. An' we'll do a real convincing job, just like you taught us."

"Fine," she said, and forced a sweet smile to her lips. She rested a quick hand on Stephen's arm and then withdrew it. She noted that he could hardly keep his eyes off her, and that he was shivering a bit, even in the warmth of this spring night. My, but her clever John André would be proud of her, she told herself as the five men filed out the back with Merry's things and she propped the notes she'd forged for her father and Polly to find on Merry's table.

You're learning fast, Peggy Shippen, she told herself. And if you play the rest right, you'll have John André himself eating out of your hand someday, and begging for every scrap, too!

Merry paced the wharf. Lapping water and fog bells sounded in the distance as the mist rolled in. This was not a busy place after dark. Now why hadn't Darcy told her exactly where to meet him along the length of the wharf? From the recesses of her hood, flipped forward to hide her light hair and face, she scanned each passing man for his height, his walk, his face.

Finally, she dared to ask the question that worried her the most, and learned there was a French packet weighing anchor at dawn. At that news, her stomach felt as if she'd been devouring sour green apples. She strolled out just a bit to look at the ship, a three-masted sloop with several guns named the *Audace*.

"Daring," she said aloud, "I think *Audace* means daring." Her voice sounded strangely distant, as distant as the creaking ropes and the muted bells.

Her heart began to beat very fast. What if Darcy was leaving here . . . leaving her? She needed him, she loved him! With all the trust they had built lately, surely their love affair would blossom to a permanent commitment!

She could feel her pulse quicken. Little panicked butterflies inside her fluttered for freedom. She feared she might be sick as she stared down through the drifting scrim of fog at the inky water slapping against the wharf. She almost thought she had fallen in when the hempen bag whooshed down over her head. At least two persons held her, gagged her. She fought for breath; she fought their hands. She felt she was drowning as they dragged her off her feet and carried her away.

Chapter Eleven

Two men with brusque voices carried Merry aboard a ship, one of them pressing the sack over her head against her mouth so that she couldn't scream. They carted her down steps, into a hall she could tell had to be narrow from the way her feet grazed the wall. They bumped her head against a door. They laid her on a bunk and tied her wrists and ankles. Only then did they loose her mouth and lift the sack from her.

She blinked in lantern light at two strangers leaning over her. "Who are you? I demand—"

"Quiet, lady, or we'll gag you, too!" one of the ruffians threatened, and shook a fist in her face until the man behind him pulled him back.

"If you'll just behave, you'll be much better off, Mistress Morgan," that man, a red-haired one, said, snatching off his cap as if to tip it to her. He seemed ludicrously polite despite his rough garb; his eyes darted nervously everywhere, even in this closed room. "You'd best get comfortable. Sleep if you can. You'll have a bit of a wait till just before dawn, and then we'll give you a little while to get prettied up. We'll insist on that. Your clothing is here, and if you don't choose something proper I will. What you have on just won't do for your own wedding," he added, and the man behind him snickered.

"My—my own wedding?" she choked out. Her mind raced. She was here to be forced into a wedding? Toller Devlin! Had he stooped so low as to hire some sailors to abduct her for him? But Toller would never be able to face his precious Philadelphia society once she told everyone he'd forced her.

"If Toller Devlin's paid you for this, I promise to pay you more to let me go, so just—"

"Toller Devlin? No, ma'am, you'll be leaving for Paris at dawn as bride to Darcy Mont, who's aboard, anxiously awaiting the happy event."

She gasped as one man snickered again. She sputtered another demand. She wanted to ask a hundred questions. Nothing made sense, and her insides rocked, while this ship only shifted restlessly in its berth.

"Get some rest now," the red-haired man, who was obviously in charge, ordered. "You'll have an armed guard right here with you all night, so just stay put and keep quiet."

He turned down the lantern hanging on a wall peg by the bed until it flickered out but left the other burning by her guard as he went out. Still stunned, she surveyed the small, low-ceilinged cabin. Just this recessed bed, a table and two chairs. And yes, in the corner, her traveling trunk and two satchels with her clothes piled in haphazardly and spilling out the tops. She tried to think. Darcy; they had said Darcy. Had he arranged all this? Did he mean to wed her before they sailed for France? But why in this furtive fashion, when she had made it so plain that it was all she longed for? No, it could not be.

The night stretched on. Her attempts to question her guard met with brusque refusals. She tried to relax, but couldn't. Surely the Shippens had missed her by now and sounded an alarm. Drat, how had this happened? She wasn't dreaming, but it wasn't real. She drifted through a sea of fears and possibilities. And then, as dawn pearled through the single porthole she had not noticed last night, she heard a snatch of French in the hall outside. Not Darcy's deep voice, but French nevertheless.

The door started to open, and she sat up as the red-haired man came back inside and untied her feet and hands. He set down a bowl of water and a chamber pot, then rummaged through her things and tossed her best satin gown at her. It was badly wrinkled. "Five minutes alone, as we're in a rush since the fog cleared," he said. "When I come back, I'll lace you up. Five minutes and then your bridegroom will be in."

She trembled as she hurried. Whether Toller Devlin or Darcy was her captor, nothing made any sense. But she pulled on her ruffled and ribboned sky-blue satin gown, and struggled to pin up stray tendrils of her disheveled hair. She washed her face and hands. Straining to reach behind her back, she had herself partly hooked into her gown when two of the men came back. The redhead finished the job for her, thrust a nosegay of early spring flowers in her hands. Funny, she thought as the fog cleared inside her head, they were the very hues and kinds from the Shippen yard, so perhaps the Shippens knew all about this and had sent them. Shaken and stunned, she faced the door as the other guards came in with yet another man—and Darcy!

"Darcy!" She started for him, arms outspread. "I can't believe this! I wasn't sure whether—"

She stopped in horror. Darcy's face was rigid as a stone mask. Cold hatred iced his eyes. One of the guards stepped closer to Darcy's back.

"*Sacrebleu*, get this over now!" Darcy clipped out. She didn't need his tone to tell her something was very, very wrong. There was dark stubble on his face, and his frock coat was wrinkled. Wouldn't he at least have shaved and changed?

"Darcy, just explain to me—"

The red-haired man's voice rang out, interrupting her. "Stand here, Mistress Morgan! Minister, proceed." He shoved a short, balding man in front of her and Darcy.

The man cleared his throat and began, "Dearly beloved . . ."

No, Merry thought, the red-haired man stood close on her other side, this cannot be happening. But when she opened her mouth to protest, her captor poked a pistol barrel in her ribs. And when she glanced behind her she saw that the man at Darcy's back had a pistol pressed between his shoulder blades.

So they were both being forced, Merry thought. But by whom?

"Darcy Mont, count of Belfort, do you take this woman to be your lawfully wedded wife, to have and to hold, in sickness and in health, in penury and prosperity, from this day forward in perpetuity, so help you God?" the minister was asking.

"I think God had best help her," Darcy said. From behind him came the distinct click of a pistol being cocked.

"Do you so pledge, sir?" the minister repeated.

"I do take this woman," Darcy intoned.

Merry was suddenly very afraid to dart another glance his way. Take her where, how? She saw that Darcy had gripped his hands so hard before him that his big knuckles had gone white. She shuddered to think of the violence and fury he was holding in—for now. Then the minister's words spilled over her and, despite her inner turmoil, she grasped what ones she could.

"And you, Meredith Morgan, do you take this man to be your lawfully wedded husband, to honor and obey, till death you do part?"

Despite the gun in her ribs, she almost refused, for the sight of Darcy's anger had shocked her. But since someone had cruelly set this up to force them both, surely Darcy would understand that she had had no part in it when she explained. Together they could clear this up, arrange to get back to Philadelphia if he insisted, find whoever had perpetrated this marriage she had wished for so fervently, though not like this.

"I do," she choked out.

"What God hath joined, let no man put asunder," the little minister concluded, his haste apparent. He handed a paper to the red-haired man and beat a path to the door.

"This whole affair is legal and binding, Darcy Mont," the man told him, waving the paper once in his face. "It will go in the public books here in Philadelphia. If you do not keep this woman for a wife, you and your country's honor will be publicly sullied. And now, before we leave you two to sail off together, a word with you, Mistress—I mean, Mrs. Mont."

When Merry turned to face the man, she saw no evidence of the gun he'd held on her earlier. "Now you look here," she began, but he pulled her out into the hall. There was no protest from Darcy, who still had a cocked gun in his back. In the narrow corridor, the red-haired man shoved Merry against the wall and covered her mouth with his hand. And then he spoke, supposedly to her, but the loud words were obviously meant for Darcy inside.

"Sorry to pull you away from your bridegroom, ma'am," he said clearly, "but you promised the rest of the money now, remember? After all, we did everything you said."

Merry tried to claw at him, but he grabbed both wrists in his other hand and went calmly on. "Thanks, ma'am. And I want to wish you luck with your new life—and your new fortune! Guess I should call you countess now, eh? Good going on catching that big fish, even if you did need help netting him!"

Here he paused, as if she'd said something quietly back to him. Then he plunged on with his obviously rehearsed speech. "No, don't worry a bit about the wedding night. Like you said earlier with your face and body he'll get used to having a wife real fast. And Mistress Shippen says you can pay back the rest of the money you borrowed for this after you get your hands on his fortune."

Quickly the man dragged her back to the door and shoved her in past Darcy's guards, who quickly exited the room. She was jolted to see that Darcy was now tied on the bed, naked but for his breeches! She gaped at him wide-eyed while he glared daggers at her.

"Have a good trip then, countess, and hope the British cruisers don't get you," the red-haired man behind her said. "You may kiss the bride, count!" The sound of the door being slammed and bolted mingled with the men's laughter and the distant cries of French sailors to cast off.

She ran to Darcy and fumbled with his wrist ties. His legs were bound, too. His boots, stockings, coat and shirt lay strewn on the floor, and his breeches were half unbuttoned.

"Darcy, none of this makes sense! I'm so sorry!"

"And stupid to untie me now. I am just waiting to break that pretty neck of yours for this trick!"

Her hands halted on his ropes, but she had undone enough that he yanked himself free in a fury.

"Trick?" she cried. "But I didn't know a thing of it, I swear! Both of us have been duped and forced! I don't care what they said! I had a gun on me, too! You can't believe that I—"

"Can't I?" he roared as he threw his ropes away and fumbled with his ankle ties. "I did not see a gun on you! It all fits! You are guilty as hell! You could not get me any other way!"

She backed away from him toward the door as he freed his legs. "We'll make the captain take us back!" she cried. "I'll prove it to you! Peggy will have to admit that I borrowed no money—'' And then she crumpled against the door as if she had been struck by lightning. Peggy Shippen! Surely even she would not go to such lengths! And why? Had losing John André actually unbalanced her? How could Peggy have known this would make Darcy hate her, would make her suffer more than if Peggy had just sent him away! But she had no time to think it through as Darcy grabbed her arm and yanked her into his harsh embrace.

He reached behind her to pound a fist twice on the door, though he must have known well enough that no one would come to let him out. Then, one bare arm around her waist, he hauled her over to the wooden porthole and slammed it open. He clipped out a string of oaths in French. They were out into the Delaware already! The spires and rooftops of Philadelphia were shrinking fast.

''Damn you, Merry Morgan.'' He leaned his face on the porthole, and his voice was muffled for a moment. ''We are going to France when I said I would never take you. But—'' he lifted a cold, austere face to glare at her ''—it seems you are taking me—temporarily. But do not think you have me where you want me. I heard what you said to that lackey you hired, but do not think I will be 'so besotted by your face and body' that I will forgive and forget and take you to court as my wife. You want to play wife, you can do it at night in that bunk to amuse me en route, but I will be damned if I will parade you politely in the daytime!''

''This isn't my fault, I said. Let me go, you're hurting me!''

'''To honor and obey,' I believe these farcical wedding vows you planned declared. It is a relief to know—'' his voice was mocking now ''—that this voyage will not be dull or boring with you for entertainment. But I will be sending you straight back as soon as we land!''

''I—I have no money with me for a return fare!''

He shook his mussed head. That little cleft in his chin that heralded anger looked hewn from stone. ''I would never have taken you for a fortune hunter. You would think I would learn not to be deceived and betrayed by beautiful women! Do not worry about your fare back, my dear. Since I intend for you to be my whore and not my wife, I will keep track and pay you good French livres for your...services!''

"You insulting bastard! Don't you dare speak to me that way!'' She tried to pull away as he sat back on the bed and roughly began to unhook her gown. He held her there with his legs clasped around her knees. "We have to talk this out, figure it out,'' she babbled. "There's an explanation!''

"Quiet! I detest being held captive, Merry, and you've tricked me into this! You do owe me a wedding night, even in broad daylight! So, instead of lying *to* me, you are going to lie *with* me!''

He felt so trapped and furious that he saw crimson behind his eyes, heard his blood roaring through his veins. He wanted to punish her for what she had done to him—for what she was doing to him even now, so that he wanted her when he should detest her. For making him want to believe her when she had to be lying!

He knew he was none too gentle in stripping her garments off; her struggles availed her nothing. When flowers cascaded all over them, they both looked surprised to find she was still clinging to her ragged bouquet. Curse her, she had been prepared for this wedding even to the point of flowers. Why should he give her a choice when she had taken all his choices from him?

He tumbled her over him into the bunk with a quick roll of his body. She smacked flat on her back on the hard bed, which was barely wide enough for two. He finished divesting her of the chemise caught around her lush hips and yanked his breeches down and off. He was glad when she looked frightened, when the tears started. *Sacrebleu*, if she thought she could lead him around by the nose after forcing him to this, she had a good lesson to learn!

"Darcy, don't, not this way. I didn't—''

He pressed against her to still her thrashing, then tangled his hand in her loosed golden hair and held her head still. Tears glimmered in each blue eye, tearing his heart out. Damn, damn, damn her, he raged silently, for her looks reminded him so of another who had led him on and then sought to ruin him. For one moment his mind hazed over with the terrible memories of that woman. And then Merry's pleading voice jolted him back to the present.

"Darcy, whatever you do to me in anger and revenge, I want you to know I—I have loved you."

"Do not say that! Am I supposed to believe that now?"

"Yes! Yes, it's the truth!"

The truth? Could he trust this? Could a woman be telling him the truth at last? "Convince me," he choked out. "Do not be just wife or mistress, then. Be my woman, and make me stop thinking all these awful thoughts," he rasped before his mouth took hers.

She shuddered at the demanding power of the kiss, but it softened suddenly and turned tender and beseeching. She stopped struggling. His hand loosed her hair, and his fingers brushed, then kissed her tears away. Gently his tongue probed for entry to her mouth. With a moan, she let him in. Smoothly, carefully, he inserted a knee between hers and lifted it so that she lay open to him, as if he would enter her instantly that way, too.

She thought to protest, to tell him how fast he was taking this, how he had frightened her, but the aura of danger in Darcy had always been part of his appeal. She responded now because she knew that despite his anger he still needed her. And he had calmed himself to be the considerate lover he had always been, however passionately possessive. If she could only batter through his inner walls, so high and ice-coated, to let her trust and love free his trust and love! And maybe then, even if he refused to honor this mockery of a marriage, he would grow to want her for a wife someday—

The rolling of the ship seemed to lull them. They slowed and savored their kisses and caresses even more. The harshness of the morning faded. Nothing else existed; the locked door, the hasty, forced departure didn't matter in these moments. She stroked the angular planes of his back, massaged the stretch of muscles there and his taut waist while he kissed her everywhere. She kneaded his hips and lean buttocks until she had him moaning, too, though nothing stopped his slick-tongued marauding up and down and around.

And then, when she was certain they would both explode before they were even joined, he rolled onto his back and lifted her above him, his hands holding her hips hard. He lifted her clear off him and slid her up until her head almost bumped the top of the recessed bunk; he nibbled and kissed and licked the trembling length of her again, breasts to loins, while she dangled there over him, hair and hands dragging over his face and chest to drive him on.

"You evidently want to be in charge," he muttered, breathing hard. "So...you...are." And he pierced her and settled her down on him as if she would ride him. With the defiant challenge on his face, he must expect her to do just that, she thought, dazed.

"Oh, Darcy, I don't know how—"

"Learn. Such a bright woman, to figure this abduction and marriage out. Now figure *this* out too."

She froze, her weight impaling her on him. "I told you all this was not my fault!"

"I think it is, so make the best of it," he ordered, his voice both terse and teasing. "On our voyage, I will teach you everything I like—wife!"

She ignored the bitterness of that last word. "Before you send me back alone?" she challenged.

He bounced once so that they were joined deeply, perfectly together. Then his hands lifted to fondle her breasts. Suddenly her urge to fight him fled. She felt emboldened; excitement coursed through her. She didn't want to fight this man but to fight for him.

"Are you telling me no right now?" he asked.

"What if I do refuse?" she dared, propping herself up a bit, her hands flat on his hard belly. "Lock me up? Chain me? Torture me—more than this, I mean?"

But she could not know how much her words about his chaining her and locking her up hurt him. He lowered his hands to grasp her thighs and squeezed his eyes shut. Memories of what the scandalmongers had whispered about him at court sliced through him. He was not going to let them say it again of him, not with another wife, not after that other tragedy! And yet he could not stop wanting and needing Merry! What had possessed him to think he could force her? Even now he had to make amends. He opened his eyes to drink in her lovely, bold face. His words came more quietly than he intended.

"You've held me captive from the first day we met, Merry," he whispered. "That's why I lost my temper. We shall stop this, then. I regret this . . . between us . . . so rough. It was my mistake from the first!"

But then Merry Morgan did, indeed, take charge. She began to fight for him in another way. She dazzled him with a shaky smile as she began to move against him. He could only suck in a breath as her sweet, supple body caressed and loved his. They rocked in rhythm with the ship, then even more wildly, as if plunging through crashing seas. He closed his eyes and pulled her down against him, savoring the very scent of her. He moaned her name and love words he could not hold back as his motions matched hers and sent them spinning off into the vastness of sweet oblivion together.

The first few days, until they were far out at sea, two armed sailors brought them food and wine three times a day and then relocked their door. When Darcy demanded they be allowed to meet the captain and have the freedom of the ship, they never even promised to pass the message on. But the fourth day he was taken out alone and came back down to say that the captain had been told they were political prisoners—French people spying for the British, no less!—being returned forcibly to France. Darcy thought he had convinced the man of their story and they would have the freedom of the ship. If only she could convince Darcy of *her* story, Merry thought, and make him believe she had never tampered with the personal freedom he cherished so for everyone.

Their door was unlocked daily now; that seemed, at least, to unlock their pent-up feelings about their plight.

"Merry, I admit I never thought you were one for tricks and lies, but maybe I have created a monster."

"And what is that charming compliment supposed to mean?" she demanded, hands on her hips over the same flower-sprigged dressing gown she had worn that night he'd come through her window and they had almost made wild love on the floor of her room. Even the memory of that made her want him again, she fumed.

He tipped back in his chair while resting his booted feet on the side of the bed on which she sat. Her beautiful, alluring body was entirely too close for him to think clearly. "I mean that I am the one who taught you deceit and trickery so that you could survive as a spy," he explained. "You had to do it as Freedom Flame, and you evidently took to it a bit too well."

"You stupid, stupid man!" she threw at him as she jumped up to pace about the room. "I hated every minute of it, and I have never lied to *you*! I tell you, I did not plan your abduction! If so, I would have not have told you how much I wanted to go to France with you! Or how I desire you! Or love you! And all that is the truth. I think Peggy Shippen masterminded this mess we're in!"

"But Toller Devlin has always had her ear, and he wanted you from the first for his own!" Darcy insisted. "She would not have crossed him to ship you off with me!"

"Don't you see?" She spun to face him, her hands lifted. "I've been thinking and thinking about it. Toller was John André's friend as much as he was Peggy's—probably more, with their fierce Tory ties. Maybe Toller even knew André was using her just to amuse himself while he was in Philadelphia. And when André left without taking her away as his bride she blamed Toller, too! And if Peggy set this whole thing up, it would explain the note she handed me personally to come to you, my clothes delivered, my bouquet from the Shippen garden."

"I remember the hatred in her eyes when she looked at us together at the dance celebrating the French alliance," he admitted. "But I still can't believe she was clever enough to plan all this! She hasn't had the practice in underhanded dealings you have." He shook his head and raked his fingers through his loosened hair. How he wanted to believe this, and yet he had once been so thoroughly taken in by another woman he adored—by another wife. "And had you talked to Peggy about my being a count?" he asked. "About my so-called fortune that red-haired bastard mentioned outside this door just before they left us?"

"No, not a word." Merry's long, loose tresses brushed her shoulders as she shook her head. "It's the only part of it I can't figure, but perhaps she heard gossip somewhere else."

He rocked on the back legs of the chair. He had his hands stuck under his armpits as if to keep himself from hauling Merry into his lap as he wanted to. He had been thinking about something their captor had said to her in the hall. She had supposedly told the man that with her face and body Darcy would not long protest being wed to her. But Merry Morgan had always been quite modest and unaffected by her beauty, so it had been eating at him that she never would have boasted that, and especially not to some stranger. Also, if she had been lying to him just now about Peggy Shippen, she could have said she had let it slip to Peggy about his title and his wealth—both of which he'd have forfeited right now to believe Merry.

He smacked his chair down and stalked away from the bed to the porthole and glared out. The sky boiled with gunmetal gray clouds; the waves rolled black, slashed with crests of angry white. A storm suited him. He had to think, away from the temptation of Merry. Even if she had his body in thrall, he would not surrender his heart! He had vowed it. Anyway, she would want out of this marriage by the time they reached France after living in such close quarters with a bitter man who could not forget.

"I'm going up on deck. The sea is kicking up. Stay here," he said. He grabbed his frock coat and yanked it on as he went out and slammed the door.

Merry paced and prayed for what seemed hours as the ship rolled and plunged. Cabin furniture scraped back and forth across the floor. But the pitch did not bother her stomach as much as she had feared. She remembered how she'd been sick over the side the night of the retreat from Long Island, when Darcy had held her shoulders. They had come so far together, and yet he was not here to hold her now!

She stopped pacing, since it was only making her reel like a drunk. Rain rattled down outside. That would bring him back down, she thought. But it did not.

The wind howled to match her own fears, and the rocking of the waves seemed to suit her own inner turmoil. Perhaps that was why Darcy had welcomed the storm and rushed up to embrace it instead of her. She would have to tell him he had every right to send her back home the moment they arrived in France. Her dreams that she could be his wife seemed so tenuous and tattered now. She had been foolish to think she could win him over, a man with such dark, secret demons. But even if she were going to lose him for good, she could not bear to forgo one moment with him. Only twenty or so more days to France, and this spring storm was surely pushing them even faster toward their destination *and* their separation. Suddenly, storm or not, she had to be with Darcy.

She wrapped her blue cloak around her and wobbled down the companionway and up the stairs to the deck. Just once around to find him, holding on to the guy lines she had seen on their strolls, she told herself. If she did not find him then, she would assume he was with the captain again and come back down to wait.

But she halted at her first step out on deck: the scene was terrifying yet magnificent. Waves smacked the hull and swept sideways on the deck. The wind whistled. The *Audace* lunged and smacked, lunged and smacked, as it rolled. Yet it plunged sturdily ahead, and she must, too. Then she saw Darcy just down the deck a little way, pressed back against the cabin house near a swinging, shuttered lantern.

Holding the strung ropes, she bent into the blast and stumbled toward him. "Darcy!" she shouted, but the wind ripped her voice away. Yet he turned toward her, startled, and reached to haul her hard against him.

"I told you—"

"I wanted to be with you!"

"I told you one other time," he roared above the wind. "Women on a ship—bad luck!"

"I'm sorry if I've been that for you! I just wanted to know you were all right!"

Salt spray drenched them both. Her hood ripped back, and her hair yanked free to whip both their faces. Together they bent along the rope to go back inside and stumble down the steps to their room. Panting, sodden, they leaned against the door of their cabin together. And then he pulled her close to tuck her wet head under his chin.

"You are much braver than I, my Merry."

"I've never known a braver man."

"Reckless, maybe, because I just did not care what happened to me at times. Now I have found a thing or two to care about." He thought of Amélie then, as he had not for days. She needed him, she loved him. And the cause of American freedom—freedom for everyone. And this woman in his arms.

"Let's take these wet things off and get warm in bed," he whispered against her cold cheek. "I will dry that hair."

"Yes, all right," she murmured, but she knew things still weren't settled between them.

They fell into a pattern that suited them both—a truce of sorts, though a formal peace treaty had hardly been negotiated. They were quite domestic in their habits of meals together or with the captain, their regular constitutionals about the deck, their conversations. And he was teaching her French, since he had admitted that she'd need it if it took several weeks to find a packet to send her back. If only there would be no ship available and she could stay on and on! Though she hated the pretending, she did so in a way to protect herself. She pretended that their lovemaking and compatibility in bed and out meant he might want to keep her with him.

America and the war seemed very far away, and they both regretted not knowing what was happening. But he had much to do at home to help Ambassador Franklin get more aid, he told her, though he did not tell her the old man would tease him, saying "I told you so!" when he showed up with Merry in tow. He feared what the court would make of her and do to her, but he knew as the voyage went on that he could not bear to send her away. And the closer they got to the shores of France, the more he became obsessed with how he would keep Merry from hearing both the lies and the truth about his past. Whatever jumble of emotions there was between him and Merry, he could not bear it if her hatred of him was added to the mix.

They sat today, the twenty-fourth day out, across from each other at the small table in their room chattering in French. Her good ear and the basic vocabulary she had picked up on her own impressed him. It was only when he spoke quickly that he lost her. He was trying very hard to focus just on their conversation, which today was about fickle fashions and prickly protocol at court, things he prayed she would never need to know. And yet he could not help but wonder if Merry Morgan, now the comtesse de Belfort, his little *rebelle américaine*, would not stand King Louis's courtiers on their ears.

As the May day was sunny and warm, she wore only her dressing gown over her chemise, and that was taking its toll on his concentration and composure. He kept remembering their delicious bout in bed last night, and even the crashing release he had achieved there didn't keep him from wanting her again now.

He glanced guiltily at her and shifted his position on the hard chair. Sunlight from the porthole glanced off her loosed golden hair and lit the tip of her pert nose. The fabric clung and stretched over her full bosom. Her breasts might not be in style at home, but they were the most beautiful he had ever seen. A pity French fashion had women's breasts pushed into such an unnatural shape—flat below, then shoved up above the neckline in bulging mounds. He did not like the idea of Merry on display to the court *roués*, and he vowed he would buy her some tippets and fichus, as well as gowns. He cleared his throat. Here he was at his age, feeling the guilty schoolboy staring at forbidden fruit, when it had been his for the asking these past few weeks.

He reached slowly for her hand across the table. She stared wide-eyed at his move in the midst of talk on varied curtsies to courtiers of different ranks.

"*Qu'est-ce que c'est?*" she asked.

"I just wanted to be sure you know the word for palm of the hand," he said, shifting to English. He scooted his chair around the table to hers, turned her hand palm up and kissed and licked her there.

"Oh! I think it's *la paume*. And what has that to do with curtsies?" she said, but her voice went lazy and languorous.

He ignored that question. "So clever, my Merry. And the word for fingers?" he inquired as he put each one of hers in his mouth in turn and sucked warmly, wetly on it before going on to the next.

"*Les doigts.* Mmm. Darcy Montour—" she murmured and leaned her head back against her chair to study him through half-closed eyes "—you do know how to change the subject."

He pulled her into his lap. She came willingly, her cheeks slightly flushed. Always his Merry seemed so natural and untouched, so very much herself. She could never have dreamed up the terrible scene of their forced marriage, he told himself for the hundredth time. But neither could she remain so untouched at the French court, even with—especially with—him at her side. But now she leaned her head trustingly on his shoulder while he caressed her throat and untied her robe.

"What word is next?" she whispered breathlessly.

"*Le bras*—the arm. *La cuisse*—the thigh. *Le sein*—the breast," he rasped as his hands moved over her with only the thin cotton chemise between them.

She nibbled on his earlobe when he picked her up and carried her to the bed. "*Le sein,*" she murmured. "But that means 'heart,' too. You have my heart, along with the rest of me, Darcy. Please, please, don't ever forget that!"

He forced himself just to take her hand, to look straight into her eyes. They both sensed that what he was about to promise was as close as he could come to trusting her, and that he was fighting even that in the lonely, still, secret places of his soul.

"Merry, I swear to you I will take good care of you the time we are in France together. I will try desperately to care for your heart as for the rest of you. On my sacred honor I swear!"

That had to be enough for now, she told herself as they slowly savored disrobing each other. For the first time in weeks she felt she had won a little victory, not only over Darcy, but perhaps over Peggy Shippen's terrible plans for her, too.

Merry lay in Darcy's arms in the dead of night. She was not certain what had awakened her; the sea rolled gently, and the May night was mild. Perhaps a sudden shift in his body. They had not minded the narrowness of their bunk in the long, sea-sweet nights. When a bump of stray elbow or knee wakened them, it often led to an even more intriguing sharing of the small mattress.

But then she realized what had waked her. His arms went tense. He jerked and muttered something garbled and held her very close. But when he spoke in his sleep, perhaps snared in some dream, she could hear each distinct, horrid word he said.

"You lying bitch," he ground out through obviously clenched teeth. "I ought to kill you, even if they do all talk!"

Merry froze, terrified, as his arms tightened again, then suddenly relaxed. Slowly his thrashing stilled; his breathing returned to normal; he shifted slightly away.

Her heart fell. He had been dreaming of her and thought that—that she was still lying—that she was a bitch. The hatred in his voice had been unmistakable! Tears stung her eyes and splashed to her cheeks with the first blink of her thick lashes. And here she had thought in these last days and nights, when they had been so close, that he believed her.

The tears of disappointment and remorse, even fear, tracked down her cheeks as she lay silent and stunned in his arms. There was nowhere to go to hide from him if he went into a rage. She was dependent on him for her very safety and sustenance. But what pained her most was that the love she had thought she saw in his waking words and his daily deeds merely cloaked his hatred and mistrust of her. And she had thought she had left all that somewhere back in the vast deep of the sea!

She lay awake until morning, trying to master her fear. She couldn't let Peggy Shippen win, if she had indeed done this to her and Darcy. Surely the better, kinder aspects of Darcy's nature would overcome his bitter inner self. She scrubbed tears from her cheeks as he awoke and hoped the morning kiss he took would not taste salty. She intended to go on fighting for him, whatever the risks.

I'm like a soldier leaving harsh Valley Forge for a new campaign in another theater of war, she told herself. I'm a soldier fighting for what she believes in strongly enough to die for it!

Chapter Twelve

They disembarked from the *Audace* in Le Havre, the great port city of France, and took a smaller packet up the Seine. On May 20, 1778, Merry caught her first glimpse of the gray spires and blue-gray roofs of Paris.

She pressed her face to the glass of the carriage Darcy had hired to take them just a mile outside the city to the little village of Passy, where he owned a house. "I sold my Paris mansion and gave up the *appartement* at Versailles before I first sailed for America," he told her. Ordinarily she would have asked why, but today she was too busy taking in the sights. She had been so impressed with the fact that the roads were paved as much as fifty miles outside Paris, but she was disappointed when she saw the venerable capital city up close. As their high-slung coach and four crawled and jerked along at a snail's pace through the mass of humanity, she saw that the inner streets of Paris were anything but grand.

"Why, they're small, crooked, crowded and dirty," she said to Darcy. "Even New York is cleaner, and Philadelphia's streets are much straighter and wider!"

"Paris and even Versailles will not be all you have imagined, Merry. A glittering, enticing shell, but within—" His voice dropped to nothing and he shrugged.

Merry pressed her face to the window again. She prayed that Darcy hadn't just been describing himself. That he didn't really believe those words he had gritted out in his nightmare—that she was a lying bitch who was trying to deceive or somehow betray him.

At least the sight of the king's vast blue-green hunting preserve, the Bois de Boulogne, and the lovely faubourgs, those fashionable garden towns along the edge of the city's sprawl, pleased her more. And when they rattled through forests and vineyards into Passy itself in the late afternoon, she breathed a sigh of relief.

"Oh, Darcy, it's lovely!"

Her head turned to take it all in as they rolled into the small stone-housed village, which was set on a hillside. Darcy's big house was of muted dove-gray stone that had been softened by the years. It hardly looked the mere country cottage she had imagined. He helped her down in the flagstone-paved courtyard, where a moss-lipped fountain splashed quietly. She looked up and around, awestruck at the overhang of a fine slate roof studded with chimney pots above three stories of shuttered windows.

"We are hardly expected," he said, as if to apologize, "and I only keep a staff of nine when I am away. Let me escort you in."

She hesitated on the broad stone steps, her hand grasping his arm tightly. That simple, unassuming comment and the reality of his wealth and position panicked her, as it had not since the day at Valley Forge when she first learned who he really was.

"Will you tell the servants who I am?" she asked, suddenly shy. "If you don't want to admit we're married, we could—"

"Of course I plan to admit it. Welcome to my—our, I should say—home, *ma chère comtesse*."

And so it started out as the most marvelous welcome to Darcy's French life she could have had.

The first day and night they were in Passy flew by on gossamer wings for Merry. Darcy was solicitous. The house was spacious, elegant and lovely. The servants were quick and kind—and they understood her French! They were too well trained to appear curious or judgmental, as she had feared they might.

Their suite of seven large rooms on the second floor overlooked a flower garden laid out in the new style Darcy had told her of in which man-made art imitated nature. The distant vista merged with hazy hillsides strung with grapevines that were like green ribbons. As busy as she was, from time to time Merry would just stand and look around, dewy-eyed. How she wished she could share all this with her sister! When Libby and Cam heard she had gone away, they would be so worried. She would try to write them, of course, and perhaps Judge Shippen, too, but meanwhile, what would everyone at home think? Perhaps they would know that she was with Darcy, that everything was well. But was it?

She reminded herself that Darcy was being a dear husband. She tried hard to shut out the danger signs: the threats when he talked in his sleep; the bitter tone that too often crept into his voice; his, as the French put it, *ennui* instead of *joie de vivre* at being back in France. But even when she blinked her eyes the fantasy was real, at least for now. Oh, she prayed, if only Darcy could overcome his inner mistrust and hidden dislike of her to love her enough! If only he wanted her for a wife and would not send her home without him!

Their first morning, at their breakfast of hot chocolate and delicious flaky rolls with honey, the butler came in to announce Ben Franklin, whom Merry was pleased to hear rented rooms in Passy, had come calling. At Darcy's bidding he was escorted in. Leaning on his walking stick, looking very much the same, in came the gray-haired, bespectacled old man, beaming.

"My dear friend," Merry told him as she kissed his cheek after Darcy's hearty greeting, "there is no one I would rather see for our first visitor!"

"Best tell your lady not to kiss cheeks at court, Darcy," Ben Franklin observed, winking at her. "Still, I believe she'll set her own styles there and get away with it, however much that vulture Lord Stormont storms!" he said, laughing at his own pun. "You'd think that with war declared between France and Britain the whining wretch would go home. We need something more to dislodge him from hanging on both the king and the queen!"

"Lord Stormont or no Lord Stormont," Merry told them, "I know of no one else here to peck on the cheek but you! But what is wrong with it at court, pray tell, Mr. Franklin?"

"Quite rude to smudge the layers of powder and rouge both men and ladies wear," Franklin said with a droll grin after a sip from his Sevres saucer full of hot chocolate. Merry's eyes darted to Darcy. He had forgotten to tell her that. And what else, she wondered nervously, had slipped his mind? Would she be walking into a hornets' nest if he took her to Versailles with him? He'd never promised he would, and she hadn't asked, but she longed to go.

"I hear," Ben Franklin was saying, "that you two are wed! I couldn't wait to come with my best wishes before everyone else descends with theirs!" He sent a smug smile Darcy's way. "Surprised I found out so fast, eh? Ah, but France is teeming with spies, and at least a few of them are mine! Now, both of you, tell me everything about your sudden nuptials and how things are going at home in my Philadelphia. And then we have a great deal to do to plan our next assault at Versailles, the three of us!"

Darcy managed to get old Franklin off alone for a garden stroll, despite the elderly statesman's gouty legs and the fact that he was still sputtering angrily over the details of Major John André's billeting himself and staff in the Franklin house. But Darcy went straight to the point anyway.

"My marriage was not my idea, Ambassador, but I have an idea or two about not dangling my little lamb before the wolves at court. And so I want her kept out of our machinations there."

Franklin plopped himself down on a stone bench amid the myrtle and pink oleanders and glared up at Darcy. "You don't really intend to keep her imprisoned here in this rural nunnery like some holy sister who's taken vows, do you, Darcy?"

Franklin saw Darcy's temper flare at the word *imprisoned* and knew why. In the more than two years he had been here in Paris, he'd learned a lot about the personalities at court. Among other things, he'd learned why the elusive comte de Belfort had left under a cloud of scandal to throw himself so wholeheartedly into the fight for American freedom. But it was time, the old man thought, for Darcy to come out from under that cloud, and Merry Morgan was the sunshine to make it happen.

"I hardly intend to lock her up!" Darcy insisted. "But she was never happy embroiled in all that secretive espionage back home, and she would not be here, either!"

"Good, because I've had my fill of that, too. I believe we're ready for open frontal action on the king and his queen. By the by, Darcy, Marie Antoinette has at last become his queen in every sense of the word."

Surprised, Darcy sank down on the bench beside Franklin. "She's bedding with His Majesty now, you mean? After five years of marriage, it is about time!"

Franklin nodded. "Advice from her Austrian Hapsburg family—and the knowledge, I believe, that however much one enjoys one's little *coterie*, it is best to share in the life of one's mate, king or not. I would venture to say they are quite the happy pair now, something we should all take to heart. And—" he grunted as he got to his feet and turned to stare pointedly down at Darcy "—that's the reason we now court the queen, too. And," he threw back over his shoulder as he started away, "that is the reason you will decide to take your beautiful young bride to Versailles when the queen's invitation comes today."

Darcy jumped up to head the wily old man off. "You *have* been busy, Ambassador Franklin, considering that we arrived only yesterday afternoon, and quite unannounced."

"Temper, temper my friend," Franklin scolded as he leaned on his walking stick. "I value Merry Morgan, in some ways more than you do. And so I tell you that taking her to court and simply letting her be herself is nothing you should fear. She's natural, independent, bold and bright—like our new country. I recall you told me some such yourself about her once."

"But—"

"And, friend Darcy," Ben Franklin interrupted when he saw that the handsome, brooding man would protest more, "I have heard about your wife—your first wife—and what happened. But however beautiful or influential or despicable that woman was, this is Merry Morgan you are wed to now!"

"Ma chère rebelle," Darcy said, as the anger he had thought he felt at the old man dwindled to nothing but gratitude.

"Exactly. They'll flock to her like honey and give our cause a needed boost." Franklin patted Darcy's arm as if he were one of his grandsons before he shambled back into the house.

The next night, the elegant crowd at Versailles swarmed toward the Salle de Spectacle for the queen's command performance by the Comédie Française. Merry's breath came quick and shallow; she held tightly to Darcy's brocaded arm. Rapid French buzzed about her everywhere; she had been introduced to numerous new rouged and powdered faces, and they and their names began to blur, too.

The sky-blue satin gown she had been wed in felt heavy with the new pearls sewn to the bodice. They matched the stunning necklace Darcy had given her. She had not had time to order a new costume, and she regretted that now. The other women's gowns looked absolutely encrusted with jewels and embroidery; their whalebone panniers dwarfed hers. And their elaborate coifs towered over hers, though her new maid, Chloé, had padded and piled her hair a bit. She had worn powder, but no rouge, which was obviously the rage. She knew she looked as pale as a cameo next to their vibrant faces.

"You are the most stunning woman here tonight, bar none," Darcy told her, squeezing her arm.

She smiled up nervously at him, her eyes aglow with gratitude. "As long as you think so, that is all that matters." she told him in French. In the flow of this bejeweled, beribboned river of French nobility, he escorted her into the theater with its gold-and-blue curtain and its gilded and painted walls.

"So, *mon cher comte*," a petite, ravishing woman said to Darcy even as her wide-set hazel eyes minutely dissected every inch of Merry, "you have returned to us with a new wife, but maybe not so new." Her eyes were now traversing Darcy so slowly and thoroughly that she might as well have stroked him from lips to crotch!

Darcy quickly introduced the woman as Jeannette, the marquise de la Senart. Marquises outranked mere comtesses, Merry knew, but she suddenly couldn't recall the particular nuance to what particular curtsy was due a marquise, so she simply bobbed her knees. *"Enchantée, madame la marquise,"* she managed, though at home a rude woman like this might have been cut cold, or at least reprimanded by her husband, who stood there gawking as if he gave not one thought to his wife's other interests. Merry could tell the marquise was about to scold either her or Darcy, but suddenly everyone dropped grand, low curtsies or bows as Marie Antoinette and her entourage swept into the back of the room.

Merry emulated the marquise's show of deference, while Darcy swept a low, elegant bow beside her. Merry tilted her head and looked up through thick lashes to study the queen as she approached.

The Austrian-born Marie Antoinette was an interesting blend of beauty enhanced and homeliness disguised, Merry decided. Her complexion glowed with a transparent sheen, and her eyes were clear cornflower blue. Her radiant smile and charming oval face were framed by reddish-blond hair piled ever so high with poufs of feathers and diamonds that would have made Peggy Shippen's concoctions look like mere birds' nests. But the queen's forehead and lower lip bulged, unbalancing her profile and giving her a heavy facial appearance that belied her graceful, quick movements. Her garments glittered with both brocade and satin. Her rubies winked; light from her diamonds danced to dazzle the eye. And Merry greatly admired how she handled the same sort of narrow, three-inch-heeled shoes that were making her feel she had to totter along at Darcy's side.

"Ah, *mon cher comte* returned to us from America with a most charming bride," the queen said as she stopped right before them and gestured to them both to stand. Merry was thrilled to find she understood every word the queen said. And she was smiling at them while everyone else hovered and stared. After all, Merry thought, if she could get by the queen herself, surely nothing else here could cause distress.

"If only I could bring my American countrymen and women to see you, Your Gracious Majesty," Merry told her after they were formally introduced. "They would all be as honored and fortunate as I."

"So, better French than that Frank*leen*, eh?" the queen asked of Darcy, and he smiled back proudly in agreement. "But did you not teach him French, too?" the queen demanded with a tap of her painted fan on his arm. Darcy admitted it was true. "Then tell Frank*leen*," she went on, "this lovely bride of yours, your new blond and beautiful comtesse, she is wiser than him for all his sage sayings, yes?"

Merry did not catch the last of it, but she laughed along with everyone else. It seemed the entire court was leaning toward them, examining her as if she were a rare new species. Suddenly the queen asked her yet another question, and she was uncertain whether it was mere inquiry or blatant insult.

"Your gown, it is like *les femmes américaines* wear in your country, eh?"

"I...I wore my best gown, Your Majesty, not as fine as those of your court, but the best I had for now. And the way you all wear your hair...lovely." Merry chose her words carefully. "But, you see, at home women are so very concerned with the war and showing the British we refuse to let them set the styles—"

"The British!" the queen said, as startled as if Merry had slapped her. "The British never have set French styles, never shall!"

Merry bit her lower lip. That was not what Ben Franklin had complained. She had done it now. It was a snake pit here, where one wrong step could ruin everything! And poor Mr. Franklin was hovering over there along the pillared wall, thinking she and Darcy could help the cause with the queen.

"No British shall ever set the styles again, because the King and I believe in the American cause of liberty for all," the queen was declaring in a voice that was a bit too loud to be ladylike. "And so anyone here in King Louis's court who favors the English had best go home and forget a truce in this war." The queen's eyes were obviously challenging the frowning Lord Stormont's across the sea of elegantly coiffed heads. "And so we shall favor this new style of *la révolte américaine, à la comtesse de Belfort*," she declared, "who is just one more link between us and our dear rebel friends."

With another slanted glare Lord Stormont's way, the queen swept down the aisle to her seat and then sent back a liveried servant to request that the Belforts come down to sit just behind her group.

"I believe you are good luck, after all!" Darcy teased in English as he escorted Merry past the banked rows of gilt-and-velvet chairs filling with whispering courtiers. "Franklin's grinning from ear to ear, and Lord Stormont has seen fit to vacate the premises." Yet Darcy was frowning, Merry noted, as if the whispers still bothered him, despite the initial success they had made with the queen.

But Merry's hopes soared. At least her hair and gown had been accepted, if only for the fact that she'd explained that it was inspired by the *révolte* and not the British. Ben Franklin had said that Lord Stormont had long held sway over the young queen, but now she had as good as publicly insulted and dismissed him. Merry had not been happier in a long time, and she wished Darcy would just stop looking so very grim, as if everyone were whispering about him. It was no doubt her plain and almost peasantlike gown that set off these sibilant whispers that were following them like the waves of the sea. But, despite Darcy's obvious unease when she had feared she might fall flat on her unrouged face, she had never felt warmer toward him. That is, until just after they took their places and the queen whispered back over her shoulder against her fan.

"Do not fret for your bride's looks, my Louis Philippe D'Arcy, for I shall invite you both to the Petit Trianon soon."

The gold-and-blue-velvet tasseled curtain lifted, and the play, a tragedy, began. Merry's heart did not need a tragedy to break again. Though she sat stock-still and did not whisper a word to Darcy about what she had just overheard, a spate of new questions ate at her. Why had the queen accepted her so kindly if Darcy should fret for her looks? And what was this Trianon? Most unsettling of all, if her husband was named Louis Philippe, as well as D'Arcy, he had never seen fit to share that with her in all their so-called heartfelt conversations! Suddenly Merry's little triumph at Versailles seemed as sad as the tragic heroine bemoaning her losses on the stage.

* * *

"And what did that stunning Jeannette de la Senart mean when she said I'm your new wife and yet not so new?" she demanded of Darcy after Chloé had ungowned her and she had joined him in their bedroom. "And how dare she look you over, lips to crotch, that way?"

"I told you court morals would not be to your liking, Merry," he said, and leaned his shoulder on the window to gaze out into the warm late May night as if the discussion were over.

"Drat it, Louis Philippe, if that's your name—another name I had to find out from someone else! I suppose lots of ladies like la Senart have whispered that name in your ear, and here I didn't even know it!"

"I don't like those names. They are the names of kings. I go by D'Arcy among my friends," he said stubbornly, still looking out into the darkness. "I left those names behind me with my Paris house and my apartment at Versailles and a few other things when I went to America to work toward freedom and democracy."

"But you didn't leave the memories of your first wife behind, did you?" She approached him at the window and touched his arm. "They all knew her, admired her, didn't they?"

He flinched. "I'm just tired, Merry. Tired of the court already. But your uniqueness has garnered us an invitation to the Petit Trianon, the queen's country hideaway."

"But that's good for our cause, isn't it? Or are you tired of me already, too?"

He spun to face her. His countenance was grim. "Hardly. Never a dull minute with Merry Morgan, especially not as countess of Belfort. I am going for a little walk outside. Do not wait up."

"A walk sounds lovely. I could go along."

"Not tonight," he said, and pecked a chaste, quick kiss on her cheek. "It is one place you have not been invited," he threw back over his shoulder as he walked straight out of the high-ceilinged room and slammed the door.

She stood there in her chemise and dressing gown, very alone, very lonely. She had thought things had gone well at first, but they hadn't, and she was not certain why. It was as if some knowledge of the court—even of her husband—was just beyond her grasp, like this language that floated by too fast sometimes, however hard she studied it.

She sank down on the big soft bed and stared at the hands clasped tightly in her lap. *It's one place you haven't been invited.* Louis Philippe D'Arcy's words echoed in her head to torment her. She hadn't been invited to be his wife, either, she told herself, and it was then that the first tears started.

Merry slept poorly that night. Darcy did not return; he was nowhere to be seen the next morning. Chloé said he had ridden out, but she did not know where. Merry took her breakfast on the stone bench outside, where the butler had set a little table and insisted on serving her personally. Even the morning sun did not warm her. And then, it seemed, though Darcy did not return, the world began to come to her.

"*Madame*, a request has come from Simon Renart, the great Paris sculptor, to do a marble bust of you.... Oh, look, *comtesse*, an invitation from the Noailles family to a *soirée* today—that is the family of Lafayette, you know—and a man is inside to beseech you and the comte to attend a dinner in your honor given by the French foreign minister, the comte de Vergennes...and this card says if only you could find time to sit for a portrait by the court painter, Richard Laurens, and..."

It was like that throughout the day. Merry's head swam with the rush of people calling and the flow of invitations. Still, Darcy did not return, but she knew now that he would be proud of her. She was going to have many chances to promote the American cause. And she had somehow won over the court, which he had obviously feared would not accept her. If he mourned the loss of his first wife, who must have been beautiful and popular with them all, surely this would cheer him up! Yet, in the deepest recesses of her heart, she knew she would have traded all these gilt-edged invitations for his simple one last night to walk the gardens or to ride out with him today.

Darcy did return that evening and saw her joy at the day's events. He told her he was glad for the boost to the American cause, but he said little else. He apologized for being away so long, but acted as if the topic were then closed.

He didn't believe she could do it, she thought—become really popular at court, the way his first wife had been. He believed she attracted attention not for herself but for her "uniqueness," as he put it. But she would show him! Then he would love and want her as much as he obviously had his first wife!

She had learned that the woman's name had been Claudine de Mirabeau, and that she had come from a wealthy noble family. Without being too obvious, she gleaned from others that their marriage had been arranged when they were both quite young.

Drat it, Claudine, Merry agonized silently more than once, as if she were speaking directly to the faceless, departed beauty. I cannot regret you died to leave me Louis Philippe D'Arcy Montour, comte de Belfort, but you've left me a difficult precedent to follow. Now we'll just see if I can't win his esteem in this arranged marriage of our own!

The days rushed by. Merry, whom many courtiers jestingly called *Sainte Marie de la Révolte Américaine*—Saint Mary of the American Revolution—modeled for busts and porcelain miniatures and sat for portraits, one of which she ordered herself to surprise Darcy. She was astounded to realize she was actually revolutionizing the *toilettes* of the court ladies: gowns were simplified; panniers shrank; some sacrificed their rouge; hairstyles deflated to emulate Merry's lower, simpler one in what was called *coiffure à la révolte*. Even courtly giggles, smothered for years behind a fan or a ringed hand, gave way to an emulation of Merry's more open laughter.

But she made her share of enemies, too. Lord Stormont went back to England cursing her and vowing revenge. The doyenne of Paris designers and a former intimate of the queen, Mademoiselle Bertin, protested heartily at the simpler fashions. After all, she had made her reputation and her fortune decreeing constantly changing ornate styles. She had even created a new color every month, from queen's color—the hue of the queen's hair—to puce—the color of fleas, when the queen moaned that her little dog had them. But now the favorite hues were those of Merry's sky-blue gown or the colors of the American flag. The famous jeweler Bochmer detested Merry, because his income was devastated. All he could sell were simple gold frames to display miniatures of painted American themes—the new rage—and paintings of the smiling face of the countess of Belfort herself. But, despite these few drawbacks, Merry plunged ahead with making herself popular and her cause known—and her husband proud.

She was sure she was achieving all those goals the night she and Darcy were invited to the queen's private palace, the Petit Trianon. Resplendent in a new gold satin-and-lace gown with simple lines, Merry was still floating on her bubble of excitement and expectations. The dinners, dances, soirées and salons she had enjoyed in her first month in Paris were nothing compared to the June afternoon when they were included among the queen's most select *coterie* at the Petit Trianon, within the Swiss-guarded, gilded gates of Versailles.

"It's so beautiful here!" Merry murmured as they alit from their carriage, which had the Belfort crest painted on each door.

"This so-called *petit palais* was a gift of the king to his queen four years ago," Darcy observed. Then he added, more to himself than to her, "Out of duty, since he hardly loved her then."

Merry chose to ignore that comment. She had been so busy these past few weeks that she had given up agonizing over every dark, brooding look or comment her husband made. After all, she was doing all this to please him and to promote the cause they shared.

Merry's eyes drank in the sights and cherished them to tell her sister at home someday. She was surprised, though, how many people playing games or strolling about the lovely grounds were evidently considered "intimates" of the queen. People in pastels played at Battledore with wooden paddles and feathered shuttlecocks; others darted through lilac bushes imported from Judaea playing hide-and-seek or blindman's buff in front of the stunning, honey-hued palace that was the Petit Trianon. Platters piled with delectable food and crystal bowls swirling with iced wines and punches carpeted linen tables thicker than the tuberoses that carpeted the lawns.

When the queen spotted Merry, she pulled her into a group cavorting on a velvet-cut stretch of grass before the palace. Soon Merry was teaching everyone what she told them was the fashionable dance in America, Burgoyne's Surrender, which commemorated the great victory over the British at Saratoga. Soon, perspiring, laughing courtiers were pressed everywhere about her, and she had somehow lost Darcy in their midst. When she could extricate herself at last, Merry took two cold crystal cups of wine and went looking for him.

Servants attired like rural lads were lighting torches on poles now that daylight was fading. Merry strolled past the octagonal building called the Belvedere. Her feet crunched on the narrow gravel path winding past lakes and a grotto with a rushing cascade toward the Temple of Love, which Darcy had described to her earlier. She sensed he had come this way, since no one was about and he had spent a goodly amount of time alone lately, off on private rides for the day, as if he couldn't abide *société*. But she couldn't wait to share this triumph with him. Imagine, Merry Morgan, from a cottage on Staten Island, she marveled, shaking her head, teaching the queen of France to dance.

She had been right, she congratulated herself as she emerged through a screen of yellow jasmine and scented gardenia bushes. Before her stood the rounded, pillared Greek-style cupola called the Temple of Love, set on an artificial island in a man-made stream. Darcy sat alone on the top of eight steps that led to a nude statue of Venus on a pedestal inside.

"Hello!" she called. "I thought you might be here!" She hurried over the little arched footbridge toward him.

He did not answer or rise to greet her, but he took the wine she offered. "Best not sit. You'll sully that gold gown *à la* Saint Merry," he told her, but his voice bore no teasing lilt.

"I . . . I didn't see when you wandered off."

"So I noted." He downed the wine and set the glass aside.

"Or maybe I'm just getting used to it," she tossed back. Drat him, she fumed silently. Why did he have to always be grim lately, when things were going so well? Ben Franklin was thrilled at the progress they'd made toward obtaining funds, arms and even the promise of a fleet of ships while they had been here, so why couldn't Darcy unbend and rejoice a bit, at least on a lovely evening like this!

"You didn't mind my dancing with other men until they got the idea of the steps?" she asked, her tone tentative now.

"I believe I have seen worse at the French court."

She tried another tack. "Why doesn't the king ever come to the queen's revels, now that they're happily married?"

"Just because they sleep together now and hope to produce an heir, you mean?" he asked, both big arms sprawled across his bent knees. "Appearances aren't everything in a marriage, you know."

"Yes, I do know," she dared. "You've been very cold lately, at least during the day, and—"

"And I've singed the bed at night in my uncontrollable lust for you." He stood.

"That's not what I meant."

"Good. I'm relieved we haven't progressed—or regressed—that far yet."

"I just do not understand your bitter moods! Is it that you want to send me back now and think it's too late? I realize our forced marriage was not done at all civilly, as your arranged marriage to your first wife—"

He swung to face her, and his big hands cupped her shoulders to twist her to him. She dropped her cup, which shattered on the stone base of the marble goddess of love.

"You realize nothing about my first wife, Merry, absolutely nothing!" He was raving now. "But you'd like to know all about her and our marvelous marriage, is that right?"

"I would certainly like to understand it—and you," she began. She was holding her temper in check, but her voice was beginning to rise. "To know why everyone gives me those squinty gazes sometimes and whispers about my looks. I'm sure I can never hope to match her in beauty, in style, in cleverness, in sophistication. Or do I resemble her? Is that it?" she demanded. "And if so, is that why you were attracted to me in the beginning, because I looked somewhat like the woman you had loved and lost?"

He stood abruptly, pulling her to her feet. "You only want to know everything, is that right? You want to know it all because you think it can smooth over everything between us? *Sacrebleu*, you don't know the real me at all, never did! But, if you want to, just remember, you asked for this!'' He grabbed her wrist and began to pull her away from the Temple of Love and across the little bridge.

''Where are we going? What are you doing?'' she cried.

He swung her around and seized her upper arms for one quick shake that almost lifted her from the path. ''Do you want to know, my little prying spy? You are going to hear and see— and experience—everything, right from me, from beginning to end. And I do not want a moment's fuss from you when I call for the carriage, because we are leaving here now!''

She knew better than to protest when he marched her back and summoned their equipage around and hustled her up into it without so much as a farewell to the others. He conferred with the driver, then climbed in to sit on the leather seat across from her, his long legs on either side of her skirts, as if to block her from escape. The carriage jolted off, plunging into the dark with only its own exterior torches to guide it once they were outside the gold-tipped gates of Versailles.

They rode for a time without speaking. And then, when they took another turn into yet another forest, Merry realized that they were not headed home.

''Where are you taking me?''

''To have all your questions answered, once and for all.''

''But you can do that in Passy. I want to go home.''

''Home, is it now? Poor America, without the presence of its patron saint.''

''I resent this tone and this trick! Now turn this carriage around!''

He reached for her in the dark and hauled her to him so quickly that she half sprawled across his lap before he righted her. ''You resent this trick?'' His breath singed her face. ''I am only taking my wife to another of the fine places she might have married me for. My fifteenth-century ancestral home, Belfort, twenty miles from Paris.''

Merry gaped. Yet another surprise from this man. His arms went around her back and under her knees to anchor her to him.

"She...Claudine..." Her heart was thundering through her taut bodice and against his chest. "She *is* dead, isn't she? That's not to be my next surprise—that she's imprisoned or something there, waiting for you?"

To her amazement, he shouted a bitter laugh. He sobered instantly, however. "Join the crowd if you think she was ever imprisoned there. She is dead, Merry, very dead. But she haunts me yet, and all I've ever wanted to love. Yet perhaps, together, we can exorcise her ghost!"

He lifted her clear off his lap and crushed her to him. His hard mouth devoured hers as the carriage rumbled on into the black, black night.

Chapter Thirteen

The ancient Belfort château was set like an antique gem in the vast park called La Chasse Belfort, east of Paris. Although they were not expected, torches flared at the old drawbridge entry to the walls, and dim lights wavered in the four turreted towers as the carriage clattered into the cobbled courtyard. As Darcy helped Merry alight, a crisp breeze sprang up to pull at her skirts and hair. Lanterns burned on both sides of the front door to throw the carved Belfort crest in stark relief. The beige stone house was a ghostly white under racing clouds obscuring a full moon. Though it stood silent, the château seemed to breathe memories of earlier times and lives.

Their groom banged the big brass knocker on the front door for them. The sound jolted Merry. She felt stunned by Darcy's almost desperate passion on the rough ride out and by fear of what she might discover here, the ghost of his first wife, he had called it. She scanned the facade of the house and the inner courtyard, but long shadows reached out toward her, and she stared at the huge front door again.

It yawned inward. They were greeted by an elderly servant who exchanged a few whispered words with Darcy. He was introduced as Jules Bruay, the majordomo of the estate. But Jules's "Good to see you again so soon, *monsieur le comte*," made Merry realize where her husband had been on at least some of his solitary, secretive rides of late. Did he care so much for this place then, or for the memories it held?

To her chagrin, Darcy took the lantern from Jules and hardly broke stride as he hurried her up the wide, sweeping flight of stone steps inside. The stairs had been worn uneven by the feet of centuries. When she stubbed her toe and almost tripped, he slowed at last.

"I know it's late," she managed, her voice trembling, "but can't I even look around?"

"Tomorrow. If you stay," he muttered, and escorted her on.

They met a dark-gowned old woman with a butterfly lace cap in the upstairs hall who bobbed them a curtsy. "Is she asleep?" Darcy whispered to the woman.

"Oh, yes, *monsieur le comte*. It's after ten, and your orders are for eight, *monsieur—*" Darcy hurried Merry on before she could be introduced to the woman or ask of whom they spoke.

Merry's heart thudded with each step. This place was alive with shadows, and Darcy was rushing her deep into the heart of it. She sensed there was some terrible secret hiding here that would keep them apart, something that would make her lose him!

"Darcy, wait! I will not go on until you tell me—"

"We are here, wife."

He halted halfway down a huge hall hung with dark portraits of staring faces, guarded by standing suits of empty armor. He unhooked an ornate brass latch and shoved the carved door inward. Merry tugged back against his strength as he stepped in. He pulled her to him, grappling her to his side with his free arm. He lifted his lantern and dragged her in another step.

Wan light wove itself into the distant corners of an elegantly appointed bedchamber. A huge flowered rug was soft under delicate-legged gilded furniture and their own feet; a massive canopied bed loomed before them, its dull blue velvet coverlet emblazoned with the Belfort crest. But the entire lovely room smelled of disuse and dust. It tickled Merry's nose. She sneezed, but he pulled her closer to the bed and thrust the lantern toward the gilt-framed portrait of an extravagantly gowned woman that gazed down at them from the head of it.

"Claudine, the comtesse de Belfort!" he announced, as if to formally introduce the painted first wife to the living, breathing wife at his side. "God help me, Merry, I want you to understand it all. Look at her. Just look!"

She did, and she gasped. But for the gown and the elaborate coiffure—and the haughty set of the perfect features—it could have been one of the portraits of Merry the painters of Paris had done this last month. Merry looked more like Claudine than she did her own sister! Claudine stared down. Merry stared up. No words came at first as Darcy turned his stern face from one to the other.

"So that's what they have all been gawking at," she whispered.

"Those who knew her. Yet that is not all."

But Merry's mind had snagged on just one terrible possibility. "Is it...because I reminded you of her...that you first were attracted to me?"

"No! Just the opposite! I couldn't bear to look at you! I mean . . . I did not want you at first because of her."

"It made your lovely memories too painful." She choked back a sob. "No one could ever replace her."

"That is not it! I am making a mess of this, just as I did before. Merry, come over here so I can explain." He pulled her farther into the room. "This damn place smells of deceit and death!"

He loosed her waist, and it took all her desperate, threatened love for him not to run from the room so that she didn't have to hear the rest. She wanted to throw her arms around him and beg him not to send her away. She feared he loved this woman still; she could never take her place in his houses, at court, in his life!

But she stood rooted to her little piece of carpet as he leaned over a cushioned window seat to fumble with the lock on the narrow window. He pulled the casements inward and shoved the shutters open. A gust put out the lantern, leaving them standing in the dark, and it seemed to Merry that she could hear the portrait breathing behind them.

"It is not that I loved her, Merry," he began haltingly. "Not at the end. Actually, I hated her for all she did. Others know, or think they do, all about it. I brought you here to risk telling you, and then you can judge for yourself."

As her eyes adjusted to the dark, she could see his profile sketched by the gray night sky outside. She could not see whether tears glimmered in his eyes, but she could almost hear them, sense them. She found the courage to rest her fingers on his rigid arm. Together they sank down on the cushions of the window seat, which gave up a musty puff of breath.

"Our families arranged the marriage, but when I saw Claudine the first time, she was so beautiful and gay I adored her from the start," he told her. "We wed when we were both nineteen. We inherited this place and the mansion in Paris when my father died just after. The house at Passy was a gift from her family. We were wealthy, young, idealistic and, I thought, very much in love—if there is any such thing. I couldn't wait to get her with child—" His voice broke, but he cleared his throat and went on. "After two years of what I thought was married bliss, we started to live off and on at court. We were still happy, I believed, but three years later, after nearly five years of marriage, there was still no child!

"Though marital infidelity was *de rigeur* and something of a sport at Versailles," he went on, "we had vowed from the first that we would always be true to each other. She was like a glorious, gilded, flittering butterfly there, and I was so busy with new assignments that I was often away. But I trusted her. I came home to her whenever I could. Often we came here to Belfort and this château. She loved me, she vowed, counted the days until I returned, because she found no joy in anything else when I was away. I told her not to go back to court then, to wait for me here. I even teased her about locking her up here, but she said court life was her patriotic duty. Duty!" He spat out the word and then drew in a painful-sounding breath. "And then, finally, after six years of marriage, Claudine bore a child."

Merry gasped. "And the child died, too! But you said you could not father a child!"

He shook his head, and she quieted, her mind racing. "To make a pitiful life story short, Merry, three years ago, when the child was four, I discovered she was not mine. The marriage I had thought was solid was mere sham. Sometime in our earliest years at court, Claudine had begun reveling from bed to bed. And everyone knew but me, damned fool that I was—their harlequin to laugh at—Claudine most of all. The child was not even from the lover she left me for, but the one before, she told me in the note she left when she fled. So it was I who was . . . deficient in the years we had no child."

"She ran away with one lover but took another lover's child?"

"No. Her last one, an attaché at court—British, no less—did not want the child, so she deserted her four-year-old daughter, too."

Merry's arms were clamped tightly over her belly. It was twisted in knots at his heartache and his pain. "Oh, Darcy, I am so sorry! And I—"

"There is more," he interrupted, but for the first time he was looking at her. His eyes glittered like polished obsidian in the dusk of the room. "As I said, I didn't know the child was not mine until Claudine left me. That was the year before I first went to America and met you. When she ran off, Claudine made certain the courtiers and I knew my daughter—who had been my pride—was not mine at all. *Sacrebleu*, I suppose I should be grateful for that, but I almost wish she had not told me, so I would have had something left. And she again fostered the ugly lies she had been spreading through the court for months about me to gain sympathy and attention."

"She said that you'd been unfaithful all those years, too?" she prompted when he did not go on.

He shook his head. "They all knew me—the honorable young laughingstock—too well to believe that. No, she told them that I was obsessively possessive, that I had locked her up here at Belfort, literally chained to our bed at times—" He bit off the words and flung out his hand as if to accuse the bed and the portrait guarding it. "How she must have enjoyed embellishing the details for her lovers, and anyone else who would listen! Again, I was the last to know these slanders. Finally someone showed me one of the letters she had written to her so-called friends at Versailles just before she ran away to London with the English bastard—and was drowned with him in a storm on the way."

"Oh, Darcy..." Merry managed, her voice as breathy as the wind that shifted the heavy draperies. Now she knew the root of his bitterness, his distrust of her—of all women. And she glimpsed the reason for his passionate, reckless risking of himself for the cause of freedom—even for a country and people that were not his own. She did not believe for one moment that he had kept his wife prisoner here and done the things that Claudine had accused him of. Though they both might have been better off if he had indeed locked her in this room with her portrait glaring down as if to challenge any other woman who might lay claim to that bed. And, the devil take that horrid witch, that was just what Merry Morgan intended to do!

"I promised myself," Darcy was saying, his voice very quiet now, "that I would never wed again. And with no hope for an heir anyway..."

"But are you sure?"

"Merry, I tried to have one by her for ten years. And you and I have not exactly been celibate!"

She bounced to her feet. "I am deeply saddened by your wasted life with her," she said, pointing at the wall above the bed, "but I'll not have you mention my name with hers! I cannot help it if I resemble her in the face, Darcy. *I am not her!*"

He seized her hands. "I know, I know. You're nothing like her. But when I thought you had deceived me to hold me captive on that ship and trap me into marriage, I lost myself in rage at the past again."

She stepped against him and cradled his head to her breasts, just holding him there. Despite his litany of sorrow, her heart was soaring. His sleeping mutters about the lying bitch he wanted to kill must have referred to Claudine, not to her! Her grief at the thought he believed those wretched things of her dissolved and gave her the strength to go on even in the face of all this.

"I understand you better now, my love. And I know you well enough to realize you never imprisoned her. The woman must have been evil incarnate to treat you that way—to tell all those lies, and to desert her own daughter."

Suddenly his arms came hard around her hips to clamp her to him. "Merry, I've fought so hard against you—against us. And when you took to the court at Versailles that way, so popular, when they still whisper about the other—"

"I understand! Compared to our happiness, the court doesn't matter a bit to me, none of it. I only wanted to help

America's cause and—I thought—to make you proud." She bit her lower lip as his words about Claudine's lies about going back to court because it was "her patriotic duty" echoed in her head. No! She was nothing like that other wife to him! She cared for all the things that woman must have instinctively detested.

"Darcy, what happened to your—I mean, Claudine's—daughter?" she asked, her hands stroking his thick, mussed hair.

"It tore my heart apart to tell her I was not her father after her mother deserted her, but I was sick of lies. I promised her this would still be her home. I cannot bear to be around her, Merry, to see that expectant look of love on her face that I cannot return. She knows her mother has died, but not how or with whom. Amélie is sleeping down the hall, her nurse says."

He had kept the daughter of that woman and her lover! Shock turned to sympathy, for the child, as well as for Darcy. He clung to her yet, like a little boy who needed comforting, this big, often austere man she had once considered dangerous. Her love enveloped him; she had never cared for him more, despite—or because of—all he had told her.

"So that old woman was her nurse?" she asked. "Then may I see Amélie?"

"All right," he agreed, but he didn't budge.

"None of this tragedy is the fault of a seven-year-old child, Darcy," she prompted. "And, in her way, I'm sure she's suffered as much as you."

He loosed her and stood slowly. He spoke at first as if he hadn't heard her gentle pleas for the child. "I have had a room prepared for us, so we can stay the night, as long as you want, if you like the place and can forgo the court. I did not know how you would feel about it all."

Her voice came shaky, but it steadied as she talked. "About you? I love you and want to be your wife. About Amélie? I want to meet her. About the court? I prefer it here with you by far. About this place? It seems grand and lovely, but for this wretched mausoleum of a room and that portrait I won't have in my house. I've ordered one of me from Richard Laurens in Paris, and I'd like it up there, if you agree. And if so, I want you to know that it and its model have not one thing to do with all that came before!''

Even in the dark, he looked dazed. "I adore you, my Merry!" he said, and gripped her shoulders hard.

It wasn't quite the declaration of undying love she had hoped for, but it was a start. She knew that her love had fostered his trust when he took her hand to lead her down the hall and into another bedchamber, where the child slept. They tiptoed in, as if, Merry thought, they had just returned from Versailles to peek in on their own little lamb. But the dream disintegrated before her as she realized that that might be exactly what Darcy was thinking—about the other wife, before tragedy had struck.

He held aloft a lantern that the watchful nurse, standing in the door behind, had given him. The light pearled down to reveal a moppet with dark, curly hair, sprawled on her back, her thick lashes like streaks of soot against her pale cheeks, her mouth slightly open in heavy slumber. Black hair like Darcy's, Merry thought. And she reminded her of Darcy, with that determined jaw and the way she clung to the second ruffled pillow in the bed as if she were hugging someone to her. They turned and tiptoed out.

"She's lovely," Merry told Madame Gravier, the old nurse. "I'm sure you do beautifully rearing her."

The woman beamed, displaying crooked teeth. "If only she were not so lonely. She swears she has a sister. She talks to her, calls her Marie," she admitted with a shrug. "That is who Amélie thinks she is hugging with that pillow next to her, and woe betide me if I try to tell her Marie is all fantasy! When you meet her, *comtesse*, you might try to tell her it is all stuff and nonsense."

"Good night," Darcy told the woman, and hustled Merry away to a small but airy bedroom two more doors down. She did not protest his haste, though there was so much more she would have liked to ask Madame Gravier.

They talked for hours after, side by side, at first holding hands, then wrapped in each others' arms as she inched closer to him. They made love quickly, almost desperately. Later still, Darcy flopped over on his back, sound asleep at last, but oblivion eluded Merry. She kept embroidering plans for their future happiness. Now that the truth was out, everything could build from here. She cuddled her own pillow to her, then thought again of the child down the hall. This was not like clinging to a pretend friend; this was hope for a new future. Surely now there was no reason to pretend about that!

Early the next morning, Darcy himself took her on a tour of the turreted château, with its crenellated roof line, which still seemed as if bowmen might be crouching there waiting for attack. The place seemed weighty in size and age, room after high-ceilinged room with ponderous stone fireplaces. But through the mullioned windows Merry could see the beauty of the grounds and the encircling blue-green parklands. Perhaps, if the windows were just larger, she mused, to pull the outside in, and if big bouquets of flowers could be put here and there, the place would seem more charmingly rustic and less like an old fortress.

Outside, ivy laced the beige stone walls and flowers ran rampant in the planted parterres sloping down to the gravel riding paths. Darcy even showed her the old stone stables, though the horseflesh there was meager compared to the old days, he told her regretfully.

"I will select a nice mare for you, and we'll go riding this afternoon," he promised as they walked from the stables into the slanting midmorning sun.

"Does Amélie ride, too?"

"She's learning, among her other lessons," he told her. She had learned he did not like all her questions about Amélie. "French and English, geography, literature, mathematics—" he ticked off on his fingers "—embroidery, decorum, and—"

"Does she have any time for play?"

"Of course." He smacked his gloves against his thigh. "I have given strict orders she is to have—though supervised, of course—the freedom of the lawns. When she is sixteen, she will be given a generous allowance and told the entire story about her mother. She will then be set free from here to live her own life as she sees fit—with an appropriate chaperone, of course. Since I have been to America and seen how such things work, at least usually, I hope she makes a marriage of her own choice someday.''

Merry's heart plummeted. Then he still regretted his lack of choice in their own situation, as well as in his first marriage. And to tell a young girl all that and then just turn her loose in the world, allowance or no allowance! Merry would see about that when the time came! Besides, she had to convince him somehow that to a woman who loved—whether she was wife or would-be daughter—freedom from the man she loved was sometimes not freedom at all.

"See—" Darcy pointed "—that is Amélie playing over there, with not a book or an embroidery hoop in sight. I loved her once. I am no slave driver!''

I loved her once. The words echoed in Merry's mind as she pecked Darcy on the cheek and strode off alone to meet his once-upon-a-time daughter. How could he say that of someone so dear, so in need of his love and approval? He might say of his dead, deceitful wife Claudine, *I loved her once*, but drat it if he would ever repeat those words about Merry Morgan!

The nurse, Madame Gravier, sat on a bench half hidden by a lilac bush. "I thought I would come to meet Amélie," Merry explained. "If you would enjoy a little respite from your duties, I would be happy to remain here with her."

"You know, she does wear one down," Madame Gravier confided. "Especially on the days the two village girls come to play. But that's tomorrow, and I'm not certain that with all her boundless energy I will even last till then."

They shared a little laugh, and Madame Gravier rose to summon Amélie. The girl was gowned in bright blue sprigged cotton with small panniers. Her cloth slippers were grass-stained and dirty from running about. Merry felt better when she saw that. The child's eyes were clearest blue—evidently her mother's, but she could have passed for Darcy's child, Merry thought as the child dropped her a charming curtsy.

"Madame la comtesse." The sweet voice repeated her name just as Madame Gravier had said it. *"Enchantée.* That was my mama's name, too, you know. Since she is with the Virgin and the angels in heaven now, did she send you to take her place?''

"No, Amélie," Merry managed, taken a bit aback by all that, "but if we had a map of America I would show you on it where I grew up as a little girl. Perhaps I can just explain anyway." She assured Madame Gravier that she and Amélie would be just fine for a while, and the two of them strolled on around the house together while the old nurse went inside.

"It is only that after your mother died the count was—well, lonely, Amélie," Merry began. "And so I am now his wife to love him and keep him company, and I would like to be your friend."

"*Merci, comtesse,*" the child replied, wide-eyed and serious-faced. "But I do have my dear sister, Marie, and so I don't need another friend, you see."

"Oh, yes, I have heard about Marie. Where is she now?"

"Climbing that tree over there, but I can call her down to meet you, I suppose. I'm not to climb trees, but Marie is allowed. Do you like to climb trees?"

"I have climbed a few in my day. You know," Merry admitted as the memory hit her, "I climbed a tree, or climbed down from one, with your fath—with the count—once. And then we hid in a hayloft."

"Really?" Amélie beamed up at her. "What fun! Does he like being with you, then? He's too busy to see me much, and he is rather angry with me, too. But he loves Marie."

They stopped under the young chestnut tree Amélie had pointed out, and Merry watched her squint up into its thick leaves. Her heart went out to the child, for it was obvious that she clung to a fantasy of a sister who loved her to replace the parents she had lost. And in the fantasy Amélie pretended Darcy loved the part of her that was Marie as he could not the child herself.

"Marie, Marie!" Amélie shouted up into the tree. "Ah, there you are! Come down, you silly goose, and meet the new comtesse!"

"My name is Merry in English, really almost the same name as Marie," Merry told her. She gawked as the child actually reached up to mime helping her invisible friend down to the ground. "You know, dear Amélie, I think all of us can be friends," Merry said. "And if we can get a pony saddled for you this afternoon you can come riding with the count and me.''

"If Marie can come, too, I would be delighted!" Amélie told her with another eager smile that quickly faded. "If the count won't mind."

"Merry, I asked *you* for a ride," Darcy protested when he heard an hour later, "not the child. She will slow us down, and we will have to watch her every minute. And we are most certainly not saddling another horse for a figment of Amélie's imagination! I thought Madame Gravier asked you to help her discourage this pretend little friend Amélie insists on!"

"She will relinquish the friend when she can. I used to have a fantasy or two myself as a child, though I was fortunate enough to have my own sister and two parents to love me. She's just lonely, and—"

"Lonely! She has a nurse, a governess and a household staff who adore her and two village girls who come here twice a week! And all the lessons and fine things in life money can buy. I suppose you are going to tell me I am cruel to her!"

"I think under the circumstances, you've been wonderful to her," she said, choosing her words carefully, "but she longs for your love and approval. After all, she had that for the first four years of her life and then lost her mother, as well. And, you know, she does resemble you, so—"

"The fact the little minx has black hair does not mean a damned thing! You do not know anything about it! And I am going to tell her that if she wants to go that is fine, but not Marie!" he insisted as he stormed for the door.

"But if you do," she called after him, "tell her it's because you especially want her to go with us!"

He slammed the door, and she wondered what he would tell the child. She had to find a way to convince him that, even though Amélie was not his, he could love her anyway. And even though Claudine de Mirabeau had been evil and Merry wanted nothing around to remind her of her presence here, somehow this innocent, charming child was not part of that.

At that thought Merry marched into the master bedroom, which she had already ordered aired and cleaned. She greeted the three maids, busy with feather dusters, who jumped aside as she entered. "Pardon, one minute," she told them.

She lifted her riding skirt to kneel on the stripped mattress. Stiff-backed, she lifted the heavy, dusty portrait of Claudine off its hook. There was a lighter rectangle on the wall where it had hung all these years. She scooted back on the bed with the heavy thing and carted it from the room. It was going up in the attic, she decided. When Amélie was sixteen and had her precious freedom, she would see that she could take this with her. Until then, it was out of her room and her sight!

A maid raced along at her side to open the attic door and light her way up as she had asked. The wooden steps creaked all the way up under the eaves. The dust was worse up here; Merry couldn't wait to put this down and go out riding with Darcy and Amélie in the good, clean air.

"Where shall you put it then, *comtesse*?" the pert maid asked.

"Just over here, I guess. What are all these trunks?"

"Oh, you know," she said, not meeting Merry's eyes. "The previous mistress had so many gowns. They were just put up here when—when she left."

"I see," Merry said, but her mind was racing again. They wrapped the painting with an old petticoat Merry took from a humpbacked trunk that emitted a musky smell of roses. She wondered if that was just the scent Claudine had used to store her things, or whether that had been her personal scent. Sumptuous garments were piled in the trunk, things that should by rights be Amélie's someday, and perhaps that had been Darcy's intent. But some good charity could use these things, too, and she decided that when the time was right she would ask Darcy if she could go through it all. Drat it, the petticoat alone had the finest delicate embroidery in gold thread on it, as if it were a gown itself. She banged the trunk lid closed.

She squinted out through the small semicircular dormer window as the maid hesitated at the top of the steps. Suddenly this place oppressed her, the portrait, the clothing, the musk scent, as if Claudine still reached out to scatter evil and pain. Promising herself she would return another day when things

were better between Amélie and Darcy—and her—she turned
and hurried down the stairs.

In the two weeks that followed, there were other rides
through the park. There were picnics for Amélie and her village friends, and even, though Merry did not tell Darcy, a private picnic with her, Amélie and the invisible Marie. Merry and
the girl took to each other beautifully, though Darcy still re-
sisted Merry's efforts toward a real reconciliation between him
and the child. The day Ben Franklin had come out by carriage
for a visit, the old man had showered Amélie with attention,
and she had blossomed before their eyes and quite forgotten her
imaginary friend Marie. Couldn't Darcy just see that and let
himself get closer to the child? Merry agonized. But when she
tried to broach the subject with him again, she was rebuffed.

"Merry, just because I have forgotten Claudine, I cannot
forget Amélie is not really mine!" he protested on a walk one
day. "Do you think that did not tear me apart—both the torment of losing Amélie and the agony of keeping her around?"

"Don't love her as a daughter, then, if you cannot! Love her
as your ward, or as an orphan you've taken in, even as an
adopted daughter, but let your feelings for her show! I know,
you see, what it is to love you fiercely, Darcy Mont, and not
know where I stand!"

He pulled her around to face him in the fringe of forest. She
had not called him by that first name she'd known him by for
a very long time. His mind darted back to their early times together: the flight from Long Island and their flight from the
Hessians. But he had been fleeing from things long before
Merry had come into his life, and even though he'd shared
those things with her he still felt very alone and afraid sometimes. He desperately wanted to feel free of the guilt of the
past—the guilt that came of loving the wrong woman, of be-
lieving her, of being made to look the ultimate fool. He wanted
to be free of it happening all over again with this woman he
adored despite himself. He needed to show everyone, including Merry, that he would risk all for freedom—her country's
and his own. So he had said yes when Ben Franklin had

broached the challenge of a new, dangerous assignment. And now he needed to explain that assignment to Merry.

Coward that he was, afraid to hurt her, he let things coast until the last few days before he would leave. He let himself relax in the company of the beautiful, vibrant woman who was his wife and had resurrected Belfort for him. The château was now ablaze with flowers, the rooms were being repainted, and she had plans to modernize the old hulk of a place. To please Merry in return, he had made a greater effort to keep Amélie about. Amazingly, he found the child's company pleased him, too—when he could forget whose daughter she was and whose daughter she was not.

But he was desperate to get Merry alone his last night, to explain and get past that which could shatter their tenuous joy. She had sacrificed being with him before for her new country when he had had a mission; perhaps, even if he had to leave her in France for a while, she would be willing to sacrifice being with him again. Surely his Freedom Flame would understand that the task was worth the risk.

He dreaded leaving her alone here in France, exposed to the corruption of the French court, and yet this fear had been what drove him to plan this test for her. When he had gone off to do his duty years before, Claudine had betrayed him. But Merry never would; Merry could be trusted. He knew that in his mind and heart, didn't he? The trouble was, he had believed and trusted Claudine once, too.

Deep inside, he wanted to give Merry the chance to prove herself to him by waiting here for him—and perhaps even going to court when he was away. When he came back from his mission, she would be waiting faithfully to purge all the old pain. She would be there to prove to him and the court that Louis Philippe D'Arcy, comte de Belfort, was worth loving, worth waiting for, worth being faithful to, and then—

"My darling—" Merry's voice sliced through his frenzied thoughts as she joined him on the big bed "—you're frowning. Whatever is it?" She propped herself up on one elbow next to him and stroked his brow. She wore only a light chemise of wispy fabric, embroidered white on white. All he wanted to do was crush her to him, but before he did that he had to tell her. He sucked in a breath and nervously arranged the folds of his brocade dressing gown over his naked body. He stretched out on the crisp linen sheets. The bed and room had been redone, and a smiling, softly pastoral portrait of Merry now hung over the bed on the freshly whitewashed wall.

"When Ambassador Franklin was here last week," Darcy began, staring up at the underside of the new bed canopy, "he and I talked some business when you were not around."

Her hand jerked to a stop along his brow. "And?"

"And, although I think you and I should head back to Philadelphia sometime this autumn, there is something else I must do alone first. General Washington and Congress desperately need to know the real condition of Americans being held captive by the British."

Her breath caught in her throat. "Held captive where? New York?"

"London."

"London!" She sat up abruptly, cross-legged on the bed, and tugged her chemise down over her knees. She had not heard that the British had shipped any captives to London! "But that would be worse than your sneaking around at home to find things out! Lord Stormont knows you, and he's gone back to London! And you don't know London!"

He sat up, matching her position. It was as if they faced each other over an Indian powwow fire such as Washington had told him of. "England is a very big, busy place, and I promise not to go looking for Lord Stormont, Merry," he said to placate her. "Actually, I do know London. Where do you think I learned my English, though I had to work like the devil to change some of my Brit pronunciations when I first went to America. Those times I was away from my first marriage I was French attaché to the Court of St. James, and I've even met the king, old German George himself, a time or two."

"Drat. I can see why you never told anyone that in America! They might have thought you were a double spy or some such!"

"I did tell Washington, and your brother-in-law, too, after I got to know them," he admitted sheepishly.

"Damn you, Darcy! But you never told me! It's one wretched surprise after the other for me yet, isn't it? You told them after you got to know them! Do you think you don't know me yet?"

That, he thought, is one of the reasons I have to go, so you can prove yourself and rescue me forever, dear wife. But he hated himself for that. He leaned over to tumble her toward him. He rolled them both over on the big bed, him on top. "Merry, Merry, I do know you will let me go and will give me a fine farewell. I do know I can trust you to tell you exactly where I am going, what I will be doing, when I could have claimed secrecy the way I used to. And I do know—" his voice caught before he plunged on "—you will be waiting for me here when I return. Two to three weeks, that is all, and old Franklin said he would escort you to Versailles while I am gone if he thinks you could help things there again. Or...or if you would want to go on your own, since you had such a fine time there."

She had gone tense in his embrace, but she exhaled now and forced herself to relax. She admitted to herself she was glad for anything he could do to help the American cause. And, as he said, at least he was sharing it all with her. She lay, pressed under him, her hair splayed across the bed, her chemise twisted up around her thighs.

"You do know me rather well, *mon cher comte*. When do you leave, then? We can make these last few days something to warm you on your way!"

He grinned down at her, despite it all. No one would ever best his Merry when it came to boldness and bravery. And then he told her: "Tomorrow at dawn."

"Drat you!" She tried to shove his weight off her, but he would not budge.

"Now that's my Freedom Flame." He bent to nuzzle her arched throat. "All heat, but I am going to have to stoke the fire still higher."

"Darcy, I resent your not telling me this until the very last moment!" she began, her voice sulky, her lips pouted. But he only kissed them to soften the pout. "I just could not bear it if anything happened to you," she got out before she moaned at his determined ministrations lower than her lips.

His mouth captured a tip of breast right through the chemise. It pointed hard between his lips as he nipped and rolled it. The soaked, thin fabric cooled her there as he bent to sweetly assault the other one while his free hand lifted and cupped the first one. He trailed kisses between her breasts and ventured lower while his free hand tracked an enticing trail up under the hem between her thighs.

"We have tonight, all night, to say goodbye for just a little while, my Merry, *ma belle, ma belle*," his raspy voice crooned to her. She untied and opened his dressing gown, then pushed it impatiently back from his big shoulders; he tugged her chemise clear up to her chin to bare her to his hot gaze and hotter hands. His emerald eyes meandered slowly, meaningfully, up and down the trembling length of her. "My beautiful Freedom Flame, burning higher and brighter before we can even begin to put the fire out," he murmured, his hand working wonders at her very core.

She could not hold still, could not keep the waves of flame from licking at her, burning her, consuming her. She shuddered with the ultimate rapture, and yet he did not stop. Again he lured her to the brink, but then settled hard against her and plunged in to cool his own wild ardor. He rocked in her; they thrust together. She clung to him, all voluptuous soft skin and legs around his waist, like her ties around his heart. He exploded into her, calling her name in her ear as she was ravaged by another release under him. When it was over, she clung hard to him and he to her. This way, she thought dazedly, the way they loved, perhaps there could be a child for them someday. Just because he and that woman didn't . . . hadn't . . .

"Come back to me, please, my love," she murmured when he began to touch her everywhere again. "We have come this far, but there is so much more to do—together! Come back to me! Promise me!"

He lifted his flushed face. His hair, all tousled, made him look quite the pagan. Some thought or emotion that she could not quite read, but that scared her, flitted across that handsome, rugged face and then was gone. And then the thick lilac-scented candle by the bed flickered out.

"I will be back for you, Merry, I do promise," he whispered in the dark. "Yes, we have much more to do together. I will be back! I swear it!"

Chapter Fourteen

The first two weeks Darcy was in England passed in a flurry of activity for Merry. She ordered several new pieces of furniture for Belfort and personally picked out the upholstery for each; she entertained guests, including Ben Franklin, who also escorted her to court several times. When she visited the Belfort house at Passy, she took Amélie and her nurse along, despite Madame Gravier's protests at traveling. What would the old woman say, Merry thought, if she took her and the child back to America? And what would Darcy say?

Not knowing how he was doing on his dangerous mission was a continual torment for Merry. She thought of him all the time and tried to send him her love. She found herself dreaming of him both asleep and awake: he came to her at night by riding through the park and climbing in the bedroom window.

One dream was very confused. He threw gravel against her window to wake her. A rock sailed in with a message from him vowing, "I will always trust and love you, my Merry, *ma belle, ma belle*." But as she gazed down at the words on the paper, they melted invisibly into the air. He climbed an apple tree to come in her window. He began to make lazy, wonderful love to her on a bed of straw, and she responded joyously. But then the portrait over their heads came to life! Claudine screamed down at them that she would ruin their happiness yet. Merry seized Darcy's hand and they ran down the hall to grab Amélie. Claudine and Peggy Shippen sent the Hessians running after them. Peggy was throwing things at them, shattering her chance to have Darcy. Running, running, then sailing on a ship, they fled together, Merry and Darcy and Amélie—

"Darcy!" Merry cried out as she groped for him, only to find the bed beside her empty. She sat bolt upright, damp with sweat, her heart pounding, the bedclothes clutched to her breasts. To calm herself, she went down the hall to watch Amélie sleeping safely, her arm still holding the sister of her dreams. At least, Merry told herself as she returned to her lonely bed, things had gone more like a dream than a nightmare at court lately.

Ben Franklin and the French foreign minister, Vergennes, were delighted at the good luck they boasted she had brought them. The fleet that had been promised to help the American rebels was now being provisioned. It was to be commanded by the comte d'Estaing, who was also to fight the British in the West Indies. If a campaign could be mounted in the southern states against the English foe, the king's advisers told them, d'Estaing's fleet could slip up from the Indies to help next spring.

"Next spring! Slip up to the southern states?" Merry complained quietly to Franklin and Vergennes as they left that interview. "But we need help *now*, and all the main action has been in Philadelphia or farther north so far!"

"Things may shift south soon," the ever-optimistic Mr. Franklin said. "As always, we must take what we can get. When Darcy returns, we shall send his information about prisoners in London with a letter to Lafayette, asking him to come back to help us plead for more permanent use of the fleet. Meanwhile, as for help in the southern states, perhaps General Washington ought to leave the north and give more attention to other places—"

More attention to other places. Merry's mind had clung to those words. Her attention drifted off to Darcy again, wherever he was. When he was not at her side, even the elegance and excitement of Versailles faded for her. Now she saw the heart of the place beneath the glittering shell Darcy had spoken of. Why, the very foundations of the rambling structures of Versailles were in disrepair, despite the topiary and flowers arranged to hide that. And at the foot of the most stunning sweep of marble stairs lurked noisome public privies, as if to prove that the creatures who walked these marbled, gilded halls were indeed mortal.

And worse than mere mortal, Merry had learned. She felt as if scales had fallen from her eyes. The pretty, rouged young women at court snickered over lewd jokes about their being not really "very much" married as they stalked new lovers. She heard the backbiting that Darcy must have suffered once. Not one of the king's ministers had been elected or was accountable to the heavily taxed people jammed in the crowded streets of Paris or bent over the grapevines in Passy. She saw the labyrinthine government grinding away, greased only by the whims of the royal family and their favorites.

Though that same favoritism shone on her at court for the faddish cause of the *révolte* in America, Merry had come to understand she could soon enough be yesterday's amusement. Now the perfumed halls of Versailles made her long for America, with its fresh winds blowing, even in the face of war. She had come to truly understand the part of Darcy that was rebellious and bitter and critical of this place where "Madame Etiquette" ruled over "Madame Morals." If only—if only!—she had her beloved husband at her side so that she could tell him all she had learned.

Darcy Mont stood on the banks of the broad Thames, just below London, squinting into the clearing morning fog at the sprawling naval yards at Greenwich. The August day would make a steambath of this place by noon, but his sweat was not because of that. He was actually nervous that things had gone so well so far, for he had one more task to do.

He stared through the spiked iron fence surrounding the naval yards. But it was not to observe the repairing or provisioning of British men-of-war or transports setting out for America that he had come here. Out there, through the masts of vessels along the docks, he could see the hulks of old derelict ships at anchor. Ships incarcerating a cargo of captured American soldiers and colonial political prisoners. Even in this rising heat, he knew he could not begin to imagine the sickening, stifling scenes that were rumored to exist aboard those ships. But it was not even that he had come to see today.

He wore workman's attire and carried tools of the carpentry trade over his shoulder as he strolled closer to the guarded gates of the yards. Hundreds of civilian laborers and sailors from nearby neighborhoods and barracks poured in. He glanced back once again. For the past few days, ever since he had made that new contact here at Greenwich who had sold him a partial prisoner list of the hulk named the *Somerset*, he had imagined he felt eyes boring into the back of his skull.

He shrugged and shook his head. Just his imagination. Or perhaps, he thought, trying to buck himself up, it was Merry thinking about him, mentally trying to watch over him. The thought calmed him. After all, tomorrow he would head back to Dover to return to France over what the British brazenly dubbed the *English Channel*, as if they owned every damned drop of it.

Today he intended to pick up a little firsthand information when the guards on those ships changed. He would ask how things really were out there, maybe collect a few more names, tell the guards he thought he had an American cousin or brother-in-law out there somewhere and just wondered how he was. Maybe he would even use Cam Gant's name. As far as Darcy knew, Cam was still safe in America, but it would let him give Washington's staff a good laugh when he and Merry went back over.

Trying to blend in with the converging swarm of men, he sucked in a breath and strolled past the guards at the gates.

But then he felt that prickling on the nape of his neck again and turned slowly back once more. His eyes skimmed the busy scene of carpenters and sawyers, the carts of foodstuffs and building materials coming in off the streets. He breathed more easily now. No one was paying one bit of attention to him. Just goods to stock the ships and feed the poor wretches he had heard were nearly starving out there on the *Somerset* and ships like her.

Then his gaze was caught by a face he knew! The man was pointing him out to another! He knew both of them! His Greenwich informer was pointing him out to none other than the former British ambassador to the French court, Lord Stormont! And he had laughed at Merry's fears that he would see that man!

Despite his carefully assembled ruse, he decided not to just try to blend in. If they closed the gates he would be trapped here. He dumped the heavy tools he carried and backed away, hoping to circle around and out. But they saw him go.

He ran. He darted through the crosscurrents of people, bouncing off a few. He heard shouts behind him and prayed it had just been the two of them, with no accompanying soldiers to arrest him. Damn, but if he had only spotted them before he was inside the gates!

The hue and cry followed him. "There! Stop him! That man running there!"

In desperation, he charged down a narrow passageway between two buildings, praying it came out the other side where he could scale the fence and hide in the brush along the river. But his prayer, like too many others in his past, went unanswered. A ten-foot brick wall behind the buildings loomed before the iron fence.

He heard the men behind him enter the narrow passageway. He hoped they would not shoot, but he had to chance that. Trapped, he looked upward to see if there was some eaves to grab, some way up and out. His heartbeats tore at his throat. It was all out of his reach. He wished he could soar into that clear blue sky and fly like a bird across the Channel to Merry. He made a desperate run and lunge for the top of the tall brick wall but only scraped his hands and face sliding back down. A warning shot cracked through the air as he fell to his knees. He crouched, then spun to face them like a trapped animal, ready to spring.

"Halt there, froggie spy!" a man he did not know ordered. "Now get your hands on your head so Lord Stormont can take a good look at you!"

Darcy did as ordered. Six soldiers with pointed muskets, and his informer, who had evidently been working for the English, as well as the French, glared at him as Lord Stormont himself caught up and shoved through his little crowd of captors.

"Ah, indeed, that is the man," Lord Stormont announced. "So nice of you to come calling on me in England, Count Belfort, since you and your American countess made sure I am no longer welcome in France." His eyes glowed triumphantly; his voice mocked. "And since I've heard you are so very interested in who is out on those prison hulks, I am going to show you. And there we'll have the nicest little chat about all you know of things both in Paris and in Philadelphia! Put the manacles on the bastard!" he ordered crisply, and turned away with another laugh that stabbed Darcy like a dagger.

He did not struggle when they clapped the manacles on and even fastened ankle irons connected by a short chain that made him hobble like an old man. But he screamed and screamed inside. His dual plan to help the American cause and then return to Merry to free himself from his past was now doubly damned. He had failed in his mission and would be imprisoned here. And she was back at Versailles, the center of everyone's attention, just as his first countess had been.

"Move, prisoner!" a soldier ordered, shoving him. The irons chafed and burned. Fear sapped his strength while fury stoked it. But nothing penetrated the sharp regret and slashing pain of how he had ruined everything.

On the sunny September day that marked the end of the third week Darcy had been gone, Merry was going through Claudine's things stored in Belfort's attic. She had propped the two dormer windows open to let in a little air. She had things in piles all around her on old sheets on the floor, deciding what to keep for Amélie and what to donate to charities, as Darcy had said she could. But her mind was on him again and her intention to go to Ben Franklin tomorrow, the first day Darcy would be over the maximum time he had said he would be away. Not to complain, of course, for she knew the importance of the mission. But at least to ask Mr. Franklin to use his many contacts to learn why Darcy had been delayed.

The scent of musk and roses permeated everywhere when Merry opened the last chest and took things out: a whalebone-stiffened bodice sewn with gold thread; a stomacher so finely embroidered it seemed real leaves and vines were twined around it; two huge quilted petticoats to stretch over panniers; and a winter muff of ermine trailing velvet ribbons. Merry stroked the sleek beauty of the fur muff despite herself and thrust her hand into its satin interior.

"What?" she said aloud as her hand touched crinkly vellum. She drew out a pack of three letters tied with a thin blue satin ribbon.

She frowned down at her discovery, for the scripted letters on the top envelope read *Pour la comtesse de Belfort*. Merry's pulse pounded faster as she shakily slipped the ribbon away. After all, she told herself grimly, though she knew nothing could have stopped her from looking inside anyway, it was her name on the letters, too!

The top epistle crinkled open, and she skimmed the French message. It was from Claudine's lover—one of them, at least. No, it must be from the one she had run away with, for it spoke of departing with him for England before her husband learned of their love!

Merry's wide eyes skimmed down for the closing. That alone was in English: Together forever, your James.

"Together forever at the bottom of the English Channel," Merry muttered, shaking her head.

The next letter was much the same, as James tried to convince Claudine to leave for England with him. The words were so impassioned—and so explicit about his feelings for her—that they almost burned her fingers on the page. Seduced by letters, Merry mused. It flitted through her thoughts then: could Darcy perhaps partly deem the English his enemy because one of them had stolen his wife? She opened the last letter and skimmed it. More of the same in this billet-doux that Claudine had evidently saved and then forgotten in her haste to leave. But then, halfway down the page, a section grabbed her eye and stopped her breath:

I told you, my dearest Claudine, I want my own children from your luscious body, and your Amélie would only be in the way when Lord Stormont posts me to Canada and you accompany me. I can offer you everything in our new life together, but only if you can come to me without such a hindrance as the child. You fear the count's anger so much when he discovers your love for me? You hate him, you declare, for his pompous piety and proud possession of you? For the way he held you prisoner and used you there, as you have told us all? Then take your toll in more than just the other letters you have written to your friends at court!

My dearest love, leave him a letter, too, telling him he may have the child—but that she is not his. A simple lie— one he deserves for not appreciating a woman like you enough to keep a better eye out for one who worships at your feet, as I do.

You must leave Amélie behind. Then he will surely not pursue us, and yet he will not have the recompense of a daughter either. What is one more little lie concerning the child's paternity? And be certain he does not believe I am the father, for I do not wish to fight him in some duel if he follows us to London or beyond. Besides his precious reputation it pleases you to sully, be certain he is so distraught that he is quite destroyed!

Merry gasped at the stunning wickedness of both Claudine and her James. And Lord Stormont was mentioned! Had he perhaps even known of their illicit tryst? But she blessed the words that showed that Amélie was indeed Darcy's child! Would he trust the words of such a man as this James? He must! She'd tell him as soon as he returned! She jumped up, her eyes closed, holding the letters to her breast and pirouetting in sheer joy.

"Oh," said a quiet voice. She jumped as if the letter had spoken again.

Her skirts swayed around her as she came to a halt. "Amélie, I did not hear you come up here," she told the child, who stood wide-eyed at the top of the attic steps.

"Why are you dancing?" she asked as she came across the floor toward Merry.

"Not dancing, dearest. I'm just happy."

She stooped to hug the girl to her. How she longed to explain this good news to her, but Darcy must be the one to hear it first. If he would not accept this, or if he believed she was playing a trick to save Amélie, it would be worse than before for the child—especially if she told her now. And then the best thought of all struck her: if Amélie was the child of Darcy's body, she and Darcy could have children of their own, too!

"You didn't hear that the count is coming back?" Amélie asked when she saw tears shimmering in Merry's eyes to match her shining smile.

"No, I—I'm just happy to have these days with you, that's all. And tomorrow we're going to Passy, because I have to speak with Mr. Franklin about when the count is coming back."

"What's this, then?" Amélie inquired and slid the dusty petticoat from the portrait of her mother to gaze at the imperious face. "Oh, that's where Mama went," she said.

"Well, yes. I'm glad you can tell her picture from the one of me."

"But of course. You smile at me. I like yours better, and Marie does, too. But she's staying in her room today."

Merry's heart almost melted with her fierce, protective love for this child. And the imaginary Marie was staying in her room so much more lately that she really thought there might be a hope she would soon be locked away forever. Holding the precious letters to her, she took Amélie's hand, and they went down from the attic together.

Darcy regained consciousness when one of his two inquisitors threw another bucket of salt water in his face. He sputtered for a breath. He hurt all over, for once again they had beaten him while one of Lord Stormont's lackeys shouted questions. He was still tied to the post in the belly of the prison hulk, shoeless and naked to the waist. If he had not been tied so tightly, he surely would have slithered to the floor with the stinging wash of water.

He tried to buy some time by staying limp. He fought to pull his mind from the maze of pain he had undergone for hours, maybe days. But this time he couldn't remember if he had told them anything they wanted to know in the endless blur of questions that had accompanied the blows:

"Who runs Washington's spy network for him? Is Lafayette involved? Were you? What are the Americans planning next? An attack on New York City? A campaign in the southern states? Did the French king send Lafayette to America? Who sent you here to Greenwich? What exactly were you to find out in the naval yards? Who are Benjamin Franklin's key contacts in Paris? Lord Stormont demands to know if your grudge against him is still personal, or political, as you claim!"

That last demand kept spinning through his brain. So Lord Stormont knew that he knew. Knew that the British bastard who had run off with Claudine, James Edgar, had been a favored aide of his. Worse, that Lord Stormont had encouraged Claudine and James's affair and had helped the two of them find the ship that had accidentally taken them to their deaths in that storm of God's justice.

"He's conscious, mate. Douse him again, and let's get back to it. No more cursing at us in French, you froggie!" a voice roared at him. Another slap of water was followed by more questions and then another rain of fists against his midsection. Another broken rib, he was certain. He tasted blood from biting his lip.

Merry, he thought, and searched for her lovely defiant face between the blows. There she was, drifting in and out of the fog in his mind. Merry the day he first seized her in the Gant town house in her petticoat and bodice, Merry daring to come across to help on Long Island, Merry naked and so lovely by that little pool in faraway New Jersey. Merry, his *rebelle américaine*, riding out to Valley Forge in the bitter cold. Merry, his wife, in his arms on the ship in a roaring storm. He reached for her. He tried to hold her. Amélie stood there, too, her little arms clasping him. He tried to cling to them, but the pain yanked them both away.

"Damn the man, he's out again, mate. Cut him down and toss him in the brig again till he mends a bit or we'll kill him, and Lord Stormont said not to."

"Not till Lord Storm-a-lot's here himself to see it, you mean," the other man groused as they cut the big, bleeding man down.

* * *

"Merry, my dear, what a lovely surprise!" Ben Franklin told her with a smile as she was brought into the study in the house he rented in Passy. "I would have come calling if I'd known you were back from Belfort."

They exchanged hasty kisses on the cheeks. None of that hesitant silliness about smearing rouge for these two pale, puritan Americans, they had always jested. But today, he saw, she looked even sadder than she had of late.

"Nothing on Darcy yet," he told her quickly, "but some news from home in the last dispatches you'll be most interested in."

Her face fell when he mentioned no news on Darcy, but she inquired as brightly as she could, "A victory for our army?"

"I'm afraid not. They're busy planning where to go into winter quarters this year, I daresay," he told her. "No, this is rather personal, and I shall save the best for last. First, your old friend Peggy Shippen is betrothed to General Benedict Arnold, and with her father's permission, I take it."

"So she really did it," Merry marveled. "Poor Judge Shippen's probably been harangued for months to agree. I only hope General Arnold has a good supply of money he can spare and china she can break. And that I get a chance to accuse her to her face someday for what I think she did to Darcy and me. But there's better news?"

"Your sister, Libby Gant, has given birth to two girls! Yes, two, named Martha and Meredith!"

"Twins? Libby? But I didn't even know she was with child!" Merry bounced to her feet. Joyous tears stung her eyes, and she clapped her hands. Anything emotional set her to crying lately, but this was wonderful news. "I'm an aunt, Mr. Franklin—and one is called Meredith!"

The old man grinned. "No doubt they'll call her Merry, and a fine heritage she has to live up to!"

That last news cheered her immensely, Merry thought on her short walk back to the house at Passy after coffee with Mr. Franklin. Her patriotic sister had two daughters, as well as her *Liberty Gazette*, to care for while Cam was away at war! And she wouldn't be a bit surprised if the baby Martha was named after Mrs. Washington. After all, the French named their children for royalty, and the Washingtons were the closest the Americans had to that.

Then Merry's steps slowed. When Darcy returned, she would love to give him a child of his own, one to be Amélie's half brother or sister. Though Darcy did not wear a uniform, he was away fighting the war, too, just as Cam was. But Darcy had to return soon, or she was going to England herself to look for him!

It was the first of November when Merry finally heard what had happened to her husband. She sat before her drawing room fire at Belfort, hunched over as if in pain, while Ben Franklin rested his hands comfortingly upon her shoulders. She could hear Amélie's voice reciting her geography lesson in French down the hall as if the world had not just tipped upside down.

"Your—your informants are very certain they have Darcy in London?" she choked out. "Thank God, at least he's not dead!"

"The description fits him, my dear. Few men are as tall or as—as hard to convince as he. He's evidently been a prisoner on the prison hulk *Somerset* for over two months."

"Darcy, who wants everyone to be free, a prisoner!"

"But, you see, now that we know they have him, I can begin to make some circumspect and roundabout inquiries about trading for him."

She stood and whirled to face him. He grabbed for the back of her wingback chair to steady himself. Her expression had transformed itself from frightened rabbit to formidable tigress, he noted with awe.

"Circumspect and roundabout inquiries?" she demanded. "We must do something now! Who knows what those sadistic brutes have done to him already! At least those horrid Hessians aren't there! And what do you mean they might trade him? For what? I can raise money! I can sell this house!"

"And give them funds to carry on their war in America? To work against what Darcy and you—all of us—have been striving for? Besides, I doubt they would be willing to take a ransom for him. No, my dear, I'm speaking of trading him for their own prisoners of war we hold back home."

She sank to her chair as if her bones had melted, her head in her hands again.

"Merry, I'm sorry. I know it can't help much, but try to think of this as I and the rest of the American government does, that this is war even here in France, and your Darcy is one of its finest soldier heroes, especially because he's an American only by choice, not by birth."

"Thank you," she managed. "It does help. A bit. But there's one thing I've meant to ask you that's been bothering me," she said. "In all the time you've been about the court, have you ever heard of a man named James something-or-other who was an attaché working for the British ambassador, Lord Stormont, maybe two years before you came to France?"

She glanced up in time to see the surprised look on the old man's face. "Why do you ask?" he said.

"He's the man who ran off with Darcy's first wife, the one who was drowned with her. My mind has just been going over it all so much, you see."

"I understand, my dear. And since it's a day for bitter truths all around, I might as well say, yes, I've heard the stories of him. His name was James Edgar. Unfortunately, the lecher was an aide to Lord Stormont, and rather like a son to him, I believe."

She leapt up again and slammed her fist down on the unmoving stone mantel. "Then if Stormont knows the British have Darcy it could be worse than ever. I knew he was bitterly opposed to Darcy because we managed to get him dismissed from the French court, but this would be far worse. The fact that this James and Claudine drowned was not Darcy's fault, but does Lord Stormont see it that way? You've just got to get Darcy out of England, Mr. Franklin!"

"I will try with all my heart. I've come to admire you both—and to adore little Amélie—more than you can know. But the request for information and a trade cannot come from me. It will be best through the normal channels for trading prisoners—from home."

"But we don't have that kind of time!" she insisted, her face a mask of agony. "We're just across their dratted English

Channel and not an ocean over and back away! It will take months just to send the messages."

"I don't know how to say this kindly, my dear Freedom Flame," the old man told her, still staring at her over the tall back of the chair. "But it is time, as well as France's aid, that will win this war for us against the overwhelming power of Britain. And it is time that will bring your Darcy safely home to you."

If he is still alive, considering what I've heard of how they've interrogated him, Franklin thought, turning quickly away so that she would not read that on his face. He had never seen anyone look so frightened and yet so furious all at once as Merry. Well, maybe just once, Franklin thought, recalling the day five years ago when Congress had first informed General Washington that the new nation's war was his to win against Britain, even though they had no army.

Merry chose to retire from court so that any English spies there would have no excuse for taking her actions out on Darcy. She spent more time with Amélie, even sitting in on her lessons to study things she had never learned at home—in both French and English. She not only donated most of Claudine's clothes to a charity for the poor in Paris, but she started one of her own for donations for American soldiers, so they would not ever have to spend another winter such as the one they had spent freezing at Valley Forge. She oversaw Darcy's vast properties and wrote him every day, although of course she never mailed the letters. But her inability to help him festered in her heart, as did the fact that she had not been able to tell him soon enough that Amélie was, indeed, his child.

In February of 1779, Gilbert du Motier, marquis de Lafayette, sailed home to France and stayed until the spring to plead for more rebel aid. Through him she became friends with his wonderful wife, Adrienne. Both were a great comfort to her while she awaited word of Darcy. Merry and Adrienne read and discussed everything together—from the Bible to Racine, from Voltaire to rearing daughters. The Lafayettes' daughter, Virginie, became like a sister to Amélie. Merry saw that Lafayette and his "dear heart," as he called his wife, were a true and faithful couple, and that did much to restore her faith in the French nobility. But that very love that inspired her saddened her, too, as she faced those lonely months without Darcy.

Lafayette returned to America. The French fleet under d'Estaing sailed up from the West Indies to help win the siege of Savannah but then left the colonies again. Merry was beginning to entertain thoughts of going home. Ben Franklin insisted the deal to get Darcy back must originate in America along with the demands for other prisoners. They did not want to single Darcy out as an especially valuable prize, he said. But perhaps if she was back in America she could speed matters up, since she knew Washington and others in charge. It would at least give her the illusion of helping.

If worse came to worst, she decided in the black depths of the long, lonely nights, she would even humble herself before Peggy Shippen—or blackmail her, if she had to. In those sleepless hours, Merry thought of the events that had happened before her own departure from Philadelphia, and theorized that perhaps Peggy had wed Benedict Arnold at John André's urging to wheedle information from the American general for the Tory cause. If Peggy still had secret ties to Major André—something she did not put past either of those plotters—then she could be blackmailed into asking him to help get Darcy back. It sounded dangerous, but Merry would have risked anything for Darcy. If Amélie didn't need her, and this would be especially true if Darcy never came back, the countess of Belfort would have stormed London itself!

That autumn Amélie came down with agues and fever and almost died. Merry was frantic, but she personally nursed her past the crisis. A letter came through from her sister telling her all about the twins, Merry and Martha, born last July, and how she knew the very moment they were conceived, when Cam had been home on leave!

"Libby, Libby!" Merry whispered aloud as she sat by Amélie's bed while the girl napped. "You always were one for bedroom stories!" But her eyes misted over, because she had no current bedroom stories of her own. How she longed for Darcy! How she dreamed about him, so vividly that at times that she not only felt his love sustain her but felt that she was almost touching him across the miles.

But then she would remember that Darcy still had not exactly said he loved her. He had called her "my Merry" and said, 'I want you, I need you, I adore you' numerous times.

"Drat, he'll say 'I love you,' when he comes back!" she vowed.

Amélie's sweet, quiet voice came from the bed. "What, *ma chère comtesse*?"

"I just might have been saying I love you, *ma petite*!" Merry told her, forcing a bright smile. "Here, your other pillow slipped on the floor while you slept. The one," she said, hoping the time was right, "you used to pretend was your friend Marie."

"Yes," Amélie said as she rubbed sleep from her eyes without reaching for the abandoned pillow. "But now I have real friends like you and Virginie de Lafayette."

Merry bent to hug the girl, and the letter crinkled between them. "And someday we'll have the count back to share between us, Amélie. We just *have* to!"

When the summer of 1780 came and Darcy had been imprisoned for over eighteen months, Meredith Montour, countess of Belfort, put her husband's estates back in their managers' hands. She bid a teary farewell to Ben Franklin, her friends and even the queen, and then to her beloved Amélie. She sailed from France for America on July 16, having promised the child that if Darcy did not return to France by the time the war in America ended she would come back for her. They would live together in France until Amélie was sixteen and then go to America. It pained Merry even to entertain the thought that Darcy might not return with the other prisoners, but who knew how Lord Stormont was treating him? Racked by strange forebodings that her beloved was being cruelly questioned and brutally kept, she prayed for the best but steeled herself for the worst.

But this month there was good news for her country's struggle. Thanks to the efforts of Lafayette and the American delegation in France, a new French fleet of ships, and 55,000 soldiers under the comte de Rochambeau, were sent to the colonies to help fight the British seapower that held the new country hostage. Also, another fleet under a new admiral, the comte de Grasse, was in the West Indies and could be summoned if there was need. Merry herself had done what she could to encourage the aid, but her refusal to mingle at court without Darcy at her side meant that her direct contribution came only through her letter writing now.

Merry stood at the stern rail of the French packet bound for New Haven, Connecticut, and her sister's family. She knew she was a far different woman from the one who had left Philadelphia with Darcy more than two years ago. She had seen the best and the worst of France and its gilded courtiers. She had both liberated the American cause at Versailles and been a prisoner of it. She was far more educated and more sophisticated. Those were things she had once been certain would help to win Darcy's heart. And yet she knew now that it was not sophistication that would keep him, or mattered to him at all. She felt older, wiser, happier, stronger and richer in many ways. But she was also sadder and more afraid, since she had infinitely more to lose.

But, she thought, as the shores of France slipped into the blue-green eastern horizon, she was the same woman in one way. She was still desperately in love with the only man she would ever love, a man she feared she might yet lose. And, more than ever, she would still risk her very life to make Darcy hers again. She only hoped, this big war and ocean aside, there would not be other things within Darcy himself to keep him from really loving her when—and if—he returned.

Darcy Montour scratched his chin through his full black beard and squinted through his favorite chink in the hull of the prison hulk *Somerset* to watch the distant daily hubbub in the Greenwich naval yards across the stretch of river. He was no longer chained, but he would have gladly accepted that to be back in the main hold among the American prisoners he had befriended in the nearly two years he had been held aboard this ship. What an array of men he had come to admire: impoverished apprentices and landed squires, pewterers and coopers, young and old, as noble and brave gentlemen as any aristocrat born in France. But a month ago, for no discernible reason but Lord Stormont's whim, he had been moved into isolation.

He wondered exactly what Merry was doing today, though it hurt him more and more to ponder that. Was she still the center of everyone's eye at Versailles, as Lord Stormont, in his erratic visits, had led him to believe? At first he had refused to listen to what he was certain were lies about Merry's conduct there—her little *liaisons*, as Stormont had put it with a leer. But after hearing it for so long—with his previous horrible failure as a husband always in mind—in the dark of night, he sometimes wondered. And feared. And became so angry he almost thought he could pound his way out of this hulk and swim all the way to France to see if it was true.

He heard the lock on the door to his cubbyhole rattle and turned away from the tiny slit that gave him access to sunshine and the outside. Surely it was too early for food. For some reason, his rations had increased, if not improved, these past few weeks. He hoped this meant the war in America might be coming to an end and the British were afraid to give living skeletons back in trade for their own officers and soldiers. He was down to skin and sinew and bone, though he exercised whenever he could even in this hole in the hulk and ate every scrap of the terrible food they allowed him.

He blinked into the light in the corridor when the all-too-familiar form of Lord Stormont entered, waving his hand before his face at the stench the prisoners no longer even noticed. As far as Darcy was concerned, it was Stormont who brought the real stench, and he was fiercely proud that he had told the British nothing. The beatings had stopped months ago . . . but now? What now?

Stormont came right to the point, leaning in the narrow door of the cubby. "I say, Count Belfort, I've a bit a news for you—and a proposition."

"Am I finally being traded?" Darcy asked, his heart in his throat. He did not stand. He tried not to look eager.

"I told you I'd never trade you, and I meant it, man. But in exchange for a simple favor from you I could let you go and ship you to New York this very afternoon."

Darcy's pulse began to pound; he fought to keep calm. Too much to hope for! A trick, a ruse! Maybe they would hang him there in British-held New York as a spy and an example to others. He began to sweat in his eagerness, but tried not to show any physical signs of his excitement to Lord Stormont.

"A simple favor?" he said mocking, daringly. "Such as what? Assassinating General Washington? Turning traitor? Telling you everything I haven't these last long, hellish months?"

"All right, then, if that's your attitude, I'll just spit it out. Your wife is sailing home to the northern colonies this week, and I thought perhaps you'd like to join her there. Quite simply, I have a bone to pick with her for not only getting me dismissed from Versailles but using her influence with the king's ministers since—she's very persuasive in bed and out, I hear— and I thought you could settle my anger with her when you settle with her yourself for her adulterous deceits—"

"I told you I believed none of those lies!" Darcy shouted, only just restraining himself from vaulting at the man to beat the truth from him.

"Then let's just say I'm letting you go so that you can learn they were not lies! After her very successful days getting things for her country—and herself—from the French king's courtiers while you were our guest here, she's heading home for a— how do you froggies say it?—a *rendez-vous de coeur* with a previous American lover, one Toller Devlin. I've never met the man, but he must be quite the one that she'd give up all her frolicking at Versailles for him!"

Darcy's brain screamed, Liar! Liar! but no words came to his lips as he gaped at Stormont. How could Stormont know of Devlin? Had General Howe told Stormont all that had gone on in Philadelphia when the British held it? Merry had not liked Toller at all, had she? Until Darcy himself had suggested she cozy up to him, she had hardly given him a smile, even though she had spent hours in his company for the cause. Wasn't that the way it really was? But for Stormont to intimate out of the blue that Devlin had been Merry's lover and that she was sailing back to him—

"Have a pleasant journey to the colonies, then, Count Belfort. You'll thank me someday. Perhaps I feel I owe you this chance, since there was no way you could get justice from the last two who betrayed you like this. Despite our adversarial position, I've regretted I knew of that and told you nothing. This time, I have made amends. Men, get him out of here!" Stormont yelled, and stepped back into the passageway while two sailors appeared to grab Darcy's arms and drag him out and up the steps to the waiting longboat that would deliver him to an outbound transport.

Damn Belfort and that American rebel wife of his, Stormont fumed as he heard the man daring to curse him even as they hauled him off toward freedom. It pained him to let Belfort go when he had not broken this man he hated so, had not even gotten one piece of incriminating evidence from him. But he had been scolded harshly by the king's ministers when they had discovered he still held a French citizen of Belfort's stature with no solid evidence against him. This would be even sweeter revenge on both the Belforts, however. He'd just set up the stubborn Frenchman to take revenge for him on that clever rebel in skirts. At last, his contacts with British spies in America were paying off for personal gain. The story his New York correspondent, that clever fellow Major John André, had told him about the Yankee Tory Toller Devlin's lust for the Belfort woman had been the final piece he'd needed to make his plot work.

Now, he mused, if André and his little dupe, Peggy Shippen Arnold, only came through with that biggest catch, if they could just turn General Benedict Arnold traitor. Then this double trap he had arranged for the Belforts would be his own personal revenge. Even if England eventually lost this long, bloody, damned expensive public war with that ragged band of colonies, his private retribution would be a success. At that comforting thought, Lord Stormont strutted up on deck to get the reek of this fetid ship from his lungs in the good, clean breeze from the Thames.

Chapter Fifteen

Libby, you've smeared printer's ink on one of your daughters!" Merry said with a laugh as she hefted her niece above her so that the two-year-old could join in the laughter.

"It's the only way I can help Cam tell the two of them apart. Isn't that right, proud father?" Libby teased Cam, who was home on a week's leave. "The one with the smeared cheek is Martha, my love," she added with a quick kiss on his cheek.

Cam grinned and playfully swatted Libby's bottom through her skirts as she collected and placed his two squirming daughters on his knees. They looked quite the angelic mirror images, both reddish-blond, blue-eyed and grabbing at their father's smart gold buttons on his uniform. But poor Libby, Merry thought, had a terrible time watching these charming rambunctious cherubs. Besides that, her print shop in New Haven put out as many weekly papers as it could to be smuggled down to New York City. It had been with one such bundle of *Liberty Gazettes* that Merry's letter requesting help from John André to see Peggy Shippen Arnold had been sent.

In the month Merry had been visiting Libby in New Haven, she had first written Peggy herself in Philadelphia, but Peggy had refused to see her. So she had wagered that John André—in the enemy ranks or not—might yet pull Peggy's puppet strings. And her daring gamble had been rewarded. André had written back that Peggy would be willing to meet with Merry at Arnold's new home near West Point, thereby not only giving Merry the opportunity to try her plan but also showing that there was still a link between the wife of the American general

Benedict Arnold and the man who was now the adjutant general of the British high command in New York. Cam would pass that information on when he returned to camp tomorrow. The French army was in Newport, and Washington was parlaying with them about a future campaign together.

Cam was not the only one leaving New Haven tomorrow. Despite his request that she wait a few days, Merry was setting off to confront her old nemesis, Peggy. Merry had decided she would first ask, then demand, that Peggy use her ties to André to plead for Darcy's release. If Peggy would not help, Merry would threaten to tell her husband, or anyone else she had to, about the abduction of her and Darcy. If Peggy still refused, Merry would then be forced to write again to Major André himself. She hated the thought of it, but that way it would be a distraught wife asking, not the American high command, as if Darcy were someone important to them. Yes, Merry was dedicated to her decision: to help free Darcy, she would bargain with Peggy, with André—with Satan himself if she must!

"I don't know how we're going to keep Mistress Merry and Mistress Martha in food any more than we are the army with this rampant inflation." Cam was teasing Libby. But he pretended to address the twins, as if they cared one bit that the Continental dollar was now worth a mere two cents. He was so thrilled to be home with them during his leave. The poignant joy and looming separation of the reunited Gant family was breaking Merry's heart. She kept picturing Darcy here with her—with a child of their own, of course—but knew the practical truth was that he was still rotting in some British prison ship! Her long-tended romantic fantasies had been shattered by reality at last.

Fighting tears, Merry left Libby and Cam to their children. She walked to the door of the narrow brick building that served Libby in exile as a combination print shop and house. Even on the front stoop, the smell of printer's ink mingled with the tart tang of autumn in the air. Already the maples were edged with gold and crimson on the Commons across the street. By the time the leaves fell and winter came, Merry wondered, was there any hope she would have her beloved Darcy back? And next year or the next, would they have children to dawdle on their knees like this?

"Merry, come back in, dearest," Libby said behind her, putting her hands on her sister's shoulders to turn her. "I know you're worried about leaving to see Peggy tomorrow, but those two military escorts Cam got will be with you, and you'll be safe in American territory all the way. I just wish I could go with you, too!"

"With two wriggling, hungry cherubs in tow?" Merry said in an attempt at levity. She gave Libby a quick hug. "I only hope someday they are as close as we've been through whatever hard times they have to face, that's all."

"And both find men to love them, just like ours!" Libby added.

Merry nodded and smiled as they went back in. Her longing for Darcy to come home to her as Cam had to Libby made her realize again that she was very much afraid. Still, she felt she had no choice but to risk dealing not only with the tricky Peggy but with that Satan himself, John André. And, thank God, for whatever reasons, André had seen fit to speak to Peggy on her behalf. Cam had balked, arguing with her over the dangers she would face, for he did not trust anything John André was involved in, but she had convinced him that it was worth anything for her to save Darcy. And, loving Libby as he did, Cam had been beaten down by the strength and determination of her sister's woman's heart.

Mrs. Benedict Arnold waited nervously with her son in her arms to greet her old family friend Toller Devlin on the lawn of her temporary home in the thick forest that bordered the Hudson River. She had not spoken to Toller since he had sided with John André and insisted that he leave Philadelphia without her. Though Papa had ranted and raved at the time, she refused to so much as be in the same room with Toller—though Papa had invited him to the wedding—since Toller had agreed she sell herself to Benedict Arnold for the cause. He must have known her heart had once been only André's, yet he had not given a fig for that!

Still, all that roiling passion seemed quite distant now, though her need for André had not faded. She watched as Toller rode down the lane and spoke with the guards at the gate. Her husband had left behind a double contingent from his garrison across the river today. General Arnold was supposedly over there himself right now, visiting the fortifications of West Point, across the river.

Two months ago Benedict Arnold had been given command of that fort and the entire essential stretch of the Hudson River by General Washington, who, fool that he was, Peggy thought smugly, trusted Benedict yet. Benedict had asked for West Point when he could have gone back into battle as commander of the left wing of the army—an assignment that Washington should have known he would greatly prefer. But some friends were loyal and blind to the end, the way she had once been to both John André and Toller Devlin himself, Peggy thought.

But Benedict, thanks to her urging and their secret correspondence with John André, had asked for this assignment because the British wanted West Point. That and the 3,000 or more American soldiers General Arnold would hand over to them when he turned on his native country for revenge and money and glory—and his wife's continued admiration—very, very soon. For if the British held West Point they held the Hudson, and with that they could cut off the northern states. Then they would isolate the south and achieve final victory.

But Peggy Shippen Arnold cared not one whit for all that military maneuvering. What absolutely mattered was that Benedict had actually gone off today to meet secretly with John André to arrange the final plans for his defection. Peggy just couldn't wait to get out of here to British-held New York City, where she could bask in the glow of being a famous turncoat's wife and inspiration. She wanted John André dependent on her for her husband's cooperation and goodwill. She wanted John André for herself, one way or the other, for the rest of her days. Still, life with Benedict Arnold had not been so bad in the interim.

As his fiancée and then his wife, Peggy had truly reigned as the social queen of Philadelphia during the months Benedict had governed it as Washington's commander. Benedict might be thirty-nine to her twenty, but he was still virile, dashing and exciting. She got everything she wanted without fussing, as she had had to with Papa over the years, though she surmised Benedict was often in debt. He was both humbly romantic during the day and passionate at night—and she had borne him a lovely son he doted on. Yet—she could not help it—he was not John André. She jerkily fingered the locket she always wore, the one that hid a lock of André's hair. She had not laid eyes on her brilliant hot-and-cold lover for over two years. Yet her obsessive need for him grew ever stronger, as did her willingness to do whatever she must to have him groveling before her in the end.

"Peggy, you *are* looking well!" Toller told her as he dismounted and one of the guards led his horse away. "And is this baby Edward? How is he? I promised your father I would ask at once."

"The baby's not changed one bit from when Grandfather Edward saw him only last month. At least my son has won him over to my marriage," she added as she escorted Toller in without taking his proffered arm.

She told him a bit about the place as they walked. Two miles from the shore, and outside the range of British guns, this fine house went with the command at West Point. "Yet I find it all terribly primitive," she admitted with a sigh, "isolated in these mountains and forests. I told my dearest Benedict I'm a city girl, but you know, Tory Toller," she rattled on, "the house did belong to the Tory colonel Beverley Robinson, a wealthy landowner who was once a friend of George Washington. Its safety and grandeur are the only reasons Benedict says he let me travel here with the child to join him."

"Peggy, before we go in..." Toller said, fumbling with the buttons of his riding cloak in the doorway. "I'm sorry you felt I let you down over losing André. And I am grateful we are all friends again."

"Best beware whom you include in your 'all,' Toller," she told him tartly as she stepped inside the elegantly furnished house. "The fact that I'm helping to set this up between you and Meredith Morgan, the so-called countess of Belfort, when she arrives here tomorrow is because John asked it, not you!"

"I see. So you and André are still a pair. Amazing!"

"You know nothing of it!" she insisted, hoping he had no inkling of the Arnold-André plotting, no matter how tight he had once been with André.

"I do know that your first plan to ruin Merry Morgan by trying to ship her off with Darcy failed. So now you evidently think I'm up to finishing the job for you!"

"I did not say any of that. You're as bad as Papa, jumping to conclusions and then raving about them!"

"Peggy," he said, more fervently than he'd intended, catching her hand to press it between his own, "you're going to ruin your life if you're still carrying some sort of torch for André. He's in New York with the British, and you're here with a great American general who was kind enough to let a Tory like me visit. And André will never be wed to anything but his own ambition."

She yanked her hand back. "There was a time, I recall, when you urged me to do *anything* for your friend John André! What's the matter? Has he let the splendid Toller down somehow? You're a fine one to talk about ambitions, carrying torches, never marrying!" she shouted. The baby in her arms fussed and then wailed, but Peggy plunged on while she bounced it.

"You have never loved anyone—just things, Toller. You don't love, you want to possess things. And when Merry Morgan wouldn't have you, you included her in that list. Now I'm telling you, she will be here tomorrow, and you can just see if you get her to go to Philadelphia with you! I say she never will unless you abduct her by force, so don't lecture me!"

"Peggy, I didn't mean to—" he began when she paused to take a breath, but she cut him off.

"Oh, yes, you did! Merry Morgan's love for that Frenchman—and his for her, I guess—evidently turned out to be too strong even for what I intended for them! She'll never go with you as long as she's married to that man she far preferred to you, even if he is yet a prisoner in England. You may think you have a plan up your sleeve to make her go back to Philadelphia with you, but maybe you'd be better off with a pistol. But, yes, if you want to know, I still hate her, and I'll be damned before she'll have something I can't!"

So that was it, Toller realized as he stared at her, aghast at the torrent of emotion. This whole tirade centered around the fact that Merry had managed to keep the man she loved through all sorts of catastrophes and Peggy had not. Astounded at the depth of her desire for revenge, he glared at the pretty young woman he had once thought his naive friend and innocent confidante. Revenge should be for men, men like him, with reputations and honor and fortunes at stake, not for the likes of her, he thought.

But it amused him that her beloved John André was deceiving her still. He had evidently not told Peggy that Darcy had arrived in New York on a British transport and was to be sent here tomorrow, only to find Toller Devlin and Merry together. André had suggested Toller make it look as if Merry shot Darcy when Darcy challenged them. That would either tame or ruin Merry, André had insisted. And then, a grieving, guilt-ridden new widow, she would return on Toller's protective arm to Philadelphia, where he could make of her what he would— whore or mistress, perhaps even wife.

But Toller Devlin still hadn't decided if he really wanted to take orders from John André, though it might make Peggy Shippen Arnold a happier woman. But, damn her, Toller thought, if this sullen, bitter woman before him thought she had John André where she wanted him, she was indeed the queen of fools!

The next day, Merry rode along at a good clip between the two soldiers Cam had been able to pull from the garrison at New Haven. After two days on the road they were approaching the Arnold home near West Point. Merry had insisted on leaving New Haven when Cam did, though both he and Libby had tried to talk her into waiting to see Peggy until Lafayette and his network of spies could be told that the young woman still had some sort of secret ties to John André. But Merry felt that Peggy's link to André, which General Arnold presumably knew nothing of, might be another weapon to use to force Peggy to help her beg for Darcy's freedom.

They had spent last night in an inn not far from here, and Merry had urged the soldiers to set out right after breakfast. She hoped it was late enough that General Arnold would be away, though. She had to see Peggy alone first so that she knew how to play things. She was scared, but she spoke words of courage to herself as the large house in the woods came into view and they were let through by the American sentries.

And then Peggy came out on the lawn to greet her, beautifully gowned and with an infant in her arms. Merry's heart sank. Did everyone in the world have husbands and children but her?

"I did not know you had a child," Merry said.

"A son, named Edward for my father."

Cam's men helped her down and she introduced them to Peggy. Peggy suggested they take the horses to the small barracks across the lawn where the guards stayed. Merry agreed, despite the fact that she could tell that the men did not want to leave her, for she wanted to speak to Peggy alone.

"The general's gone out," Peggy said, trying to calm her voice. It was not facing this woman again that made her jumpy, Peggy assured herself, but the fact that Benedict was still out meeting with John André on the British man-of-war *Vulture*, just downstream. And, if all went well, when he returned he would have traded his plans for handing over West Point for their future in New York and London. She wanted Merry out of the way when he returned! She wished she had never given in to John André's request, but perhaps Toller could make it quick and get Merry away from here.

"I can actually say I hope you are making General Arnold happy, Peggy," Merry said as they stood facing each other on the still-dewy grass. "He's a fine general who has not always gotten what he's deserved."

Merry saw Peggy's frown pucker her pretty face. She didn't wear her hair so high out here in these forests, at least. Merry wondered what she was thinking, but she would have been shocked to know.

How Peggy would have loved to spill in this detested woman's face all her glorious plans! Benedict Arnold had not gotten what he deserved, Merry had said. Did she mean the horrid way Congress had treated him or the fact that she herself had married him? And how dare she look at her that way just because she had been to the court of the French king! How could her sister Polly or her stupid father have adored this spoiled, vindictive Morgan woman so!

"So," Peggy told her, "let's simply conclude our business as quickly as we can. Come inside."

"If you wish," Merry said as they started at a good clip toward the house. "Peggy, I need your help to get my husband released from a prison in London. And, if you cooperate, I shall choose to ignore your hired abduction of the two of us."

"Really?" Peggy sputtered, gripping her son so tightly he wailed. She bounced him but shouted over him. "Choose to ignore? You're demented. I simply haven't the vaguest notion what you mean!"

"It all fits, and believe me, I've had enough time to think about it! You hired some ruffians to abduct Darcy and me and make it seem I had done it to force him into marriage. Now, unless you want your father, your husband and your adored John André to get involved—and General Washington to know of your ties to André—"

Peggy gasped. Even the baby quieted. "You know, you leave me no choice but to give in—on one condition. Enter, then," Peggy said, and pushed open the front door to the house.

Merry's insides cartwheeled. Was it the mention of André that had made Peggy so easily acquiesce? On the doorstep of the house, she darted a look back at the two guards Cam had sent with her. One of them leaned on a fence near the sentries. She waved to him to let him know things were well and hurried inside after Peggy. But she was barely down the entry hall and into the well-appointed drawing room behind her hostess when she saw that Peggy had a surprise for her, too. A man, elegantly attired in silver velvet and satin, rose from the settee under the window where he had evidently been taking late breakfast on a tray. She gasped as his gray eyes met hers.

"Toller? Here?" Merry choked out.

"My dearest Merry!" He affected surprise as he rubbed his hands on his linen napkin. "We're together again!"

Merry could have fallen through the floor. She backed toward the door and bumped against it as he strode forward to take her hands. "Old reunion week all around, isn't it, my dear?" he said. Peggy couldn't mask a smirk.

"My single condition to agreeing to your demands, Merry," Peggy said, "is that you go back to Philadelphia with Toller right away while I ask for your Darcy to be released. And that you do anything Toller asks while you wait. That's all."

Merry was still gawking at Toller as if he were a silver serpent waiting to strike. "No. Not that—I couldn't."

"But you can, my dear," Toller said with a grin as his eyes raked her. "No one need know. You can and you will. Now, promise me!"

Before she could protest again, he yanked her to him, one hand in her hair, as Peggy went out and firmly closed the door behind. Peggy knew Toller had a gun, just as she'd suggested, so she didn't think a thing of the silence in the room. But just in case Merry raised a fuss after Toller "reasoned" further with her, she'd best go out and tell Merry's companions that all was fine.

She had just started across the lawn toward the barracks when two riders hurtled in from different directions. With a grin and a broad wave that told her all was set in his negotiations with André, her husband came pounding down the lane from the river. It had been galling her for days to know that John André would be so close by with her husband, when it should be with her! But she couldn't believe Benedict was back already—and so early in the morning! She did not want him to know about all these other goings-on with Merry and Toller. But, worse, from the other direction came Darcy Mont, riding like the wind!

Peggy stared and gasped as if Darcy were an apparition. If he were back, why had John not let her know? He had vowed they were working together, and she had kept her side of the bargain by helping turn her husband to the British cause. Her insides twisted. And Toller was inside with Merry! Had Toller known somehow? Or had all this been Merry's trick from the first? If so, she and Toller would be caught, and Benedict would learn all about her earlier trickery!

"My dearest love, all went so well," Benedict began as he dismounted stiffly, favoring the leg that had healed shorter and made him limp.

"My darling...good!" she cried, and was off like a shot for the house, despite the puzzlement on her suddenly deserted husband's face.

Darcy passed through the guards and reined in. General Arnold recognized him but thought he looked thinner and paler. That's right, he'd heard this man had been imprisoned in Lon-

don for a year or so. A shudder shot through Arnold. The
man's eyes looked haunted. He must be very certain that his
plan to defect did not go awry, because he could never bear
prison. Far better that the Americans should hang him or shoot
him, as they did spies and traitors. Arnold almost went for his
gun, frightened by Darcy's expression and the speed with which
he had arrived. What if his plot had somehow been discovered
by the Americans?

"Darcy Mont! Whatever brings you here?"

"My wife."

"She's not here, but mine is—"

Cam Gant's two soldiers came running toward Darcy. "Sir,"
one shouted up at him, "Mrs. Mont thought you were still in
London, and—"

"Is she here?"

"Inside with Mrs. Arnold."

Darcy raced for the house with the surprised General Arnold limping behind him. Peggy Arnold stood just inside the
first room, as if she were expecting him, holding the infant to
her and pointing at a closed door. Darcy strode over and shoved
it in. Merry was within, locked in a frenzied embrace with none
other than Toller Devlin, the lover Lord Stormont had told him
she had come back to America to see!

"Merry!" he yelled, lunging at Devlin, despite the gun he
saw the man held in his hand.

He yanked Merry away from Devlin's grip. The man leveled
the pistol at him. Darcy ducked as it exploded. Merry screamed
his name and kept screaming. He smashed first one fist, then
another, into Devlin to send him flying. He grabbed Merry's
wrist to pull her to him.

"Is this true? Is any of it true?" He shook her while she hung
limp and stunned in his arms.

Peggy shrieked and the baby cried until General Arnold
himself fired a pistol shot into the ceiling and roared, "Silence!"

All but the baby quieted. Merry crumpled into Darcy's arms.
He held her to him, cradling her now, stroking her disheveled
golden hair.

"Sit down, all of you!" Benedict Arnold commanded. "I
need to know exactly what is going on here. Mrs. Arnold, take

little Edward out, and fetch a cold compress for Mistress Morgan—ah, Mrs. Mont." He motioned to Cam's men, who had charged in, too, to help Toller up from where he lay sprawled in the ashes of the hearth.

Darcy collapsed on the settee with Merry in his arms. In this first moment of really seeing her, touching her, it suddenly did not matter one bit that he had found her in Devlin's embrace. After all, the man had had a gun, and she'd been struggling. And Darcy, stunned as he was, considered again the sources of his information: it was Lord Stormont's advice that had angered him, and it was John André who had told him she would be here with Devlin. Claudine was long dead, and this was his honest rebel, Merry! And yet it gnawed at him that he had seen Merry's note to André in which she had asked for this visit. And to find her here like this, after all the time she had been in France with him locked away!

"Merry, Merry..." He shook her gently as she looked dazedly around.

"Oh," she said, her face glazed with tears. "You're really here, and it isn't a dream. Hold me, just hold me!"

When Peggy came back in without their son, General Arnold pulled her back out by her arm. "What in blazes is going on here today?" he demanded.

"André," she said, not looking in his eyes even when he gasped. "André set all this up, too. But he obviously did not know the timing—"

"Set what up? That British bastard had better not be playing both ends against the middle when my neck's at stake! I'll not have some petty personal goings-on endangering all this about to happen here."

He lifted his head when he heard another rider thunder in. Not intending to let his wife out of his sight until she'd finally explained this chaos to his satisfaction, he pulled her to the door behind him.

"Damnation," he whispered to her. "It's the man from the British ship *Vulture* who rowed André over to the shore so that we could meet."

He loosed Peggy, then limped down into the yard to greet the man as she hurried in his wake. "Two things quick, gen'ral," Peggy heard the man say breathlessly. "André's been cap-

tured with a letter in your hand and the map of West Point you
gave him in his boot. And General Washington's coming here
to breakfast, though he don't know a thing 'bout your dealings yet, I take it.''

Quickly the man wheeled away and rode out. But Peggy's
legs had given way at the news that André had been captured
and Arnold had to hold her up. Her face crumpled, and she
sobbed aloud.

"Not now, Peggy, not now," he said, thinking that her grief
was all for his endangered plans. "Washington doesn't know
yet—or at least it's likely he doesn't. I presume he was riding
through the area and thought to have a simple breakfast with
me, as he often has before. The fact that this other matter has
occurred may have nothing to do with it."

"You can't stay...can't stay to face Washington if they
have...have...André," she sobbed. She gasped when she saw
Darcy standing in the door behind them. Arnold's hand went
to his pistol again, but the Frenchman evidently noted nothing
amiss but Peggy's tears.

"My wife is dazed and not making much sense, either
General," Darcy told him. "If I could take her upstairs and lay
her down, it might help. I believe our wives had an argument
today and opened up old wounds, you see, but it is not the time
now—"

"No, I agree it isn't. There's a guest room at the top of the
stairs."

"Thank you. And I have two soldiers guarding Devlin until
I can talk to him," Darcy added, but General Arnold was already helping Peggy upstairs. Darcy carried Merry up, then
went down for water for her. He had never seen her this distracted, and it frightened him.

Merry lay there frozen on her back, staring up at the ceiling
after Darcy promised to be right back and went out. She was
still stunned: Toller grabbing her, saying all those things, then
Darcy appearing when she had been certain he was in prison in
England. Where had he gone now? Her mind raced. To question Toller? Had she somehow imagined all these shocks today, imagined Toller telling her she must be his or Darcy was
as good as dead. Where was Darcy?

She wanted to be with him! She had to be! She sat up and scrubbed the tears from her cheeks. She shoved her loosed hair back. And then she heard the breaking glass and sat stock-still as Peggy's muted but passionate words seeped through the wall, just as they had in those earlier days.

"You can't leave me. You can't! We're in this together! If you go, I do, too! What will I tell Washington? Tell all of them! She is back with Darcy, and you'll not leave as André did. You have to save him if they've captured him! You have to!" Peggy cried, and another piece of glass shattered the wall where Merry pressed her ear. Whatever was Peggy ranting about?

Merry stumbled to her feet and opened the door to the upstairs hall. She had to find Darcy to make certain he was real. She had to find out what Peggy meant! She had to be sure Toller told Darcy the truth!

Then General Benedict Arnold flung open the next door in the hall and slammed it behind him. He rushed right by her without so much as a glance. He clambered down the stairs, his shorter leg clumping with every step. In the room he had just left, yet another piece of glass smashed against the door.

Merry stood wavering in the hall. She heard General Arnold give a command below, then more than one horse gallop off. She heard Darcy's voice raised in anger and started down the stairs. She threw herself in Darcy's arms the second he started back up toward her, despite the fact that she spilled the pitcher of water he carried.

"I love you, I love you so, Darcy! And it wasn't what you think with Toller!" she sobbed against his chest. He felt thinner, harder, but this was Darcy come back to her! "Peggy had Toller here!" she went on. "You can ask him! Make him tell!"

"I cannot right now," Darcy told her as he took her back to the upstairs room where he had left her and sat on the bed to hold her in his arms. "For some reason, General Arnold told Cam's men to free Toller on his way out while I was fetching this water. The general and Toller are both gone."

"Maybe because Peggy and Arnold had a fight. She broke things," Merry told him.

Peggy again, Darcy thought. Until he got his hands on Toller or cleared up things with the strange-acting General Arnold, he intended to speak to Mrs. Arnold, even if she was throwing a fit and breaking things. But still he held Merry. She was telling him the truth, of course she was. She always had, his Merry.

They heard many horses coming in the yard. Darcy went over to the window, and she went right behind him. They stared out in disbelief, but it was a morning for surprises. "Washington and Lafayette!" he cried. "There must really be something up, and here Arnold's just missed them."

Peggy Shippen presided at the late breakfast, looking like a chalk-white ghost. All color had drained from her face but for her bloodshot eyes. Her hands trembled; she knocked over the sugar cone, trying to cut off the tip, and slopped coffee on the pristine linen when she poured. She seemed not to be listening, not even to General Washington, who regretted that he had missed his friend Benedict. Instead, she kept her head cocked, as if she were awaiting someone else outside. Perhaps, Merry thought, Peggy had finally taken leave of her senses.

Once again, as she had years before, Merry found her resentment for Peggy tempered by sympathy, if not understanding. Perhaps Peggy had never gotten over losing André and today General Arnold had discovered that and stormed out. Perhaps it had unbalanced her for good. She herself had been dazed by everything. Why couldn't General Washington see that Peggy was ill and send her upstairs?

And then what Peggy had evidently been listening for occurred: a single rider's fast hoof beats over the men's chatter and the ding of silver and porcelain. Peggy stood and turned toward the doorway, then walked out of the room without a word. And screamed. They found her in a heap on the doorstep, a messenger of Washington's leaning over her. He straightened and saluted when he saw his commander-in-chief, breakfast napkin still tied around his neck.

"General, a spy, John André, Commander Clinton's adjutant general, no less, was caught this morning near Tarrytown, sir." He glanced down at the prone woman as Merry bent over her, then back up at Washington. "The map he had, and a letter, too, were written in General Arnold's hand. The guards say the general rode out a bit ago, sir. All our evidence suggests Benedict Arnold's gone turncoat and tried to take West Point with him. And if this is Mrs. Arnold, sir, I swear, I didn't tel her a thing of it before she just fell over like this when she saw me.''

Shouts of shock came from the men who pressed together in the hallway of the house as Merry and General Washington himself stooped to help lift Peggy.

Darcy and Merry left the Arnold house early the next morning. Washington and Lafayette and their entourage had ridden out yesterday, leaving the hysterical Peggy under guard. Washington had seen her alone, and—a gentleman to the last— he had declared poor Peggy innocent of all the general's doings, because that was what she claimed. Merry was disappointed in Washington, but Darcy sympathized with a man of honor who could not recognize deceit from an attractive woman when it hit him in the face.

Peggy had been given laudanum to quiet her hysteria. When she was better she would be sent back under guard to her father in Philadelphia. So Darcy gave up hope of talking to her for now. He suggested that he and Merry head for Philadelphia, where he would assume the post of liaison between Washington and the French commander, Rochambeau.

In the bedroom next to Peggy's at the Arnold house the night before they set out, Merry and Darcy had lain side by side and talked most of the night. Of his imprisonment, of her days without him in France, of her decision to return. Merry shared with him news of Amélie's progress and told him of the letters from the trunk in the attic at Belfort. They rejoiced together about his Amélie and the children that they now hoped they could make together in the future. Darcy told her the things Lord Stormont had said of her, and she marveled at the wickedness in the world and the enemies they had made. And now Toller had been freed by the turncoat Arnold. At least General Arnold himself had been exposed before he could ruin all they had worked for so hard by handing over half the new nation to the British in one fell swoop.

''Washington's doubly grieved about Arnold's treachery,'' Darcy said the morning they set out, after they had parted from Cam's men at King's Ferry. The soldiers headed for Newport to report to Cam, and Merry and Darcy crossed the Hudson and rode on into New Jersey on their 130-mile trip ''home'' to

Philadelphia. "He's lost a great general, and a man he thought was a good friend. Deceived by one he thought he knew, one he fully trusted..." His voice trailed off.

"But that sort of thing is over for us!" Merry declared. Then, when he still seemed lost in frowning thought, she cried, "Look, darling, do you realize what road we're on? The one the British and Hessians stopped us on when we fled New York together!"

He reached over to her to cover her hands on the reins with one of his. "I am not certain we were 'together' then, but we are now. And I wondered when you'd stop staring at me long enough to notice where we are. I am here, Merry, and I am real. And I believe you, not Lord Stormont or that damned John André. Though I should not speak that way of him, for they will no doubt execute him for his part in all this." He frowned again. He still had to find Toller Devlin and talk to Peggy when they brought her back to Philadelphia. He believed Merry, but he needed it settled once and for all before his private wars were over.

He looked around on the road to get their exact bearings. "We're not far from where the enemy stopped us," he announced. "There's a certain farmhouse just up ahead with an apple tree in back where we might stop to have a bite to eat and visit a brave farmer's wife and her two daughters."

Merry breathed more easily, without her great burden for the first time in years. Nothing could defeat her and Darcy now! They had their whole life together ahead, and perhaps with children, too! But they found the farmhouse and the barn where they had hidden burned and deserted. They rode on along the road toward Pennsylvania, as they had four years before, afraid they might find other destruction.

But everything seemed secure here, even the little footbridge they had hidden under. For Merry the years dropped away. She felt young and nervous again with this dangerous, darkly handsome man. But she would never want to go back to those days, she assured herself, the days before she had known and understood his pain and he had completely trusted her, as he did now.

"Merry, *ma belle, ma comtesse, ma femme*," he murmured as they reined in to water their horses at the same pond where she had hidden while he'd gone off to find her some suitable clothes to wear to meet the Shippens. He reached up to lift her gently down from her horse, his green gaze linked with hers. She smiled, suddenly so shy that her lower lip trembled.

"I have dreamed of that other time," he admitted as his eyes left hers to take in the beauty of the sheltered spot. Through trees edged with flaming autumn hues the sun filtered down, gilding the water and warming the air.

"I recall when that poor nag you bought came to get a drink and startled us—while we were busy," she told him as they walked hand in hand down to the pond.

"During the long months in prison, I have thought of this very place so many times," he told her. "When I could picture you here bathing, beautiful and nude, when I could recall that we were—busy, as you put it—I could get myself through another damned day. Merry, loving you—despite all those things I worried about with you back at court, and then Toller Devlin—kept me going."

Loving you, he had said. *Loving you!* Her heart soared. He pulled her to him, and they clung, rocking against each other by the fringe of the mossy pool. And then their motions quickened, their breathing accelerated in unison. Soon they were laughing and tugging off their shoes. They waded in knee-deep despite the crisp tang of the water, wetting breeches, stockings, skirts and petticoats as they struggled out of them.

"And when I saw that you dared to stand there naked that day," he muttered through their frenzied kisses and hasty showering of the bank with garments, "I could not believe my eyes."

"Believe your eyes now, my love!" She tossed her final scrap of undergarments to the grass. "Believe I love only you, and always will!"

They splashed and laughed, kissed and caressed. They churned the placid little pond of memory to a wavy ocean. He carried her up on the grass just before they would have drowned. Half hidden beneath a bush, they melded perfectly, as if they had never been apart. For both of them, so long distant in body if not in heart, it was wilder and more wonderful than ever.

Chapter Sixteen

Merry and Darcy leased a house on Crown Street in Philadelphia, not far from the Shippen home. Darcy traveled a great deal to set up and keep open the lines of communication between Congress and his countrymen, Rochambeau in the north and Lafayette in the south. Lafayette had been assigned to chase the traitor Benedict Arnold, who was harassing Virginians in his first undertaking as a British general. Whether or not Washington took his old friend's raids in his home state as a personal affront no one knew. But his private orders to Lafayette, Darcy told Merry, had been quite explicit: find the turncoat dog who was destroying American warehouses, tobacco crops and plantations and bring him back, dead or alive. Meanwhile, Rochambeau and Washington spent the winter of 1780-81 planning possible attacks on New York City and a southern campaign to bolster Lafayette's efforts.

In October Mrs. Benedict Arnold had been sent back to her father's house with her six-month-old son, where she became an enforced recluse. Though Washington had been magnanimous with her, most citizens were so incensed by her husband's deceitful and bloody deeds that they did not believe she was innocent at all. By the spring it was considered best for all that she be handed over to the British in New York City, to which her husband had been recalled from Virginia. Either Lafayette had gotten too close to capturing England's prize turncoat general, or the British themselves had sickened at the viciousness Arnold had displayed in Virginia. At any rate, one week in April, when Darcy was out of town, Merry received a surprise summons from Judge Shippen: Peggy wanted to see her before she left Philadelphia for the last time.

Merry pondered the invitation for a long time. She had made her peace with the Shippens before Peggy had returned, and she wanted to put that earlier part of her life behind her. Besides, Darcy had asked to speak with Peggy, and she had turned him down each time. And he had been unable to locate Toller Devlin, whose vast holdings in Pennsylvania had now been confiscated, since he was under suspicion of collusion with Benedict Arnold. Merry had worried that Peggy's refusal and Darcy's inability to locate Toller would keep Darcy from trusting her. But all that had evidently been resolved last November when she had given him the joyous news that she was carrying his child.

"I have a surprise for you," she had said over an intimate little breakfast before the fireplace in their bedroom. "Something we will want to include in the letter we're writing to Amélie."

"That her imaginary sister is also welcome to come live here with us?" he had teased, his green eyes warm on her over his saucer of coffee.

"Not that," she had said, hardly able to keep herself from exploding across the table to hug him in her joy, "for Amélie won't ever need an imaginary sibling again. I myself have been able to give up dreaming of things I want since I wed you, you know. So I thought a real brother or sister would be preferable to the invisible Marie."

He had banged his saucer down with a ding, and he had gasped. "You mean—" he managed, his big hand rattling silver against his plate.

"I do. In late August or early September, I calculate, though I'm rather new at all this, and—"

It was he who had exploded then, with grins and shouts and a trembling in his big body that touched her heart. He had whirled her around and then tenderly cradled her in his lap as if she were the child yet to come. She had never known a deeper love than at that very moment. After that she had shut out the possibility that he still did not trust her, just as she had shut out thoughts of the possible danger to him when he rode out on his assignments to link the French and the Americans in this war.

She knew she could not bear it if she were to lose again the only man she had ever loved, now that she really had him at last. And that was the real reason she had finally decided to see Peggy Arnold today. Though Peggy was being sent to her husband in New York City, it was in Tappan, New York, last October, that Peggy had lost John André, the only man she had ever loved, to a hangman's noose.

The two American soldiers acting as sentries at the front door of the Shippen house opened it for Merry, then turned back to stand at ease, staring down the people gathered along the walkway as she went in. Judge Shippen greeted her in the elegant foyer. "My dear Merry, so good of you to come after all the unpleasantness Peggy has caused you and your husband."

"That crowd, Judge Shippen," Merry said, "surely they are not just waiting for a glimpse of Peggy when she leaves today."

"I'm afraid so. Some rabble is always out there. Notoriety, when she only wanted fame," he muttered as he escorted Merry in to wait in the downstairs drawing room. It was curtained and lit only by muted daylight—and memory. She looked around, noting that nothing had changed here, where Toller Devlin and John André had called on her and Peggy during those long months of British occupation. Poor Peggy, Merry mused. She truly pitied her. Perhaps everywhere she looked, here or in all of Philadelphia, she recalled her lost love. It had been that way for her when Darcy had left France for his dangerous mission in England, when he had yet had every chance of coming back.

Judge Shippen drew her from her reveries. "And Polly, who has always admired you, has asked me to thank you for your kind invitation to visit at your new home. When Peggy is out of my other daughters' lives, I daresay, they will be better off and can resume calling on their own friends—those who will still receive them, in spite of the Benedict Arnold taint on us all. Ah, I shall fetch Peggy, then. She's nearly packed, you know," he said, and rattled off something else that she could not catch as he stepped out. Merry waited by the low fire on the hearth. It seemed barely a moment before Peggy came in and closed the door behind her.

"I did not know if you would come," she told Merry. She was as beautifully gowned as usual, in a stunning scarlet almost the hue of the British uniforms. Her face seemed a carved mask of imperious disdain. Her hair, as in the old days, was padded, piled and ribboned, though to Merry's eyes, used now to the intricate French coiffures, it was no longer shocking.

"Perhaps I came for your family's sake," Merry told her, standing her ground behind the settee by the hearth. "Or perhaps because I'm amazed you still try to carry off the lie that you were innocent of the collusion between John André and General Arnold. Even now the city awaits your appearance, just as you always wanted—if for all the wrong reasons."

Peggy's gaze fluttered around the room. Her hands flew to her throat, where Merry saw she still wore the locket with André's hair. They could both hear the murmur of the restless crowd on the street even in here, though it was muted by the walls and closed drapes.

"My reasons—and my innocence—are no one's concern but my own," Peggy told her, not moving one step from the closed door. "And I asked you here not for my family or to make some confession, but to suit myself. I wanted to see your smug face when I told you I have seen to it you will not be able to keep the man you love."

Merry's insides tilted, but her eyes did not waver from Peggy's hard, triumphant stare. Let this woman rave! She knew nothing of the way things were now between her and Darcy. Merry would never tell her of this child of love she carried, nor of all the pain she had gone through to earn Darcy's trust. And that trust, Peggy could never touch. She would not give Peggy the slightest pleasure by showing any fear. Besides, this time, her threat had to be a lie. Peggy had been under American military escort everywhere she had gone, and she was under house arrest here. Her confederate, Toller Devlin, tainted as he was by association with Arnold, dared not set foot in Philadelphia, where everyone recognized him. If he did, he would be arrested. And Peggy's ties to André had been cut with his death. Yet this final, cruel attempt to harm her and all she held dear undercut the pity Merry had long felt for Peggy Shippen Arnold.

"Threaten all you will, Mrs. Benedict Arnold! I've been attacked before, and by liars far more adept than you. As for your reasons being your own, that isn't true, either. You might have fooled General Washington, your husband, your father—all the men in the world, for all I know. But I know you're a greater traitor than your husband. Because I know you did everything for an unworthy, deceitful man named John André, who brought you not love but a living hell that's only beginning!"

Merry moved then. She darted to the front windows and yanked the draperies apart to open the room to sunlight and the stares of the crowd. A chant of "Hang all the traitors! Hang all the traitors!" got louder and louder. Someone heaved a stone, and a pane of the large window shattered. Merry jumped to close the drapes as Peggy screamed and tore out into the foyer with Merry behind her.

Judge Shippen and his two youngest daughters ran down from upstairs, Edward Arnold in Sally's arms. Peggy ran right into her father on the stairs and then snatched her child from Sally.

"I am sorry, Judge Shippen," Merry said. "I made the mistake of opening the drapes, and someone threw a stone."

"Oh," Merry's old comrade, Polly, said, her eyes owlish behind her reading spectacles. "You mean for once it wasn't Peggy?"

"I think," Merry said, staring up at the distraught Peggy, who clutched her son to her while the crowd's chants rose and swelled outside, "Peggy's done with breaking things. I'll just go out the back way by the mews now."

Her own words, *Peggy's done with breaking things,* echoed in Merry's mind as Polly followed her to the back of the house. Peggy was done with breaking things because she'd shattered everything.

Merry gave Polly a quick goodbye hug on the doorstoop where she had once seen John André kissing Peggy. Yes, Merry thought mournfully, Peggy has broken everything, including her own heart, and all for a man not even worth loving.

On the first day of September, 1781, as the combined armies of France and America marched south toward Philadelphia to take on the British at Yorktown in Virginia, Merry Morgan Mont gave birth to her first child. It was harder than anything she had ever done, except getting through those times when she had thought she had lost Darcy. But she felt so exhilarated and triumphant when the birth was over that she knew it was a sign of victory, for the troops must surely be here soon.

"*Sacrebleu*, my Merry, he is a wonder!" Darcy told her when he held his son for the first time, sitting gingerly on the side of the bed next to her. His hands spanned the length of the infant's body and trembled with joy as their son kicked his tiny legs and waved his balled fists before they wrapped the blanket back around him.

"When it was happening," she told him, her voice weary, "for a few moments I thought I was in the big bed at Belfort." Every muscle in her body ached, but her heart sang.

"Better he be born here," he told her, "heir not to the old Belfort name but the new American name Mont we have made together for him." He nestled the child back in the crook of her arm where she had held him for his first nursing only moments before. "Our son, born of the union of old France and the new America," he told her with a moist-eyed smile. "Andrew Thomas Mont, our proud, bold American boy."

He had been adamant about their not naming the child for anyone else, neither king nor general, and she had gladly agreed. This child was their link to the future, not the past. Now she held the child in her arms as she held Darcy in her love. And, she thought fiercely as she cradled their child and drifted off to sleep again, no threats from a bitter woman now far away in New York or from that raving rich Tory, Toller Devlin, running for his life somewhere, and no dead, deceitful spirits in their graves, could ever threaten her and this new life she had made with Darcy.

It was but three days later when first the American and then French armies marched through Philadelphia on their way south to join Lafayette, who was skirmishing with Cornwallis and the British army at Yorktown, Virginia. Word had just come that Benedict Arnold had led a devastating raid on his home state of Connecticut in which patriot blood had mingled in the streets with melted sugar from burned warehouses. But not even that could dampen Philadelphia's enthusiasm for this day and the coming battle. Only those close to Washington knew that the entire cause might yet be lost if the French fleet under Admiral de Grasse did not arrive from the West Indies in time to help in Virginia. Without ships to hold off British reinforcements, the battle and the war might yet be lost.

Though Merry was still weak from childbirth, she insisted on getting dressed and going out in a hired sedan chair to watch the troops march by. Andrew was asleep in his cradle back at the house, but she was here to cheer Darcy and his countrymen on! She craned her neck and squinted into the sun, looking for her husband. He would ride in the vanguard of the parade, just behind Rochambeau, the French general, who spoke not one word of English and sometimes used Darcy for a translator.

And there they were! Rochambeau rode by with General Washington with an escort of Virginia light horse. Rochambeau was a big smiling bear of a man whose troops lovingly called him "Papa," though not to his face, Darcy said. And there came Darcy on a prancing black horse, right behind the generals! The man who had done so much to arrange this liaison of powers was finally getting his due, Merry thought. Proud tears stung her eyes.

Darcy spotted her at her appointed place and rode over to lean down and kiss her. Then Washington, usually so grim-faced, smiled and doffed his cockaded bicorne to her. When someone evidently told Rochambeau who she was, the portly man bellowed, *"Vive la belle comtesse de Belfort!"* over the music and the cheers. Then Darcy hurried back to his position and Merry stood in her sedan chair and waved until the front ranks disappeared from sight.

She fluttered an American flag she had ordered from Betsy Ross and cheered when the veteran Soissonnais regiment, favorites of the French queen, went by in their brilliant pink trimmings and their grenadier hats with white ostrich plumes. Philadelphians, so used to the plain uniforms of American motley and wearied by the days of scarlet British coats, went wild at the new sight of the rainbow ranks wheeling by. Their smart, colorful attire and sharply disciplined steps tore cheers from American throats.

Darcy had told Merry earlier that the admiration between the two armies was mutual, for the French had lauded the cleanliness and quick, quiet marching of the Americans, though they were appalled that the colonials ate their meat, vegetables and salad on the same plate and used only vinegar to dress their salads! And it had been quite a shock that the Americans considered their wives out of bounds to the handsome foreigners, but in time they had adapted even to such a primitive custom!

Fifes, drums and field guns saluted the crowds. Exotic tiger skins bounced by on polished saddles; barons, counts and viscounts paraded as finely as they ever had in the paved streets of Paris. Some even frizzed their hair or rouged their faces, reminding Merry of Versailles. However fickle life was there, she was grateful that the strength of France had come here to help her country. The troops were all so splendid that even the hundreds of servants and the massive baggage train trailing behind could not dampen the excitement of the day.

French soldiers, used to Flanders and the Rhine, Darcy had said, now had learned how to charge on narrow tracks, traverse primeval forests and use pioneer resourcefulness. They were proud of fighting here in America, and today they showed it. Soon, she knew, they would make camp with the Americans so that they could meet up with the French navy in Virginia. And it was 25,000,000 livres from a French loan that was holding everything together for the coming big assault on the British at Yorktown. Her eyes alight with the freedom flame, Merry waved her flag. And she cheered, as well, for her and Darcy's own contributions to this glorious day.

That night, when Darcy rode back to have dinner with her before heading south, he tucked both the baby and her gently in their beds.

"I will send word when I can on how things go, my love," he told her, "but I am finally as optimistic as Mr. Franklin. Now we have a trained army under Washington, who has learned his military lessons the hard way since that retreat from Long Island. A French army, and money for provisions, arms and food. Everything is ready for the final victory except the arrival of Admiral de Grasse and his fleet. If they arrive, we will finally have those British bastards right where we want them!"

"And I've got you, Darcy Mont. That's my victory." She smiled up at him.

"You have me," he said just before he kissed her and turned the wick down to gut out the lamp. "And, no matter what, you always will."

Two days later, the first afternoon Merry was really up and about on her own after Andrew's birth, was a hot, fitful day. Thunder rumbled in the distance; the breeze was hot. The baby fussed, and Merry finally fell asleep with her head on her hands writing to Libby at Darcy's desk in the small library downstairs while Andrew slumbered in his cradle across the room. The house was silent but for the wind against the shutters. Her mind was dead to all but her dreams. The cook was shopping; Merry had given the maids the afternoon away, since she felt stronger at last. But one of them was shaking her shoulder now, when she had barely fallen asleep.

"What? The baby?" Merry mumbled before she turned her head. A man was standing there, holding both a gun and her child. Though he wore a gray beard and tattered clothes, Toller Devlin stood in her house, as if he had stepped from the depths of her worst fears.

She snapped instantly alert. "Give me that child," she demanded, standing and reaching out her arms. "You're wanted in this town, and you'd better get out before they find you."

He leveled the gun at her and stepped back with the child. "Your telling Washington and who knows who else about me has seen to that." His voice was bitter and raspy. "I'm hunted high and low, and American soldiers are swarming all over my town house and out at Devlinton, damn you! I did not have a damned thing to do with Arnold turning! But at least Peggy smuggled me some information and funds through her sister Sally before she left town. My dearest Meredith, I've just been hiding until the time was right to come calling on you, and now it's here."

She recognized his desperation, something entirely foreign to the usually smooth Toller, despite all the times she had frustrated his desire for her. Even that day last autumn when she'd seen him near West Point he had not had this crazed look in his eyes. The suave sleekness of Toller Devlin had departed, leaving behind this frightening-looking man. She feared for the child, and for herself, too.

"I'm sorry about all that," she said quietly. "It is truly not my fault. Please give me my child."

"Boy or girl?" he asked, startling her. She had been agonizing over a way to stop him, but as long as he had a gun and the child, there was nothing to do but obey.

"A boy. What do you want, Toller?"

"Judas Priest, even that traitor Arnold has pretty Peggy with him, so I'll take you. After a score I have to settle south of here, we'll head for England. Don't think I didn't squirrel some money away there. Now sit back down at that desk and we'll write your beloved husband a note telling him he can have the child if he swears to let us be in England."

She gasped. Anything but doing that to Darcy! She wanted to scream. But she just stood stock-still, staring at Toller. Was this just blind, cruel chance that he demanded she do to Darcy what his first wife had done? Surely Toller could not know of that. Forgive me, Darcy, she thought. I can only pray you will understand and see through this. I am not Claudine. Our precious little Andrew is not your Amélie, deserted by her mother. Even though you found me in Toller's arms after those long months we were apart, it is not what you think!

Quietly she said, "I will do what you say if you just swear to leave the child here."

"No bargains," Toller said. "You will do what I say *because* we're taking the child, my dearest Meredith. Now sit and write."

She did exactly as he told her, though she took her time, praying that one of the maids would come back in time or someone would come calling. But the day was silent except for the pounding of her heart and the rumbling of thunder. Then she thought of something that might help. As Toller snatched the note he had dictated and skimmed it to be sure she had not tricked him, she said, "I'll just address this envelope then, as he's headed south and they'll have to send for him." Quickly she unstoppered a bottle of greenish invisible ink Darcy still had and dipped another quill in it.

"Toller forced me. Beware trap. Later, England," she scribbled on the piece of paper she would use to enclose the letter, then grabbed her other pen to write "Darcy Mont, My Husband," on it with black ink, much more slowly. She blew on it as she wrote. Just before Toller took the envelope from her to read it, too, she managed to underline the *H* in *Husband*, that sign in the time of Freedom Flame that meant to develop an invisible message with heat. She held her breath, praying the ink on the envelope was dry enough that Toller would not notice it. He did not. He jammed the letter in it, nearly dropping the child.

"Let me take him!" she cried, but he shoved her away with the barrel of the pistol.

"Out through the back way," he ordered. "We take the note with us. I know well enough where your husband is. If you behave when we're out of town, we'll see then about your holding the child."

That was the last promising thing he said to Merry all day.

The combined French and American armies, marching south, had camped near Chester, Pennsylvania, along the broad Delaware River, when Merry's note reached Darcy the next day. It was delivered to him in a meeting in Washington's field tent by a farm boy who was gone before the sentry handed him the note. He started when he recognized Merry's writing, then ripped it open. He prayed nothing had gone wrong with the baby, or even her, since she was just out of childbed. Officers looked up at him from their canvas camp stools around the table with the maps of Yorktown spread all over. They saw the frown on his face changed to a furious scowl as he read silently:

Darcy,
Now that the child is born, the game is up, and I must go with the man I love. Toller Devlin has been my life, and I can no longer pretend to keep that secret from you. If you want your son, come alone by night to the old Willis farmhouse near Riverbend, east of Chester. Bring no one else, and ride in unarmed. And in trade for the child, you will not follow us to that life we deserve elsewhere.

Merry

"*Sacrebleu*, no!" he yelled. Men jumped to their feet. Washington came over to clasp his shoulder.

"Bad news, man? Merry? The child?"

But Darcy could only stumble from the tent with the envelope and letter crinkled in his fists. He ran behind the tent and started for the rope stockade of horses at full tilt. His feet worked, but his brain would not. Only rage and pain roared there, making him see red, making him relive that other betrayal he had thought buried forever in his love for Merry.

Merry!

He stopped! Merry. This was his honest Merry. He had seen the love in her eyes all the years she had fought for his love, even when he had struggled against her and had not deserved her care and adoration. He had seen the pride on her beautiful face when she had given him his son, had seen the flare of independence and truth that was always there. Something had gone wrong. Someone else had done this to Merry and him when he had thought they were so safe. Peggy Arnold? Her hellish husband, reaching out with his long arm to punish those who had once believed in him? Lord Stormont's influence from England? No, it must be the elusive Toller Devlin, whom he had written off as a fugitive, for his name was mentioned in the letter. If he just knew a little more, he would know how to fight back, how to save her and the child.

He crouched right where he was and spread the note out on the grass to look for a clue to what had really happened. No, nothing hidden in the note. He lifted the letter up to the noon sunlight and squinted at it. General Washington walked slowly up behind him. Without a word, Darcy handed him the note and uncrinkled the envelope. And then he saw it. Bless his Freedom Flame! She had underlined the *H* in *Husband* to tell him she had interlined the letter and he should use heat to read it.

"This cannot be, Darcy. Not Merry." Washington shook his head. "Is there anything I can do? Troops to go with you?"

"Thank you, general, but I cannot risk that, whoever has her and the baby. But if you could find an officer who has someone in his regiment who might know the layout of this Willis farm—"

"Done!" The commander-in-chief was off at a good clip, his sword clanking.

Darcy ran to the nearest cook fire and explained he needed a skillet to read a hidden message with. The French soldier shrugged with Gallic charm and immediately poured their bubbling sauce over their uncooked roasting hens. Darcy pressed the paper to the skillet so fast that he burned his fingers. Nothing! Absolutely nothing appeared in the lines between the note! Could she have underlined the *H* accidentally?

He stared down at the wrinkled envelope again, and then it hit him. His hands shaking, he pressed the envelope itself to the skillet and read Toller's name and the rest of it. He had taught her well, his Freedom Flame! By that time a young, freckled boy had reported to him on the double, a tattered, dusty bicorne in his hands and General Washington hovering right behind.

"You know the Willis farm at Riverbend, east of Chester?" Darcy asked the lad.

"Raised up jest down the lane, sir. It's deserted now, right on the river."

"General Washington," Darcy said, "I realize that our Yorktown plan will never work without a fleet, so I'll need two riflemen to go with me—and a rowboat."

"A rowboat?" Washington said, but he quickly nodded his assent. Since those early days of warfare in New York, he had learned to trust this Frenchman's judgment.

"A rowboat on the bank of the river, posthaste!" he said to a lieutenant behind him, who jumped to it. But why had Darcy mentioned the plans for the crucial campaign at Yorktown, he wondered as he watched the Frenchman and the boy sprint for the river so fast that he could only call, "Godspeed!" after them.

The night before, Merry had been exhausted and sick, but she had convinced Toller to let her hold the baby at last in the woods just off the road where they had stopped to await the dawn. On the long ride out he had only let her touch the child to nurse him and then had taken him right back on his own horse. It had been a nightmare. They were following the same well-traveled road south the two armies had taken, and there was little food left along the way. At least the baby had her milk, and, amazingly, he did not fuss at being outdoors at night. Merry held him close to her and wrapped her skirts up around him for warmth, despite the fact that it bared her lower legs to Toller's avid view.

It was torment to think she was drawing closer to Darcy and yet closer to the trap Toller was setting for him at some place near Chester called the Willis farm. "This farmhouse is obviously someplace you know well," she prompted him, hoping to get some information she could use to help warn Darcy if—when—he came looking for them. She hoped desperately that he would come knowing this was a ruse and that she was nothing like Claudine, that other countess of Belfort.

"A Tory friend of mine owned the place once," Toller told her, willingly enough. "We used to have some wild goings-on in the barn there," he mused. It appalled her that Toller kept pulling on a flask of liquor, even while he held the gun on them. His speech was starting to sound a little slurred. If he would only drink himself asleep so that she could grab that gun! "I'm gonna take John André's advice on this," he added, half to himself.

That jolted her. "André's dead. What do you mean?"

"He suggested I kill Darcy at West Point and make it look as if you shot him. I just may do that yet, when he comes to get his child—before he kills us both in a jealous rage. I wish he'd bring his friends Washington and Rochambeau so I could do Mother England the great favor of killing them, too. Judas Priest, I'd be as big a British hero as Peggy's Benedict then. I saw Washington and Rochambeau near your Darcy in the parade, you see, my dear Meredith. I've been watching you for months, waiting until you had the child, for he's my assurance of your good behavior. I was just waiting until the time was ripe. And now it is, just as you are," he said, and yanked her to him. He punished her with a grinding kiss that crushed her sore breasts between them as the child squealed. His hand still lewdly placed on her full breast, he sat back at last and half glowered, half leered at her.

She pulled back when he let her, but she kept quiet, since she had the baby and he had the gun. "When you've healed a bit more from birthing that one, we'll make a few of our own. You

know, I always did love my rare collections, but now those are
lost to me. I'll collect things again, starting with you," he
muttered, and snorted a drunken-sounding laugh. But he
managed to stay awake all night, glaring at her and the child in
the dark.

Merry sat gagged with her hands tied behind her in the hay
loft in the barn at the abandoned Willis farm the next afternoon. The baby lay asleep on the dirty wooden floor beside her.
She prayed he would not wake and cry to anger Toller again as
he had a few moments ago. Toller, with a loaded and cocked
musket and two pistols that had appeared from his saddlebags
this morning, stood gazing out over the scene below by peer-
ing around the second-story meant for bales of hay. Its block
and tackle still hung over it. Below him, she could see, though
not the whole expanse as he could, the grassy, weed-strewn
square that had once been the barnyard. He was listening for
the sound of a rider coming in, and he could see the lane to the
road both ways. Behind the barn, the green Delaware River
which they could not see from here, glinted through the ranks
of tall maple and chestnut trees.

Merry bit down on the handkerchief stuffed in her mouth,
trying to swallow. Again she almost retched. It was like waiting for a trap to close, for the disaster she and Darcy had
avoided for so long to clang shut with iron jaws.

Her mind skipped back to that other hayloft, where they had
hidden from the Hessians in the straw five years before. There
she had dared to dream they might be man and wife, sharing a
marriage bed, someday. Now, she could not even summon up
a fantasy to comfort her. Her dream life with Darcy had come
true, but she could lose it all now, and the pain would be worse
for having had it and lost it.

The baby stirred again and fussed behind her. The most she
could do to keep him quiet was to move her leg against his little body and rock him slightly. And then she heard the noise,
but Toller did, too. There was a rustling down below in the
barn, though Toller had obviously seen nothing come up the
lane. And then a dog barked below.

Toller tore over to her and lifted her to her feet, leaving the baby. He marched her to the opening of the loft and hid behind her, pointing his pistol nervously outside.

"Darcy won't shoot you any more than he would the baby," he muttered, more to himself than her. "I've got to know what's down there. Maybe the dog's just a stray, here on its own."

"Devlin, I am here." Darcy's voice suddenly rang out below, and he appeared beside a tree trunk before he stepped back behind it again. "And I cannot believe," he continued from behind the tree, "that you would consider risking the woman who wants to run away with you. I will pay you for the child if you just come down. Now!"

That shouted "Now!" was the signal for chaos. Another man across the yard from Darcy stepped from behind a tree and leveled a gun at Toller, then fired just below their feet so that the bullet raised splinters. The dog below barked. A freckled boy charged up the ladder, firing a pistol in the air, while the baby woke and wailed. And then, just when Merry thought Toller would shoot Darcy or her amid the bedlam, another shot rang out and Toller spun away to grab his shoulder.

The boy in the loft dived at Toller. Merry hit the floor hard with her hands tied behind her. The boy and Toller grappled, rolled. They both fell out the loft opening, and she heard them hit the ground with a sickening thud. Merry screamed through her gag, again and again. The baby quieted. Sobbing and choking, she rolled toward him and huddled like a protective roof over him. And then Darcy scrambled up into the loft. He tore her gag off and cut her ties to hold the baby and her in his big embrace.

"Darcy, Darcy, are you all right? You didn't believe Toller?"

"Believe him? About you wanting to leave me? My love, nothing short of death will take either of us from the other in this world. I know that now."

"Those men . . . the boy . . ."

"Two sharpshooters, one American and one French. The boy has a broken leg, but his mother will be glad enough to tend him at the farm down the road instead of having him risk his life at Yorktown. He has been hero enough this day, although his dog followed us as we rowed in on the river and almost gave us away. And Toller is dead."

They huddled together in the loft while the men below retrieved their horses from the next farm. They threw Toller's body over one and took the boy to his house. And then, with the Mont family all riding on Darcy's big stallion, they made their way back to the camp of the two armies as the sun sank blood red in the west.

"I had been staring at our battle plans for Yorktown so long, sir, it was what came first to mind when I had to save my family," Darcy told General Washington at breakfast in his big field tent the next morning while Merry cradled little Andrew. She had been exhausted the day before but had caught the sense of excitement at the coming battle from these men after a night with her family in a borrowed officers' tent nearby. "I knew we could never pull it off against the British at Yorktown without the help of the fleet," Darcy went on. "That is when it hit me that I needed a fleet of my own, that I could use a rowboat to get us to the Willis farm without a sound."

"So you besieged that barn on all sides, using your 'fleet' for a surprise attack and to cut off possible escape," Washington said with a grim look. He stood and sighed. "Now if only our fleet would come so we could trap Lord Cornwallis and his army at Yorktown! Well, then, I shall leave you here to bid farewell again. I will see that Merry and the child are escorted back to Philadelphia while we all push on. And may I say that from the first, Freedom Flame—" he was addressing Merry now "—it seems victory had followed for us wherever you go. Whoever it was said ladies in war are unlucky was dead wrong. If it were not for that fine little boy there, we would just take her along to Yorktown as our token for good fortune. Yes, Darcy?"

"Yes, indeed, General," Darcy agreed, but even as he rose in deference to Washington's standing his eyes were on Merry. "I have never been so sure, so confident, about anything," he told her when the tent flap closed and they were alone with only their child. He leaned over to kiss her soundly.

"Sure of us, as well as the war?"

"Of us, as we have lived through our war. My beautiful wife, I have never loved you more! Let's send for Amélie to join us here in America, whatever happens. We can sell the French houses and build a home on the Schuylkill River when the stonemasons and the carpenters come home from the war!"

"Oh, yes, my darling. Yes and yes! Look, Andrew's smiling. He's gurgling his yes, too!"

Their next passionate kiss was interrupted by a commotion outside. Startled, they walked to the flap and lifted it. The usually staid General Washington was hugging the grinning French general Rochambeau, and they were both dancing a crazy jig while officers around them clapped and cheered their American *"Huzzahs!"* and French *"Vives!"*

Merry and Darcy hurried out to join them. "What now? What now?" Darcy shouted to the French officer next to him.

"Ah, *alors*," he told them in broken English with moist eyes and grandiose gestures. "Word eez just come! Admiral de Grasse and zee thirty French ships did blockade the Chesapeake, eh, and zee British are doomed! Yorktown and this whole beeg war— The victory eez ours at last!"

Their hope for the future in their arms, the light of freedom in their eyes, Merry and Darcy joined in the wild dancing, too.

* * * * *

Author's Note

The victorious American siege of Yorktown was indeed the last big victory the Americans needed to win their war for independence. Ironically, it was the only battle in which the American and French troops fought side by side, although the French nation continued to give aid in other ways. Besides the French love for *liberté*, many scholars believe the American drain on the French king's already overburdened treasury was one of the causes of the French Revolution, which began eight years later and overthrew the power of the aristocratic class.

Lafayette, however, unlike Louis XVI and Marie Antoinette, was one French noble who escaped the mobs and the guillotine. Lafayette named his son after George Washington, the man he considered his adopted father, and returned several times on triumphal tours of America as a national hero.

Benedict Arnold sailed to England shortly after the American victory at Yorktown. He became quite unpopular there, a reminder of a lost war. Ironically, he petitioned Parliament for reparations for *his* losses in America, when he had destroyed so many other Americans' property in his vindictive raids. He died in England in 1801, without funds or reputation. However, his intrepid wife, Peggy Shippen Arnold, reared their two sons after his death, and both boys joined the British army, where they served with more honor than their father had. It is said Peggy still had a locket with a snippet of John André's hair years after she left America behind.

Although the Treaty of Paris, which formally ended the American Revolution, was not signed until 1783, the elderly

Benjamin Franklin's struggle to obtain French aid was for the most part over after the glorious victory at Yorktown. When he returned home to Philadelphia, it is said, the entire town turned out to honor the great American genius and statesman. He found his beloved home there quite intact, except for a favorite portrait of himself that John André had taken with him as a memento of his days in the occupied rebel capital. Any clue to André's true feelings for Peggy Shippen, whose misguided devotion to him had caused herself and others much grief, died with him on the scaffold.

Although today Americans feel more closely bound to England than to France, it should be remembered that French aid played a large role in helping us achieve our independence from Great Britain in the "mere" seven years it took our forefathers to win the Revolutionary War.

Caryn Cameron
June, 1989

CELEBRATE THE SPIRIT OF

1776

If you enjoyed the story of Merry Morgan and Darcy Montour in FREEDOM FLAME, then you'll want to see how intrepid newspaperwoman Libby Morgan and Tory aristocrat Cam Gant fell in love in Caryn Cameron's first American Revolution book, LIBERTY'S LADY (Harlequin Historical #39).

As the American colonies rose up against the oppression of mother England, spirited journalist Libby Morgan fed the fires of rebellion—and clashed head-on with the prime target of her rabble-rousing. Dashing New York aristocrat Cameron Gant was an avowed Tory, a spy—and her sworn enemy. But Cam Gant was not what he seemed, and in his arousing embrace, Libby's contempt quickly dissolved as passions flared.

If you missed LIBERTY'S LADY the first time around, order it now!

Take 4 bestselling love stories FREE

Plus get a FREE surprise gift!